SO
OTHERS
MAY
LIVE

LEE HUTCH

Cover design and Formatting by Damonza
https://damonza.com

ISBN: 978-1-7337909-0-1 (hardback)
ISBN: 978-1-7337909-1-8 (paperback)
ISBN: 978-1-7337909-2-5 (ebook)

http://leehutchauthor.com

For my girls, Elizabeth and Anastasia
And
For those who face the flames

PART ONE
21 NOVEMBER 1943
DAY

*Man that is born of woman is of few
days, and full of trouble.
He cometh forth like a flower and is cut down; he fleeth
also as a shadow, and continueth not.*

Job 14:1-2

CHAPTER ONE

"What was it you needed to talk to me about?"

Michael lay sprawled on his back on the bed in his shirt sleeves, his collar unbuttoned and his tie unknotted. He watched Grace, who stood with her back to him, as she slipped into a gray skirt.

"It's nothing, really," she said over her shoulder. "We can talk about it later."

"I only have a weekend pass, you know," he said. "Have to be back at 6 p.m."

"It can wait until…" She froze for a moment and then turned to face him. Her light blonde hair framed a young face with lines of worry etched into the corners of her green eyes. "Until after… you know."

"Have it your way then," Michael said as he sat up. "It'll be soon enough. I imagine we'll have another go tomorrow night. That should finish things. One way or the other."

Michael need only fly one more mission to reach the magic number, thirty. He'd get a spell off operations and a cozy posting as an instructor somewhere for several months. With any luck, it might turn into a permanent assignment with another promotion and medal almost assured. And, of course, marriage. All he had to do was survive.

"I wish you wouldn't talk like that," Grace said.

"I'm just being realistic. Of the fifteen of us from my flight school who got assigned to Bomber Command, only three of us are still on ops. Two are prisoners. The rest are dead. It's really not good odds at all, you know."

"I *know* that! You don't need to keep reminding me."

"You're right." Michael straightened his tie and grabbed his tunic from the back of a chair. "Truce? Come on. Let's go find something to eat. I have a few more hours before I have to catch the train back."

Twenty minutes later they were sitting in the hotel dining room. When they had checked in a few days earlier, Michael listed their names in the registry as "Mr. and Mrs. Churchill." Many hotels frowned on unmarried couples who shared a room, but the presence of a uniform, especially that of a pilot, discouraged questions. The clerk did not ask them to show their identity cards. Michael could tell the clerk knew the game, the absence of wedding rings being an essential clue, but he said nothing and passed the room key across the counter. Michael slid a couple of one pound notes to him with one hand as he snatched the key in the other. This was only the second time they'd managed to spend more than just a few hours together; the last was nearly two months ago. War had a way of magnifying things as though the proximity to death made one more alive.

"So where do you want to get married?" Grace asked as she sipped her tea.

"In a church, I guess," Michael replied. "Isn't that what you want?"

"Your church?"

"I don't know about that," he said. "I think they have

some kind of rules about marrying Protestants, though I don't know exactly what they are."

"There is a small chapel near my parents' home. We could use that?"

"'Tis fine." Michael shrugged. "But first don't you think you should tell your father you are engaged? How will he take the news you are marrying a Catholic boy from Belfast?"

Grace frowned.

"I'll tell him," she promised. "But I'm twenty-one years old. I hardly need his permission."

Michael tapped his fork on his plate in time with the music which drifted across the room courtesy of the radio on a table in the corner. *One more*, he thought. *Just one more. Then I can pack it in for a while.*

"Michael?"

Her voice broke into his stream of thought, and he looked at her.

"Sorry," he said. "Just thinking."

"About what?"

"Only about how much I love you," he said as he forced a smile. She blushed slightly. Michael liked that about her. Though she was friendly enough and relatively outgoing, underneath it all was a shy girl unsure of herself.

A sudden noise turned their attention to the front of the room as three members of Michael's crew staggered through the door, a little worse for wear from the night before. A few days earlier, Michael had flown them to Berlin. The Big City had a way of aging a crew ten years in the space of a single night. They returned home in the early morning hours with two of the crew dead and a third badly wounded. The group commander thought it best to give the crew a few days off, and so he arranged the weekend pass they now enjoyed. Michael would have preferred to stay on ops to finish up his tour, but he was overruled. The Wing Commander had pointed out that Michael's plane, P for Paul, needed repairs and the bits of blood and tissue which clung to the interior needed to be removed.

"And how are the lovebirds this morning?" Angus McKenzie, a burly Australian with a bushy moustache and a ready grin, asked with a lewd wink as he dragged a chair across to the table, sat down, and helped himself to some of Michael's food. "Everything shipshape then?"

"Of course it is," Richard Lawton, a squat young man from Yorkshire with old eyes, said as he clapped McKenzie on the back. "He's a bleedin' officer, ain't he?"

"Just shows our desperation," Fergus Cameron added. "When we had to start commissioning paddies. Should've stuck with Scotsmen. We know how to fight a war."

"Other than Culloden, you mean," Lawton replied.

Michael made an obscene gesture towards Cameron, who, in turn, tossed a breakfast roll at Lawton's head, which drew laughs from everyone. Michael's commission was almost an accident. Many of the pilots in Bomber Command were sergeants. When he enlisted, he was sent to Canada for flight school. He proved particularly adept and graduated second in his class. The top four graduates received a commission, and the rest were told they might get one if they completed their first operational tour. Michael had hoped that graduating second in his class would mean an assignment to Fighter Command behind the controls of a Spitfire. Alas, Bomber Command went through crews as fast as they could be assigned. *Still, it's no small feat for a Catholic boy from North Belfast to sit behind the controls of a plane.*

When he returned to England to train on multi-engine aircraft, all the pilots and aircrew with the exception of the flight engineers gathered in a large room. They divided themselves into crews just as they might split up into football teams. The flight engineers were assigned later when the crews began to train on the aircraft they would fly on operations. It was a matter of chance, or luck, really. You picked a man because he looked like he knew what he was doing. He might. Or he might have a breakdown the first time the plane got caught in a searchlight over Germany. The three men who now shared his table proved themselves time and again, as had those whose broken bodies were lifted out of the plane just a few days ago. *One more*, he thought. *Just one more. But with three new men whom I don't know feck all about. I hope they're experienced men and not fresh out of school. Maybe I should talk to the Wing Commander about that.*

Grace smiled politely as McKenzie recounted the crew's adventures on the town the night before. Wartime London, though littered with leftover bomb damage from the Blitz, provided many avenues for entertaining men on leave. Michael and Grace had started off with them, but then made their way back to the hotel. The men spoke with the easy familiarity of those who had faced death together and survived. Rank did not matter to them, and they joked with Michael as they did with each other. At twenty-two, Michael was the oldest. Mere boys, who in another era would be in school, now flew machines which dealt death on a nightly basis while other young men in different uniforms did their best to kill them in return.

"So Grace," McKenzie said in a tone which suggested he'd known her his whole life instead of two days, "has Mick told you about the trip we made a couple of weeks back?"

"No," Grace replied. "He doesn't tell me much about what he does."

"And for a good reason," Lawton said as he lit a cigarette. "There isn't much to tell."

"Shut up, you Tommy twat," McKenzie said.

"Mind the language," Cameron said. "There's a lady present. You must forgive him, Grace. Colonials behave like wild animals. Mixed company or not."

"Go bugger a sheep, you kilt-wearing catamite," McKenzie replied. "Now back to the story—"

"Hold on now," Michael said, raising his hand. McKenzie ignored him and continued.

"So we were over the Ruhr, can't tell you where. But it was bloody awful. Flak everywhere. Planes going down in flames left and right. We got coned by a searchlight. They zeroed in on us. Flak pinging off everything. Mick twists and turns, but we can't get out of the light. I had just about shat myself when I heard something over the intercom."

"Mick was bloody whistlin'," Lawton said.

"That's God's truth," Fergus added. "I heard it too. I looked up – I sit just down and behind him, you see. I looked up and there he was whistling to himself while we corkscrew all over the sky. Cool as a cucumber, he was. I've never seen the likes of it. We're all checking our chutes and hoping we have time to bail out after we get hit, and he's acting like he's out for a stroll down Piccadilly."

"And you got out of the searchlight?" Grace asked with a face gone slightly pale.

"Of course," McKenzie said. "We're here, aren't we?"

"Getting coned by searchlights is like getting caught naked in a crowded public place," Michael explained. "Once they have you, they'll pound you with flak and if that doesn't get you, a night fighter will."

"Come on," Lawton said as he stood up. "Let's shove off and leave the lovebirds be."

The men politely said goodbye to Grace and arranged to meet at the train station at 3 o'clock to return to their airfield. They made their way out of the restaurant with the boisterousness of a team taking the pitch.

"They're nice men," Grace said.

"A bit rough around the edges," Michael said, "but they're good lads. So were the two we buried Friday morning."

Grace's bottom lip quivered slightly.

"I'm sorry," Michael said. "I shouldn't have said that."

"It's fine, really." Grace brushed away a tear with the back of her hand.

They had met by accident. After a month with an operational training unit, Michael received a seven-day pass before he reported to his permanent post. He caught a train to London with Simon Daniels, a Canadian and his best friend from training. They wandered around the city with all the wide-eyed enthusiasm of tourists. At a theater where they stopped to catch a movie, Michael and Simon sat in the only two seats available. As it happened, this put Michael next to Grace, who was catching a movie with a friend after they left their jobs as secretaries in a shipping firm for the evening.

When the lights came on, Simon, the more outgoing of the pair, struck up a conversation. The four went out for a drink that night, and spent the remainder of the evenings that week together. They said goodbye at the train station and went their separate ways. Simon went to a different squadron and three nights later went down in flames over Essen.

Michael continued to write to Grace and call once a week. Whenever he got a pass, he traveled to London to see her. On his last pass, six weeks ago, he proposed and she accepted. He sent most of his money home to his father, a widower who was much taken to drink, so Michael lacked the money for an engagement ring. His father had gone over the top on the first day of the Battle of the Somme as a young private in the 36th Ulster Division. They were butchered by the German defenses. As a child, Michael never quite understood why his father spent so much time in a bottle, but after twenty-nine nights over German cities as flak exploded and searchlights swept the sky, it had begun to make a lot more sense.

Though she was attractive enough, it wasn't looks that drew Michael to Grace. He sensed in her the same loneliness he felt in himself, as though an essential part of life was somehow missing. Their relationship moved ahead and at a pace accelerated by war and the desire to not lose what they shared in whatever time the war allowed them to have.

Michael checked his watch.

"We've got a few hours left," he said. "No need to spend it sitting here at the table."

"What do you want to do?" Grace asked.

"I could use a month's sleep," Michael replied.

Night bombing missions over Germany made it difficult for his body to adjust on three-day passes. At night, his reflexes and brain woke up and fought off sleep for as long as it could. And when he did manage to drift off, images of burning planes and bursting flak filled his thoughts and made him jump and twist in the bed. Though Grace never mentioned it to him, Michael knew it kept her awake. *Maybe it'll calm down when I come off ops. If I come off ops.*

"Maybe a walk will wake you up," Grace suggested.

Michael nodded and the two of them set off, arm in arm. Men and women in uniforms of various sorts filled the streets of London. From large, suntanned Aussies to Yanks, who walked with a bit of a swagger as if they had just stepped out of a cowboy film, the whole of the free world was gathered in England. Some trained for the eventual invasion of Europe while others carried the war to the German heartland by day or by night. The navies were well represented as they protected the vital convoy routes which brought men and material to the British Isles. The couple did a bit of window shopping, and Michael spent a couple of pounds on a hat Grace liked. After a quick lunch, they made their way to the train station, where they found the rest of the crew sitting on a bench, a bit more somber than they had been in the morning.

"Well, sir," McKenzie said, "are you ready to get back to the war?"

"Once more unto the breach, dear friends," Cameron replied as he scratched his face.

"Or close up the walls with our English dead," Michael finished the quote.

"Hear that," McKenzie said with a laugh. He slapped Lawton on the back. "You're gonna buy it on our last mission!"

"Fuck off," Lawton growled. He fished a cigarette from his pocket and stuffed it into his mouth. His hands shook and the match would not light.

"Here," McKenzie said, producing his own lighter.

"How about we go ahead and climb aboard the train," Cameron suggested. "You can catch up with us after you say your goodbyes."

"Thank you," Michael said.

Grace shook Cameron's hand, and then Lawton's. When she attempted to shake McKenzie's, he brushed it aside and scooped her up. He spun her around in a circle and kissed her on the cheek. She laughed as red crept into her cheeks.

"We're family now," he said after he sat her down.

"It was nice to meet you all," Grace said. "I hope you'll all be able to make the wedding."

"Wouldn't miss it," Cameron said. "You just tell us when and where."

Grace smiled, but her eyes watered. McKenzie noticed and leaned down to whisper in her ear.

"Don't cry now, luv. We'll make sure to bring Mick back to you in one piece. You're our good luck charm now."

Michael put his arm around Grace's shoulders as the three men walked towards the train. He tried to think of something, anything, to say. A slight lump rose in the back of his throat. *I'll not see her again*, he thought. *I know I won't. My luck's run out and here I've gone and made her fall in love with me. I didn't mean it to happen. Not like this. I can't marry her, even after I finish this tour because there'll only be another one. I'll not make her a widow. I love her too much for that.*

"They're good lads," he finally said. "The best there is."

"I know." She turned her face and looked up at him. "Just a few more days and we can get married and live together for a few months at least. I'm looking forward to it."

Michael put his hands on Grace's shoulders and turned her towards him. His brown eyes bored deep into hers.

"I'll call you the second I get back from the next raid," he promised. "Even if it is five a.m. You won't mind, will you?"

"I won't, but my roommate might."

Grace shared a small flat with a girl from Liverpool.

"Sod your roommate," Michael said. Grace laughed.

"She'll be in the wedding, you know."

Michael started to speak, but the train whistle cut into his words. From the train, he heard McKenzie yell, "Come on, you bog trotter! You can't miss the train!"

"That's come on, you bog trotter, *sir*!" Michael yelled back. Then he turned back to Grace. He leaned down and kissed her. She locked her arms around his neck and held on tight. After a minute, he pried her hands loose.

"I promised myself I wouldn't cry," she said.

"There's no shame in tears," Michael said. "Goodbye, Grace. I, well… I'm glad I met you. You've made this war a bit more tolerable."

"Only a bit?"

He leaned down and gave her another quick kiss. With a sad smile, Michael walked over to the train and climbed the steps. He paused for a moment before entering the car. As the train began to pull away, Michael raised his hand to the visor of his cap in a gesture somewhere between a wave and a salute. Grace waved back, both at Michael and at his crewmen, who blew her kisses through the open window of the railcar. *Once more unto the breach*, Michael thought. *Once more unto the breach.*

CHAPTER TWO

AT THE SAME moment Michael boarded the train, Karl Weber surveyed the young faces who stared at him from their places at tables set up in an upstairs room in a fire station in Berlin. It was an imposing building, erected in the late 1880s, and took up half a city block a short distance west of the Tiergarten. Three stories tall, with stately windows which looked out over the street, the station housed an engine, a ladder, and now an ambulance manned by a middle-aged nurse, a Dutch youth conscripted from the labor service, and a French POW who had been a military doctor. Red doors faced the street, though when the city built the station, it housed horse-drawn fire engines. With modern fire equipment, the doors were hardly wide enough to allow the trucks much room.

The classroom where Karl now stood had tables on either side of an aisle. On one side of the room, young women clad in baggy gray coveralls and blue garrison caps sat with expressions which ranged from interested to amused. On the other side of the room, Hitler Youth boys of fifteen and sixteen, clad in their brown uniforms with fire protection badges freshly sewn on the cuffs of their left sleeves, stared at him with bright, eager eyes. Some seemed excited, though about him or the young women, Karl was unsure.

Though he preferred to wear work coveralls, Karl forced himself to dress in the official uniform, green tunic and pants with a peaked cap and the ribbon for his Iron Cross, First Class received on the Russian front in his buttonhole. Though entitled to wear all his decorations on his tunic, the Wound Badge, Close Combat Medal, and Infantry Assault Badge never left the drawer of his station desk, lest they be lost or damaged on a fire scene. Prior to 1938, members of fire brigades wore blue and, in fact, the voluntary fire brigades still did. As part of the National Socialist obsession for organization, professional fire brigades were placed under the police and given a national command structure. It necessitated a change of uniforms and also a change in the color of their engines, now a dark green. Three older men, similarly dressed in their official uniforms, stood in the back of the classroom, arms folded across their chests.

"Right," Karl began. "Welcome to my station. And it is *my* station. I am Oberwachtmeister Weber. You will all be under my command, though behind you are three more men of long experience."

He paused to allow the young people to turn and look at the back of the room where Ludwig Baumann, Thomas Frei, and Claudwig Fischer – men he had been serving with on this brigade before the war – scowled back at them.

"They speak with my authority. Obey them as you would me. Is that clear?"

"Jawohl, Herr Oberwachtmeister!" the class responded, though the Hitler Youth boys put considerable more enthusiasm into it than did the young women.

"I know you have had some training," Karl continued. "And your decision to volunteer your services speaks to your character, but spraying water on burning haystacks is not what we are about here. With us, you'll face stern tests. Some of you may not be able to handle it. Nothing wrong with that. We'll find something else for you to do. Now, what is our purpose here?"

The five Hitler Youth boys all raised their hands. Only one of the young women raised hers. She had intelligent blue eyes, so Karl motioned for her to speak.

"Our purpose is to protect the citizens of Berlin from all hazards relating to fire, and to assist in rescuing people in the aftermath of an air raid, Herr Oberwachtmeister."

"Precisely, Fraulein…"

"Schneider, sir."

"At all times," Karl said, his voice serious, "you must obey the orders of we professionals as if they came from the Fuhrer himself. Instantly and without question. We know what we are doing and we will do our utmost to keep you as safe as we can. Remember this, the Fire Brigade is the noblest of callings, especially in wartime. Now, any questions before we start today's lesson?"

One boy raised his hand. He had a cocky air about him which Karl found distasteful. *I'll have to keep an eye on this one*, Karl thought.

"Yes?" Karl asked.

"Forgive me, Herr Oberwachtmeister, but I did not realize the Iron Cross was awarded to members of the Fire Brigade. How did you receive it?"

"You are correct," Karl replied. "It isn't awarded to Fire Brigade members."

Cheeky bastard, Karl thought. He launched into the lesson, and the class turned their attention to their notebooks and scribbled furiously as he described various types of bombs, their effects, and the particular dangers associated with each. Of all the ways to die in an air raid, Karl feared phosphorus incendiaries the most. The little balls of flame which erupted from them burned through anything, and kept burning. Water did nothing to stop it.

Five months ago, Karl and other members of the Berlin Fire Brigade traveled to Hamburg to assist the firemen in that city during the midst of a week-long bomber offensive. Americans by day and British by night. In the midst of the firestorm created by a particularly heavy raid, one which killed tens of thousands of people, Karl saw a crewman from an engine pull out a knife and carve out a hunk of his flesh to stop a phosphorus ball as it burrowed into his leg. The man stuffed a handkerchief into the hole and kept on with his work until a thousand-pound bomb blasted him, his engine, and four other firemen to pieces.

All firemen feared the glowing balls of death. Karl considered giving this anecdote to the class, but decided against it. *Better to let them see it for themselves. They wouldn't believe me if I told them. The boys are all full of love for the Fuhrer and think themselves invincible. The girls are wondering why they didn't decide to train as nurses with the Red Cross instead of being here.*

After the hour-long lesson, Karl left them to study their notes and, when finished, to polish the trucks on the ground floor. He and the other experienced men walked down the stairs to Karl's second floor office.

"You really put the fear into them," Ludwig Baumann said as he lit a cigarette. He was a large, balding man who'd joined the Fire Brigade after two years in the trenches in the Great War. Though Baumann was the senior man at the station, he resisted any efforts to promote him and happily drove the ladder truck. He knew every inch of the city.

"I'm giving you two our Hitler Youth boys," Karl said, turning to Thomas Frei. "They are probably better suited for scrambling up ladders and into piles of rubble, you think?"

"Yes," Frei replied. "You are probably right."

Thomas Frei served on the ladder truck as its crew chief. Like Baumann, he'd fought fires in Berlin for twenty years. In August, Frei's wife had died in an air raid the same week the Russians killed his son on the Eastern Front.

"Drill them hard." Karl dug around in his desk drawer and pulled out a crumpled pack of cigarettes. "Try and beat all of the Hitler Youth shit out of them. This isn't the Reich Labor Service. They won't be felling trees and singing Party songs here."

"We'll do it," Baumann promised. "Those young bastards won't know what hit them."

Karl turned to the other man in the room, Claudwig Fischer. Like Baumann, he fought in the first war and joined the brigade at the age of nineteen. Now, at forty-three, he boasted twenty-four years of service and drove the engine. He too opposed any promotion.

"We'll keep the women with us," Karl said. "But we must keep them away from the boys. That's why I won't mix the crews."

"Girls as firemen," Baumann grumbled. "What's the world coming to?"

The manpower needs of the Wehrmacht drained the abilities of fire brigades to respond to emergencies. The Eastern Front, a meat grinder which devoured lives as a hungry man devours a meal, pulled larger and larger numbers of men from all walks of life. The Hamburg raids jarred the government into action, and so they created more voluntary fire brigades and recruited teenage boys and young women to the fire services. The professional men left behind were either grizzled fire service veterans too old to be much use to the army or men who had served until wounded and thus returned to the fire brigade.

Karl fell into the latter category. He had joined the brigade in 1929 at the age of nineteen. After six years of service, he joined the army as a reservist. Called to active duty a month prior to the invasion of Poland, Karl saw action in Belgium, France, and then Russia. A year ago in Stalingrad, a machine gun round and a dose of shrapnel put an end to his military days. He'd laid on a cot at the airfield for two days awaiting evacuation. Doctors ran out of morphine long before he arrived, so he gritted his teeth and bore the pain as best he could. Planes came in one at a time. Enlisted men loaded as many wounded men as they could and the planes took off. Every so often, Russian anti-aircraft fire hit one and it would crash in flames, all within the view of men who waited for their turn. *I hope I never see Russia again*, Karl thought. *Leave it to the Reds. I saw nothing there worth having in the first place.* The army discharged him after a four-month stint in various hospitals, and he received new orders to return to his previous occupation.

So much has changed, Karl thought. When he arrived in Berlin, Karl found most of the familiar faces from the brigade gone, but Baumann, Frei, and Fischer were still at the station. They were pleased at his return and supported his promotion, as it meant they got to stay at their present rank, but the war had left a mark on them as well. Men no longer joked with each other around the station. The pranks which kept them entertained between calls vanished. Few even played cards anymore. Now they sat and smoked as many cigarettes as they could, given the rationing requirements, in utter silence, each lost in their own thoughts.

Despite the war, the men still responded to the day-to-day calls as they did in peacetime. Train accidents, car accidents, chimney fires, fires in apartment buildings, or rescues. Every day brought more incidents. But now, the men faced death from the air. Since his return to the city, a few raids had hit Berlin, some heavier than others. The last raid took place just a couple of days prior, but in each case the bomb damage was enough to create a nuisance but not enough to cause the same terror Karl had seen in Hamburg. *Thank God we haven't had that here.* Through it all, the men still took pride in their job now that it was all the more important due to the war.

"Are you going to draw up a duty schedule for them?" Frei asked.

"I don't know," Karl answered. "I suppose we could have them work nights, in case of air raids, and then we can handle the daytime calls."

"That might work," Fischer agreed. "We really only need them during a raid."

The men froze as a large bell mounted on the wall sounded. Four bells, followed by two bells, then five, and a final three. The men stood and walked out of the office and into the large open room which served as a day room and a bunkroom for the men. They walked over to a row of doors which resembled closet doors but, upon opening, revealed a brass pole instead. The Hitler Youth boys came tumbling down the stairs from the third floor, followed closely by the girls.

"Get back up there," Karl ordered. With sheepish looks, they complied. Karl slid down the pole to the ground floor and walked over to a row of pegs on the wall. He slung his gas mask canister over his shoulder with the strap across his chest so that it rested just behind his right hip. Then he buckled a belt over the strap to hold it in place. The belt held an axe which dangled along his left thigh. Karl removed his uniform cap and picked up his helmet, similar to those worn by soldiers but with the addition of a leather flap to cover the ears and the back of the neck.

"Know where we are headed?" Karl asked as he climbed into the cab of the truck alongside Fischer, who tugged a rope which hung down from the ceiling. As he did, the station doors began to open.

"Box 4253. Yes, I know the intersection," Fischer replied as he put the engine in gear and pulled out of the station. Berlin, like most urban centers, used a telegraph alarm system. Fire alarm boxes on street corners contained a handle which, when pulled, sent an alarm to a central receiving station. The person on duty noted the box numbers and notified the nearest fire stations, also by telegraph. Calls came in by telephone as well. During air raids, the civil defense authorities gave out assignments by phone or, if the phone system got knocked out, by messenger boys on bicycles.

"I'm too tired to fight a fire right now!" Fischer shouted over the sound of the engine and the clanging bell. "The raid the other night made a mess of my internal clock. Now I can't sleep at night."

"You'll sleep when you get tired enough," Karl yelled back. Though, since Russia, Karl slept little. When sleep did come, so did the memories. The Russian he killed with a knife, the dead child in the burning apartment, and Hamburg. Always Hamburg.

They saw nothing amiss when they arrived at the intersection the bells dispatched them to. No smoke, no flames, not even an overturned car. The four men climbed down from their trucks and walked around. Karl looked up at the windows of the four-story apartment buildings on either side of the road. In the event of a fire, the streets usually filled with people from inside the buildings, and with curious onlookers, but no one greeted them with shouts or waves. On occasion, boys pulled the fire alarm box and then hid to watch the fire trucks arrive, but the stiff penalties imposed by the government put a stop to most of that behavior.

"Should we go back?" Ludwig asked. "Doesn't seem to be any work for us here."

Before Karl could answer, the door to one of the buildings flew open and a young woman with red hair hurried out to the middle of the street where the four firemen stood. She went right over to Karl and took his arm.

"I'm so sorry," she said.

"For what, miss?" Karl asked.

"You see, I was cooking supper and I left something on the stove too long. I had gone into the bedroom and when I returned to the kitchen, it was full of smoke. I opened the door to my apartment and saw the neighbor boy. He went to pull the alarm box."

"And is your apartment on fire?" Karl asked.

"No, no," she said. "I turned the stove off and ran some water over the pan."

"I'll have to check," Karl said. "You three wait here. I'll be right back."

He indicated for her to lead the way. She wore a green dress, her red hair pulled back in a tight bun as many women wore their hair these days. As they walked up the stairs, she looked over her shoulder and said, "Sorry, but I'm on the top floor."

"Naturally," Karl replied with a pained expression.

"Are you okay?" The woman stopped.

"Yes, yes, I'm fine. Just a nagging injury that hates stairs."

"From the war?" she asked as she resumed her walk.

"Yes. From Russia."

The woman was silent until they reached the fourth floor landing.

"My brothers were killed in Russia," she said in a whisper.

"My sympathies, Frau…"

"Fraulein," the woman corrected. "Müller. Ursula Müller."

When they reached her apartment, Karl took a quick look around. The smell of burned fish filled the air. He wrinkled his nose. She had few furnishings, just a battered couch and chair in the living room. The table near the kitchen looked as though it would be better utilized as firewood. Karl used his hands to feel around for heat near the stove.

"Everything seems in order," he said. "Do you live here alone, Miss Müller?"

"No," she said. "I have two roommates. We work as telephone operators. Today is my day off, so I'm in charge of supper."

He studied her face for a moment. Light blue eyes. A few freckles across her nose. He felt something he had not felt for many years. *Not since Ilse. No, best not to think of her now.*

Karl extended his hand, and she shook it.

"Pleasure to meet you, Miss Müller. I hope you'll have a safe evening."

"I'll keep a better eye on my cooking in the future," she said with a laugh.

"I... I mean, we would be happy to come back any time you need us," Karl said.

"I'll keep that in mind," Ursula said.

Steady, Karl warned himself. *She's ten years younger than you.*

"Good evening," Karl said with a slight nod. He made his way down the stairs to the street where the three other firemen sat on the bumper of one of the trucks.

"'Bout time you got back, Weber," Baumann said.

"Checking more than her stove, eh?" Frei asked.

"Shut up," Karl said as he got into the cab of the engine with Fischer.

"Is it true then?" Fischer said. "I've always heard that girls with red hair are sex fiends, though I have not had cause to find out myself."

"Unless you want me to personally push you under the next bomb to fall on this city, you'll shut your mouth."

I should have, I don't know, asked if I could call on her some time, Karl thought as he frowned. *No, I can't do that. Now isn't the time for such things.*

CHAPTER THREE

GRACE LEFT THE train station and hailed a cab. The driver, a middle-aged man with a cockney accent smiled at her as she climbed into the back seat.

"Sayin' g'bye to yer man?" he asked.

She nodded, not trusting herself to speak. He kept up a running commentary on Churchill, the war, Yanks, and the driving habits of other motorists, most of it indecipherable, as he weaved his way around the Sunday afternoon traffic. After the second near collision, Grace closed her eyes. *I should have told him*, she thought. *He has a right to know. When he comes off of ops, I'll tell him then.*

"Alright, miss," the cabbie said after a drive of twenty minutes, "here ya go."

Grace got out of the cab and paid the fare. She and a roommate rented a third floor apartment in an older building west of the center of London. Grace had made her way to the city in 1940 with the intention of training as a volunteer nurse. The last words her father spoke to her before she walked out the door had echoed in her mind through the whole train ride to the city.

"You'll not make it as a nurse," he had said. "You haven't the constitution or the character required for it. You spend your time in books. Maybe a position as a typist or a secretary would be more suitable."

Stung by his words, Grace took a job at a shipping firm and rebuffed the numerous attempts her parents made to entice her to return to the family home forty miles outside London. During the Blitz, Grace spent many nights in the basement shelter with the other residents of the apartment building. Though bombs hit nearby, none caused damage beyond a few broken windows on the ground floor. The air raid sirens still sounded from time to time, and each time the screech penetrated the walls, a series of shivers raced up and down her spine. Memories flooded back of nights below ground while the walls shook with the concussion of explosions and the shriek of bombs as they plummeted earthward. You never knew where one might hit. In the middle of a particularly heavy raid, Grace could no longer stand the damp confines of the basement with its smell of mildew and fear, so she ventured to the roof where she watched flames devour part of the nearby block. Searchlights probed the sky. She gasped when one light caught a German bomber almost directly over her head. Bombs tumbled from the belly of the plane. They hurtled towards her and she put her hands over her eyes and waited for the end, but they exploded a few streets away. After that night, Grace remained in the basement, mildew smell or not.

"How was your weekend?" Helen asked when Grace walked into the apartment. They had met three years ago when they both got hired the same week. As both needed a place to stay, they made a decision to find an apartment together. Given the bomb damage in London and the influx of servicemen, accommodations were difficult to come by. Grace contacted her father, who made a few calls on her behalf.

Though he lacked a title, Dr. Chester Robinson had an extensive network of contacts from his days as a young officer on the Western Front in the Great War. He'd won a Victoria Cross during the last German offensive in 1918 when his company held out against an onslaught of German shock troops for six hours, long enough for relief to arrive. When the war ended, he returned to Oxford and studied medicine, which gave him even more persons upon whom he could call for favors. Grace heard rumors that her father also offered discreet treatments for venereal disease to politicians, army officers, and even vicars from the Church of England. Always a stern, cold man with no apparent emotions, Dr. Robinson had become even more withdrawn since the death of Jimmy, his only son, during a raid on Dieppe in August of 1942. Jimmy had served with the Commandos and longed for a chance to prove himself as brave as his father. Instead, death claimed him along with so many others Grace knew from her childhood.

"We had a grand time," Grace replied, "but it was too short."

"It always is," Helen said. Her easy, confident nature drew men as a flame attracts moths. Slim, with brown hair and hazel eyes, her goal in the war, as she stated to Grace many times, was to snag an American, preferably one from California, so she could settle in Hollywood. Though she dated a few, none of the relationships developed beyond the casual stage.

"He should get one, maybe two, weeks off before he gets his posting to a training unit – as soon as he completes his next mission."

"When will that be?" Helen asked.

"As early as tomorrow night," Grace said. "He thinks he'll go up again very soon."

"Nervous?"

"Me or him?"

Helen shrugged. "Either."

"I don't know about him. We don't talk much about what he does. But I'm bloody terrified," Grace admitted. Her eyes watered. "Damn. I'm not going to cry about it."

"Have you set a wedding date then?" Helen asked.

"No," Grace said. "We will do it when he gets his leave. Get married, I mean. It won't be a large affair, but you'll be in it, won't you?"

"Only if you promise to be in mine?"

"Of course!"

"Let's go out tonight," Helen suggested.

"I don't know…"

"Come on!" Helen urged. "If we don't, you'll just sit around and worry. He won't be flying tonight anyway. Then tomorrow, we'll be at work and we can stop for a drink on the way home. How about it?"

She has a point, Grace thought. *I'll be dreadful company around the apartment tonight. I'll still be dreadful company if we go out, but maybe a little less. Besides, Michael wouldn't want me to worry, would he?*

"Okay," Grace said. "We can go out. But where?"

"Oh, I know a few places," Helen assured her. "But, Grace, did you tell him before he left?"

"Tell him what?"

"You *know*, about… about *that*."

Grace shook her head to indicate she had not. Helen was the only living person, apart from Dr. Robinson, who knew of the baby Grace's parents had forced her to give up when a summer relationship when she was sixteen had suddenly turned serious. Grace had grown up on the fringes of the family, with just enough attention to make her feel loved, but not enough to make her feel liked. After the pregnancy, she no longer felt the love either.

Her mother died two months after word of Jimmy's death reached the family. The doctors said it was a heart attack, but Grace knew a broken heart really killed her mother as Jimmy was the favorite. Dr. Robinson had wanted a son and barely hid his dismay when his firstborn child turned out to be a girl. Two years later, the hoped-for son arrived. There were no more children. Both parents doted on Jimmy, who grew into a confident, if a little cocky, young man. His temperament suited the Commandos. *I know father needs me now*, Grace thought with a twinge of guilt, *but he never showed much interest in me when I needed him. That's why I came to London in the first place. He'll not want me around anyway.*

"Will you tell him?" Helen asked.

"I'll have to," Grace said. "I just didn't want him thinking about it before his last flight."

"You don't *really* have to tell him," Helen suggested. "It's not likely he'll find out on his own. You'll get married, the war will end, and he'll take you to Belfast. I rather doubt he'll spend time investigating your past, now, don't you?"

Grace shuddered.

"I'd not like to live in Belfast," she said. "Michael doesn't speak very highly of it at all. With him being a Catholic and me not, it might cause trouble. No, I think we'd stay here. But I can't keep it from him. It wouldn't be fair. If I were him, I'd want to know."

"And would it change anything?" Helen asked.

"Well, no—"

"See," Helen interrupted. "You're just borrowing trouble then. So come on. Let's get ready to go out. Shall I call a few other girls too?"

Two hours later a doorman clad in a white jacket and black tie held open the door to a nightclub near Piccadilly Circus. "Come along, quick as you like. Mind the blackout curtain!" Heavy black curtains designed to keep any light from spilling onto the street hung just inside the door. Helen and Grace stepped inside and saw Ruth and Catherine, two of their co-workers, as they sipped drinks near a second door which led to the interior of the club. Ruth, a somber-faced girl with black hair and eyes, smiled when she noticed them and nudged Catherine, a tall brunette with piercing blue eyes, more striking than pretty. The sounds of a jazz band drifted through the interior door, rising above the sounds of voices and laughter. The smell of stale beer mixed with perfume and sweat drifted across the dance floor as the group walked in and found a table in the corner. Grace sat with her back to the wall with Helen beside her. The others sat across from them.

Most of the men wore uniforms, and most of those were American. *No wonder Helen picked this place*, Grace thought with a wry smile. *Plenty of Yanks for her to choose from.* The band switched to a cover of Glenn Miller's "Moonlight Serenade." All of the musicians were black, and they too wore American uniforms with stripes on their sleeves which ranged from PFC to Staff Sergeant. Since her firm did business with the US Army, Grace picked up the differences in officer and enlisted ranks, though she could not figure out the same for the British Army. Michael took the time to explain the RAF ranks to her on their second date when she asked exactly what his was. Across the dance floor, a group of four young men zeroed in on the group of women and began to walk towards them with the slow, easy confidence many of the Yanks exhibited. Each sported a set of wings pinned to the left breast of their tunics.

"Would you ladies care to dance?" asked the tallest one when they reached the table. He had reddish hair trimmed short and a scar along his right cheek. The others gathered beside him. Helen nodded and rose and took his hand. They disappeared onto the dance floor. Two of the others claimed Ruth and Catherine. Grace found herself looking at the last of the men, a slim youth with shy eyes.

"Well?" he asked.

"I'm terribly sorry," Grace said, "but I'm not much of a dancer, really."

"In that case, may I join you?"

Grace nodded and he sat down across from her.

"My name is Doug," he said as he extended his hand across the table. He spoke with a slow, soft accent. "Doug Murray. I'm from Louisiana. Ever heard of it?"

"I've heard of New Orleans," Grace admitted. "I'm afraid I don't know much else about it. Are you a pilot?"

"Yes, ma'am," he said. "I fly B-17s. You know, the big four-engine bombers."

"I know," Grace said. "My fiancé flies a Lancaster."

Doug emitted a low whistle.

"That's rough. We've heard they take heavy losses." When he saw the expression on Grace's face, he quickly added, "I'm sorry. I shouldn't have said that."

"It's okay," Grace replied. "You are correct. They do take heavy losses. He's only got one more mission and he'll come off ops for several months. We'll get married then."

"I envy him," Doug said. "Not only does he get to marry you, but he's finishing up his tour. I haven't flown a single mission yet."

"Really?"

"Honest truth. We just got here a month ago. They've had us doing all sorts of training. Navigation, practice bomb runs, formation flying. You name it. We got some leave because we'll be operational in a few days. I think the brass wants us to blow off some steam before we go into action."

Grace nodded politely but said nothing.

"So how did you meet your fiancé?" Doug asked.

"Michael," Grace said. "His name is Michael."

She told him about the movie theater and their first real date the next night when Michael took her to a fish and chips shop and then another movie. Grace had listened as Michael told her about growing up in Ardoyne in North Belfast and of his flight training in Canada. When he asked, Grace talked about the large house outside of London and the loss of her brother. Michael reached across the table and squeezed her hand as she told him of how her brother's death also killed her mother. She was drawn to the sadness buried deep within his brown eyes which contrasted with his ready laugh and caring nature. In Michael, Grace found the empathy she'd never gotten at home.

"I hope I can meet someone like you," Doug said when she finished her story.

"She's not really like me, but my friend Helen loves Americans, though she is really interested in ones from California."

Doug laughed. "I've been to California. I'll take Louisiana any day. I just want to finish this war up and get back home. Preferably in one piece."

"You don't have a girl at home, then?"

"No," Doug said with a grimace. "I had a girl, but when I went off to flight training she sent me a letter and said she wasn't going to wait for me like she promised."

"I'm sorry," Grace said. "Sorry I asked and sorry about what happened."

"Naw... it's okay," Doug replied. "It's for the best. To tell you the truth, I'm terrified of going into combat. We hear all these stories about how new crews don't last long. Did, or does, what's his name? Michael? Does he ever talk about being afraid?"

"He never tells me much at all about what he does," said Grace as she remembered the story McKenzie told earlier that day. *Searchlights, flak, getting 'coned.' I want to know but at the same time I'd prefer I didn't. The men on his crew says he doesn't show fear, but I've heard him at night when he is asleep.* The first night they spent together, Grace and Michael shared a lumpy bed in the corner room of a seedy motel tucked deep inside the East End. The clerk did not raise an eyebrow at an unmarried couple. The hotel's best days, if there ever really were any, were decades past. Grace feared she might contract a virus just from the sheets. Michael assured her that was not a likely event. She hadn't planned on sleeping with him, at least not that quickly. It just happened. It was late and Michael didn't have a room to stay in. Grace could not take him back to her apartment, so they settled on a hotel. *It's the war*, she told herself. *It changes everything. What if this is the last chance he gets to be with a girl? He could die tomorrow. I could die tomorrow. Don't we deserve some happiness?*

When they fell asleep, Michael lay on his back with his arm around Grace's shoulders. During the night he began to squirm and twitch. *Watch out*, he yelled. *Fighter on the port beam. Jesus Christ! Make sure your bleedin' chutes are on! Lanc on fire just ahead. Get out! Jump! Goddamnit! They blew up!* She lay there next to him, frozen, unsure what to do. After several minutes, a person in the room next door pounded on the wall and yelled, "Shut up! We're trying to sleep in here!" Michael bolted upright in the bed, nearly tossing Grace onto the floor in the process. He looked around the room, eyes wide. His breath came in ragged gasps.

"What?" he asked. "Where am I?"

He jumped when Grace squeezed his arm, and then the present came back to him. Michael apologized profusely, and kept doing so throughout the rest of the next day. Grace tried to reassure him that she didn't care, but he insisted he had ruined their time together. *As if a nightmare could ruin our first time*, Grace thought. When she left him at the station, he said very little and gave her a chaste kiss on the cheek before he disappeared into the train. Two days, two very long days, later he called and apologized for his behavior. In their few nights together since, though the nightmares still came, Grace never spoke of them and did not attempt to wake him. *Better to leave that subject be, just like… just like the other.*

"Ma'am?"

Grace turned her focus back onto Doug, who looked at her with concern in his eyes.

"Sorry," she said as she stood up from the table. "It's been very nice to meet you, Doug. I wish you all the best when you get to your squadron, but the smoke in here is getting to me. I think I'll walk home. It isn't far. Would you tell my friends for me?"

Doug rose from his chair.

"I'll walk with you," he offered.

"No!" Grace said a bit more forcefully than she intended. "That's nice of you, really it is, but I'll be okay. I hope you find a nice girl while you're in England, Doug."

She reached over and squeezed his hand and, before he had time to say another word, she drifted across the dance floor, dodging happy couples locked in each other's arms, until she passed through the door and out into the street. She took several deep breaths, filling her lungs with fresh air.

"Everything okay, miss?" the doorman asked.

"Yes, fine," Grace said. "I'm not feeling very well, that's all."

She turned to walk away and then paused and faced the doorman again.

"Do you remember the girl I came here with?"

"Of course," the doorman said, "I'd not soon forget a bird like that."

"Well, when you see her leave, could you tell her I walked home?"

"Certainly, miss," the doorman said. "I hope you feel better."

Grace smiled. *I won't feel better until Michael calls me and says he's safely back from Number Thirty. I should never have gotten involved with a pilot, but I've fallen in love with him. The war… the damn, bloody, war. Why can't it just be over? We can't hardly make a life together when he's bouncing around from assignment to assignment. Dear God, just let him come home one more time. That's all I ask. Just one more time.*

CHAPTER FOUR

URSULA STOOD IN the window and watched as the fire engines drove away. The smell of burned fish did little to improve the appeal of the small apartment. Still, with well over 100,000 homeless residents in Berlin, a small apartment was better than no apartment at all, even if she shared it with two other people. *The fireman seemed nice*, she thought as the engine disappeared around the corner. *I would hate to have his job, especially now.* As a telephone operator, she did not worry about conscription into another occupation as the government considered her job essential to the war effort. The clock struck five, and she closed the window and drew the heavy curtains closed. Night would descend on the city soon, and to show any light risked the wrath of the air raid warden for the block, Herr Schroeder, who, drunk with the power of his office, imposed stiff fines on those who violated the government standards. Repeat offenders received a referral to the police. *I need to steer well clear of him. And the police.*

Ursula crossed over to the small bathroom in the hallway situated between the two bedrooms. She coaxed enough water from the sink to splash some on her face. *It's time*, she thought. Grabbing a threadbare gray overcoat from a rack by the door, Ursula ducked out of the apartment and walked down the stairs. The government rationed clothing along with food, which forced residents of Berlin to wear clothes they'd have thrown away just a few years earlier. When she reached the door which led to the street, Ursula paused and surveyed the area before she stepped outside. Nothing appeared out of place. She produced a white scarf from her coat pocket and tied it around her head. A few strands of red hair poked out from beneath it and she tucked them back inside before pushing open the door.

Now comes the fun part, Ursula said to herself.

After another quick glance, Ursula began to walk down the block, headed east towards the city center. She took no notice of a man seated on a bench with a newspaper in front of his face. When she reached the end of the block, the man stood up and began to follow from a discreet distance but she did not see him. Every few blocks, Ursula stopped and made a show of looking into a store window. After a minute, she continued to walk. On the left, an alley ran between two large apartment buildings. She turned into the alley and followed it to the next street. When Ursula reached that street, she turned and began to walk in the direction she'd just come from. After an hour of walking a zig-zag route, Ursula reached her destination, a scant six blocks from where she started. After another check of her surroundings, she moved into another alley and knocked on the back door of a squat, gray warehouse. Three knocks. A pause. Two more. Another pause. And then four. She heard movement inside.

As she waited, the pace of her heartbeat slowly returned to normal. The thrill of secret meetings and assignments filled her with excitement, though it was mixed with a twinge of guilt. *What we're doing is important for the future*, she lectured herself, *it isn't like a spy film. It's for real and with real consequences.*

The door opened and a middle-aged man in a ragged suit motioned her to enter. He closed the door behind her and beckoned her to follow him down a dark corridor which terminated at a large bookcase. The man pulled it open. Inside was another room, lit by a single lightbulb which swayed from the ceiling. Two other men, younger, and a woman who appeared to be in her late teens sat around a small table. Blue cigarette smoke covered the ceiling. Six months of weekly meetings and Ursula still did not know their names. *Better that way*, she thought as she stepped into the room as the bookcase door closed behind her. *Less to say if we get caught by the Gestapo.*

"Did you bring them?" the man who opened the door for her asked. She mentally referred to him as Beard Man due to the long white beard which hung down to the middle of his chest.

"Yes," Ursula replied. She removed her overcoat and placed it on the table. Then she lifted the hem of her skirt and produced a small package wrapped in brown paper held in place by her garter. The eyes of the men followed her skirt up and then back down. Ursula picked up her coat and dropped the package on the table, where one of the young men – Blondie, she called him – picked it up and unwrapped it. The package contained two sets of forged identity papers and two ration books, also forged.

"Perfect," Blondie said. He handed them to the third man, Blue Eyes, who stuck them into the inside pocket of his coat.

"Were you followed?" the woman asked.

"No," Ursula said with a shake of her head. "I was careful."

"As well you should be," Beard Man said as he walked to the center of the room. "As well we all should be. Last week the Gestapo grabbed one of our agents in Munich. Thank God he doesn't know very much."

"But what he does know he'll tell," Blue Eyes said. "The Gestapo can be very persuasive."

Ursula suppressed an intense desire to shiver. Most people in Berlin knew at least one person who had disappeared since the Nazis came to power. She'd been thirteen years old that spring. Her father ranted at the radio in the living room of their flat in Wedding. Her younger brothers, Thomas, nine, and Erich, eleven, seemed excited by it all. Uniforms, torch-light processions, and the joy of belonging to a group appealed to them. Each joined the Hitler Youth at the earliest opportunity, much to their father's dismay. Herr Müller referred to the National Socialists as 'those damn idiots' or 'Hitler and his circus full of clowns' in private. Soon, with his sons both enthralled with the movement, Müller no longer spoke of the Nazis at all unless it was in a hushed whisper to Ursula. She was the only family member he could confide in.

A car had struck and killed Ursula's mother in 1937 as she crossed the street in front of their apartment. Her father died on the day the government announced the invasion of Poland. *Better that way*, Ursula thought. *He'd fought in the first war and at least he was spared from the death of his sons.* Erich fell near Leningrad in 1941 and Thomas in Stalingrad last winter. As their next of kin, Ursula received the official notices. Many families in Berlin received the same terse death notifications after the invasion of Russia. You never complained though, at least not in public. If a comment made its way to the Gestapo, agents might come to your home and 'invite' you to accompany them for a chat, provided the comment wasn't too extreme. If it was, Gestapo agents pounded on your door around sunrise, their preferred time to strike, and hauled you away, never to be seen again. A single arrest yielded many more as they forced a person to denounce others as well. Ursula, like everyone in Berlin, heard rumors of beatings, fingernails yanked out, or electric shocks in sensitive places, but no one knew for sure what they did unless they did it to you. And if so, you never told a soul because you'd never see the light of day again.

"We've got another assignment for you," the woman said. "If you are up to it."

"I am," Ursula said. She had inherited her father's distaste for the regime, which grew to outright disgust as time passed. The boarded-up windows of shops once owned by Jewish merchants, the beatings of political opponents in the streets, and the heavy, palpable sense of being watched filled her with shame for a country that had once been a center of European culture. Yet, despite the shame, she longed for a Germany rid of the Nazis. Six months ago, Beard Man had approached her in a café and asked to sit with her. They made small talk, and he dropped little hints, sly comments really, about the Nazis. When she responded with a laugh rather than outrage, he asked to meet her again the next day. After two weeks of feeling each other out, Beard Man brought her to the warehouse and introduced her to the others.

It was only then that he told her that he'd known her father, which was why he decided to contact her in the first place. The group provided forged documents to those on the run from the government. Some Jews, some not, but all of them wanted. Ursula served as a courier. She picked up the paperwork and delivered it to the group, which then distributed it to the people who purchased them. The others never spoke of why they risked their lives in such a pursuit. It could have been money or it could have been patriotism. The less she knew, the better. Ursula refused to accept any pay no matter how much or how often they offered. *To accept pay would make me a what? Mercenary? Spy? I'm not doing this for money. I'm doing this because I love Germany as my father did.*

"We need you to pick up another package for us," the woman said. "Tomorrow night."

"Certainly," Ursula replied.

"It's not documents this time," Blondie said as he took a deep drag on his cigarette, eyes fixed on her face.

"It's a gun," Blue Eyes added.

"A gun?"

"Yes. A pistol. It won't be with the same person you normally meet," Blue Eyes said as his fingers drummed on the top of the table.

"Good." Ursula thought of the printer who made the forged documents. He always made a point to stand as close to her as he could, and his leering eyes gave her goose bumps.

"Read this," Blondie said, handing her a scrap of paper.

Ursula took it and read the address. It was in Charlottenburg, twenty blocks away from her apartment.

"Got it?" Blondie asked. Ursula nodded, and he reached over and took the paper from her hand. He lit it with the tip of his cigarette and then dropped it in the ashtray.

"When you get there, give the same knock you give here," Beard Man instructed. "When the door opens, ask for Herr Furst. The person will say, 'I'm sorry but Herr Furst is not here at the moment.' That's when you say, 'Oh, what a pity.'"

Say it exactly that way. Exactly. They'll let you in and get you set up. You'll need to come straight back here once you get the package. Questions?"

"Yes," Ursula said. "What time should I get there?"

Beard Man turned and looked at Blondie, who said, "9:30."

"9:30," Ursula repeated. "And you'll be expecting me here?"

"Yes," Beard Man said. "Take your time getting back. Make sure you aren't being followed. I don't need to tell you what the Gestapo would do to you if they caught you out in the blackout with a pistol..."

Ursula failed to suppress the shiver this time. *What was the gun for? An assassination? If they catch me with it they won't waste time with interrogation. It'll be straight to Plötzensee Prison and the guillotine.*

"May I ask what the pistol is for?" Ursula asked.

"Better you didn't," Beard Man said. "Less to say if you get caught."

"And if you do get caught," the woman said, "forget you ever met us. Try and think up a story you can tell them about how you came by the gun that they might believe. The Gestapo men aren't stupid, but they are men. Use whatever you have to. Understand?"

Ursula nodded.

"I cannot stress how important this is," Beard Man said. "If you think you are about to be nabbed, you'd better off pulling the pistol out and using it on yourself. It'll be easier than what those goons will do to you."

Dear God, Ursula thought. *What have I gotten myself into?*

Blue Eyes pulled a knife from behind his back and

slammed the point into the table with such force that it rattled the ashtrays. Everyone jumped, even Beard Man.

"And just so we are clear," Blue Eyes said, tapping his index finger on the hilt of the knife as it wobbled back and forth, "if I find out you are working for the Gestapo, you'll wish it was them who had you and not me. If we get caught, I'll know it was you. And there are others who know where to find you. Understand?"

A thin trickle of perspiration ran down the side of Ursula's face and dripped onto the floor. She wiped her damp palms on the front of her skirt and tried to swallow with a mouth gone suddenly dry.

"I'm not working for the Gestapo," she protested. "If I was they'd have grabbed you long ago. You know that!"

"Come on," Beard Man said as he patted Ursula's back and glared at Blue Eyes. "No need to scare the girl. She's done good work for us. You've said so yourself."

"Just making sure she knows the score," Blue Eyes replied in an even tone.

"You remember what you are to do?" Beard Man asked.

Ursula nodded.

"Alright then, I'll walk you out."

By the time she stepped into the alley, a heavy darkness covered the city. With the blackout, you took a big risk if you ventured out after dark. The government preferred people stay off the street, but many residents sported black eyes and bandages from running into things in the dark. Ursula wore a small device on the lapel of her coat. It absorbed sunlight during the day and glowed at night. It did not provide enough illumination to see, but rather allowed her to be seen by others. Each night brought collisions between pedestrians, between people and lampposts, or, more tragically, people and vehicles. In this, the fourth year of the war, fatal accidents had decreased as the public grew more accustomed to the darkness. Ursula kept her shoulder close to the buildings and ran her hand along them as she walked lest she stray into the street. *It wouldn't do to get hit by a car before I pick up the package.* Unlike her earlier walk, Ursula took a direct route home this time. Right as she reached her door to her apartment building, the eerie howl of the air raid sirens rose about the city and sent electric jolts up and down her spine.

Not again, she thought as she pushed the door open. Residents hurried down the stairs towards the basement. Some carried suitcases while others clutched pillows or even pets. Several years ago, the city government instructed all buildings in the city to establish their own air raid shelters though they provided public shelters as well. Her apartment had a deep basement which had been converted into a shelter. It contained rows of wooden benches, more practical than comfortable, buckets of water in the event of fire, an air shaft which ran up to the ground level, and several buckets behind a curtain for use as a toilet. To prepare for the possibility of a blocked exit, some of the men in the building knocked out bricks from the wall which divided their shelter from the neighboring building and then carefully put the bricks back. In an emergency, the bricks could easily be removed.

Two nights prior, a large formation of bombers flew over the city, but most of the bombs fell well outside the city center. Months had passed since the last raid to do any serious damage. On some nights, people stayed in their shelters until almost dawn. Other times they might take shelter, then return to their homes when the all clear sounded only to be sent back to the shelters an hour or two later. *It's almost as if they don't want us to sleep*, Ursula thought as she pushed through the people on their way downstairs as she tried to go up. She bumped into her roommates, Gisela and Monika, on the third floor landing.

"Where have you been?" Gisela asked. She was a short, thick girl who'd grown up on a dairy farm before she moved to Berlin to find war work.

"Sorry," Ursula replied. "I went to visit a friend."

"There's no time to go upstairs," Monika, a girl with dark hair and dark eyes, protested. Like Gisela she wore a house-coat over her nightgown and carried a suitcase in her hand.

"I'll be alright," Ursula said. "I'm just going to get my suitcase and then I'll meet you down there."

"*Hurry*," Gisela urged as the press of those behind her propelled her and Monika down the stairs.

Ursula made her way to her apartment door. The siren seemed louder now, but she did not hear the sounds of the heavy anti-aircraft guns from the center of the city. She grabbed her battered suitcase from under her bed and joined the others who waited until the last minute to seek shelter. The government urged people to keep certain items in a suit-case or bag so that they did not waste time in getting to a shelter. Ursula had no important papers other than her iden-tity documents and ration book, and those she kept in the inside pocket of her overcoat. She carried a change of clothes, a sturdy pair of shoes, a flashlight, and a battered copy of *Gone With the Wind* in her suitcase to pass the time in the event of a false alarm. Even then it might take several hours before the all clear sounded. Other women brought their knitting with them and some board games for the children. Anything to pass the time and keep the mind from pondering whether the next bomb might hit your shelter. Ursula heard rumors from other cities, Hamburg in particular, which spoke of massive fires and thousands of deaths, but the government made no official announcements of casualties. Based on their fierce denunciations of the British *terrorfliegers*, Ursula assumed they must have been heavy indeed. Otherwise, the government would have boasted about a great victory in the sky rather than lamenting the destruction wrought by an invisible enemy overhead. *All worth it to end the war, I suppose.* She pushed open the heavy oak door which led to the basement stairs and made her way down the steps in the dark as her left hand ran along the smooth, cold stones. At the bottom of the steps, a heavier door opened into the shelter. She stood for a moment and looked into the shelter as her eyes adjusted to the light.

"Ursula! Over here!"

She caught sight of Monika, who waved above the heads of those gathered around her.

"We saved you a nice comfortable spot on our bench!" Gisela shouted.

Ursula sighed, walked into the shelter, and closed the door behind her.

CHAPTER FIVE

As SOON AS he arrived back at the base, Michael made his way to the Wing Commander's office. After two hours on a train, he welcomed the chance to stretch his legs a bit. The evening chill bit straight through his dark blue overcoat. Despite twenty-nine nightly visits over Germany, the cold still bothered him on the ground and in the air. *Why couldn't I have been stationed in North Africa,* he thought as he trudged across the damp grass towards the simple wooden building which housed his squadron office along with the wing offices. *But then I wouldn't have met Grace. Maybe that would've been better for her. She wouldn't be shackled to a corpse that way.* Three RAF clerks warmed themselves around a wood stove as Michael entered the office. None turned in his direction, so he hung his coat on a rack as noisily as he could. When that failed to attract their attention, he cleared his throat.

"Oh, Flying Officer O'Hanlon," a spectacled young airman said as he walked towards Michael, "back from leave, are you, sir?"

"So it would appear," Michael replied. "I need to see the Wing Commander."

"Is he expecting you, sir?"

"No," Michael said. "But I need to see him all the same."

The airman nodded and walked past a row of desks where three WAAF women typed furiously without even a glance at the activity around them. All wore determined expressions as they banged away at their typewriters. The chatter of the keys sounded like gunfire.

"Tea, sir?"

Michael turned and accepted a mug from another airman who'd managed to tear himself away from the stove long enough to pour a cup. As soon as Michael's hand closed around it, the airman retreated back to the stove. The liquid burned his throat as it went down. *Damn English and their damn tea. How'd these people ever get an Empire?* As a Catholic in Belfast, Michael saw firsthand the arrogance of English rule, with their discriminatory laws against adherents of his religion. His own father, though he fought in the trenches in the Great War, served a year in jail after he and a group of other young men raided a police station during the war against the Black and Tans. The RIC shot two of the men dead and arrested his father and three others. *Yet here I am, in a British uniform. Ironic, that.*

"Fer fuck's sake, boy," his father had said when Michael announced his desire to enlist in the Royal Air Force, "why do ya want to go and do that for? They'll only use you fer cannon fodder like they did in the first war. Mark my words, lad. You'll be sorry you took the King's shilling."

Michael mentioned his desire to fly, which Sean O'Hanlon found hilarious. Michael became enthralled with the idea of being a pilot after seeing *Dawn Patrol* a year before the war began. On September 3, 1939, Michael listened on the radio as the British Prime Minister announced that Great Britain was again at war with Germany. While many greeted the announcement of war with trepidation, Michael was elated. *This is my chance*, he had thought.

"They'll sooner let you be King of England before they'll let you in an airplane," Sean O'Hanlon said. "You'll be handed a rifle and packed off to die like so many of me friends in the last show."

Michael performed well in front of the Aircrew Selection Board, which approved his application for aircrew service, and in his initial training. Before long the RAF sent him to Canada to train with pilots from all over the Commonwealth. The trip across the Atlantic made him glad he joined the RAF rather than the navy. During one submarine alert, a German U-boat hit a nearby ship. Michael had shivered on the deck, clad in a life jacket, and watched as the ship burned. Through the smoke, he saw men onboard the stricken vessel take the lifeboats, but Admiralty rules forbade any ships in a convoy from stopping to take on survivors lest they too fall victim to a submarine. For the first time since he'd enlisted, Michael realized what going to war meant. Or at least he thought he did. Later, in the night sky over Germany, he learned far more than he ever wanted to know about the business of killing and dying. Each mission brought new dangers or new ways of experiencing old ones. The sound of shrapnel as it pinged off the side of the aircraft. The chatter of the machine guns on his aircraft. The whoosh of a cannon shell from a night fighter. The glow of a German city as it burned. The roar of the engines on his Lancaster. The scream of a wounded crewman. *I've got a bellyful of this war. Even if it ends tomorrow, there'll only be another one in two years, maybe ten.*

"WingCo will see you now, sir," the airman said. Michael handed him the half empty mug of tea as he walked past him and into the office. Wing Commander Hugh Simpson, a stocky, dour man with a bushy black moustache, sat behind a desk piled with papers. He motioned Michael to sit across from him.

"Have a good leave?" he asked.

"I did," Michael replied. "A bit short, but aren't they all."

"You'll get a longer one soon enough," Simpson said. "And on that note, I know why you are here. There's not much I can do for you, I'm afraid."

Michael stiffened.

"But, sir," he protested, "surely there's some veteran crew who are missing a pilot right now. I'd be happy to take on any of them."

"Can't do it," Simpson said. "I am assigning your replacements from Z for Zebra's crew. They flew their first mission a couple of nights ago. Went to Berlin. You were on that op, right? Anyway, the pilot pranged on landing because of some battle damage. Broke his shoulder and both legs. He won't be flying for a long while, if ever. I'm splitting the rest of the lot up. Three to you and three to T for Tom. So they won't be brand new. They'll have one flight under their belts. Best I can do for you, old chap."

"And there is no one else?" Michael asked.

"No, thankfully," Simpson replied. "The losses weren't as bad as the August raids. Sure, they'll be a little green around the gills, but I'm sure you can whip them into shape. I truly wish I could give you some with a little more experience, but I just can't."

Michael had flown over Berlin three times between August 23rd and September 3rd. The squadron lost planes on each mission. He knew each of the crews who failed to return and, for two of them, he also witnessed their demise. On the run over the target on the second mission, his bomb aimer had called out corrections. "Left, left. Steady on. Right. Right. Steady. Steady." A tremendous burst of flak lit up the sky. A Lancaster to his left drifted in front of him with both wings a mass of orange flame. Mentally he urged the crew to jump, but the plane rolled over on its wing and lost altitude. He strained to see if any chutes appeared. None did. On the third mission, searchlights coned a Lancaster just ahead of him in the bomber stream. A night fighter dove on the stricken plane even while flak continued to burst all around. The gunners tried to keep their gunsights on the target while the pilot took evasive action, but flashes in the cockpit marked where the fighter's cannon rounds struck home. His own gunners took a few shots at the fighter but it slipped away into the darkness. Michael worried about the location of the fighter for the rest of the trip. *He's out there somewhere. Stalking us. I know it.* He did not breathe a sigh of relief until his wheels touched down on the runway.

"Are we working tomorrow night, sir?" Michael asked.

"Since you mentioned it," Simpson said, "we just got an alert order for tomorrow. We don't have any of our planes up tonight. Your plane should be ready in the morning. Your ground crew have been working on it around the clock since you got back. Take her up after breakfast tomorrow and make sure everything is in order."

"Yes, sir," Michael said.

"With your new crewmen, of course," Simpson added. "I've told them to expect you to stop by and chat with them this evening."

"I will. And, sir... any word of the target for tomorrow night?"

"No idea," Simpson said. "But even if I did know, I couldn't tell you. Come on. You know that."

"Figured it wouldn't hurt to ask, sir."

"My God, you Irish are a crafty race!" Simpson exclaimed. "Let's hope it's to somewhere with no ack-ack and no night fighters, eh? It wouldn't do to get the chop on your last mission before you come off ops, now would it?"

"No, sir."

"That'd be a damned bad show. Have one of the airmen run you over to the enlisted men's quarters. Have a chat with your new men. Scare them. Bribe them. I don't care. Just make sure you get back here after the next one. We haven't had a crew complete a tour in a few months. Bad for morale, you know. I'm sure the lads would love to lay one on for you when you get back."

The airman who fetched his cup of tea earlier drove Michael towards the enlisted quarters in a truck which bounced and swayed its way along the ground. Michael kept a bicycle at the hut he shared with five other officers as the base was spread out to minimize the potential for damage from German bombers which, though the air raid siren sounded on occasion, never came. A few slit trenches and sandbagged bunkers dotted the landscape around the base, though few used them during an alert. The truck lurched to a sudden stop outside a collection of wooden huts and a few of the metal Quonset type.

"They are in the first one on the left there, sir," the airman said as Michael climbed out of the cab. "Want me to wait for you, sir? So's you don't have to walk back when you are done?"

"Thank you," Michael replied. "It won't take long."

When Michael walked into the long, narrow barracks, six

empty bunks caught his attention. Enlisted crews from three planes shared one living space, eighteen men total. Enlisted pilots had their own accommodations. If a crew failed to return, the others in their quarters went through their belongings to ensure no embarrassing material made its way to their next of kin. It wouldn't do for the parents of an eighteen-year-old gunner to receive a stack of dirty magazines or condoms along with their personal effects, much less a wife if the man was married. Inside he found six men at a card table near a wood stove and another six gathered around a radio. He stood in the door for a full minute before one of the card players looked his way.

"Look lively, lads," the man said. "We've got an officer in the door."

Some made an effort to stand, but Michael waved his hand at them to tell them to remain seated.

"Where's Zebra's crew?" he asked.

Six men raised their hands.

"Which of you are assigned to me? P for Paul?"

Three hands went down. Three stayed up.

"Right. You three come with me."

He walked outside and waited for them to join him. When they did, Michael led them around the side of the hut out of earshot of any eavesdroppers.

"Which of you is which?" Michael asked.

"I'm Graham, sir. Wireless operator," said a pimply faced youth with crooked teeth.

"How old are you?" Michael asked.

"Eighteen, sir," Graham replied.

He's lying, Michael thought. *I'd wager a pint he's barely a day over seventeen.*

"Williams, sir. Gunner," said a short, stocky lad with thick black hair when Michael's eyes wandered in his direction.

"Welsh?" Michael asked.

"I am, sir. Father and grandfather were coal miners. I'd be one too had I not joined up."

"We're a bit of a mixed crew," Michael said. "I'm Irish as you can tell. We have an Australian and a Scotsman. May as well add a Welshman too."

Michael turned to the third man.

"Turner, sir. Navigator." He was a bit taller than the other two, but still an inch or so shorter than Michael.

"Welcome to my crew," Michael began. "As you know, we've one more trip to make and we come off ops. You are replacing three men who, well, they won't be going with us on the next one. I know you've been over Berlin. But don't kid yourselves into thinking you are veterans now. At fifteen missions, you think you've seen it all. At twenty-nine missions, you realize you haven't. That's what makes a veteran crew, which my crew was until you lot came along. All I ask is that you do your jobs. If one of my men dies because you screwed up, I'll personally boot your arse out of my plane over Germany without a parachute. Got it?"

They nodded with considerable vigor.

"Good. One more thing, we took some battle damage last week. The WingCo assures me it is fixed. We'll be going up in the morning for a shake down flight in case we visit Herr Hitler tomorrow night. Be at the plane at 0800. You can meet the rest of the crew then. You'll need to learn the way I run my aircraft before we go on an op, not during. Any questions?"

"Where do you think we'll go tomorrow?" asked Williams.

"How the bloody hell would I know?" Michael asked. "I

find out at the same time as you. All I know is that we're alerted for an op."

"I hope it isn't Berlin again," Graham offered. "I've had enough of that place."

"Listen to me, boy," Michael said as his face tightened into a sharp frown, "I've made three over Berlin and all in the same week. You've a long way to go before you have a right to be tired of any target. You think Berlin was bad? Try the Ruhr."

"Sorry, sir," Graham said, a sheepish look on his face.

"Get some rest. That's an order. Get a good meal in you tomorrow morning too."

Michael turned to walk away but stopped and called back over his shoulder, "And 0800 tomorrow. Sharp. Don't be late or I'll have your guts for garters."

With that, he hopped into the cab of the truck and signaled the driver to go. As the truck crossed the airfield in the gathering twilight, Michael pondered the new men added to his crew. *They're bloody children*, he thought. *Schoolboys. Christ! They are just a year or so younger than McKenzie and the rest. Have we aged that much in the last four months? I suppose we must have looked the same to the old hands when we arrived here. None of those old hands are still around. They are all pushing up daisies or cooling their heels in a POW camp now. And we'll be with them soon enough, either in the grave or in a camp.*

"How was it, sir?"

Michael turned and looked at the airman behind the wheel who picked his nose with one hand and drove with the other. He removed a piece of snot, held it in front of his face and studied it for a minute, and then flipped it out the window.

"What?" Michael asked.

"How was the new lot you've been assigned? Eager to have a crack at the Hun, are they?"

"They'll do. They'll have to. It isn't like I've got a choice in the matter," Michael replied. "The place seems deserted tonight. Where is everyone?"

"At the pubs, most likely," the airman replied. "No mission tonight, so most of the aircrew went to the villages. I think the last mission shook them up a bit, sir. If you don't mind my saying so."

Michael's airfield, Thomas Green, made up a complex of three large bomber bases. Each of the bases had a village nearby, and all three villages were a long bicycle ride or a short bus trip away. The airfields, on evenings with no operations, often allowed the aircrew and some of the non-flying personnel to visit the pubs. Bases ran trucks to shuttle them down and back. The last trucks typically left the villages at 9 p.m. and woe unto anyone not on the last truck. If you missed it, a walk through the darkened countryside awaited you unless you managed to entice a local to use some of their precious fuel to run you down to the airfield in their own car. This was not at all likely as the villagers, though they enjoyed the money spent by the aircrew, did not necessarily like them. A spate of hasty marriages and, worse yet, unwed mothers among the young ladies in the vicinity served to make the populace less than welcoming. *Still*, Michael thought, *at least we aren't the Yanks.*

"Here you go, sir," the driver said as the truck stopped outside a series of buildings no different than those used by the enlisted men. Michael nodded his thanks as he climbed out of the cab. Rather than go into his hut and escape the chill of the evening, Michael leaned against the wall and stared up at the sky. *Tomorrow we'll be up there right about now. Heading off to God knows where. Six lives depend on me, and tomorrow I'll let them down. We won't come back. Not from this one. I know it. I can feel it.*

A sudden craving for a cigarette hit him. Michael smoked on rare occasions, usually after a rough mission, or sometimes before to calm his nerves. *Damn*, he thought as he patted his pockets and found no cigarette pack. *Maybe one of the lads inside has some.* As he turned to walk into his quarters, he took one last look up at the sky. *Surely heaven's not up there. Up in the clouds filled with flak and Hun planes. I guess I'll find out soon enough.*

CHAPTER SIX

WHEN THEY ARRIVED at the fire station after the call, Karl walked upstairs to the third floor, where he found the Hitler Youth boys gathered around the table where the four young women sat. The young man who had earlier questioned Karl's Iron Cross ribbon was in the middle of a story. He made wild gestures with his hands as he talked. Karl waited in the door for a full two minutes. No one noticed him.

"What is the meaning of this!" he asked. The young men and women turned to face him and immediately snapped to attention. "Do you think this is a summer camp?"

He glared at the boy who had been engaged in storytelling.

"No, Herr Oberwachtmeister," the boy said. "We were just... just taking a break. That's all."

"A break? And what have you done to deserve that?"

The boy made an attempt to speak, but Karl cut him off.

"Silence. You boys go downstairs and report to Frei. You'll be in his charge. I expect he has some work you can do."

I'm being too hard on them, he thought. *I left them no instructions and it is only natural they would want to talk to the girls.*

The boys gathered up their notebooks, helmets, and gas mask canisters and trooped down the stairs. Karl turned to face the young women, who gave him a sheepish look. All, that is, except Schneider. The corners of her mouth turned up in a smile as her eyes locked onto his.

"My apologies, ladies," he said. "Those boys are hard cases. They think they've seen it all. I'd give them a wide berth if I were you. Now, you four will be with me and Fischer. He's a good man, if a bit old fashioned. Now tell me, how much training have you actually had?"

"Two weeks," Schneider said. The other three girls nodded in agreement.

"What exactly did they have you doing?" Karl asked.

"Obstacle courses. We drilled on putting on our gas masks. And using the hoses," the younger of the four girls added.

"And your name?" Karl asked.

"Hartmann," she replied. "Erika Hartmann."

She's a pretty little thing, Karl thought. Shorter than the other girls, Hartmann had sandy blonde hair and green eyes, but her erect posture and determined expression spoke of a wisdom beyond her years.

"How old are you?" Karl asked. "Be honest?"

"Seventeen, Herr Oberwachtmeister," she replied.

"And you, Schneider?"

"Twenty."

Karl looked at the other two. Both had the stocky build of a farmer's daughter. Broad shoulders, hair in pigtails and pinned on top their heads, tough expressions on their faces.

"And you two? Names and ages, please?"

"Ingrid Koch, nineteen," the taller of the two replied.

"Elisabeth Becker, eighteen," the other girl said.

"Since you are here on a voluntary basis," Karl said, "I

mean, voluntary in the sense that you won't be paid, I have decided to put you on this schedule. Report here no later than 5 p.m. You'll be on duty until you are released, which could be several hours, or even days, if we get a big raid. If no raid comes, I'll try to relieve you around 3 a.m. so you can get some rest. I assume you have jobs during the day?"

They all nodded. The RAF did more than just drop bombs. The constant threat of air raids meant the sirens sounded more often. In most cases, no planes appeared, yet the threat of an inbound raid meant Berliners spent much of their nights in shelters, either those provided by the government or in basement shelters under their own buildings. Bomb damage made the commute to work difficult as well, so a ten-minute walk might turn into an hour. Disruptions of the S-Bahn and the U-Bahn caused more delays. All of this had a detrimental effect on work productivity, especially for those employers engaged in war industries. The government exhorted the population to keep up. Some employers adjusted their work schedules so that employees could arrive home no later than 4 p.m. to catch some sleep before a raid. However, when the bombs fell, workers often could not get into work until mid-morning, or even later. Commutes of two hours each way after a big raid, such as those in late August, had become more and more common.

Even the Fire Brigade's hours shifted as the war dragged on and raids grew more frequent. In peacetime, firemen worked a series of rotating day and night schedules. In 1939, the department switched to a forty-eight-hour tour followed by twelve hours off duty. By November of 1943, the military had called up most of the younger men. Those who remained did more work with less manpower and equipment. Firefighters stayed on duty more or less continuously, with a few hours off here and there. The routine calls did not go away just because there was a war on, and the war-related calls piled on top. Karl, like the men in his crew, sported large bags under his eyes. His limbs hurt. His back hurt. A week's sleep might help, but he knew no one would get any rest until the war ended, one way or the other. Their job entitled them to a bit more food than the average Berliner as the government calculated the daily calorie allowance based on the age and the type of work the person did. Even with the increased rations, the firemen still ate far less than they did in peacetime. The constant gnaw of hunger never moved far from their thoughts unless they were out during an air raid when the fear of death pushed everything from the mind. The lack of food made them lethargic at times, particularly after a full night's work during a raid that stretched well into the next day. *We're like horses who have to pull heavy wagons with nothing to eat but bits of grass or the bark off of a tree. I ate better in the army.*

"Will we be here on duty tonight?" Schneider asked, a note of hope in her voice.

"Yes," Karl replied. "You may as well start now. Go down to the second floor and select a bunk. Grab some rest if you want, but do not remove any articles of clothing. We have to be ready to go at a moment's notice."

"I'm not taking off anything in front of those boys," Hartmann said.

"Be professional with them and nothing more," Karl suggested. "Come on. Let's get you sorted out."

Karl led them down the stairs to the second floor and waited as each of them selected a cot. He then showed them the office, the bathrooms, and instructed them on how to use the fire poles. When he finished, Karl brought them down to the apparatus floor and showed them where to hang their helmets and gas mask canisters. A breeze blew through the open station doors and Karl heard Frei yell, "Come on! Get up that ladder! You climb as slow as my grandmother! Go! Go!" Karl poked his head out and saw the truck's ladder raised to the roof. One boy struggled to climb as the others gathered around the truck and looked up at him in apprehension as they awaited their turns. Karl suppressed a laugh as he turned back to his female charges.

"What happens during a raid?" Koch asked.

"What do you mean?" Karl asked.

"What do we do?"

"When the alert comes in," Karl said, "we check our equipment and stand by. One of us mans the telephone since that is how we are notified we are needed. If the phones are out, a messenger on a bike will come and tell us. If it is a heavy raid, we just head to where the bombs are falling."

"You mean we go out during the raid? Not after?" Becker asked.

"Of course," Karl said with a chuckle. "That's when they need us the most. The biggest threat is fire. Once those are under control we can shift our focus to rescue work. We have help from the Luftschutz, the police, and civilians. It's not so bad, really. When you are focused on putting out a large fire, you don't even notice the bombs."

Unless they hit near you and you get splattered with shrapnel, Karl thought. *Best not to tell them that. We can only pray we have no Hamburg here.* Karl and the others from Berlin, fighting alongside the Hamburg firemen, had made a valiant effort, but a firestorm started anyway. *Like a tornado of fire sweeping over everything in its path!* The winds which flowed into the base of the flames pulled people off their feet and sucked them into the pyre. Even the streets burned. Damage to the city water supply rendered the firemen impotent in the face of the combined assault of high explosives and incendiaries. When the bombers finally switched to other targets, civil defense authorities started the long process of recovering the dead. Bodies lay in heaps in the streets, charred beyond all recognition. In some shelters, fifty or more people looked as though they might have fallen asleep when in fact they died from carbon monoxide or from asphyxiation as the massive fire sucked all the oxygen out of the air. Others died of blast lung when the concussion of a blast wave ruptured their lungs. They too gave little outward indication of what happened. Karl had wanted to shake their shoulders and tell them to get up. He'd seen death in Poland, France, and Russia, but nothing prepared him for the countless dead he saw in Hamburg. Men, women, children, elderly people, or babies, the bombs did not discriminate and dealt death to all without regard for age or gender. After two weeks, he returned to Berlin only to face heavy raids in his own city a month later at the end of August. *Still*, he thought, *as bad as that was, it was nothing like Hamburg.*

He walked back upstairs and went into the office, where he found Fischer seated in front of the radio.

"Something's up," Fischer reported. "There may be a raid on. The radio said something but I didn't catch what. Should we tell the kids?"

"No," Karl said. "Let them enjoy themselves for a little while. There is no reason to get them excited or scared if it turns out to be nothing."

Fischer nodded. The sound of laughter drifted through the open office door. The young women were gathered around one of the bunks and Hartmann produced a deck of cards from inside the bag she carried with her.

"How do you think they'll do?" Fischer asked.

"I don't know," Karl replied. "It's hard to know how anyone will act until they face danger. Then you find out."

"Remember that kid we had here back in… '36 or '37? What was his name?"

"'36. It was right before the Olympics. Heinz was his name, I think."

The station had received a new recruit with the standard training course of two weeks' duration, which the department used at the time. When he arrived at the station, the young man managed to anger all of the old hands in a matter of two days. It just so happened those two days were much slower than normal, with plenty of downtime. Heinz spent the time boasting of his prowess in training and all of the people he planned to rescue during his career. When a call came in one afternoon for a fire on Bismarck Strasse, Heinz put his gear on and hopped on the engine. The officer sent Karl and Heinz into the building with a hose line. They found the fire in a back room on the ground floor. Karl held the nozzle and, as he sprayed water back and forth, the hose got suddenly heavy. He turned and saw no one where he expected Heinz to be. His shouts, muffled by his gas mask, got no answer so he focused on his effort to put the fire out. With that accomplished, Karl began to search for Heinz. He finally found him crouched in the corner with his knees drawn up to his chest as he rocked back and forth. It took ten minutes for Karl to coax him to get up. They brought him back to the station, where

Heinz gathered up his personal items and left. The men never saw him again. Karl laughed as he thought of it.

"It wasn't much of a fire either," Karl said.

"Better he find it out at a small one than at a big one," Fischer said. "What do you think happened to him? After he left us, I mean."

"He's probably in the army by now," Karl said. "If he is still alive. I rather doubt he'd be much use in a combat unit though."

"Shhh! Listen!" Fischer said as he gestured towards the radio.

"*Achtung! Achtung!*" An official voice filled the room. "Enemy bomber formations are in the vicinity of Hannover and Braunschweig. Possible targets include Berlin. Stand by for more information."

"Shit," Fischer said. "Do you think it is the real thing or another decoy?"

"I don't know," Karl said. "I guess we'll find out soon enough."

He heard the sound of the ladder truck as it backed into the station seconds before the air raid sirens began to wail. The laughter from the bunk room stopped as the sound of the siren sucked all the conversation out of the building. A tingle ran up and then down Karl's spine. He stood and stretched in an attempt to ward off the heavy sense of gloom which enveloped him every time he heard the sound. Fischer followed him into the room where the young women were putting their cards away.

"Come along," Karl said. "Let's go check your equipment, and I'll show you where we wait out the raids until we are called. It's fairly safe."

The women looked more nervous than scared, which reassured Karl. *I'm nervous myself. No shame in that.* Downstairs the Hitler Youth boys stood around their truck with helmets on and gas masks at the ready. Frei saw Karl as he descended the stairs and shook his head like a man who knows his life depends on things outside his control.

"Tonight of all nights," Frei said. "Damn Tommies."

"Put your gear on the truck," Karl said. "We don't go rushing off just because the air raid sirens go off. Sometimes we do and sometimes we don't. If this is a real raid, we'll know it soon enough. I promise."

Karl watched as they complied with his instructions, then he led them all into a room in the back of the station. Chairs lined the walls, and a small table in one corner held a phone and a radio. Karl plugged the radio into a receiver set to give air raid updates. As bomber formations approached the coast, radio stations went off the air. The receiver set allowed people to listen to updates and a second channel allowed them to hear radar and flak communications. In the event of a raid on Berlin, Karl tuned it to the flak channel and used a large flak map pinned to the wall to chart where the bombs were most likely to fall. Fischer took up the spot nearest the phone and kept his hand poised near enough to answer quickly. Karl unbuttoned his tunic and draped it over the back of his chair. Then he produced a pack of cigarettes. He offered them to the others present. Schneider took one as did the cocky Hitler Youth boy, who coughed explosively when he tried to inhale. Karl caught Baumann's eye and Baumann smiled. When he finished his smoke, Karl crossed his arms and tucked his hands under his armpits. *Don't show them you're scared. Don't let them see your hands shake.*

"What happens if we can't get the trucks out?" Hartmann asked.

"In that case, we try and catch a ride with another engine," Karl said. "Or we go on foot. The government has discussed getting us bicycles to use as a backup."

"I wouldn't worry about that," Frei said. "If a bomb hits close enough to pile rubble in front of our station doors to the extent we can't get our engines out, then we'll probably be buried in it ourselves."

"Correct," Baumann said. "Unless, of course, we've already been burned up by incendiaries."

"That's enough," Karl replied. Though a certain amount of ritual hazing took place with all new arrivals to a fire station, he did not want them to upset these new recruits before their first call.

The door opened and the crew from the ambulance shuffled in. They sat in the unclaimed chairs. The French doctor closed his eyes and fell asleep within a minute. The teenage Dutch labor conscript who drove the ambulance sat next to the doctor and began to tie his shoes. He untied them and then tied them again, over and over. The nurse produced some knitting from her handbag and began to work on a half-finished scarf. The government rationing of soap and toothpaste, and the presence of so many unwashed bodies in the confines of a small room, created a foul-smelling fog which clung to the ceiling. Karl, like most Berliners, had grown so accustomed to foul odors in public places that whereas in the past, such smells might have induced him to vomit, these days he barely noticed. To pass the time, Fischer began to tell a story about a call the men went on several days ago, one which Karl did not remember. Most of Fischer's stories involved various levels of lewdness, and with young women present, Karl felt the temptation to tell him to stop, but decided it was better to let something, anything, distract them from the bombs he hoped would not fall.

Karl leaned his head against the cool brick wall and shut his eyes. Images of flames and charred corpses danced their way back and forth across the recesses of his brain. The smell of burned flesh still lingered in his nostrils. It grew stronger every time he closed his eyes. Screams, bombs, bodies, explosions. *Why can't I get it out of my head? What is wrong with me? Why won't it stop!* Karl let out a deep sigh and opened his eyes. Everyone in the room appeared absorbed in their own thoughts, so Karl sat back to wait for the bombs.

CHAPTER SEVEN

THE BASEMENT SHELTER stank of unwashed bodies and the stale odor of fear. The fifty residents who occupied the wooden benches all sat in silence, lost in their own private worlds. When the war started, civilians treated air raid alerts as something akin to a holiday. They laughed and joked with each other as they waited for the all clear siren to sound. After the first heavy raid on Berlin, the jokes and smiles stopped. To experience a raid meant to sit in near total darkness as the shriek of bombs rose to such a pitch that they drowned out the sound of the sirens while the walls shook from nearby blasts and plaster dropped from the ceiling. Children sobbed. Men cursed the bomber crews and, on occasion, the government. On long nights underground, the smell from the buckets behind a curtain created an almost visible miasma which clung to the clothes of everyone in the room. Some women kept handkerchiefs dipped in perfume inside their emergency bags and discreetly dabbed their noses. Each time the siren howled, the citizens had no idea if it meant a heavy raid, a small nuisance raid, or a false alarm. The strain of it pressed down on them with the crushing weight of a heart attack. Even a nuisance raid could kill if the bombs fell on your street. The threat of bombs hung over the city like a giant sword of Damocles.

"So which friend did you visit?" Gisela asked as Ursula settled onto the bench next to her and Monika. Across the room a young mother began to read a story to her small children. Her voice shook as she read.

"Mutti," her daughter said, "are the men in the planes the same ones who killed daddy?"

"No," the mother replied. "The Russians killed daddy."

"Ursula?" Gisela asked.

"Oh, I went to visit Heinrich," Ursula lied.

Heinrich did not exist. Ursula invented him after she began to meet with the other members of the group. Since childhood Ursula had found pleasure and escape in books and, even now, with living space in Berlin at such a premium, she found room to keep her collection of novels. Since her roommates did not share her love of the written word, a fake literary friend seemed the easiest way to avoid questions.

"And all you do is talk about books?" Monika asked.

"Yes, that's all," Ursula said.

"You should invite him over for supper sometime so we can meet him," Gisela suggested.

"He's not very social," Ursula said and then shifted to a whisper. "Besides, with rationing being what it is, cooking for a guest is almost impossible."

Any public criticism of the government, the war, or the lack of food invited a denunciation to the Gestapo. It was as if the walls themselves heard every word. Prior to a statement about the government or a joke about the Nazis, Berliners first checked over their right and left shoulders lest anyone overhear their words – a mannerism that came to be known as the Berlin Glance. As the war dragged on and casualties and air raids mounted, people sometimes questioned the reason for such destruction, but they rarely criticized the government outright. Fear necessitated silence, but others maintained an intense belief that the Fuhrer would see them through no matter what.

"I don't know that I'd like to meet him," Monika said. "No offense, Ursula, but he sounds dreadfully boring. I'd much rather go out with an officer, preferably a pilot though maybe a U-boat commander would be nice too."

"I don't go out with him," Ursula said. "We just talk about the books we are reading. It's not like I'm planning on marrying him."

"Maybe you should," Gisela said. "Men worth marrying are scarce enough as it is. And why isn't he in the army, anyway?"

When she invented Heinrich, Ursula had anticipated this question so she said, "His eyesight is terrible and his lungs are bad. He tried to enlist but they wouldn't take him. He works as a clerk in a shop."

"His eyesight is probably bad from all the reading," Gisela replied. "That's why I stick to magazines and pictures."

"I doubt you've so much as cracked a book since you were in school," Monika said as she nudged Gisela with her elbow. Gisela slapped her arm lightly in return as she laughed.

"How long do you think we'll be down here?" a female voice asked from across the room.

"Why? Do you have an appointment to get to?" a man's voice replied. Several others laughed.

Ursula leaned back and rested her head against the rough brick wall. It took her a moment to find a spot where a piece of mortar didn't dig into the back of her skull. She closed her eyes and drew several deep breaths. Though confined spaces did not bother her under normal circumstances, a basement during an air raid alert was far from normal. Her ears strained to hear the sound of planes as they approached the city, but only the sound of muffled conversations and the occasional snore reached her. Some of the residents in her building managed to fall asleep each time they went to the shelter, even during raids when bombs fell close by. When the all clear sounded, someone shook their shoulders to wake them and they shuffled back up the stairs to catch a few more hours sleep before they went to work. *To be that oblivious would be wonderful,* Ursula thought. Instead, adrenaline caused her senses to heighten as she tried to piece together the events outside through sound alone. Several men who shared the basement had served in the last war, and they assured everyone that as long as they heard the sound of bombs, they were okay. The ones you didn't hear killed you.

One hour stretched into two before the steady tone of the all clear rang out from the sirens. Everyone breathed a sigh of relief, but only a partial one. The government determined alerts by the projected courses of bomber formations. If they turned away, the all clear sounded. The British knew this, however, and often had their bombers make doglegs and feints. One formation might pass a city only to double back and hit them. Small and fast Mosquito fighters flew over some cities just to make the sirens sound. Ursula and the others knew the all clear meant little until the sun came up. On several occasions, she had left the shelter only to have a second warning go off an hour later that sent her scurrying back down the stairs.

People rushed to get out of the shelter with more urgency than they rushed to it. Ursula and her friends stood near the back wall to allow all the others to leave first. Each shelter had its own unspoken code of conduct. In their building, the residents allowed women with small children to leave first, followed by the elderly; next came middle-aged persons, and last but not least, young people. No military-aged men lived in their building as they were all serving on one of the many fronts, so young women always left the shelter last. Ursula wondered how orderly their exit would be in the event they had to get out quickly in the middle of a raid. *Every man for himself, no doubt*, she thought as the last of the residents started up the stairs.

When the shelter cleared out, Ursula and her roommates walked back up the stairs into their apartment. The city shut off utilities during an air raid alert, so the late November chill had penetrated the stone exterior and turned the apartment into an icebox. As the women discussed their day, their mouths emitted a puff of frost with each exhale. Telephone operators staffed the city phone system to connect essential services in the city to the military and government. Operators worked around the clock, even during air raids. This week, the women worked the day shift and next week would switch to nights. Thus far, there had been no daylight raids while they were on duty, but with the American bombers starting to hit targets in Western Germany, they knew it was just a matter of time. Thus far luck prevented them from working the phones during an attack which, they learned from others who had, was a terrifying experience. The switchboard was located deep inside a building but not underground. If the bombs hit the building, they would destroy the system and the employees.

But at least you'd be occupied while it went on without having to sit in the darkness and contemplate your own death, Ursula thought. *I'd rather be busy than to sit patiently and wait for a bomb. For all its terrors, the war is at least exciting.*

"How long do you think this war will last?" Gisela asked as she dropped onto the sofa.

"As long as it has to," Monika replied. "Until the Bolsheviks are no longer a threat."

"The British and Americans will come to their senses," Ursula added. She found it best to assume an outwardly pro-Nazi stance. "And then they will help us fight the Russians. Isn't that what the Fuhrer wants?"

She left them to discuss the war and made her way down the short hallway to her bedroom. When they moved into the apartment, they drew straws to determine who would get the room to themselves. Ursula drew the short one. New government regulations instituted after the August raids dictated two adults or three children per bedroom, and Ursula knew it was only a matter of time before they received a new occupant for their apartment. Thus far the registration officials had not made it to their building, but once they did, a new roommate would arrive in short order. *That will make things a bit more difficult,* Ursula thought as she sat down on the edge of the bed. Gisela and Monika never went in her room without permission, but Ursula preferred not to keep any items associated with her nocturnal activities in her room. She kept them on her person instead. With no one else in the room, this proved to be easy enough, but a roommate would make it almost impossible. *I'll worry about that when the time comes. If the time comes.*

Ursula placed her emergency suitcase near the bed, handle

up for easy access, and removed her dress. She draped it over the back of a wooden chair in front of a small dresser with a mirror. Her hands shook slightly as she unpinned her long red hair and shook her head to loosen it. *Why am I so nervous?* she wondered as she sat in the chair and began to work a brush through her hair. *I've done plenty of tasks for them before and nothing has come of it.* Before the war, Ursula had worn her red locks as a badge of honor. With the wartime shortage of soap, she could not properly care for it. The government rationed water too, and she only managed a simple wash in cold water once a week. Though a black market existed for both luxury and necessary items, Ursula stayed away. The government knew such a trade existed and imposed harsh penalties for those caught buying or selling items, though the attempts at enforcement seemed half-hearted at times. Still, better to not draw undue attention. Gisela had a connection with a man in Pankow and brought home cigarettes and the occasional meat – chicken or rabbit – from time to time. *We'll survive the war somehow*, she thought. *We have to.*

Before he died, Herr Müller said, "Politicians come and go, but through it all, Berlin will survive." When the government removed the lime trees from the Unter den Linden to widen it in the mid 1930s, her father had exploded with anger.

"Do they not know of the legend? As long as the trees stand, so will Berlin, but if the trees are gone, Berlin will go too," he shouted as he slammed his fist on the table with enough force to rattle the dishes.

"I'm sure they'll plant other ones, Father," Ursula said. Indeed, the government did. They imported lime saplings from the United States and braced them with black stakes to make them look like miniature lanterns. Now, the street was sometimes called the Unter den Laterne.

"That's not the point, child," Herr Müller said as his faced flushed a deep shade of crimson. "It isn't just any old trees. It is *those* trees. The ones the bastards removed. These clowns in office now will have a lot to answer for. I assure you. A lot to answer for."

"You mustn't say such things, Father," Ursula said.

"I fought for Germany," he said, pointing his fork at her. "I received two – *two* – Iron Crosses in the Kaiser's army. Not one like our halfwit Austrian corporal in the Chancellery. I can say whatever I want. I earned that right."

Ursula had shaken her head and returned to her meal. When her father had his blood up, any attempt at rational thought or conversation went out the window. He spent most of his time in their apartment, a blessing lest he speak in public as he did at the table. On Saturday afternoons he met three of his wartime buddies in a small café where they played chess and drank coffee. Ursula never met the men, but she assumed they were of like political mind as her father or else he would not spend so much time with them. Both of her younger brothers joined the Hitler Youth when it became mandatory, though their father threatened to not allow it, no matter what the government said. He tempered his comments whenever they shared the table at supper. By 1939, no one trusted anyone around them, not even their own children. Ursula heard stories of the government giving awards to young boys of ten or eleven who denounced their parents at a Hitler Youth meeting. Neighbors used denunciations to settle feuds which sometimes dated back before the National Socialists even came to power. When the war came, the rate of denunciations increased. The best way to get rid of a person you disliked was to contact the Gestapo and report the person as a defeatist, a black marketer, a person who harbored Jews, or a spy. You were only limited by your imagination. Chronic manpower issues plagued the Gestapo and they relied on citizens to report behavior. On occasion, they'd conduct a simple investigation and find nothing warranted further action while other times the target of the report disappeared, never to be seen again. It depended on the specific charge, but it also depended on the agent assigned to the case.

Ursula placed the brush down and walked over to the bed. She reached under the pillow and pulled out two small framed photos, one of each brother. *What did they die for?* Like many families, she took out a small notice in the newspaper to list each of their deaths. Early in the war, death notices often included a phrase stating that the deceased died *For the Fuhrer and the Fatherland.* As casualties mounted in the eastern campaigns, a large portion of them switched to the simple *For the Fatherland* or *For the Volk.* The notices she placed for her brothers stated they died *For the Fatherland.* She did not mention the Fuhrer. *Were they fighting for him?* she wondered. Never close to her brothers as they grew up, she ignored the Hitler Youth propaganda they sometimes indulged in, but had they really *believed* in what they said? She did not know and, to her great regret, never found out. Seeing them go from children to soldiers, only to die on behalf of the regime, made her resent the Nazis even more. After they left for the army, she saw them on rare occasions and never at the same time as they served in different units and went on leave at different times. She last saw Thomas, the youngest, three months before she learned of his death. From the date on the terse message from the army, it was obvious he died within weeks of his return to the front. *And so many others. Too many others.*

Most of the boys she grew up with in Wedding went into the army as soon as they turned eighteen. They fell in Poland, France, North Africa, and Russia. *We've watered half the world with the blood of our young*, she thought as she put the pictures back under her pillow. *And it will go on until someone makes it stop! Either we do it ourselves or we wait for the British, Americans, or – God forbid – the Russians to end it for us.* Though the Russian Army was still a thousand miles away, the war news indicated they were moving steadily closer. Berliners might curse the British bomber crews, but they feared the Red Army. Soldiers home on leave filled them with stories of Soviet atrocities at the front. They never spoke of German atrocities. Ursula heard of those from the men she met with in the warehouse as they had contacts in the East. *If half of what they say is true*, she thought as she slipped under the covers of her bed, *then we deserve whatever the Allies do to us. It's a war for survival, and no matter how much the government says otherwise, we are destined to lose. And we deserve to lose after all we've done.*

Like most boys, her brothers had come to think themselves smarter than their father once they reached their early teens. As the gulf widened between the boys and the elder Müller, Ursula grew closer to him. He shared stories of Berlin as it was before the first war and the ensuing political turmoil. His chest swelled with pride as he spoke of marching in a military parade under the eye of the Kaiser himself. Herr Müller loved his city and loved his country, and it was that love that made him despise the Nazis. Yes, they'd restored Germany to a position of prominence in Europe, briefly, but at what cost?

The only way to atone for our sins and reclaim what Germany once was is to get rid of them. She shivered as she pulled the blanket up to her chin.

No sooner had she drifted into sleep, when an air raid siren sounded again. With a groan, she rolled out of bed and grabbed her suitcase and her coat. Gisela and Monika met her in the hallway and, blinded by sleep, they stumbled down the stairs to the basement.

CHAPTER EIGHT

THE PHONE RANG as Grace walked into the apartment. She placed her coat on the rack near the door and answered.

"Hello?"

"Grace?"

"Michael?" she asked. The sounds of men talking and laughing in the background made it hard for her to hear. "Is everything okay?"

"'Tis fine," Michael replied. "I just wanted to let you know I got back in one piece."

"Thank you," she said. "Michael... there's something I need to tell you. I wanted to talk to you while you were here, but I didn't—"

"Sorry, Grace, I have to run. Remember, I'll call as soon as I can. Maybe Tuesday morning."

"Michael..."

He hung up before she could say another word. *Damn*, she thought. *Just when I had worked up the nerve to tell him. I couldn't even say I love you.* Grace walked over to the radio and switched it on. A newsman read the headlines in a somber voice. When he began to talk about a raid over Berlin a few nights past, Grace switched off the radio and went into the kitchen for a drink of water. Her stomach felt queasy, and she feared she might be sick. After a moment, the feeling went away. She thought of writing him a letter to explain everything, but decided against it as he would not receive it before he got his leave and his next post, and so she would see him in person before the letter reached him. *If he comes back. No, he WILL come back. He has to! You can't allow yourself to think otherwise.* Her mother always told her that to worry about an event that had not happened could cause the very thing you feared to become real. *The more I fret about him not coming back, the more likely it is that he won't. But didn't he seem to think as much himself?*

Before the death of her brother and before she met Michael, Grace had listened to the news on the BBC with rapt attention. The reports contained very little in the way of good news during the summer of 1940. Like many people in England during the Battle of Britain, Grace kept track of the score of German bombers shot down versus fighter planes lost as some might keep track of football scores. Victories, no matter how small, brought comfort to the citizens of London and other cities during those dark days. Now, with a fiancé in a bomber squadron, Grace preferred not to listen to much news as it only caused her to worry. *He's up there at night doing the same thing to the Germans that they did to us, but worse if the reports are to be believed. Is it revenge? Or is it something else?* She knew, of course, that civilians died during the raids just as British civilians perished under German bombs. Once when a nearby block got hit by a German bomb, Grace saw the bodies of three women, an elderly man, and two children laid out in the street as rescue workers covered them up with thick, gray wool blankets. The blankets were not long enough, and their legs struck out at odd angles. She'd been on her way to work when she chanced upon the scene and vomited her meagre breakfast into a gutter. No one took any notice of her when she did, and no one in her office raised an eyebrow at the small splatter of vomit which stained her shoe. Michael rained the same death upon their cities now. Grace felt sorry for the children and the animals, but shed no tears for the adults. *They started it, after all*, is what Michael always said. Even his own native Belfast was bombed as was Dublin, a neutral city in the Irish Free State. Michael never spoke of the specific cities he bombed, but from the few radio reports she heard, Grace was able to piece together some of them. The list read like a tourist guide to all the major places in Germany.

Grace had travelled to Germany with her parents and her brothers in 1935. Outwardly it seemed a happy place where foreigners received excellent treatment from the Germans. Smiling children, happy couples, quaint hotels in towns with beautiful architecture; Germany appeared to have every-thing a person could want were it not for the ever-present flag, a black swastika on a white circle with a red background, and the constant presence of uniformed men. As visitors, of course, the family did not discuss politics with anyone, but many Germans seemed all too happy to point out the new direction Hitler had taken them. Even Dr. Robinson admit-ted the country had recovered quite well from the lingering effects of the Great War and the economic depression of the early 1930s. "It's a miracle, really," he said one afternoon as they sat and ate in the courtyard of a *biergarten* in Munich.

"Don't you find all the uniforms a bit peculiar?" Mrs. Robinson asked as she sipped her beer. "Almost like they are planning to have another go."

"They won't do that," Dr. Robinson replied with an air

of authority. "Hitler kept the communists from taking over and should be commended for that. They say he fought in the trenches in the last war, as I did. Anyone who experienced that would not want to go rushing headlong into another war. I can assure you of that."

Four years later as the family gathered around the radio to listen to Chamberlain announce their country was again at war with Germany, Grace noticed her father's pained expression. *I wonder what's worse for him*, she thought. *That we're at war and his son will have to serve as he did? Or that he has to admit that he was wrong about something? It's probably the latter and not the former.* Her mother squeezed his hand and wept as the Prime Minister talked. She'd been a nurse in the last war and saw up close what men are capable of doing to one another. Her brother seemed almost excited by the prospect of doing his bit for King and country. *None of us realized how different this war would be.* Though the Germans used Zeppelins to bomb London during the Great War, that paled in comparison to the punishment they dished out to the city in the current war. *They say the last war changed everything. Well, this war will change it all again. Better or worse is yet to be determined.*

She glanced at the clock and realized Helen would not be home for several hours yet, if at all. Some nights Grace returned to an empty apartment and went to bed only to see Helen the next morning as she staggered in through the door with just enough time to get to work. Since the arrival of the Americans, people took to saying many British girls wore utility knickers. One Yank and they were off. Grace found Helen's constant efforts to meet and fall in love with a smooth-talking American who looked as if he'd stepped out of a movie screen amusing. Their access to items not available, or not available in sufficient quantities, to those in the British Isles, such as cigarettes, silk, or chocolate, made them prized catches for young women – much to the dismay of British soldiers who made far less money than their American counterparts. *I just hope she's careful,* Grace thought of Helen, *but she's as hard-headed as I am and will do what she bloody well pleases. And who am I to criticize her? Even after what happened to me before, Michael and I are not taking precautions either.*

As she sat in the semi-darkness of the living room in a comfortable old chair, Grace began to nod off. As she did, her mind wandered back to a few days previous when Michael stepped off the train. He'd phoned her at work at mid-day Friday and said he had a spot of leave. She offered to meet him at the train station. As soon as he stepped down from the rail car, she knew something was wrong. His bloodshot eyes had dark bags under them. His shoulders slumped forward, and he shuffled rather than walked. The rest of his crew piled out behind him, a bit more boisterous than he, but still subdued. She'd never met them before, and Michael went through the motions of introducing her to each in turn. They shook her hand and said a kind word or two when their turn came. She remembered, from previous conversations, that Michael had six men on his crew, yet only three arrived with him. *Where are the rest of them?* she wondered. She did not dare ask him. They went straight to the nearest pub, and Michael ordered two drinks for himself and one for her. He chugged the first and then sipped the second.

"You look stunning," he said as he wiped the beer foam from the top of his lip with the back of his hand. "I'd say being engaged suits you."

"You look… tired," Grace replied.

"Haven't slept very well the past few days," was all he said.

They finished their drinks and then walked out of the pub. He jumped when she slipped her arm through his. She withdrew it quickly.

"No, sorry, 'tis fine. I'm just a bit jumpy right now."

"What's wrong, Michael?" she asked as she stopped and turned to face him.

He kept walking and called out over his shoulder, "It's nothing. Come on. Let's find a place to eat. I'm famished."

Despite his professed hunger, Michael picked at his food with his fork when the waiter brought it to them. He took a few bites here and there while Grace devoured her food.

"I'm sorry," she said in between bites. "You must think me such a pig."

"Not at all," Michael said with a hint of a smile. "It's nice to see a girl with a healthy appetite, though with the shortages, I guess we all have one."

"You're not as hungry as you thought?" she asked as she tried to keep her voice innocent.

"Just tired," he said as he made a show of taking a bite from his fork. His eyes scanned the room around them as he ate. They never focused on a single spot for long as he checked the room as he might check the sky for an enemy fighter. His leg bounced up and down under the table, and the hand with the fork shook just enough for Grace to notice.

After dinner, they caught the subway to Central London. He told her that his crew planned to meet in front of Nelson's Column so they could plan where to stay and, perhaps the most important thing, where to drink for the night. As they waited under the steady gaze of Lord Nelson, Michael told her of the events of the past month since they'd last seen each other. *He hasn't said anything about what's eating at him*, she thought but did not say. She laughed when he described a spot of trouble McKenzie got into with the Wing Commander after he caught a harmless snake and hid it in the drawer of the Wing Commander's desk.

"He very nearly gave him the chop right there on the spot," Michael said. "He wanted him off the station and tossed in the gaol or sent over to the army and made an infantryman."

"Why didn't he?" Grace asked.

"I told him if he did, I'd tell everyone how he fouled himself when he opened the drawer and saw the snake. Besides, they wouldn't want to break up my crew. Not now."

"Did he really?"

"I don't know, but based on how quickly his anger vanished, I think I may have been on to something."

After his crew arrived, they spent the evening in various pubs and dance halls until way after the hour the government required such establishments to close. They found a hotel with dawn a scant few hours away. Before they went to sleep, Michael mentioned a rough mission earlier in the week. Grace sat up in the bed and looked down at him. He lay flat on his back with his hands tucked under his head. His chest rose and fell with each breath. With his eyes closed, Grace thought it looked as if he took deep breaths in an effort to calm himself.

"You've never really talked about what you do," she said as she placed her hand on his bare chest. "Was it bad?"

"The worst," he mumbled as he rolled over onto his side with his back to her. She moved her body alongside his and slipped her arm around him.

"Do you want to tell me about it?" she whispered.

"No," he said. "I'd rather not. I don't want to upset you. You wouldn't understand."

"How do you know that if you don't talk to me?" she asked. "I know something's wrong with you. Why won't you tell me?"

"You wouldn't understand," he repeated and said no more. Two hours later, she awoke to Michael's voice as he thrashed around in the bed. He apologized when he awoke from his nightmare but rebuffed her attempts to get him to talk. At lunch – they'd slept through breakfast – he ate little and said less up to the point when he sat his mug of tea down and said in a matter-of-fact tone, "I lost three of my crew on Thursday. On the way in, an anti-aircraft shell, flak, we call it, got Charles. Over the target, a night fighter got Ian and Christopher."

"Dead?" she asked.

"Aye, Charles and Ian. Cannon took off Ian's head and Christopher's leg. We were on the bomb run, so I had to keep the plane as level as I could. McKenzie was focused on the target and Lawton was occupied with the rear turret, and so Cameron was the only one who could help. He slapped a tourniquet on Christopher's leg and gave him an injection of morphine to stop him from screaming. It didn't help so he gave him a second one. That didn't do much good either. Finally passed out after thirty minutes or so. He came to and started again as we crossed over the coast.

"Did he survive?" Grace asked, her voice a whisper.

"So far," Michael replied. "He lost a lot of blood. The surgeon had to cut off some more of his leg, but they say he should pull through. I almost envy him in a way."

"What?" Grace exclaimed.

"He's out of the war at the cost of a leg. Seems a bargain to me. No more flak. No more fighters. No more ops. I'd trade my own leg for that, I do believe I would."

"You just need a rest," Grace said.

He didn't so much as give her a kiss until that night when they returned to the hotel room. They'd gone out with his crew again, but begged off and returned to their room after a few hours. He seemed to come alive a bit more as the evening wore on, but after they made love, Michael lay on his back with the same expression he'd worn the night before. In the darkness as she slept, the nightmares returned.

Will that be what marriage is like? Grace wondered as she went into her bedroom and began to prepare for bed. *Will we be condemned to sleep in separate rooms because of his nightmares? It scares me. I'm scared for him and I'm scared for me.* On occasion, her own thoughts turned to the air raids she'd experienced and the sight of the dead bodies under the blankets, but each time it happened, Grace managed to push them from her mind and focus on something different, something happier. For months, she used the image of Michael as he smiled at her in his blue uniform to keep the darker images away, but now he never smiled and all she could think of were his nightmares and the phrases he uttered in his sleep. *And when I tell him my secret, it might push him further away than the war already has*, she thought as she got into bed and picked up a well-worn copy of *Gone With the Wind* from her nightstand. She opened the book to the page she'd last read, marked by a photograph of her and Michael taken on his last leave. Michael had his arm around her waist, and she pressed her hip into his side. The corner of his mouth was turned up in what passed for one of his smiles. A haunted, vacant look filled Michael's eyes and turned his whole expression into one of a man faced with his impending execution.

"I'll be strong," she whispered to the picture before she kissed it. "I'll be your anchor. Just come home safe to me soon. We'll face it together. The war. Life. Everything."

She tried to find escape into the world of the pre–Civil War south, but the talk of war in the novel reminded her of her own war. *Is our own society going to get swept away by this one? Like the Great War did to my father's generation?* Frustrated, she tossed the novel onto her nightstand and held the photograph in front of her face. When she finally nodded off to sleep, the picture slipped out of her hand and floated down until it came to rest on her chest.

PART TWO

22 NOVEMBER 1943
MORNING

So man lieth down, and riseth not:
till the heavens be no more,
they shall not wake, nor be raised out of their sleep.

Job 14:12

CHAPTER NINE

MICHAEL ARRIVED AT his aircraft well before the rest of the crew. He found Smith, the crew chief in charge of maintenance, in front of P for Paul on top of a large toolbox. Smitty wore a faded blue uniform under a leather smock stained with grease. Smitty considered the plane his property and only allowed the crew to "borrow" it for missions. Every time they returned with battle damage, Smitty shook his head and scolded Michael before his own men tore into the plane with every tool imaginable to get her ready to go up again. After the last mission, Smitty said nothing and helped remove the bodies of the dead crewmen as the survivors stood in stunned silence. All of them saluted each body as the ground crew brought it out before they climbed into the truck for the long ride to the debriefing hut.

"How's the old girl?" Michael asked. At McKenzie's urging, Michael had had "Paddy's Wagon" painted on the starboard nose of the aircraft. The RAF officially frowned on such decorations, unlike the Americans who adorned their planes with scantily clad pin-ups, but they tolerated simple nose art.

"She'll do." Smitty began to run down a list of all the repairs, checking them off on his fingers as he spoke. "Patched the holes in the fuselage. Installed a new wireless set. Replaced the rudder cables. New glass on your top turret. New guns up there too. I think that about covers it."

"Thank you, Smitty. Hope we'll come back from this one in better shape."

"Yeah," Smitty grunted. "That'd be a welcome change."

"Don't blame me. Blame the Jerries."

"We've got orders to get you ready for tonight." Smitty stood and picked up his toolbox.

"How much fuel?" Michael asked.

"Loaded down," Smitty replied. "Wherever you are going, it'll be a long flight."

Michael whistled through his teeth. The ground crews learned of the target after the aircrews, but their experience with fuel and bomb loads allowed them to guess with some accuracy. A plane loaded down with fuel meant a target deep inside Germany.

"Hoping for a milk run were you, sir?" Smitty asked with a smile.

"I was, truth be told. What's your guess?"

"Hannover, maybe Berlin even."

"Jesus Christ," Michael exclaimed. "Of all the places. Berlin."

"Could be Hannover," Smitty said.

"As if that's any better, you old sod."

A truck driven by a WAAF corporal stopped beside the plane. McKenzie jumped out of the cab, and the other five crewmen climbed out of the back. They wore various manner of dress – a check flight did not require the heavy flight suit needed for high-altitude flying. The men carried their parachutes and assorted gear based on their position on the plane.

Michael wore his blue uniform pants and a white turtleneck sweater under a leather jacket lined with sheepskin. He kept his service cap on his head, though he switched to his flight cap before takeoff. Around his neck, Michael wore a green scarf for good luck. All of the men had their own personal talismans. Some, like Michael, took them up every time they flew while others only used them on missions lest their good luck wear out from overuse.

The crew made their way over to Michael and gathered around like players to a coach. *I'd rather be a bloody football coach than be here, that's for certain*, Michael thought as he looked over his crew. His veteran men looked bored, the new men scared.

"Right," he began. "So you've met the new lot?"

The three experienced men nodded.

"We have," McKenzie said. "Two pom pooftas and a sheep shagger."

"Thought the Scots were the ones who bugger sheep," Lawson said as he cast a glance at Cameron, who made an obscene gesture in return.

"Pay McKenzie no mind," Michael said to the new men. "Here is the plan for the day. We are going up to run some checks. Williams, you need to check the top turret thoroughly. It got a bit damaged last time. And Graham, do the same with the wireless. It's new. So don't muck it up. Everyone else, you know what to do?"

The men nodded.

"Any word on tonight?" Cameron asked.

"Smitty says they are layin' on a lot of fuel. Should be a long run, wherever it is."

The crew groaned. Like Michael, they hoped their last mission would be a quick one.

"No use complaining about it until we know where we are going. And even then it isn't like we can do something about it," Michael said.

He and Cameron, the flight engineer, walked around the plane and conducted the external portion of their pre-flight checklist while the rest of the crew climbed through the hatches and began to look over their own positions. Smitty kept on their heels while they looked over the plane and pointed out the various patches as if they were not obvious.

"Don't stay up too long, sir," Smitty said as Michael prepared to climb through the forward hatch. "We need time to get her ready for tonight."

"I won't," Michael promised.

He settled in front of the controls and ran through his checks as Cameron stood just over his shoulder. The engines started with a bang and a cough of smoke. Michael called the control tower and received permission to taxi to the runway, so he released the brakes and slowly navigated his way forward, aided by Smitty, who walked in front of the plane on the port side with an orange cone in his hand. When P For Paul reached the takeoff position, Michael set the brakes again and called the tower. A bored voice told him he was cleared for takeoff. With Cameron's help on the throttle, Michael ran the four engines up to full power and released the brake. The plane sprang forward like a horse out of the starting gate. Unlike takeoffs for operations when loaded down with fuel and bombs, P for Paul gained forward speed rapidly as Cameron called out every ten knots. A gentle pull on the controls and she sank down for a second and then leapt into the air.

"Best takeoff you've ever had, Mick," McKenzie said over the intercom from his vantage point in the nose of the plane.

"Shut up," Michael said. "Listen up, you bastards, I'm going to take her out about thirty miles or so and up to five thousand feet. When we get there, check everything, and I mean *everything*. Gunners, make sure the controls work in your turrets. And wireless operator, try and raise the field and anyone else you can think of. I want no mechanical problems tonight. Clear?"

One by one the crew indicated that they understood his instructions. During takeoff and landing, Cameron sat in a jump seat alongside but just below the level of the pilot. Once they were airborne, he sat in a chair facing a panel full of controls where he monitored the gauges and assisted the pilot with the control of the engines. In a pinch, some flight engineers landed crippled bombers when flak or fighters wounded the pilot. Michael had no desire to see if Cameron was capable of such a feat. A half bulkhead separated the flight deck from the rest of the plane. Behind this bulkhead on the port side, the navigator sat at a table with his charts and ground radar aids. A blackout curtain, closed when on a mission, allowed him to use light to aid in his position fixes without it leaking into the cockpit. The wireless operation station was located just aft of the navigator, also on the port side. Further aft, the mid-upper gunner sat suspended in a chair that rotated 360 degrees. The chair took up about half the height of the fuselage and made it almost impossible to crawl around or under when in bulky flight clothes. At the extreme rear of the plane, the tail gunner sat enclosed in a turret. To get into it, he had to use the portable toilet as a step and then crawl over the rear spar. In a stricken aircraft, a tail gunner's odds of getting out of the plane were not good at all. Everyone knew this but no one talked about it, least of all Lawton, whose sharp eyes had saved the crew from a stern attack on more than one occasion.

"All gauges normal, skipper," Cameron said. "I don't see any problems."

"Hello, skipper," Lawton called. "Tail turret is in working order."

"Nose turret checks out, skipper," McKenzie called from his position forward of the flight deck.

"Pilot to mid," Michael said. "How's the turret look?"

"It looks okay, sir," Williams said after a long pause.

"Looks okay or is okay?" Michael asked. "Be specific."

"It *is* okay, sir."

"Cut the sir," Michael said. "Up here you call me pilot or skipper. Nothing else."

"Understood, skipper."

Michael flew the plane east and then began a slow turn to the north as he climbed to five thousand feet. The Lancaster made a tremendous amount of noise when airborne. The roar of the engines made it difficult to understand the chatter over the intercom at times. On a mission, as flak exploded all around and the turrets fired hundreds of rounds at enemy aircraft, the noise levels reached an almost unbearable level. The vibration of the plane and the uncomfortable seats caused a deep ache in the lower back, which worsened as the mission dragged on. Often upon return, Michael found it difficult to stand up straight until an hour or so passed. When tempted to complain about his lot, Michael reminded himself that as bad as it got in the night skies over Germany, the alternative assignment to the infantry was much worse.

"Hello, wireless," Michael called.

"Go ahead, skipper."

"Raise the base if you would," Michael said.

"Aye, aye, skipper," Graham replied.

"This ain't the Royal Navy," McKenzie growled.

"I thought about bein' a seaman," Lawton said from his position in the rear turret.

"You are a bloody waste of semen," Cameron said.

"Shut up or I'll toss the lot of you out with the bombs tonight," Michael said. "Keep the intercom clear."

With the crew dispersed to different parts of the aircraft, the intercom provided a crucial link in combat. Most night fighters attacked from dead astern, so the ability of the tail gunner to shout a warning to the pilot meant the difference between life or death, between home and a POW camp or worse. Though the pilot flew the plane, all the crew served as his eyes and ears.

Combat exposed weaknesses and laid bare the souls of those involved. An airman who whizzed through training might panic in his first action. Over the course of twenty-nine missions, Michael knew several individuals removed from flight status with the dreaded "lacking moral fiber" note in their personnel file. These men vanished from the base, never to be seen or spoken of again. While some flight crews agreed with the RAF's term for such people, Michael did not. *To have the balls to say you can't hack it on ops anymore isn't a weakness, it's a strength. I wish I had the guts to do the same.* At the same time, Michael was also grateful none of his crew took that route.

"Hello, skipper," Graham called out.

"Go ahead," Michael answered.

"Radio checks out. Everything in order."

"Good," Michael replied. "Williams, is the turret still working?"

"It is, skipper," Williams replied. "I've done everything I can except shoot the guns."

"Think you can pot a Hun with it?" McKenzie asked.

"Find me a Hun and I'll bag him," Williams answered with considerable more faith in himself than Michael had in him.

"Right," Michael said. "Let's go home."

He banked the plane to the west and reduced his altitude to two thousand feet. He planned on a rest when they got back to the base. Before a mission, the Wing Commander briefed the crews in the early afternoon. From the moment they announced the target, personnel were restricted to base. After a meal of bacon and eggs, the men had a bit of time to rest or to check over their equipment. Then they dressed in their flight clothes and made their way to their aircraft. Things ran on a strict schedule as the bomber stream relied upon proper timing to do the maximum amount of damage to the target.

Less than twenty-four hours and I'll be done, Michael thought. *If we make it.* New crews lasted a few missions, four or five. Experienced crews sometimes reached fifteen or even twenty, but even they failed to return eventually. The closest a crew had come in the past two months was twenty-four missions. On the twenty-fifth, they suffered a direct hit from an anti-aircraft battery and the plane simply vanished into a cloud of smoke and debris. Their loss shook the squadron to the core as everyone had expected them to make it.

"Skipper," McKenzie called.

"Go ahead," Michael replied.

"We gotta make it home from this last one," he said.

"And what reason do you have?" Michael asked. "Other than chasing after more WAAFs?"

"I put ten quid on it," McKenzie said.

"What the bloody hell are you talking about?" Michael asked.

"Some of the lads are running a bit of a pool," he said. "If we make it back, I get around forty quid. We can have quite the bash with that."

"Jesus Christ," Michael said, wiping his hand across his forehead. He looked over his shoulder at Cameron, who grinned at him.

"You too?" Michael asked.

"Five quid," Cameron said.

"Pilot to crew," Michael said. "None of you other gobsh-ites better place a bet."

"Too late, skipper," Lawton said. "I put eight quid on it."

"Jesus, Mary, and Joseph," Michael said. "None of you other new lot better bet. You've a way to go to finish your tour."

McKenzie crawled out of the nose compartment and slapped Michael on the back as he made his way past the navigator and radio operator to the small bunk on the port side of the plane. During takeoffs and landings, he and Lawton sat on the bunk and the mid-upper gunner sat on the floor with his back against the bulkhead. Cameron moved over to the jump seat beside and below the pilot's seat when the control tower gave them permission to land. The crew sat in silence until the wheels kissed the ground and Michael finished taxiing the plane to its dispersal spot. When he shut down the engines, the roar stayed in his head for several minutes.

"Well?" Smitty asked as soon as Michael exited the plane.

"Everything's good," Michael replied. "She'll do fine."

"We'll get her ready," Smitty said. "You're getting a cookie and the usual incendiaries."

The four-thousand-pound bomb called a 'cookie' was used to blast building facades open so that the incendiary containers, as they dumped their smaller bomblets, could set fire to the interior of the buildings. Other planes carried delayed action bombs designed to go off hours or even a day later to catch the emergency personnel in the open. Those in charge of Bomber Command engaged in a cruel calculus of destruction. If they destroyed German industry, or simply destroyed the homes or lives of those who worked in those industries, they considered the job well done. Michael never gave much thought to where they bombed or the damage it did. In his mind, the Germans started it and it was up to the RAF and the American bombers to finish it. The loss of life among the civilian population, while regrettable, was no different than the lives lost in Britain during the Blitz, which included his native Belfast. *And Grace*, he thought. *She lived through the bombing of London. She could have been killed and I'd have never met her. The one bright spot in all this.*

The same truck with the same WAAF driver who dropped them off earlier picked the crew up and took them to the hut which housed the lockers where they stowed their flight gear. When they walked into the mess room, all conversation stopped and a dozen sets of eyes focused on them.

"What are ya lookin' at, ya buggers?" Lawton yelled.

People turned their attention away and resumed their conversations as the men received a generous helping of powdered eggs and what passed as bacon. Though still not up to pre-war quality, the food provided to aircrew exceeded that provided to the infantry. Michael picked at his and ate a few bites while the rest of his crew attacked their plates with a ferocity he'd not seen since they were last in action. When

McKenzie saw that Michael did not plan to eat all of his food, he reached over and appropriated his plate and ate the rest.

"Gotta eat to keep your strength up, Mick," McKenzie said with a mouthful of eggs, "but if you plan on letting it go to waste, I have an obligation to finish it for you."

"Go ahead," Michael replied, though with McKenzie half finished, a protest would have done him no good.

Michael pushed his chair away from the table and stood up.

"I'll leave you lads to it," he said. "Try and get some rest before the briefing. Especially you new lot. Smitty says it'll be a long flight, and I don't want any of you daydreaming. If you can't sleep, then lay there with your eyes closed and act like you are sleeping. I'll see you at the briefing."

As Michael turned to walk away, he noticed a slight tremor in his hands. He shoved them into the pockets of his pants so the others would not see them. *Can't let them know how scared I am*, he thought as he began to walk towards his quarters.

CHAPTER TEN

Ursula managed to get out of the basement after the second alert around three o'clock in the morning. After five hours of restless sleep, she got up at eight a.m. She did not have to report to her job at the telephone switchboard until ten a.m. for her eight-hour shift. With her assignment for the night, Ursula knew she did not have much time afterwards to make it back to Charlottenburg to pick up and deliver the package. Gisela and Monika rubbed sleep from their eyes as they joined her in the kitchen, where Ursula prepared three cups of ersatz coffee. It tasted foul, and with no milk or cream to cut the bitter aftertaste, the three women sipped it with sour expressions. Ersatz coffee was better than no coffee at all, and with the frequent alerts of late, it helped ward off the effects of interrupted sleep.

"All that for nothing," Gisela said with a yawn. "It's almost a disappointment."

"What do you mean?" Ursula asked.

"Having to spend a night down there with nothing to show for it. At least a couple of bombs would've made it worthwhile."

"As long as they don't fall on you," Monika said.

"We've been lucky," Ursula agreed.

"Still, it's a bit exciting," Gisela said with a smile. "Think of how boring our lives would be without the war. We wouldn't have a useful job. We wouldn't be living on our own. I'd probably be married to a boring accountant."

On the streets of Berlin, the phrase "Enjoy the war. The peace will be terrible" was popular among many, though they only spoke it in hushed whispers lest someone without a sense humor take offense and report the teller of the joke. In the late 1930s, a rumor maintained that Reichsmarshal Goering, popular with the people in the capital, offered to pay a nice sum to anyone who appeared in his office and told a joke about him that he had not heard. Though Ursula heard the rumor repeated on many occasions, neither she nor anyone she knew could offer any evidence of a person actually attempting to collect on the wager.

When the war began, Goering boasted, "If a single British plane appears in the skies over Berlin, you can call me Herr Meier." One night Goering and his driver found themselves on the streets when the warning siren sounded. They made their way to the nearest public shelter. All conversation stopped when the portly second-in-command of the Reich appeared in the entrance. Without missing a beat, Goering said, "Good evening, ladies and gentlemen. My name is Herr Meier." Government officials either left the cities targeted for destruction or took shelter deep inside concrete bunkers. None visited public shelters or the far more numerous shelters in basements throughout the city. They might, on occasion, visit areas bombed to reassure the civilians. Various agencies existed to help bombed out families, but nothing the government did managed to put a halt to the raids in the first place.

"How long do you think the war will last?" Monika asked as she finished the last of her coffee and placed the mug in the narrow sink.

"It can't go on forever," Ursula said. "All wars end. This one will too."

Of the three, Gisela, though not a party member, believed in much of their propaganda and never questioned the statements made over the radio about the conduct and progress of the war. Monika said very little about her political views. *She could be a Gestapo informer. I'll never know for sure*, Ursula thought. Given her own nocturnal activities, Ursula adopted a typical attitude in public of quiet acceptance of the state of the country. Most of those around her passively accepted things for what they were, and while perhaps not party members, they still went along with the government programs. Most adults knew at least one person who had 'disappeared' since the National Socialists took power.

"Final victory," Monika sighed. "Let's hope it doesn't take too long."

Ursula excused herself from the kitchen and grabbed her coat.

"I'll catch up with you at work," she called over her shoulder as she opened the door and left the apartment. A thin haze of cloud cover blocked the sunlight as Ursula walked down the street. Most of the people outdoors in the early morning chill stumbled around with sleep-deprived faces. Sleep, like soap and food, was in short supply. As she walked, Ursula's mind turned to her mission for the night. She knew where to find the building as it was not too far away from her apartment. She passed rows of shops with empty shelves where once the smell of food or the sight of racks of clothing lured shoppers.

As she passed Kleiststrasse, Ursula saw the fireman from the previous day in front of his station. He wore a stained pair of blue-gray coveralls with his peaked uniform hat tilted back on his head. He waved when he saw her and walked her way. *He seems nice enough*, Ursula thought, so she turned towards him and smiled.

"Good morning, Fraulein Müller," he called out. "Any more problems with the cooking?"

"No," she replied with a slight blush. "I'm sorry but I seem to have forgotten your name."

"Karl," he said. "Please call me Karl. Are you on your way to work?"

"Not quite," Ursula replied. "I don't have to report in until ten."

"I have a few hours off this morning," Karl said. "Would you care for a cup of coffee?"

"I don't know..." *He seems like a nice man, but now isn't the time for pursuing relationships, and he does work for the government.*

Karl leaned close and whispered, "I know a place that has real coffee."

"In that case," Ursula replied, "lead on."

Karl offered her his arm, which she took. As they walked, Karl told her a little about his job with the Fire Brigade. It did sound like interesting, if a bit dangerous, work. He steered her down an alley and stopped in front of a heavy wooden door. After a quick knock, the door opened.

"Ah, Herr Oberwachtmeister," a gray-haired man in a rumpled suit said, "it has been too long since you've last visited us. You have a guest, I see?"

"Fraulein Müller," Karl said. "She's a... friend."

"You are both welcome. Come in! Come in!"

He stood aside, and Karl placed his hand on the small of Ursula's back and indicated for her to go first. She stepped into a room devoid of any furniture. The place smelled musty, like sweat mixed with mildew.

"Come along," the man said. "Through here."

A second door led to a small room with several tables and chairs. Three patrons smiled at the pair when they entered. Karl led her to a table in the back and pulled a chair out for her to sit. A radio in the corner played military marches interspersed with the occasional news broadcast. After a few minutes, the man appeared with two cups of coffee. Karl picked his up at once and winced as the hot liquid burned his lips.

"He has coffee but no sugar or cream," Karl replied. "Even the black market has its limits."

"How did you come to know him?" Ursula asked.

"He had a fire in his shop once, maybe three months ago," Karl explained. "It was in a different location, not here. We found a stash of black market items after we put out the fire. He offered to keep our station supplied with coffee if we neglected to mention his products to the police."

"Isn't it a bit dangerous?" Ursula asked.

"No. Not very," Karl replied. "He supplies some Party officials too and they direct the Kripo to steer clear. But unfortunately, he won't be able to get stuff for much longer, I fear."

"What's his name?" Ursula asked as she picked up her mug and blew on the surface of the hot liquid to cool it before she took her first sip.

"I have no idea," Karl said with a laugh. "He knows mine, of course, but I thought it best to not ask him for his own."

Just as I don't know the name of those I work with, she thought. With the strange and creative ways the Gestapo used to get information out of suspects, even not knowing a person's name did not guarantee safety. The agents forced other names instead. No matter what, they got the names they wanted with guilt or innocence not entering into the equation. Either way, a concentration camp awaited all the suspects if they were not tortured to death or sentenced to the guillotine or a firing squad in the courtyard first.

"Have you been with the Fire Brigade long?" Ursula asked.

"Since 1929," Karl replied. "I joined when I was nineteen. In 1935 I joined the army as a reservist and I got called up in 1939. I served in various places, but the Russians pumped my left leg full of shrapnel. With the increase in raids, I got a discharge and returned to my duties here once I recovered. Last summer they sent several of us to Hamburg to help out the week of the big attacks."

"Was it as bad as people say?" Ursula asked.

"Worse," Karl said as his eyes took on a faraway look.

"I hope we don't see anything like that here," Ursula said as she placed her mug on the table, still half full. *No need to rush. I want to savor every bit.*

"As do I," Karl said, then he leaned across the table and whispered, "but I fear the worst for us is yet to come."

When the war began, the government enlisted the support of the entire population in the defense against aerial attack. Citizens received informational pamphlets and instruction on how to best extinguish an incendiary quickly before it had time to spread. Ursula even saw a film last year of men in the same dark coveralls Karl wore with gas masks and helmets put out a roof fire caused by an incendiary. They lugged heavy hoses while others prodded the wooden surface to find hidden pockets of fire. Ursula heard from a girl in the office that women were being recruited to help in civil defense efforts. She asked Karl about it.

"It's true," Karl replied. "The Luftschutz trains them to be auxiliary personnel. We've received a batch of them at our station along with some Hitler Youth volunteers. They got a few weeks of training and then arrived yesterday. We badly need the help, but I don't know how much use they'll actually be. We use them at night, not during the day."

"What do you do during the day then?" she asked. "Are there enough men on duty?"

"We make do with what we have. Most of us in the brigade now are either old men the army doesn't have a need for, or people like me who were wounded and discharged. They've even called retired members of the brigade back to service. Men who are sixty years old! That should tell you how desperate we are. God help us if we get hit like Hamburg."

"Do you ever have time to get home?" Ursula asked.

"I have no home," Karl said. "I had a small apartment, but it was destroyed in the raids in August. Lost everything. Now I just stay at the station, which is for the best because we are almost always on duty anyway."

"I'm sorry," Ursula said.

"Don't be," Karl replied. "I'm a fireman, and the city needs us now more than ever."

Ursula sipped the rest of her coffee in silence as she listened to Karl tell a few funny stories from his pre-war days in the Brigade. Each time she lifted her mug, she inhaled the steam as if she could ingest the rich liquid through her nose. Karl laughed.

"I did the same my first time here. I'd forgotten what the taste of real coffee was like."

"I need to get to work now," Ursula said with a frown. "As much as I'd like to stay here and drink coffee all day."

Karl nodded and rose from the table with her. The owner hurried over to them and shook Karl's hand.

"Come back any time. You too, miss."

"Thank you," Ursula said. *I might do that. If the cravings get bad.*

After the door closed behind them, Karl turned to her and asked, "I know it sounds forward of me, but might I walk with you? I don't have to be back on duty for another hour or two. After that, I won't get any time off for several days."

"And you want to spend it walking with me?" she asked.

"I do."

"Come on then," Ursula said. She led the way towards the center of the city, near the Tiergarten. It was a bit of a walk, but given the smell of public transportation now, Ursula didn't mind the exercise. With the rations, some Berliners gained rather than lost weight because of the heavy concentration of carbohydrates, but they were in the minority. As they passed the entrance to the zoo, Ursula felt a pang of sorrow about the state of the animals. Without enough food to feed everyone adequately, the animals suffered even more. Still, the heroic zookeepers made every attempt to keep them nourished enough to not starve, even if they couldn't give them enough to thrive. She could not bear the thought of the sad faces of the other animals too, the cats and dogs who still roamed the city. Some pet owners had their pets euthanized before the first bombs fell, but most tried to hold onto them as long as they could. The terrified faces of cats and dogs in the shelters nearly moved her to tears.

She stopped in front of a large building with a red brick façade. Young women came and went through a set of glass doors with tape on each pane. Sandbags surrounded the entrance and created an awning overhead. A sign on the door said *Rauchen Verbotten,* Smoking Forbidden.

"Must be hard to go through a shift with no cigarette," Karl said as he gestured towards the sign.

"They give us breaks," Ursula replied, "but I don't smoke."

"I wish I didn't," Karl said. "They are getting too hard to come by now."

"Thank you for the coffee," Ursula said. "I needed it this morning."

She turned to go into the building. When she reached the door, Karl called out, "Ursula! Wait!"

She stopped and turned to face him.

"Yes?"

"I don't want to be too forward," Karl said as he pulled off his cap and tucked it under his arm, "but I was wondering if you might like to go out again sometime. When I'm off, I mean. I rarely get a night, but I can probably manage to slip away for a while."

"Well…"

"Forgive me," Karl said. "I know I'm a bit older than you. It's just that I enjoyed your company."

Ursula gave him a long look. *I'm not looking for a man at all*, she thought. *I'd only put him in danger if they find out what I've been up to. But he looks so lonely. His contacts with the black market might be useful too, if not to me, then to the group.*

"I would be honored, Herr Oberwachtmeister," she said with a smile. "Provided you don't expect me to cook for you."

"I should say not," Karl said. "If yesterday evening was any indication of your culinary abilities, that is. I'll check about getting an evening free. If you stop by the station on your way to work on Thursday, we can set a time."

"Thursday morning then," Ursula replied. "Maybe we could get some coffee again."

"Excellent!" Karl exclaimed. "Until then."

He gave a brief nod of his head and walked away. As he did, Karl passed Gisela and Monika walking towards the building. Both turned to watch him go and then smiled at Ursula.

"Another one of your literary companions?" Gisela asked.

"He doesn't have the look of a reader," Monika said. "Too serious an expression."

"He's only the fireman who came to the apartment yesterday when I burned the supper," Ursula insisted.

"So why is he at the door to our office?" Gisela asked. "Does he fear you might cook something here too?"

"He only wanted to make sure we were alright," Ursula said with an emphasis on the 'we.'

"Sure he did," Gisela replied. "Come on. We don't want to be late."

Ursula sighed and followed them inside. Her life was complicated enough with her job, her roommates, and her work with the underground. *I don't need a man to complicate it even more.* Her thoughts were muddled as she hung up her overcoat on a rack in a small room and went to find her roommates. Their voices led her to the small kitchen, where the two complained over a bitter cup of ersatz coffee. Ursula smiled as she remembered the taste of the real thing, just a short while ago. She decided not to tell either of them of her newest secret.

CHAPTER ELEVEN

GRACE AWOKE AFTER a restless night's sleep in which her dreams shifted between the line of dead bodies on the pavement she saw during the Blitz and the sight of a Lancaster as it plunged towards the earth in flames. She felt relief when her alarm sounded to grant her a reprieve from the terrors of the night. Helen was sitting in a rocking chair in the living room still dressed in her clothes from the night before when Grace walked into the room. The tea kettle whistled from the kitchen as Helen stood up and stretched.

"I'm positively exhausted," she said. "Yanks can be such fun. Why'd you run off?"

"I didn't feel well." Grace walked into the kitchen and poured two mugs of tea. She handed one to Helen and then sat down on the couch.

"You don't look like you slept much," Helen said.

"Nerves," Grace replied. "I just wish tomorrow would hurry up and get here."

"He'll be fine," Helen said with more conviction than Grace felt. "All these times he's come back without a scratch. The Irish are lucky, are they not?"

"Two of his crew died on their last op, and another was

seriously wounded. I think it shook him up a bit. He seemed, I don't know, different this weekend. More somber."

"Try not to worry about it. Worrying won't change anything. I'm going to have a bit of a wash before we go to the office."

Grace finished her tea and looked at the phone, her lips turned down in a frown. *I've got to do it now,* she thought. In the middle of the night she'd decided to call her father today and tell him of her plans to marry as soon as Michael finished his tour. She walked over and picked up the phone. Her fingers shook slightly as she dialed the number. It rang several times without an answer. Just as Grace prepared to hang up, the gruff voice of Dr. Robinson barked, "Hello?"

"Father? It's Grace."

"Do you know what time it is?" he asked. "It's 7 o'clock in the bloody morning. I'm trying to enjoy my tea. What's so important you have to interrupt that? Got yourself in a bit of trouble again, eh?"

Bastard, she swore under her breath. Her father found a way to bring up her past trouble every time she spoke with him.

"No, Father," she said, keeping her voice as calm as she could, "it's something quite different really. You see, I'm to be married soon."

There. Straight and to the point. She paused and awaited his answer. After a long minute of silence, Dr. Robinson finally spoke.

"What's this? Married, you say?"

"Yes, Father. To a pilot. He flies a Lancaster."

"Got you in the family way, has he?"

"No!" Grace replied with considerable force. "It's nothing at all like that. I met him several months ago, and we fell in love. He proposed, and we plan to marry as soon as he finishes his tour. He's only got one mission left."

"And where is this boy from?"

"Belfast, Father."

"Belfast!" Dr. Robinson exclaimed. "Nothing good has ever come from Belfast. What's his name?"

"Michael O'Hanlon," Grace said. "He's an officer too, Father. A decorated one.

"You call me and interrupt my morning tea to tell me you wish to marry a paddy. And a papist! He is, isn't he?"

"He is Catholic, Father, but not very religious at all. I was thinking we could use the chapel near your house."

"I forbid it," Dr. Robinson yelled. "Put it out of your mind. This infatuation you have will pass. It's wartime. If he's a bomber pilot, he probably won't make it anyway. You want to find yourself a widow at twenty-two? You think his papist family will take you in? Of all the things you've done, child, this takes the cake."

"I'm not calling to ask your permission, Father. I'm simply telling you what is going to happen. We are to be married as soon as he finishes his last op, which will be very soon. You can be there if you'd like. Or not. I'll telephone and let you know the details as soon as we have them."

"You will not marry without my permission," Dr. Robinson snarled.

"I don't need your permission, Father," Grace said with a sigh.

"You've disgraced this family once before. I will not allow you to do it a second time."

"Goodbye, Father." He was still talking when she hung up.

"You bastard," she swore as tears sprang to her eyes. Every

time she spoke with him, Dr. Robinson always found a way to bring... it... up. *Haven't I been punished enough? How long will he keep doing this to me?*

"Guess it didn't go well?" Helen asked, walking into the living room as she wiped her face with a damp towel.

"No." Grace felt the first tear trickle from the corner of her eye.

"He'll come around."

"I don't think he will. Ever. He's gotten much worse since Jimmy and Mum died."

She wiped her eyes with the back of her hand and stood up. Grace walked into the small bathroom and ran four inches of water into the tub. The government encouraged water conservation along with rationing. The only soap available for purchase left a film on her body that made her feel almost as dirty as when she started. Without shampoo, her hair took on a matted look, especially when she used the soap on it. The army took most of the razor blades off the market as well. *Is it this bad in Germany?* she wondered as she lowered herself into the lukewarm water. *Surely it is worse.*

Grace leaned against the back of her tub and closed her eyes. Part of her had hoped her father would show some modicum of understanding, but the rational part of her brain knew his reaction would be exactly as it was. The marriage would go forward with or without his blessing, but she felt she had to tell him ahead of time no matter how great the temptation to say nothing until it was done. Michael encouraged her to talk to her father first too, and so she made the call with full understanding of what his reaction would be. She thought of Dr. Robinson's statement about Michael's chances of survival. Deep down she knew the odds of his death increased with each op he flew. He knew it too, and each time she saw him he appeared more and more aware of his diminishing chances. *Don't think of that now*, she warned herself – too late to do much good. *What if he doesn't come back? What then? How will I even know if we aren't married? They'll tell his father, who may not even know I exist.*

Michael did not speak of his family very often. She knew his dad had fought in the trenches in the last war and drank to excess. Michael's mother died when he was very young and his father never remarried. His only sibling, a sister named Maureen, died when the Germans bombed Belfast in the spring of 1941, but he had only ever mentioned her once. Grace and Michael had been walking arm in arm along the street near her flat. She told him about the line of bodies she'd seen during the Blitz but not about the nightmares she often had about them. Michael said, "My sister died in an air raid." He said it with such a matter-of-fact tone in his voice that Grace wondered if she'd heard him correctly.

"You say your sister died in an air raid?" she asked. "I didn't know you had a sister."

"I don't now," Michael replied. "She died when the Germans hit Belfast in May of '41. Killed nine hundred people, they did. It was right after I joined up."

"I'm so sorry," Grace said.

"'Tis alright," Michael said with a shrug. "We were never all that close. She married at sixteen and moved away to another part of town. Just a few miles away, but I never saw her again."

"She didn't come to visit?" Grace asked.

"No. My father is a mean shite. Meaner after my mam died. The world would be better off without him."

He said no more on the subject and, given his dark expression, she dared not ask him to say more. She hesitated to make any firm plans for the wedding until Michael's safe return, but two weeks ago Grace jotted down a short list of people to invite – just a few co-workers from her office and the men on Michael's crew. *Now I can cross three names off the list, unless he wants to invite the replacements who will go with him tonight. No. He won't do that.* It would be easier, she decided, to have a smaller ceremony anyway.

Grace eased herself out of the tepid water and grabbed a towel. She wrapped it around her body and walked into Helen's room. Helen was sitting in front of her dresser and dabbing at her face with a makeup brush.

"This war needs to end," Helen said. "The makeup shortages are impossible to deal with. Impossible!"

"Where do you get your energy?" Grace asked.

"I was born with it," Helen called over her shoulder. "Gave my parents fits when I was small."

Grace returned to her bedroom and got dressed. Each weekday morning, she and Helen left together at 8 a.m. They walked a few blocks to the tube station and caught a ride into the center of the city, where their office was located. They worked upstairs in an office above a large warehouse. The other two secretaries were already behind their typewriters when Helen and Grace walked through the door. They looked a little more worse for wear than Helen did. Grace hung up her coat in the coatroom and went over to say hello. No sooner had she sat behind her typewriter when a male voice said, "May I have a word, Miss Robinson?"

Grace turned and saw her boss, Mr. Holland, standing in the doorway to his office. He was a man of imposing height, nearly six feet four, and a somewhat dour expression. Holland walked with a cane due to an injury in the last war. When the current one began, he tried to enlist again but was denied for reasons of health and age. With so many men away, the company hired more women to do jobs normally reserved for the men. Some worked in the warehouse and moved heavy crates around with forklifts while others drove the trucks which delivered the products to army bases around London.

"Yes, sir," Grace replied. When she reached his office door, Holland placed his hand on the small of her back to usher her inside. He sat behind the stacks of paper and triplicate forms on his desk as his eyes wandered up and down her calves as she crossed her legs.

"Last week you were telling me that you may need some time off," Holland said as he folded his hands atop the desk.

"Yes, sir," Grace replied. "It's my fiancé, you see. He's finishing up his tour as a pilot, and we're to get married before he gets his next posting."

"And what does he fly?" Holland asked.

"Lancasters, sir."

"Ah," Holland said. "Yes. I wanted to be a pilot in the last show, but they turned me down. Said I was too tall. So it was into the infantry for me. My back pains me constantly now since I had to spend so much of my time hunched over to keep my head from poking out above the trench. Nasty business, all that. Much better to be a pilot."

"It is dangerous enough, sir," Grace replied as her lips tightened into a frown and then a scowl.

"Of course, of course," Holland said. "Had a nephew in the RAF. Fighter Command though. Much more dashing than bombers. He got the chop over the Channel during the

Battle of Britain. They say his plane burned all the way down. I sure hope he was already dead."

White-faced, Grace clenched her hands in her lap so hard it cut off circulation to her fingertips.

"About my request for some leave, sir?" Grace prompted.

"Oh yes, that," Holland replied. "I'm terribly sorry but I don't think we can manage without you. It's a busy time for us, you know. Perhaps if you'd wait until after the first of the year. Then I'm sure we can accommodate you."

"I'm afraid that won't be possible, Mr. Holland," Grace said as she shifted in her seat. "He'll only get a couple of weeks off before he's posted to a unit as an instructor. We wanted to marry then since we don't know for sure where he will end up. It could be in Canada."

"Yes, well, as I said, it presents difficulties," Holland said as he made a show of shuffling papers on his desk. "Besides, aren't you being a bit premature in all this?"

"What do you mean?"

"Well, he has to finish his tour first. Isn't that what you said? Why not make your plans once he has finished. No sense tempting fate. Suppose you take your holiday and he fails to return? What then."

Grace stood so quickly her chair toppled over behind her.

"Mr. Holland" – her words sounded as if they'd been fired from a machine gun – "if that will be all?"

"No need to be upset, my dear girl," Mr. Holland said. "I'm sure we could reach some sort of arrangement to our mutual benefit."

His eyes widened, and his tongue flicked across his lips.

"I'm not sure I take your meaning, sir," Grace said, her voice even.

"Come now," Mr. Holland said. "Sit down and we can talk. Would you like me to ring for some tea?"

"I think I'll just get my coat, Mr. Holland," Grace said as she moved towards the door.

"Whatever for?" he asked.

"I'm leaving, Mr. Holland," Grace said. "Michael and I are getting married, and that's all there is to it. I'm sure you can find someone to replace me easily enough."

"But this is a reserved occupation," Mr. Holland said. "I'll report your resignation to the appropriate governmental authorities, and you'll find yourself a land girl before the month is out!"

"I'll be married before the month is out," Grace said. "And you can bloody well stick your reserved occupation up your arse."

She walked out of the door and left Mr. Holland sputtering behind his desk. Helen caught the expression on her face and got up to follow her into the cloakroom, where Grace took her coat off the hanger.

"Is everything okay? Where are you going?"

"I'm going home," Grace said.

"Did you get the chop?" Helen asked as she took Grace's shoulders in her hands. "Are you alright? You look affright."

"I quit," Grace replied. "He says I can't take off until after the first of the year. And then that dirty old bugger said he could reach an accommodation with me. I told him he could sod off and now I'm going home."

"But what'll you do?" Helen asked.

"I'll go home and wait for tomorrow," Grace replied. "Michael will put it all to right as soon as he gets back."

Grace walked past Helen and took the staff elevator down

to the first floor. The chill November air bit at her face as she walked down the sidewalk. Though months had passed since the last time the Luftwaffe visited London, piles of brick and rubble marked the sight of previous raids. With so much damage spread around the city, cleanup would take time and manpower; the government had neither in large supply. Grace decided not to take the tube and instead opted to walk the two miles back to her apartment. Halfway home, with her nose and fingers red and throbbing, she regretted her decision to walk, but pressed on. *What have I done?* she thought. *What if everyone is right and he doesn't come back? Now I don't even have a job to occupy me. Mr. Holland is right. I'll end up getting called into service doing something else. No. Mustn't think like that. It's bad luck. I'm sure I'll think of something. Anything would be better than being packed off to the Land Army and having to work on a farm. I'd sooner join the WAAFs.*

When she got back to her apartment, she considered attempting to place a call to Michael's airfield to let him know she now found herself in want of a job. He'd given her the number to the duty officer a month ago in case she needed to reach him in the event of an emergency, but Michael cautioned her that if they were on an op, the duty officer would not tell her anything, not even if he was up that night. She sat in front of the phone for five long minutes and debated whether or not to call. Finally she decided to let it go. *No sense in telling him now. He'll only worry, and he'll have plenty to worry about tonight. I can tell him tomorrow.* As she sat in the parlor, her mind returned to the dream she'd had the night before. As hard as she tried to push the image of the burning Lancaster from her mind, it stubbornly clung to her consciousness and refused to budge. Though it was not quite noon, Grace went to her room and pulled a bottle of whiskey which dated from before the war from under her bed. She took several stiff belts and then lay back on the bed and watched the ceiling spin.

CHAPTER TWELVE

"Come on! Get up!"

Karl bolted upright from the narrow cot. Sweat dripped down his face and from under his arms. He tried to swallow, but his mouth felt as though it was filled with sand. Other men moved around him. *Where am I?* he thought as he rubbed his eyes with clenched fists. After a second, his senses returned. After he walked Ursula to the telephone exchange, Karl had returned to the station. Despite the coffee and the exercise, the air raid alerts the previous night left him exhausted, and so he lay down on his cot to grab some sleep. *Hamburg. Every time I close my eyes I see Hamburg again. God help me.*

"Get up!" Fischer urged. "We've got an assignment."

Karl's mind snapped into focus. He swung his legs off the cot and stood up as fast as the nagging pain in his hip and knee allowed. Baumann came into the room and placed Karl's service cap on his head for him.

"You were thrashing around a bit," Baumann whispered. "Dreaming of that lovely redhead you met yesterday?"

"No," Karl said. "Hamburg. You ever think about it?"

"Not if I can help it," Baumann said cheerfully as he made his way over to the fire pole. Karl limped after him and waited for Baumann to descend to the ground floor before he followed. The engines of the trucks turned over as Karl tossed his cap onto a peg and replaced it with his helmet. After he slung his gas mask canister over his shoulder, Karl buckled his belt and axe around his waist and climbed onto the engine.

"Where are we going?" Karl yelled over the sound of the engine as the truck pulled out onto the street. He absentmindedly pulled the cord to ring the bell as Fischer maneuvered around pedestrians and the light traffic.

"Unexploded bomb," Fischer yelled. "From the raid a couple of nights ago."

"I didn't hear the bells," Karl said as Fischer let loose a string of expletives at a car that failed to yield fast enough to suit him.

"Came in by telephone," Fischer answered.

Delayed ordinance bombs and bombs that failed to explode plagued the city after each raid. The Fire Brigade had little to do with the disposal and removal. Their job was to stand by and provide whatever assistance the army needed. Sometimes they sprayed water to cool a damaged building enough to let the disposal team get inside. Other times they just stood around and watched from a safe distance.

Fischer turned onto a side street a few blocks off the Tiergarten. A uniformed police officer waved him to a stop. Karl and Fischer walked over to meet him as the ladder truck pulled up and parked behind the engine.

"The bomb is just up there," the officer said as he pointed to the partially collapsed façade of an apartment building. "Kids playing in the rubble found it."

"What kind of bomb?" Karl asked.

"High explosive from the looks of it," the officer said. "Two thousand kilos. We've evacuated the block and sent everyone to the church."

Karl nodded and walked back to the engine. He mentally measured the distance from the bomb's location to the fire trucks and determined their placement to be safe enough. On occasion, bombs exploded while the disposal team attempted to make them safe. Last August, Karl had watched as a bomb of similar size exploded. The bodies of the men attempting to diffuse it inside the crater disintegrated into a cloud of pink mist. The blast pressure picked up a police officer who ventured too close to the crater out of curiosity and hurled him into the wall of a shop across the street. When the firemen got to him, his body resembled a rag doll as he lay on the street, limbs askew and blood trickling from the corner of his mouth.

An army truck arrived and parked next to the fire engines. Two soldiers emerged from the canvas cover over the bed of the truck, followed by two thin figures in striped uniforms. Prisoners who volunteered for bomb disposal duty received a short course of instruction and a few special privileges, usually better rations. Few lived long enough to enjoy them. The driver tossed each of them a pair of leather gloves.

"I don't envy that lot," Fischer said as he watched the two prisoners and one of the soldiers walk towards the mound of rubble.

"The soldiers or the prisoners?" Karl asked.

"Both," Fischer replied. "I done my share of soldiering in the last war and I don't have any desire to experience one of the camps."

"Now that's a laugh," Frei said as he lit a cigarette. "With all your cheek, I'm surprised you haven't ended up in protective custody by now. Fireman or no fireman."

"That happened, you know," Baumann said. "I think it was when you were away with the army, Karl. One of the men assigned to a station in Wedding. He told a joke about Goebbels and Himmler buggering each other. His mistake was to tell it on the S-Bahn. The wrong person overheard it and we never saw him again."

"At least Herr Meier has a sense of humor," Fischer offered.

"The only thing that fact fuck has a sense of is appetite," Baumann said. "I saw him drive by the other day. He barely fit in the back of the car. How in the hell did he ever fit in an airplane?"

Karl watched as the men moved bricks, one by one, to expose the shell crater. They disappeared inside, and Karl braced himself for an explosion. None came. After about thirty minutes, excited shouts erupted from the hole. The soldier who stood on the ground level and watched the prisoners work turned and cupped his hands to his mouth.

"They're jabbering in Polish, but I think they've got it!"

"Go down and check," the other soldier yelled from the front of the truck.

The first soldier's smile disappeared in an instant. He hung his head and turned towards the shell crater. One of the prisoners climbed out with a smile on his face. The soldier crawled into the hole. Five minutes later, he pulled himself out, followed by the second prisoner.

"They got it!" the soldier yelled. "Pulled the detonator right out!"

The firemen and the police officer applauded. The two prisoners gave a short bow as the soldier clapped each of them on the back. Karl flinched as a loud crack echoed down the street. He looked up and watched in horror as the rest of the building façade gave way and toppled towards the ground. The two prisoners and the soldiers tried to run, but they vanished in a cloud of dust.

Everyone ran towards the collapse. Karl found one of the prisoners on the ground. He lay flat on his back, his legs covered by heavy stones. The man's eyes were glazed over, but he was still breathing. He screamed when Karl attempted to move the first of the stones.

"Leave him be," said the police officer. "Find the soldier."

"He's probably dead. We can save this one."

The police officer began to speak, but Fischer shoved him aside and knelt opposite Karl. They began to lift the stones and toss them aside. The prisoner continued to scream. Just as they reached where his legs were pinned, a sudden gunshot, loud and close, caused Karl to hurl himself backwards. A soldier stood over the prisoner with his Mauser rifle pointed down. A bloody hole in the man's forehead marked the entrance of the bullet. Brain matter leaked from the shattered top of his head.

"You bastard," Karl growled. "We could have gotten him out."

"You expect the hospital to waste morphine on the likes of him?" The soldier gestured towards the body with his rifle. "He's no use to us with his legs shattered."

Karl stood and stepped over the body towards the soldier, who took a step backwards. Fischer got in between them and put his hands on Karl's shoulders.

"Come on. Let's get the others out. Leave it."

Karl glared at him and started to speak.

"Leave it, Herr Oberwachtmeister," Fischer said.

They attacked the larger pile of rubble. In an hour, their hands were bruised and bloody, despite the gloves they wore, but the men uncovered the body of the second prisoner. Soldiers dragged him away and dumped him on top of his dead companion. A few minutes later, Karl moved a brick and caught a glimpse of a gray field uniform.

"Here!" he yelled. The men tore into the pile with renewed vigor and soon had the soldier's body out. His helmet had protected his head from serious damage, but the cascade of brick and stone crushed his ribs and legs. Baumann and Frei carefully lifted the body and carried it towards the truck. The driver, who'd been helping dig, followed them and pulled the canvas cover back so they could slide the body inside. Karl and Fischer walked over to the bodies of the prisoners and lifted the first. As they neared the truck, the soldier who'd shot the first one blocked their path.

"Leave them," he ordered as he unslung his rifle and held it across his chest.

"We can't leave a body in the street," Karl said.

"You're not putting them in there with Johann," the soldier said.

"Yes, we are," Karl said as he and Fischer took a step forward.

The soldier worked the bolt on his rifle. The spent shell casing popped out, and a fresh cartridge slammed home.

"No," he said. "You aren't."

"It's okay," the police officer whispered in Karl's ear. "Leave them here, and we'll take care of them."

They left the body and climbed aboard their fire engine. As they pulled away from the scene, Karl glared at the back of the soldier. *Bastard*, he swore. *He's here and not on the front. A taste of Russia would be good for that attitude.* From refugee columns attacked by Stukas in Poland to the bodies of executed partisans in Russia, Karl had seen enough death for twenty lifetimes. *There'll be plenty more before all this is over. And those*

responsible for all this misery never have to see any of it up close.
Damn them. It's up to us to pick up the pieces.

"Damned unlucky!" Fischer shouted.

"What?" Karl asked.

"Unlucky," he repeated. "Imagine that. You diffuse a bomb only to have a building fall on you. Reminds me of something from the last war. One of our officers. Bravest man you ever saw. Survived Verdun and got the Iron Cross, First Class. Then a sniper got him while he was taking a shit two days before the Armistice. Gone through the whole war and then got caught with his pants down."

Fischer slapped his thigh and laughed at his own joke. Karl shook his head and patted the cover of his blue-gray coveralls in search of his cigarettes before he realized that he'd left them on his desk at the station.

"Think we'll get hit tonight?" Fischer asked.

"Perhaps yes. Perhaps no," Karl said.

Fischer nodded as he pulled in front of the station and expertly backed the engine in, followed by Baumann in the ladder truck. The men jumped down and removed their helmets and equipment.

"So Karl," Frei said as they started up the stairs, "I was looking out the window this morning, dreaming of a nice, quiet home in the country with a big-busted blonde, and what did I see? You having a chat with that redheaded girl and then strolling off arm in arm like two lovebirds."

"I was taking her to visit our friend," Karl said as he walked through the bunk room and into the office. He sat behind his desk and turned on the radio. The somber tones of "Ich hatt' einen Kameraden" drifted from the speaker.

"The propaganda ministry sure likes that song," Frei said. "Especially since Stalingrad."

"Either that or 'Lili Marlene,'" Baumann said, "though I'd sure love a roll in the hay with her."

"No, no," Fischer said as he entered the office and dropped into a chair. "I'll take Irene von Meyendorff. A goddess."

Fischer kept a photo of the actress taped above his bunk.

"Isn't she a baroness?" Baumann asked.

"What? Baronesses can't be pretty? Beautiful and rich. Just like I like it," Fischer replied.

"You'd do well to steer clear of the vons," Karl said. "I came across many of them in the army. Stuffed shirts, full of self-importance and eager to send you to die for their promotion. A few of them were alright. My last company commander was a von something or the other. He was a good sort and tried to take care of us."

"What happened to him?" Fischer asked.

"Oh, he ended up on the wrong side of a mortar round," Karl replied. "Shrapnel took his testicles clean off."

"Did he survive?" Baumann asked. "I don't think I would want to in that situation."

"Bled to death," Karl lied. When the round exploded, Karl had rushed from the cover of a pile of mangled steel and brick and dragged the screaming officer to safety. A medic tried to reach him but got cut down by a machine gun. Karl managed to stop the flow of blood with his hands. The officer reached up and grabbed hold of Karl's tunic.

"Shoot me, sergeant," he ordered.

"I can't do that," Karl said. "We can get you back to an aid station and they can patch you up."

The officer convulsed in pain but did not let go of Karl's

uniform. The man clenched his teeth and waited for the spasm to pass, then he spoke in a clear tone.

"I can't go home like this. Shoot me. Now."

As he spoke, the Russians opened up on their position with mortars and machine-gun fire. From down the line, the call came to fall back. The officer released Karl's tunic and fished his identity discs from under his shirt. He calmly broke them in half along the perforated line which ran down the middle. Then he reached up and tucked one of them into Karl's pocket. Angry shouts in Russian approached, interspersed with gunshots.

"Now!" the officer yelled.

Karl swallowed hard and then pulled the man's helmet off. The officer turned his head to the side and tapped his temple to indicate where Karl should place the shot. Karl removed the Luger he kept tucked into his boot and placed the muzzle against the man's head. He closed his eyes and pulled the trigger, then he staggered to his feet and dashed towards the rear without casting so much as a glance back at his handiwork.

An official announcement with the latest war news broke into Karl's memory. The radio reported heavy fighting in the east as the army readjusted their lines to deal with the Red menace. It concluded with praise lavished on the flak crews who defended the homeland from Allied *terrorfliegers*.

"Shortening the lines again," Fischer said. "they must be short indeed by now."

"Not even God can help us if the Ivans get here," Karl said.

The bells began to ring. Three. Five. One. Two. Karl saw Fischer mentally calculating where the alarm box was in relation to the station and the best route to get there. Karl reached into the desk drawer and pulled out his cigarettes. He tucked them into his pocket as he followed the men out of the office and down the pole to the first floor.

"You'd think we were the only crew in the city working today," Frei growled as he grabbed his gear from the wall.

"You joined the Fire Brigade to sit on your ass all day?" Baumann asked. "Maybe you should have joined the Kripo instead."

"If it wasn't for the war, I'd retire," Frei said. "Maybe I'll put in my papers anyway."

"You'll not have any luck with that," Karl said as he walked to the fire engine. "And even if they did accept them, you'd be drafted into the Luftschutz and then have to do the same job for free. So you are stuck, my friend."

"I guess you are right," Frei said as he walked towards the ladder truck. "But the day the war ends, I'm retiring. Not even Adolf himself can stop me."

As he climbed aboard the engine, Karl glanced over at Fischer and asked, "How are we set for petrol?"

"Oh, we've enough for a while. So long as they don't send us too far out of our district. We'll need more in a couple of days."

Karl made a mental note to send a requisition order for fuel once they returned from the call. The chill of the November air bit into his face. The engine pulled out of the station and moved towards whatever misery the next assignment entailed. Karl's mind moved back to the injured prisoner laying in the street and the bullet which had ended his life.

CHAPTER THIRTEEN

HALFWAY TO THE hut he shared with seven other officers, Michael changed his mind and walked to the officers' mess instead. With a few hours to kill in between the flight lunch and the mission briefing, he knew he would not be able to sleep, nor did he want to spend his time staring at the wooden walls, adorned with pin-up girls alongside pictures of wives or girlfriends. Michael had two photographs of Grace, one of the two of them together which he had framed and placed alongside his cot, and the other of just her. He kept that one in his billfold and, despite orders to take no personal items on missions, Michael taped it to the instrument panel before takeoff. *I wonder what she's doing now?* he thought. *How hard it will be on her when I don't come back.*

"Afternoon, sir," a blonde WAAF corporal said as she crossed his path. "Good luck tonight."

"Thank you." Michael returned her salute with a vague wave of the hand in the vicinity of his forehead.

The building which housed the officers' mess had been hastily constructed, like most of the base. A wooden sign above the door read "Abandon Hope All Ye Who Enter." A similar sign marked the entrance to the NCO mess. Though gunners in Bomber Command were always enlisted men, commissioned officers could be pilots, navigators, or bomb aimers, depending on the whim of the command authorities who ran the training schools. Michael's crew was entirely enlisted, other than himself, but some had two officers. A good pilot was a good pilot, regardless of his rank.

Michael hung his cap on a rack near the door when he entered the mess. A wooden bar ran along one wall, though with the squadron on alert, alcohol consumption was prohibited. Michael knew a few pilots who took sips of whiskey from flasks before each flight, and perhaps during as well. They rarely lasted long. There were a few tables on one side of the room and a collection of ragged sofas and recliners on the other. A billiards table separated the two halves. A large British flag hung on one wall, and the tail section of an Me-109 downed during the Battle of Britain took up a large section of wall opposite the flag. A few months ago, Flying Officer Jefferson had donated his rather impressive collection of female nudes and the men placed them at various points around the room until the chaplain complained, no doubt at the behest of one of the WAAF officers. The nudes came down and, soon after, Jefferson went down in flames over Dortmund. Michael wondered which of Jefferson's bunkmates made off with the photographs before the personal effects were sent home.

A few officers gathered around a battered piano and competed with the radio across the room. They took no notice of his arrival. Faces came and went in the mess. New officers often went down before Michael even learned their names. Most disappeared within their first five missions.

"Tea, sir?" the enlisted mess attendant asked.

"No. Thank you," Michael said. The enlisted man moved away to his station in the corner as Michael dropped into a chair. He winced as the ache in the small of his back reminded him not to move too quickly. The door opened and Flying Officer Sterling, a bomb aimer on K for King, walked in. He smiled when he saw Michael and made his way to him. Sterling was a tall, thin man with a young face and old eyes. Though a mere twenty years old, gray hairs around his temple spoke of the strain of his job. He often joked that if Bomber Command had a sense of humor, they'd have assigned him to a squadron which flew Stirlings rather than Lancasters. Sterling and his pilot, a dour Ulster Presbyterian named McBride, shared the hut with Michael and a handful of others.

"Can't sleep?" Michael asked as Sterling sat across from him and accepted tea proffered by the mess attendant.

"I was about to ask you the same." Sterling blew on his tea to cool it.

"I never sleep before an op. I'd just as soon take off now and get it over with."

"Tut-tut," Sterling said. "Only the Yanks are crazy enough to go over by day."

"Got a cigarette?" Michael asked. Sterling fished a pack out of his pocket and passed one to Michael, who lit it and inhaled deeply, smiling as the smoke bit at his throat. "Thanks."

"Any word on where we are going tonight?" Sterling asked in a whisper. Rules prohibited talking shop in the mess. Violators had to buy a round of drinks and stand on a table and sing a song of the mess's choosing.

"My crew chief says they are laying on fuel," Michael said. "Full tanks. Long trip."

"Jesus bloody Christ," Sterling said. "I was hoping for a quick dash to France and back."

"Apparently Butcher Harris has other plans," Michael said. Arthur Harris, chief of Bomber Command, directed the offensive from his headquarters at High Wycombe. He received his nickname not for the destruction wrought on Germany, but for the heavy losses his command suffered. Some of the more enterprising statisticians at Thomas Green determined only one in five crews survived a full tour. No crew from Michael's squadron had reached that milestone since early September. The pilot went out to celebrate with his crew, had too much to drink, and ran his car off the road and into a ditch. He was flung out of the vehicle and head first into a tree. The next morning, a child on a bicycle found him dead of a broken neck.

"This will be seventeen for us," Sterling said. "What I wouldn't give to be in your shoes."

No you wouldn't, Michael thought. *Your risk of death increases with each operation.*

"Think the WingCo will fly this one with us?" Sterling asked.

"He might," Michael said. "He seems to like to fly the tough ones."

The previous squadron leader only flew on operations to the French coast. Sure, he'd already done one full tour and no doubt had his fill, but it did not endear him to the pilots who faced hell over Germany. He'd been forced to ditch over the Channel on the way back from Le Havre one night. His Lancaster broke up on impact, and the coastal rescue boat found no human remains.

"Have you spoken with McBride lately?" Sterling asked, his voice low and serious.

"No," Michael replied. He made a point to avoid McBride

as much as possible. Though both hailed from Belfast, they might as well have grown up on two separate planets. Centuries of animosity existed between Ulster Protestants and Catholics. McBride made a point to mix references to "papists" and "shinners" into the few conversations Michael had with him.

"I'm afraid he's gone daft," Sterling said. "On the last trip over Berlin, whilst we were on the bomb run, he was giggling like a school girl over the intercom. And then, when our tail gunner took some shots at a fighter, he started yelling, "Vengeance is mine, sayeth the Lord."

"Well, Ulster Presbyterians can be a strange lot," Michael offered.

"He just doesn't seem right. I'm a bit worried about going up with him tonight."

"Have you spoken to the WingCo or the doctor?"

"No, I can't do that. If they yank him off ops, we'll be stuck with a new pilot or, worse yet, they'll break up the crew. Crazy or not, I'll have to take my chances with him."

"How does the rest of the crew feel?" Michael asked.

"No idea. I haven't spoken to them. It wouldn't be right, would it? Us being officers and all. I can't criticize a fellow officer to enlisted men. Surely there's a regulation about that."

"The King's Regulations are only fit to wipe your arse with." Michael massaged the back of his neck with his right hand. "They work wonderfully well for preserving good order and discipline in peacetime. But in a war?"

"I guess you are right about that. I'll see how he does this mission. If he cracks up again, I'll talk to the doctor when we get back. Say, how was your leave?"

Michael gave him a rundown of his weekend with

Grace and his crew. Sterling had no girl at home, and once Michael proposed introducing him to Grace's roommate. She informed him that only Americans need apply for Helen's affections. *Her loss*, Michael thought since he knew Sterling's father owned a considerable estate in the midlands. Though some members of the squadron thought him a bit of a toff, Michael enjoyed his company.

"She mentioned that she had to tell me something," Michael said as he finished his narrative. "But I didn't give her a chance to when I telephoned today. Had to give up the phone to the chaplain. I wish... I wish I'd have let her say what it was."

"Hmmm," Sterling said. "I don't mean to pry and it really is any of my business, but have you, you know, gotten to *know* her? In a marital way?"

Michael laughed at the red which crept up Sterling's neck and onto his face as he asked the question. *A sheltered life, no doubt. He's probably never so much as kissed a girl.*

"She truly is a nice girl, and we've decided to marry," Michael said.

Except I won't be alive this time tomorrow.

"Understand I really have no experience in these matters," Sterling replied. "But is it possible that she is in the family way?"

"I'm pretty sure she'd have told me that!" Michael stiffened and leaned forward in his chair. *But would she? Maybe she didn't want to burden me with it before my last flight? Jesus, that complicates things if I don't come back.*

"It was just a thought."

"You sure know how to cheer a man up," Michael replied with a faint smile.

"I say, old boy" – Sterling pulled a small white envelope out of his tunic – "if I don't make it back, would you see that this letter gets to my parents?"

"Be happy to," Michael replied. "But don't give it to me. Leave it in your locker with your personal effects."

"Yes. Of course. That makes sense." Sterling slipped it back into his pocket.

"If you'll excuse me," Michael said as he stood, "I think I'll wander back to our hut for a bit of a lie down. We still have time to kill."

And I've my own letter to write, Michael thought as he left the officers' mess and walked towards his quarters. Mentally he tried to compose his letter to Grace, to be opened in the event of his death. No words formed. *How do you comfort a person who fell in love with you on the mistaken pretext that you'd survive the war? Apologize? Say it was fun while it lasted? I hope you find someone else soon?*

With a frown, he glanced across the field towards the dispersal points where ground crews swarmed over the planes like ants. Fuel, ammunition, and bombs. The tools of the trade. The erks also cleaned the turrets and pilot's windshield, inside and out. The crews took their work seriously. A bolt not tightened, the last drop of fuel not added, and a bomber might go down with seven trained crewmembers aboard. Some took it hard when their crew failed to return. Others shrugged their shoulders and took over the next plane to arrive. The war wore on their nerves as it did the flight crews', and after a raid with heavy losses, reports of drunkenness and fistfights increased. The squadron leader allowed most of it to blow over and rarely assigned serious punishments lest an otherwise good man's record be tarnished forever as a result of a simple mistake made under great stress.

None of the other officers were in the hut when Michael arrived. He carefully made up his cot and fluffed the lumpy pillow. Then he reached underneath and slid his footlocker out. His name, rank, and service number marked the green lid. Inside, Michael kept a few emergency packs of cigarettes, extra socks and underwear, a set of rosary beads which had belonged to his mother, and a few novels and magazines. He took the photograph of him and Grace from the small wooden nightstand and placed it inside his footlocker, along with the contents of the dresser drawers. Then he slid it back under his cot as the door opened and McBride walked in, followed by Pilot Officer Jackson, a sprog yet to fly a mission.

"You ready for tonight?" McBride asked as he collapsed onto his cot.

"I am," Michael replied. "As ready as ever. How goes it with you?"

"I'm as right as the mail," McBride said. "Ready to sally forth and defeat the Hun."

"Are you alerted for this op?" Michael asked Jackson.

"Yes, sir," Jackson said. "And am I ever ready for it. They've had us doing training flights for three weeks now! The lads and I are ready to see action."

Michael smiled at the pimply faced youth's use of 'lads' to describe his crew. *I'm only a couple of years his senior, but he is like a child. All full of piss and vinegar. God help them if we go to Berlin tonight.*

"Is it true, sir?" Jackson asked. "That you are finishing up tonight?"

"If we make it back," Michael said. "Never take anything for granted in this war. We've still gotta make it to the target and home before they can go handing out gongs and promotions."

Michael had hoped for a quiet moment in his hut to write his letter, but Jackson's questions and the loud snores which erupted from McBride's mouth like a volcano made that most unlikely. He collected a few sheets of stationery and an envelope from Sterling's nightstand and took his leave of Jackson, who made to follow him until Michael gave him a stern order to stay put. *Somewhere in Germany, a night fighter squadron is getting ready to provide us with a warm reception. Flak crews are checking their guns. They are just waiting for us to open the ball.*

"Good luck, sir!" a corporal exclaimed as he rode by on a bicycle with a WAAF sergeant perched precariously on the handlebars. "Give 'em 'ell tonight!"

"Jesus Christ," Michael swore. "Can I not get a moment of peace?"

"No chance of that, Mick."

Michael turned and saw McKenzie behind him with a big grin on his face.

"Didn't realize I said that out loud."

"You Irish always seem to speak before you think. Maybe that's why you are such a combative lot. Unlike we Aussies who are the very soul of tact and demeanor."

"More like misdemeanors," Michael said.

"Where are ya off to?"

"I need to find somewhere to write a letter."

"To Grace?" McKenzie asked, his smile vanishing.

Michael nodded.

"She's a corker, Mick. A real catch. No idea what she sees

in you, of course. But you haven't written one of those letters for her yet?"

"No, I haven't," Michael said. "I guess I never thought about it."

"Hop to it then," McKenzie said. "And put in a good word for me."

"For you?" Michael asked.

"Sure. If you buy it and I don't, I plan to look her up myself."

"Seeing as how I'm flying the bloody airplane, that seems unlikely. We go west together or not at all."

"Aren't we just a marriage made in hell," McKenzie said. "Well, I'm off to pay my respects to Sergeant Plummer. She's the tasty little WAAF corporal I went to the dance with a while back. Remember her?"

"Vaguely," Michael replied. "There've been so many."

"Gotta have fun before I settle down," McKenzie said. "The war would be smashing fun if it weren't for all the dying."

With that, he turned and walked away with strides more akin to a gallop. Michael shook his head and tried to suppress a smile. *They are good lads. All depending on me to get them home. Them and their families.* Within hours of landing after the Berlin mission, Michael had sat down to write letters to the parents of Holland, his mid-upper gunner, and the teenage wife of Fuller, his navigator. He told Mr. and Mrs. Holland the truth. Their son died instantly as he blazed away at the enemy. He could not tell Mrs. Fuller the truth, that her husband died screaming in an aircraft as it bucked and twisted in the night sky. Jones, the radio operator, had been seriously wounded and Cameron had to split the morphine between them as he tried desperately to stop the torrent of blood.

Fuller bled to death, conscious until almost the very end. *No, I couldn't tell her that*, Michael thought. He'd met the girl only once, at the wedding in early September. Fuller admitted he had not known her long, but they wanted to marry nonetheless. Her parents had sad faces, but not the kind many parents have when their daughters marry. Michael thought they looked resigned to their daughter being a widow. Two days before the Berlin mission, Fuller announced his wife was pregnant to the delight of the crew, who threw him a bit of a bash. They embraced any excuse to celebrate life amidst the somber air of a bomber base.

Michael spotted a bench outside the operations office and he sat down as he fished in his pockets for a pen. He stared at the paper for several long minutes, his mind blank. *Come on, lad*, he urged himself, *this will be all she has to remember you by! You have to say something, anything, to ease her grief.* Eventually the dam burst within his mind and he began to write.

CHAPTER FOURTEEN

GRACE AWOKE SEVERAL hours later, a gnawing pain in her stomach which matched the throb at her temples. It took her brain a few moments to process where she was, and remember what had happened. *What have I done?* she thought as she massaged her forehead. *I won't need the job when Michael gets back, but what if he doesn't? No! I can't think that way. He'll be back.* Her head protested as she sat up in the bed. A splash of cold water over her face and a strong cup of tea helped clear the fog in her head, but did little to assuage the hunger. Grace decided to walk down to the tea shop at the end of the block to eat whatever they had on the menu today. Well aware of the whiskey fumes which oozed from her pores, she left the apartment.

Grace walked past windows marked with heavy tape designed to keep glass from shattering in bomb blasts. Wooden boards covered some places to mark where windows had once been. In the early days of the war, the government had drafted a list of air raid precautions and circulated them among the population. It detailed the myriad blackout regulations enforced by fines or even arrest for serious or habitual violators. The pamphlets urged the use of tape on windows though, at the time, Grace doubted a few sticky strips would do much to stop a thousand-kilo bomb blast. During the long nights of the Blitz, as bombs pounded London, Grace often felt the desire to shake her fist at the sky and curse the German pilots who made war on women and children. *And now, our lads are doing the same to them*, she thought. Grace once asked Michael how he felt about bombing German cities by night. He just shrugged his shoulders and said, "Sure, what can you do? They started it, didn't they? London, Coventry, Belfast. We're only trying to end the war. Besides, it's fair play. They get a crack at us when we fly over. They aren't entirely defenseless."

She dropped the subject after that and never asked him his opinion on his work again. And it was work. That's how he described it. As a job. *And now I find myself in want of the same*, she thought as she skirted an American sergeant with his arm around a plump brunette. "You could be a film star," he was saying to the girl as Grace passed them. The girl sounded suitably impressed with the compliment, and Grace smiled. *The Americans with their cigarettes, chocolate, and nylons. Our own poor lads can't compete with that.* Conflict often arose when British soldiers returned home from years fighting in North Africa only to find their favorite village pub overrun with Yanks who established a monopoly on the local girls. A few weeks ago, Grace read a news story about one of Monty's men who'd been in Africa and Sicily. He had returned home on a spot of leave after three years away only to find his wife playing house with a Yank pilot. He'd shot them both and then himself. *I wonder what they told the pilot's family. Killed in action? Died in an accident? They can't likely tell them the truth.*

She entered the tea shop and sat down. A waiter in a white shirt and black tie brought her a cup of tea and told her that soup was on the menu, and nothing else. Grace nodded and the man moved away to another customer. A radio behind the counter gave the latest war news. Heavy fighting in the east and on the Italian front. U-boats sunk in the Atlantic. The news reader had an optimistic tone, unlike a few years ago when each broadcast seemed to speak of some impending doom. During the fall of France and the long summer of 1940, the public listened to the news as though it narrated their own upcoming execution. As the RAF battled the Luftwaffe in the skies over Southern England, the radio gave updates on total numbers of planes shot down versus lost each evening. At the time, she had no personal connection with any of the participants in the epic aerial battle. *Before I met Michael*, she thought. *Now, when they speak of raids, it tears at my heart. It'll be over soon. And I won't have to worry.*

The news complete, the radio switched over to music as Grace took in the other customers. Each table had at least two occupants. Several couples smiled at each other over their cups. Some of the men were in uniform, but most were not. In the corner, a WAAF sergeant made polite conversation with an RAF pilot. From her exaggerated facial expressions and forced laughter, Grace determined the pilot to be more interested in her than she in him. Two older men argued back and forth about where and when the cross-Channel invasion should take place. One insisted Calais, and the other thought a landing near Cherbourg best. *Armchair generals*, Grace thought. *They always think they know better than the real ones.* The conversation reminded her of her father, and she frowned. *He's like that too. Always yelling at the radio to correct whoever had the misfortune of giving the news. Even after Jimmy was killed. What will happen when he meets Michael? He'll have to at some point. I can't likely delay it forever. Even if he's not at the wedding.*

After her bowl of watery soup, Grace considered returning home to try and phone Michael, but she realized that if he were going up tonight, he'd be busy and they might not let him talk anyway for security purposes. The soup settled in her stomach and soaked up the whiskey she'd consumed earlier. Grace determined to tell Michael her secret the second she saw him again. *Maybe he'll be so glad to be alive and off operations that he won't care. No, it wouldn't be fair to tell him like that. I'll have to wait a day or so. Maybe I could just write him a letter?*

A military vehicle drove down the street at a high rate of speed. When it hit a puddle, water splashed over Grace's shoes and legs. "Watch where you're going, you bloody fool!" an equally soaked man yelled after the car as it disappeared. Then to Grace he said, "They'd never let a bleedin' eejit like that behind the wheel if it tweren't for the war. That's God's truth." Grace offered him a polite smile and then moved on.

To kill time, Grace visited a few shops but spent no money. With her current lack of employment, she thought it wise not to give money out too freely, not that the shops had much worth purchasing anyway. The government rationed far more than just food and petrol. When she reached a jewelry shop, Grace decided to purchase a small gift for Michael to celebrate his return. When he asked her to marry him, he promised to purchase a ring for her as soon as he finished his tour. She didn't mind, as he never spoke of his financial situation. She assumed that, growing up in a Catholic family in West Belfast, he had to be of less than modest means before he joined the RAF. As a child, Grace dreamed of a large wedding at her father's house in the country. *But now? It isn't the size of the ceremony that makes you happy. It's the person you marry,* she thought.

A portly man with spectacles perched on the tip of his nose looked up from his newspaper when Grace entered the shop.

"Help you find anything, miss?" he asked in a voice that managed to convey both hope and a desire to return to his paper as quickly as possible.

"I'd like to buy something for my fiancé," Grace said. "He's a bomber pilot."

Now why did I say that? Grace thought as the man rose from his stool with slow, deliberate movements, as though each inch caused him pain.

"Fiancé?" he asked. "I notice you don't wear a ring. Could I interest you in an engagement ring? The prices are quite reasonable."

"No," Grace said, her tone a little harsher than she intended. Recovering, she continued in a gentler voice, "No, thank you. You see, we got engaged six weeks ago. He's a bomber pilot and has one more op left to finish his tour. We'll get the rings then. But I wanted to find a small token to give him when he comes back. Sort of a congratulations, you see."

"Hmmm," the jeweler said as his fingers drummed the countertop. "I don't really have much in the way of jewelry for men that isn't wedding rings or a watch. Come to think of it, a watch would be a nice gift, I'd say. Pilots need watches, or so I've been told. Never been in an airplane, myself. Spent the last war in the trenches. Mud and slime. If I had to have another go at war, I'd do it in an airplane. Providing I could fit in the cockpit, what!"

Grace smiled at the joke as the jeweler slapped his side and laughed. The rolls of fat around his midsection jiggled with such force she feared it might break the glass counter-top. He gestured for her to approach the counter and spent twenty minutes detailing the pros and cons of every watch in his inventory. She finally selected one with a canvas band and a face which had the number twelve in red rather than black like the other numbers.

"Want anything engraved on the back?" the jeweler asked. "Doesn't cost that much extra. Be nice to give it a personal touch, like. I could have it done in a few days."

"No, thank you," Grace said. "You see, he'll be going up either tonight or tomorrow, and I want to give it to him as soon as he gets back."

"Since he is on active service and all," the jeweler said, "I could do it whilst you wait."

"Very well. Could you please engrave it with 'To Michael. All my love. Grace.'"

"Certainly, and normally I don't allow returns on engraved items, but with his job being a dangerous one and all, I'll make an exception should the unthinkable happen."

"Very generous of you," Grace said evenly.

"It's the least I can do for the future wife of one of our brave airmen."

Grace slipped him the money, and he took the watch and disappeared into the back of the shop. Ten minutes later, he emerged with a small wooden case and handed it to her. Grace opened it and inspected the watch, then she smiled as she turned to leave.

"Miss," the jeweler called after her. She stopped and looked over her shoulder at him. "How about the two of you come in to pick out wedding rings once he gets back? I'll give him an RAF discount! How's that?"

"I'll consider it," Grace said.

She left the shop and walked a few blocks to her apartment. On the narrow staircase, she passed the older woman who lived in the apartment next door.

"Shouldn't you be at work?" the woman asked as Grace turned her back to the wall to give the woman room to squeeze by.

"Day off, Mrs. Prescott," Grace said.

"On a Monday? What's this world coming to?" Mrs. Prescott's voice trailed off as she disappeared down the stairs.

Grace suppressed a laugh. Mrs. Prescott kept a close eye on Helen and Grace and took a vested interest in their comings and goings. She made pointed comments disguised as questions on matters she found distasteful, such as a male visitor in the apartment. Though Helen found the busybody to be a great nuisance, Grace considered her harmless. *Just an old woman who uses us to provide a source of entertainment and gossip.* Nothing in the building remained a secret long. *Helen will no doubt murder the woman after Michael and I find a place of our own.* She'd not given much thought to living arrangements after the wedding. Michael mentioned it might be best not to make any decisions until he knew where the RAF would post him. It could be to a flight school in Canada. *It could be in Siberia and I'd still follow him,* Grace thought as she slipped her key into the lock.

She hung her coat on a peg near the door and slipped her shoes off lest she track water into the room. Barefoot, she walked to the kitchen and ran a small bit of water into a glass and drank it before she filled and drank another. Her mind raced with thoughts of Michael's impending mission. *What's he doing now? Having a briefing? Is he scared? Nervous?* To distract herself, Grace picked up a paperback romance novel and walked over to her chair. As she sat, she turned to the first page and tried to read, though her foot tapped out a staccato beat on the floor which shook the chair. As she held the book open with her right hand, she placed her left hand on her knee and tried to hold her leg still. Instead, her leg jostled her hand as well. With a loud exhale, she flung the paperback across the room. It struck the wall with a dull thud right as the door opened and Helen walked in.

"Have the Jerries invaded then?" Helen asked.

"What are you doing here?" Grace asked. "Shouldn't you still be at work?"

"Got something important to tell you," Helen replied. "Couldn't wait, so I asked Mr. Holland to let me take off a bit early. He didn't mind."

"And what is so important you had to take off early?" Grace asked.

Helen's eyes gleamed with excitement as she threw her coat over the back of a chair and began to talk.

CHAPTER FIFTEEN

URSULA SAT AT a telephone switchboard along with two dozen other young women who each had their own headset and board. Some wore uniforms which marked them as military auxiliaries while others, like Ursula, were civilians. Most of the calls that came in were from Wehrmacht field headquarters and routed through to various military or government departments. On occasion, Ursula even caught the unmistakable sound of shells or gunfire in the background as she answered calls with a terse 'Number Please.' She'd held the job for the past two years. The government expected young, single women to do their share of war work. Though strictly voluntary at first, women not working in an essential occupation found themselves dragooned into some sort of war work. A few of the civilian telephone operators volunteered for the Luftschutz or the Red Cross, which assisted in hospitals and provided coffee and sandwiches to residents bombed out of their homes. During the heavy raids in late August and early September, two of the girls she worked with died when their shelter took a direct hit. Three others lost their apartments, though the bosses quickly worked to get them rehoused with a family nearby. Though grateful her section of Berlin had not received major damage, Ursula knew it was only a matter of time before the bombs fell on them too. *God help us when it happens*, she thought. *I only hope we can all make it out of the shelter alive.*

Though the work schedules rotated between morning, afternoon, and night, Ursula had not been on duty overnight during a raid. The city attempted to keep the phone lines running for the purposes of relaying damage reports between city departments. Heavy sandbags protected the exterior from blast fragments, and a fire watch manned the roof at night with buckets of sand and water. She knew neither provided much protection from a large bomb hurtling earthward from sixteen thousand feet. It would smash through all the way to the ground floor before it detonated among the workers. Gisela had worked during the last big raid on the city in September. Though normally unaffected by hardship, danger, or privation, she confessed to Ursula how terrified she was as the building shook from nearby bombs. A few of the girls wept, yet they never left their posts. A few hardy souls sang patriotic songs until ordered to stop as it interfered with phone conversations.

As she transferred a call to the Reich Ministry of the Interior, Ursula felt a presence behind her but she did not turn around. The bosses often stalked back and forth to keep an eye on the women as they worked. Some did it for professional reasons, others leered at the girls and made the occasional suggestive comment.

"Fraulein Müller," a voice said over her shoulder, "might I have a word with you?"

She turned and saw Major Bandelin, a tall, thin man with the erect bearing of a Prussian officer. A pin held his left sleeve up, a reminder of the arm he'd given for the Fatherland during the last war. Ursula slid her headphones off and stood up.

"Certainly, Herr Major," she replied as a cold fear began to gnaw at her stomach.

"My office," Bandelin said. "Follow me."

He led her up the stairs and down a hallway. Uniformed officers hurried back and forth, each nodding at the major as he passed. When he reached his office, Bandelin held the door open and indicated she should enter first. Ursula half expected to see Gestapo men waiting inside to arrest her, but the office was empty. A large glass window looked out over the first floor so that the major could watch the women work while seated at his desk.

"Please sit," he said as he pulled a chair out for her. She sat down, and he took his place behind his desk.

"How is your wife, sir?" Ursula asked. "I heard she'd had an operation."

"Yes," Bandelin smiled. "Her appendix ruptured. She's on the mend, though I don't think she'll be moving at her usual speed for quite a while. We got her to the hospital just in time."

"I'm glad to hear that, Herr Major."

"I'm sure you are wondering why I need to talk to you." He paused for a long moment, and when Ursula made no reply, he continued. "You see, a couple of the girls have come down with a case of influenza. We are going to be short staffed for a while. Would you be willing to work a double shift?"

"Today?"

"Yes, some of the overnight workers won't be able to make it. I know it's asking a lot of you on such short notice, but it would be helpful."

Ursula's mind raced as she tried to come up with a suitable excuse. *If I miss my appointment tonight and fail to carry out the mission, the others might think I've gone over to the Gestapo and try to eliminate me. But I can't hardly tell the major that.*

"If you have plans," the major said, "then perhaps I could ask someone else. It's just that I've been impressed with your work ethic, and I trust you more than some of the others."

"Well, you see," Ursula said, "I do sort of have something planned for tonight."

"You have a young man? A soldier, perhaps?"

"A member of the Fire Brigade, actually." Karl seemed as good an excuse as any.

"Ah, I see. I thought we were down to using young women and old men in that line of work."

"He was a fireman before the war," Ursula said. "But he was a reservist and so he served in the east until he was wounded. They discharged him and sent him back to work."

"The east... I lost my only son in the east."

"My brothers too," Ursula said. "Both of them."

"That must have been terrible for your parents. And you too, of course."

"My parents were already dead, Herr Major. Mother died in an accident a long time ago, and Father died of a heart attack on the day the war started."

"Did he now? Did he serve in the last war?"

"Yes, sir. In France."

"Me too. My arm is still there somewhere. Let's hope this war ends soon."

"In victory," Ursula replied.

"Quite," the major said through a clenched jaw. He sat still for several minutes as his fingers tapped his desk. Ursula averted her eyes and studied the inside of the office, bare of any furnishing except a desk and a photograph of the Fuhrer on the wall. The major's desk contained a typewriter, a large stack of documents and forms, and two photos, one of his wife and one of his son, a handsome young man in an officer's uniform. A knock on the door interrupted the silence. A harried corporal walked in with a form. He thrust it in front of the major, who signed it without so much as a glance at the page. When the corporal left, Bandelin looked at Ursula and gave a faint smile.

"I'll not have it said that I stood in the way of young love," he said. "We all must grab whatever happiness we can."

"Perhaps I could work a few hours extra," Ursula said, and cursed herself the second the words left her mouth. "Maybe two or three."

I'll be cutting it fairly close, she thought. *But I'm sure I can make it so long as there isn't a raid to slow me down.*

"Thank you for the offer, Fraulein Müller," the major said, his face brightening. "I'm sure I can find someone to relieve you by seven. Please take care of yourself. I don't want you to come down with the influenza either."

"I will, Herr Major," Ursula said. He eyes moved towards the door.

Major Bandelin noticed the direction of her gaze. "Yes, that will be all," he said. "And thank you again for your willingness to help."

"We all must make sacrifices for the Fatherland." Ursula rose and, after a small curtsey, she walked out of the office and returned to her switchboard.

"What did the major want?" the young woman next to Ursula asked as she took her seat.

"Oh, just for me to work late," Ursula replied. "Some of the girls came down with the flu."

"He's such a nice man," the young woman said. "Devoted to his wife though. A few girls have tried to tempt him in the past and failed. They found themselves reassigned."

The woman continued to talk as Ursula slipped her headphones on. *Would Karl be like that?* Ursula thought. *He seems nice enough, but I don't want to expose him to any danger. The war is helping bring some couples together, but I'm hardly in a position to have any sort of relationship. It would be too risky. Maybe after the war.*

After two hours, Ursula took a short break. She made her way to the room where employees off duty gathered to drink ersatz coffee and smoke. A thin blue haze of cigarette smoke hung in the air. A few young soldiers sat at a table with two uniformed women. The soldiers regaled them with a blow-by-blow account of a recent football match.

"I'm telling you, Schalke will win the league again this year. Just you wait and see."

The soldiers attempted to draw her into their discussion, but with no knowledge of football and little interest in conversation, she kept silent and they turned their attention back to their two female companions. *Four more hours here*, she thought, *then I'll have time to go to the apartment before it's time for me to make the walk to the shop. I hope there is no raid tonight. That would complicate things.*

The door to the breakroom opened, and Gisela walked in. She gave a little wave to the soldiers and then took her seat across from Ursula.

"Would you like to go to a picture after work?" Gisela asked.

"I'm afraid I can't," Ursula replied. "I made other plans."

"With your literary friend or your fireman?" Gisela asked with a knowing smile.

"I'm sure Karl has to work tonight. He said they have to stay on duty at night in the event of an air raid."

"How romantic," Gisela said.

"What? An air raid?"

"No, how you met him. The only thing more romantic would be if he threw you over his shoulder and carried you out of a burning building. Lucky for you that your cooking is terrible."

"I'd not thought of it that way," Ursula said with a laugh.

"But how will your literary friend take it when you tell him about, what's his name? Karl?"

"I'm only friends with both of them. Nothing more. Heinrich and I only talk about books, that's all. Quite platonic. And as for Karl, well, I just met him yesterday. I don't even know him that well."

"Well enough to walk you to work this morning. He's quite a catch for you. A good government job. All his limbs. Not bad looking either. Better sink your teeth into him before I do."

"The only thing I'm sinking my teeth into right now is my lunch," Ursula said.

"So why don't you invite Karl to come to the pictures with us?"

"I'm not seeing him tonight. Like I told you," Ursula said, annoyance creeping into her voice, "he will be working. If you must know, he said he'll get some time off on Thursday and I'll see him then. After work."

"Excellent!" Gisela exclaimed. "Monica and I will find us

dates, and we can all go and do something together. Maybe dancing at one of the underground clubs."

The government had banned all forms of dancing while soldiers fought at the front. A brief relaxation of the rule followed the Fall of France, but it resumed upon the invasion of the Soviet Union. Still, Berliners could not be put off so easily. Many establishments still permitted dancing despite the regulations. Though technically secret, most residents knew of the location of at least one such club. Ursula visited a few from time to time with her roommates. The first time she set foot in one, she was shocked to find soldiers and party officials dancing to forbidden music alongside shopgirls and factory workers.

"I'll have to ask him." Ursula looked at the floor. "He was injured at the front, and I'm not sure if he can dance now."

"Pity," Gisela said. "Not being able to dance would be terrible. Say, I noticed a strange man hanging around near our apartment the past few days. I've been meaning to ask you if you've seen him."

"What do you mean?" Ursula's pulse quickened. "Where? When?"

"I've seen him three times. The first time was three days ago. He was standing across the street. Then yesterday, I saw him in the lobby of our building looking at the mailboxes. This morning when Monica and I left for work, he was across the street again. Just staring at the door to the building."

"What did he look like?" Ursula struggled to keep her voice calm.

"He's tall. Maybe six feet. He always wears a gray overcoat and a gray hat. If I had to guess, I'd say he looks like he's—"

"Gestapo?"

"Yes," Gisela said. "Definitely someone official. I wonder if someone in the building is up to something. Maybe hiding Jews. I wonder if they will raid the building! How exciting!"

"Maybe it's nothing," Ursula said. "He could just be meeting his girlfriend. Or watching for one of those blackout burglars."

"You are probably right," Gisela said with a frown. "Nothing exciting ever happens at our place. Other than the occasional air raid. And even then they miss our neighborhood completely."

"I have to get back." *Is he watching me or someone else?* she thought. *If he's following me, I might inadvertently lead him straight to the warehouse. Should I not make my appointment tonight? No, I have to go. I'll just have to take extra precautions, provided I have time. Damn this schedule! And damn the Tommies if they hit us tonight! That will slow me down even more.*

The remainder of her shift passed with relative speed. At six thirty, Major Bandelin came downstairs and told Ursula she could leave for the day. He thanked her again, profusely, for volunteering to help and told her he hoped she had a good time with her date. As she collected her coat, the major stuck his head in the room and whispered, "You might want to hurry home. The radio just announced that bomber formations are approaching. They are a ways off, if they come here at all, but it wouldn't hurt to rush home anyway. Just in case. I hope it doesn't ruin your evening plans."

"Thank you, Herr Major," Ursula replied. "If it does, we'll make new ones for another day. The war has taught us all to be flexible, if anything."

"That's the spirit," the major said. With a polite nod, he returned to his office. Ursula hurriedly grabbed her belongings and left. The cold November air nipped at her face as she walked down Oranienburger Strasse. She turned the collar of her overcoat up to try and ward off some of the chill. *It's going to take me a while to get to the shop*, she thought. *Especially if a raid happens.* She cast several glances around her as she walked, searching for any sign of a man in a gray overcoat, but the night sky and the blacked-out city covered everything with an inky darkness.

CHAPTER SIXTEEN

KARL WATCHED A human torch crawl down the street. Behind the burning man, a solid wall of flame swirled in the air. People ran in all directions, some burning, others blackened by soot. The wind feeding the inferno carried their screams, like those of wounded animals. With no water pressure, Karl and his crew could do nothing more than watch as the world around them melted.

A hand touched his shoulder. He shook his head to chase away the images of Hamburg which invaded his mind on a near constant basis. Frei stared down at him.

"Sorry," Karl mumbled as he rubbed his face with his hands. "I was thinking about something."

Frei leaned close, his breath warm on Karl's ear.

"We all think about it sometimes, *kamerad*. There is no shame in it."

Maybe, Karl thought. *Maybe we all do. But I cannot get these images out of my head. Every time I shut my eyes I see it. No wonder I envy the dead. They at least have some peace.*

"Best check over our equipment in case we need it tonight," Baumann suggested as he stuck his head into the office. "I've got a feeling the Tommies will pay us a visit."

"You and your feelings," Frei said. "Didn't you stand in

that very same spot not a week ago and say you had a feeling we'd have a big apartment fire that night?"

"I admit I was wrong on that point."

"Or the time you assured us we'd be called upon to extricate some unfortunate victim from under a train within the hour," Karl added.

"So I was wrong on that too. So what? This time I think I'm right."

"You should have gone into military intelligence." Karl stood with a grimace as pain stabbed his hip. "They could use someone like you on the Eastern Front. A man with your *feelings*. Just think of it. You could predict Ivan's next attacks. That would make it easier to – what does the radio say? – 'shorten our lines.' They would no doubt make you a general. Perhaps even a field marshal. We'd never lose another war."

"The only feeling I have is hunger," Fischer said from his seat at a table in the day room. "A thick, juicy slice of ham. My mouth waters just thinking about it."

The four men walked down the stairs and split up to check their respective equipment. Karl glanced over the hoses pulled on a cart behind the engine while Fischer checked over the pumps. Baumann pulled the ladder truck out of the station and raised the ladder while Frei climbed to the top. Satisfied the hoses would not leak, Karl put his gas mask on and checked the straps and canister.

"The engine could use a good wash," Karl said as Fischer put his gas mask back into its case. "The ladder truck too. Perhaps even a bit of polish. Just because we are at war doesn't mean we can't have nice equipment. A well put together engine indicates a well put together crew. Pride, Fischer. We show our pride in the job through the condition of our equipment."

War or no war, Karl thought, *we are still firemen and Berlin is still our city. There was a Fire Brigade before the war and before the Nazis, and there will be a Fire Brigade long after both have faded into memory. We are firemen, and there's honor in that.*

"You are right, but I wouldn't call us a well put together crew," Fischer said. "I'll put the Hitler Youth recruits on the washing when they get here. It'll keep them busy and out of our hair, and the hair of the young women, for a while. I remember how I was when I was that age."

"And what will we do with the women?" Fischer asked.

"I haven't thought that far ahead," Karl replied. "Though I suppose we need to show them how everything on the engine works since they'll be with us. If Baumann's feeling is actually correct for a change, it'll come in handy. And if not now, then certainly in the near future."

"Girls as firemen," Fischer said with an exaggerated sigh.

"Haven't you heard?" Karl asked with mock seriousness. "It's the New Germany. The Party says we all have a part to play. Even you, Fischer."

Some are just a bit more murderous than others, Karl thought. Before the invasion of the Soviet Union, Karl's company commander assured the men that they were about to launch a crusade against the Jewish Bolshevik influence in Europe and that history would record their deeds among the heroes of old. *It was so unlike France*, Karl thought. *The Tommies gave us a decent enough fight and played by the same rules as we. Not so in Russia.* He'd seen soldiers from his own unit laugh as they gunned down Russian troops attempting to surrender. Some joked as they set fire to small peasant cabins as the elderly occupants stood and took it all in without so much as a word of protest. While on anti-partisan operations, Karl's soldiers engaged in punitive raids on villages thought to harbor or aid Russian guerillas. They followed the same basic pattern. All homes burned. Young men, and sometimes old ones, shot out of hand. The women marched to the west for forced labor.

On one operation, they captured four partisans alive. The company commander forced Russian civilians to erect a gallows in the center of town and then to watch the execution. Two of the condemned were young women in their late teens. One had blonde hair and blue eyes, almost Aryan were it not for the round Slavic face. They stood on simple stools, alongside the two young men they were captured with, as the commander read a lengthy diatribe against Russian resistance to German rule, against Jewish crimes, and against the evils of communism. A Ukrainian volunteer translated the speech into Russian for the town's population, who looked on with faces that showed neither fear nor defiance. Finally the stools were removed. Watching the two young women writhe on the noose as they strangled, faces turning red, their bound hands twisting against the ropes, Karl had to turn his head away. His stomach heaved and he tasted bile along with the partially digested rations he'd consumed earlier. *After all I've seen*, he thought, *this is what makes me vomit? This is no longer war. It is murder.*

Two weeks later, the company commander who ordered the execution stepped on a mine which ripped his legs off and sliced open his stomach. He sat on the ground, a stunned expression on his face, with his intestines piled in his lap. When a medic approached, the commander was trying to stuff them back inside his body. The men heard later that he died on the way to the field hospital. The company returned to the front and the casualties continued to mount. *And then there was Stalingrad. Bloody, brutal Stalingrad. If I ever meet the Ivan who wounded me, I'll stand him to a drink in the nearest bar for getting me out of that frozen hell. But to die in Stalingrad or here, in Berlin, under a British bomb is still the same. No matter what, you are still dead. But at least here we are dying for something worthwhile. Maybe, just maybe, the lives we save here will outweigh the lives I took in the east.*

A few dozen Berlin firefighters died in raids stretching back to the previous August. Karl knew some of them, as he'd known them in peacetime. A few more were recent recruits. Unlike the pre-war days when a dead firefighter meant a large department funeral with representatives from departments all over Berlin, the number of wartime losses meant the man's death would get no official notice. Just one among hundreds. *Before the war, I feared death*, Karl thought. *But now it has lost its mystery. Death is a release from life's terrors, nothing more.*

Baumann reversed the ladder truck back into the station while Frei followed on foot. Karl hated every moment of the three years he spent assigned as a driver before the war, first on an engine and then on a ladder. In the pre-war days, Berlin's streets contained far more vehicles and pedestrians during the day. Navigating around them while headed to an emergency took great skill. Karl liked the act of putting out fires, which the drivers of the apparatus did not get to do since they had to stay outside and man the pumps. Now drivers dodged bomb craters and rubble rather than people, and on some nights, they dodged the bombs themselves. The men left one of the big doors to the station open for the young volunteers to enter through when they arrived later on.

Karl walked up the stairs with Fischer close on his heels. Frei entered the office and switched on the radio. Midway through the patriotic tune, a voice interrupted and announced enemy bomber formations were approaching the coast. The station went off the air once the message ended. Karl plugged the radio into the receiver connected with the phone lines and turned it back on. There was no ticking sound, which indicated the planes had not yet reached German airspace.

"I told you!" Baumann said with a grin on his face. "That will teach you clowns to give me more respect around here."

"We don't know where they are going yet," Karl said. "It could be anywhere. And as far as respect goes, perhaps you should try to be more accurate with your predictions."

"Tonight will tell," Baumann said as he shook his finger at Karl. "Just wait. You'll be coming to me and saying 'Old Baumann was right.' Assuming you survive the raid, of course."

"I hope it's Munich," Fischer said. "They could drop a million kilos of bombs on that place and it would do ten million Reichsmarks worth of improvements."

"Ever been there?" Baumann asked Karl.

"No, I have not. Perhaps I'll visit someday."

"It would be a waste of a holiday," Fischer said. "Bavarians are a nasty sort. Full of their own arrogance."

"Says the Prussian," Karl replied.

"I wouldn't go around saying too many bad things about Bavarians," Frei cautioned, "seeing as how we have so many of them in Berlin now. What would the Party do without them?"

What indeed, Karl thought. As a public servant, he faced pressure in the '30s to join the Party. Those who did so found promotions came much faster than those who did not. Karl resisted the urge, not out of any real dislike of the National

Socialists – in fact, in the early years he agreed with their stance on communists – but rather to his general desire to stay out of all politics. He'd seen enough of the violence that accompanied the social unrest after the Great War to lump most politicians together in one category: people to avoid. *Just keep your head down and do your job, and everything will fall into place.* As time passed, that mantra became more and more difficult. Everything in Berlin was political in the '30s and worse now in wartime.

He stood up and walked over to the window. Karl pulled the curtain back and peered down at the street. A few pedestrians hurried past, no doubt spurred on by the possibility of a raid. As darkness would descend over the city in an hour, Karl closed the curtains and then drew the heavy blackout curtains closed too. Fischer saw him and walked over to do the same to the other windows. The sound of laughter drifted from downstairs.

"Guess our new recruits are here," Frei said.

"I guess we should go down and greet them," Karl sighed. *These poor children. They don't know what they are in for.*

PART THREE
22 NOVEMBER 1943
EVENING

Immediately after the tribulation of those days
shall the sun be darkened, and the moon shall not
give her light, and the stars shall fall from heaven,
and the powers of the heavens shall be shaken.

Matthew 24:29

CHAPTER SEVENTEEN

Ursula hurried along the street in the gathering darkness. She caught snatches of conversation from the few others on the street. One man patted his female companion's arm and assured her the *luftgangsters*, air gangsters, would not dare visit Berlin so soon after their last raid. From the doubtful expression on the woman's face, Ursula knew she did not share her friend's optimism. *And that's all we have*, she thought. *Blind faith in the Fuhrer and Final Victory. Only a miracle can give us the old Germany back.* The Zoo Flak Tower loomed in the distance. The massive structure bristled with anti-aircraft guns. It also boasted a hospital and served as an air raid shelter for up to fifteen thousand people. A line of people snaked around the side, waiting for the doors to open in the event the aircraft approaching the coast turned for Berlin. Most held suitcases or pillows. A sign near the door forbade men of military age from taking refuge inside and suggested they try going to the front instead. As more Berliners found themselves bombed out of their houses, public shelters grew in importance. The thick concrete walls provided far more protection to the occupants than a reinforced cellar in a crowded apartment building. Ursula preferred her own shelter to any public one, despite the increased risk.

Air raids caused enough noise. She imagined the inside of the flak tower added a new level of auditory sensation as the roar of anti-aircraft guns in close proximity mixed with the sirens and the shriek of bombs as they fell from the sky. The basement where Ursula waited out raids was bad enough; the thought of spending several hours packed into a bunker with unwashed bodies and few toilet facilities turned her stomach. Still, some had no choice but to endure it after bombs destroyed their own shelters. After several months of little activity, the last week indicated the Royal Air Force had no intention of permitting Berlin to grow too complacent. *Perhaps*, Ursula thought, *this is a good thing as people pay more attention to the warnings than they did before the raids grew heavier.*

In the early months of the war, air raids took on an almost holiday atmosphere. People laughed and joked on their way into the shelters, if they went at all. Restaurants and cafes stayed open. The patrons simply moved to a back room or, if it were large enough, the basement. Waiters broke out champagne bottles and turned up the music to drown out the wail of sirens. When bombs fell in those early days, they missed anything of importance more often than not. Berliners visited the sections of town and stared at the occasional bomb-damaged house. The descriptions they gave each other of the damage, while standing in the street, often reached the ears of the affected residents. The Party promised to take care of those who suffered the misfortune of losing their home, and in the first few years of the war, citizens could expect to receive some emolument to cover the cost of new clothing and ration books. A central office found housing for them as well. Since last August, however, the government had found

172

it difficult to cope with the sudden influx of homeless citizens. Bombed-out families from all over Germany made their way to the capital in a somewhat mistaken impression they would find more resources there. The swell in numbers after the week-long destruction of Hamburg the previous summer pushed the city's resources to the breaking point. Berlin was bursting at the seams and there was little the government could do, other than to offer assurances that the residents of the Reich's capitol wouldn't experience what Hamburg's citizens had suffered through. Most believed the propaganda, and even Ursula admitted the defenses around the city looked formidable indeed. *But I'm no expert*, she thought. *And bombers will still get through.*

As she walked a few more blocks, she passed the fire station. A thin line of light shone through one of the partially open doors. Voices from inside drifted out to the sidewalk. She stopped. *With me working late, I don't have much* time, she thought. *I'll already have to rush home and then to the shop. I won't be able to take my time like I usually do. I'd like to stop in and say hello, but then I'll have to hurry even more.* She ignored the warning in her head and walked over to the station and looked inside. Karl and another fireman stood near their engine with four young women dressed in blue coveralls. Karl ticked several items off on his hand as he spoke, while the other man nodded his head with a serious expression on his face. Next to the engine, four young boys applied rags with polish to the sides of the ladder truck as two firemen watched over them and pointed out various spots the boys missed. Ursula had never seen the inside of a fire station before. Four brass poles descended from the second floor along the side wall. It smelled like a mixture of soot and motor oil. A large map of the city occupied the back wall with pins to mark something, maybe other fire stations. Or perhaps they marked the location of fires the men fought in the pre-war years. Karl cast a sideways glance towards the door and saw her. His face turned back to his young pupils for a moment, and then he snapped his head back towards Ursula. A smile spread over his face. Ursula stepped inside and shut the door.

"Take over, Baumann," he said.

"Your door was cracked," Ursula said. "I could see light on the street. I had to do my patriotic duty and bring this violation of our blackout restrictions to your immediate attention. Better I catch you than the air raid wardens."

"Thank you for your diligence and attention," Karl said. "And our local air raid warden can go take a leap off the flak tower for all I care."

"Is this a bad time?" Ursula asked as she looked over Karl's shoulder at Baumann, who lectured the young women about the proper way to attack a fire. "I just wanted to pop in and say hello. I only have a moment."

"Oh," Karl said with a laugh, "so it wasn't just the blackout regulations!"

"Guilty," Ursula said with a slight blush. *I really should get home. I have no right to involve myself with such a nice person. The Gestapo might be after me, and I'm putting Karl in danger by being seen with him. He doesn't seem like the sort to go goose-stepping through the Tiergarten, but you really have no way to know how a person feels about the state of the country.*

"Let's go upstairs," Karl suggested. "We can chat in the office."

"Do you think we'll see a raid tonight?" Ursula asked as she followed him up the narrow staircase.

"Perhaps," Karl said. "Baumann, that was him with me down there, seems to think we will. Says he has a 'feeling' about it."

"And are his feelings accurate?"

"Rarely."

Ursula paused inside the large room lined with cots and a few tables. She looked around and saw a few calendars and photographs of fire apparatus from the past three decades. Several posters published by the government with bold, angry words which denounced the 'terror fliers' added a stern countenance to the room. It smelled of smoke and the faint odor of mildew. All of the cots were made up in an identical manner, with the blanket folded down four inches. She wondered if it were a written rule or if the men just copied one another's habits after spending so much time together. The table nearest the office door contained a few magazines, mostly older issues of *Der Signal*, the official Wehrmacht publication. A neatly folded copy of the latest Berlin newspaper lay on top of one of the stacks, its creases still perfect as if it had not been read. *Not much worth reading about in the papers these days as it is*, she thought.

"We don't get as much sleep at night as we once did," Karl said as he beckoned her to follow him into the office. "I would offer you some real coffee from our friend, but with the Hitler Youth boys down there, well, I don't know if I can trust them to keep the secret."

"I understand," Ursula said. "One can't be too careful these days."

Karl looked at her for a long minute and then said, "Indeed."

The radio emitted a constant tick, like that of a cuckoo

clock. This meant Allied aircraft were now over German airspace, somewhere. Karl reached over and set the receiver to the flak communications channel. *I've got to leave soon*, Ursula thought. *Especially if the raid heads here. And then what? Am I to continue on my mission in the middle of a raid? I suppose it might give me some cover, but at the same time it adds to the danger. It would make it harder for someone to follow me though.*

"Busy day at work?" Karl asked as he turned his attention away from the radio.

"A bit," Ursula said. "Some of the girls have the flu and so I had to work a little later than planned. And you?"

"The funny thing about the war," Karl said, "is that we aren't as busy with the day-to-day type calls as we were in peacetime. We still respond to those type of calls, but they don't come as often."

"But you are busier with war-related things?" Ursula asked.

"Yes," Karl said. "Yes, we are."

"I really should get home," Ursula said. "Just in case."

Karl stood and ushered her out of the office just as the other firemen trooped up the stairs. They gathered around as Karl introduced them. Each shook Ursula's hand in turn. Baumann asked if her temper matched her hair, and Ursula assured him that he did not want to find out. This drew a laugh from the men; Frei slapped Baumann on the back and said, "She sure told you!"

"I'm glad to see our Oberwachtmeister taking an interest in the fairer sex again," Baumann said as he winked at Karl. "I was starting to worry about him, Fraulein Müller. He spends all his time here. Never seems to take more than an hour or two off, though to be fair that's all we get these days."

"Again?" Ursula turned towards Karl and raised an eyebrow.

"I was married," Karl confessed. "For a few years before the war. Then, well, then the war seemed to change everything. She wrote me a letter while I was in Russia and said she'd taken up with a Luftwaffe pilot and wanted a divorce."

"I'm sorry," Ursula said. *What a terrible thing to go through,* she thought. *No wonder he looks so weary.*

Karl shrugged, though his face took on a strained look.

"I'll walk you down," Karl said.

"I truly am sorry," Ursula said once they reached the main floor. The boys were busy polishing the engine as the young women studied the various hose attachments.

"I told them not to leave these two groups unsupervised," Karl growled. "The last thing I need is one of these girls getting pregnant or getting her heart broken. Or one of the boys to hurt himself trying to show off."

"How long will the war last, do you think?" Ursula asked as they reached the door.

"I don't know," Karl said. "Maybe years. The Russians are tough fighters. Much tougher than the government gives them credit for. They won't give up. I'm no fan of the Bolshies, but I fear our Propaganda Ministry knows little about their military abilities. If they did, who knows? Maybe we'd have never invaded in the first place. Listen to me! I'm starting to sound defeatist. I should be more careful with my words."

"Let's hope that Final Victory arrives before Christmas," Ursula said, her voice flat.

"Please take care of yourself tonight," Karl said. "If we catch a raid. I know I haven't known you for long, but I've grown quite fond of you. Maybe it's the war. Everything seems so rushed these days. Do you have a safe shelter?"

Ursula nodded.

"As safe as the next."

"If, well, if we get hit hard tonight, I'll try to come by to check on you. If you have to leave the shelter, come here. The door will be unlocked, and you will be safer here than on the streets. Even if we aren't around. Just come in."

"I will," Ursula said. "And you must take care of yourself too. Don't take any unnecessary risks. I would tell you to stay out of danger, but we both know that isn't possible."

Karl smiled. They faced each other for a minute but said nothing. *What can I say?* Ursula thought. *I've grown fond of him too, but I can't tell him what I get up to after dark. And now isn't the time for romance anyway. But still, should I let the war rob me of happiness too along with everything else?* She rose on her toes and gave him a light kiss on the cheek, then, without a word, she slipped out the door. Ursula did not notice the man in the trench coat and hat across the street, in the shadow of a building. As she moved down the street, the man walked towards the fire station.

When she walked through the door, Gisela and Monika were collecting their coats. Both jumped slightly at the unexpected intrusion.

"You nearly gave me a heart attack!" Monika exclaimed. "I thought it would be another hour or two before you got home."

"No," Ursula said. "I got home a bit earlier than I thought. The major found someone to come in early and relieve me. Still off to the pictures?"

"Sure you don't want to come?" Gisela asked. "I'm sure there'll still be tickets for sale."

"What? Now?" Ursula asked. "Don't you know there is a raid on?"

"We heard," Monika replied. "They just said the bombers were still heading east. If we leave now, we can at least catch some of a picture before the raid starts."

"But where will you go when the bombers get here?" Ursula asked.

"There'll be a public shelter nearby, silly," Gisela said. "What is it they say? Enjoy the war. The peace will be terrible."

"And where are you going tonight?" Monika asked. "Gisela said you were planning on seeing your literary friend. Is that still on?"

"I don't know," Ursula said. "I should telephone him and see, I guess."

The two girls stared at her expectantly.

"What is it?" Ursula asked.

"Well, go on and phone him," Gisela said. "We want to hear his voice."

Shit, Ursula thought. She snapped her fingers and said, "I've just remembered. He said he had to work late and would meet me when he got off work. I don't know how to telephone him at work, and I wouldn't want to bother him anyway. He might get in trouble. He says his boss is very demanding."

"Too bad then," Monika replied. "We will see you when we get back."

"Be careful out there," Ursula said. "I'm worried about you going out tonight."

"Don't worry," Monika said. "No Tommy bombs will fall

on us tonight. Maybe with a little luck we can run into some fighter pilots! And if we do, don't wait up for us!"

The girls laughed as they walked out the door. *Terrible indeed*, Ursula thought as she watched them go. *Win or lose, it makes no difference. It'll be bad for us no matter what.* The girls had left the radio on, and the air raid commander gave out the latest information. The bomber formations were approaching Hannover but still on an eastward heading. *That settles it*, she thought. *We are the target.* Her mind raced as she tried to decide if she should try to contact the others in the warehouse, or carry on with her mission anyway. *I won't be much use to anyone if a bomb kills me before I can deliver the pistol. But if the raid is bound for Hannover or Leipzig and I don't go to the shop, they might think I've turned against them or gone to the Gestapo. That would be just as dangerous as being arrested. I'll carry on. I'm a soldier too, just like my brothers, only I'm fighting for a different Germany.*

A sudden knock on the door made her jump.

CHAPTER EIGHTEEN

MICHAEL LED HIS crew into the unheated Nissen hut. Aircrews sat on rows of wooden benches, which faced a wall where a thick curtain hid a map of Northwest Europe with the target for the night marked. The walls were empty save for two posters. One showed a lone bomber about to be shot down by night fighters. It read, "Don't be proud! Stay in the crowd!" Another warned downed aircrews to give nothing but their name, rank, and serial number if they fell into German hands. Any information, no matter how small, might be of use to the enemy. For the past fifteen missions, Michael's crew had claimed the back row. A new crew, on their first op, occupied the bench. Mac slapped the pilot on the shoulder and with a jerk of the thumb indicated they should seek a seat elsewhere.

"I say, Sergeant," the young pilot officer said, "we were here first."

"Move," Michael said as he inserted himself into the situation. "That's an order."

The crew grumbled as they sought seats elsewhere. Mac thrust his face into the pilot's and said, "You're for the chop tonight." The man's face turned a deep shade of green, and he looked as though he might vomit. Chuckles erupted from the experienced crews, who all went through similar hazing when they first arrived at the base and went operational. Three new crews would be on their first op tonight. They were easy enough to pick out. The men fidgeted in their seats and cast furtive glances at the curtain which hid the target. Some puffed furiously on cigarettes. The experienced crews, though just as scared, took great pains not to show it. A few cracked jokes, usually at the expense of the new crews or the Wing Commander, but most sat with resigned expressions on their young faces as men might face their own impending execution. Michael knew several good pilots who vomited before every mission as if to cleanse their bodies of any hint of nervous fear. He felt the butterflies too, but fought to maintain a composed manner in front of his crew. *No need to let them think their pilot is going nutty*, he thought. *They've concerns enough of their own.*

Mac kept up a running commentary on which crews would fail to return from the night's raid. This was his usual pre-briefing activity. It kept him from thoughts about his own potential fate. Finally, Michael elbowed him and told him to give it a rest. Cameron pulled out a battered pack of cigarettes and passed them around the crew. Michael accepted one as a way to keep his hands from shaking and giving away his own fear. The solemn atmosphere reminded Michael of a funeral, apart from the off-color joke about a Scotsman and a sheep Lawton told to the three new men on the crew. Cameron responded with a detailed and profane description of Yorkshire and its inhabitants.

After an eternity, the Wing Commander walked to the front of the room, followed by the squadron intelligence officer, who the crews remarked showed a striking lack of it.

Wing Commander Simpson took his spot at the center of the raised platform in the front of the room and surveyed the crews with his hands on his hips.

"Well, chaps," he said, "I've got a spot of news for you tonight."

"The bleedin' war is over and we can go 'ome?" Lawton called out to the great delight of the men.

"Nothing of the sort," Simpson said. "Tonight we've got another chance to smash the Hun where it hurts the most!"

He turned and nodded to the intelligence officer, who drew the curtain back. A thin red string stretched from their airfield straight to Berlin. Michael felt cold fear grab hold of his stomach. A sudden intake of air rose from those who knew what a trip to Berlin meant. Heavy flak. A forest of searchlights. And enough night fighters to maul any bomber stream. Beside him, Michael heard Mac whisper, "Oh bloody hell."

Michael forced himself to pay attention as the Wing Commander ran down the takeoff times, positions in the bomber stream, and a short pep talk on the need to carry the fight to the enemy. He sat down, and the lead navigator gave the crews information on the positional markers and their time over target. Unlike the Americans, who flew in tightly packed formations in broad daylight, RAF crews sometimes made their runs with little knowledge of exactly where other planes were in the sky around them, other than the occasional glimpse of a bomber caught in the searchlights or the slipstream from a bomber ahead of them. The lead bomb aimer for the squadron told the men their target indicators. Michael glanced over and saw Mac furiously writing the information down.

"And lads," the man said as he finished, "don't drop your

loads until you are bloody well over the target. I'm talking to you new crews in particular. It'll get hairy up there. You'll be tempted to drop as soon as you see the indicators go down. If you do that, you will not, I repeat not, get credit for the mission. Your photo must clearly show you over the target area. You'll feel like quite the fool if you fly to Berlin and back only to not get an official mission. Am I understood?"

No one answered him, so after a scowl which lasted a minute, he sat down. After crews dropped their bomb, they dropped a photo flash and the bomb aimer snapped a picture. This served as official proof they had bombed the target. Otherwise, crews might fly around in circles over the North Sea for the estimated mission time, jettison their bombs, and return home. *I'd be tempted enough to do that myself,* Michael thought. *Especially tonight.* The meteorological officer, a balding man with spectacles perched on the tip of his nose, took the stage to give the night's weather forecast. He had the air of a country schoolmaster about him.

"There may be cloud cover over the target," he warned. "The good news is that it might hinder their night fighters. The bad news is you might be bombing blind. But that's a matter for the pathfinders. You drop where they put their flares. There'll be cloud cover over the base when you get back. Perhaps down to five or six thousand feet. So be careful. And good luck."

"Want to make the flight with us, sir?" a sergeant pilot on his thirteenth mission called out from the center of the room. "Be happy to take you along."

"I'm afraid my duties require me to remain here," the officer answered to the delight of the crews, who roared with laughter.

The last officer to take the stage was the intelligence officer, who briefed the men on the city's defenses and the general targets they hoped to hit that night.

"I don't need to remind you how heavily defended Berlin is," he intoned. "We hit them a few nights ago. They might very well be expecting us tonight and, if so, they'll put up a hell of a fight. Pay attention to any unusual tactics from their night fighters. We've word they are experimenting with a few different things, so if you see something out of the ordinary, make sure you tell us at debriefing. Good luck. Take the piss out of them."

Wing Commander Simpson took the stage again.

"I expect they'll be ready for us tonight. So stay well bunched and put your bombs on target. Let's hammer them as hard as we hit Hamburg. We all know how important a target Berlin is, so let's make this raid count. Remember, England expects every man to do his duty!"

Cameron stood. "Well, seeing as how I'm a Scot, I'll bugger off and leave the war to you proper Englishmen!"

Before Simpson could formulate a response, Mac called out, "That goes for me too. You Pom bastards can fight your own bloody war."

"I see you still have no control over your crew, Flying Officer O'Hanlon." Simpson smiled as he looked at Michael.

"I'm an Irishman, sir," Michael said as he stood up. "I'm inclined to agree with them."

The room erupted into hoots and claps. Simpson allowed it to continue for a few minutes before he waved his hands for silence. When the men calmed down he said, "Good luck, lads. Go hit Berlin and then head for home and tea. I want to see you all back here in the morning."

When he said the last line, he looked straight at Michael's crew. *I don't think you will*, Michael thought. *Hate to disappoint you.* When Simpson dismissed the crews, Michael pulled the three new men assigned to his aircraft aside. They looked scared, whether of him or the enemy, Michael could not say.

"Look," he began, "you've been to the big city before. You know what to expect. Just stay focused on your jobs and you'll be alright. Turner, I need you to be on top of our position at all times. We've a long trip to make, and it will stretch our fuel. We can't risk running out of petrol because you've got us over Moscow instead of London. Clear?"

"Yes, sir," Turner replied.

"And you, Williams" – Michael turned to his mid-upper gunner – "keep your eyes open. Even if you can't shoot worth a damn, if you give me warning, I'll get us away from the fighter."

"Understood, skipper."

"Graham," Michael continued, "work those frequencies and try to jam any night fighter communications you come across. Speak any German?"

"No, sir."

"If you hear any German, jam it. Simple as that. Check?"

"Check," Graham said.

"Let's get to it, then," Michael replied.

The crews walked over to the locker room where they dressed for missions. Michael fell in alongside Sterling, who clapped him on the back and whispered, "Nervous?"

"Bloody terrified," Michael said, his voice low. "How's McBride?"

"He was singing hymns just before the briefing," Sterling said as he nodded his head towards McBride, twenty yards in front of them. "He said God has called him forth to be his sword arm."

Michael gave a low whistle.

"Aye, he's gone daft," he said. "It's not too late to talk to the Wing Commander."

"After the mission," Sterling said. "The crew wouldn't forgive me if they yank him and give us a sprog pilot."

"Make sure you do," Michael said. "There's no shame in losing your marbles. It can happen to any us."

"You'll take care of the letter?" Sterling asked to change the subject. "Just in case?"

"Leave it in your locker," Michael said. "I'll see to it."

"Thanks awfully," Sterling said with a smile. "That gives me some comfort."

When they reached the Nissen hut where the crews got dressed, Michael extended his hand and wished Sterling luck before he walked over to his crew, who stood around in front of the metal lockers. In the past, they got ready at the same time and saw no need to start without their pilot. Given the cold environment in which they operated, command allowed them to dress in whatever way they felt comfortable. Mac was the only crewman Michael knew who flew in his necktie. When questioned about it before their first operation, he said, "I hear the sheilas in Hun Land are bloody magnificent. I want to look my best for them in case we get shot down." Michael removed his shoes, coat, and tie. In place of his uniform jacket, he put on a white roll-neck sweater under his padded flight coveralls and his green scarf around his neck before he stepped into a pair of fur-lined flight boots. He left all of his personal effects in the top of his locker, along with his letter to Grace. Though expressly forbidden from taking any personal items on operations, many of the men took a photograph of a wife or girlfriend along. Michael kept his photograph of Grace with him. Cameron kept a rabbit's foot clipped to his parachute harness. Mac kept a stuffed kangaroo in the bomb aimer's compartment. Lawton tucked a small Bible given to him by his mother in his boot.

After they dressed, the crews stopped by to pick up their parachutes from a pretty WAAF sergeant, who looked at them with sympathy. She whispered a 'good luck' to each man as he took his chute. When Michael walked out of the parachute hut, a raven-haired WAAF corporal handed him chocolate bars and an escape kit with a silk map and emergency rations. Mac grabbed a thermos of tea, and the men climbed into the back of a truck with one other crew for the drive out to the dispersal point where their aircraft awaited their arrival. Michael didn't know any of the other crew personally, though he'd seen them around the base. Their pilot was a sergeant with a red moustache which matched his hair. The man sat with his eyes closed as the truck bounced its way across the field.

"Paddy's Wagon!" the driver called out as the truck slowed to a stop. Michael followed his crew out and walked over to the aircraft, where the ground crew was gathered around, hands in their pockets. Michael thanked each of them in turn for their work on the plane while Mac, Cameron, and Lawton completed their preflight ritual of each urinating on one of the wheels.

"Good luck, sir," Smitty said as he shook Michael's hand. "You're alright for an officer. Just bring the old girl back to me in one piece."

"I'll do my best," Michael replied. He wanted to say more

but no words came, so he squeezed the man's shoulder and turned away. He motioned for his crew to gather around.

"All set?" he asked. The men nodded. "I don't have a speech planned. Just do your jobs. Gunners, keep a close eye out for fighters and other bombers. Call out anything you see. We are going straight in and straight back out, so expect trouble. We've got some time yet before we take off. May as well get comfortable."

The men sprawled out on the ground to await the flare to signal takeoff. Michael lay on his back, eyes closed, as his brain tried to recall the words he'd not spoken since the last time he attended mass, some seven years ago. *Hail Mary, full of grace, the Lord is with thee. Blessed art thou among… women? Blessed is the fruit of thy womb, Jesus. Holy Mary, mother of God, pray for us sinners now and at the hour of our death. Hour of our death. The hour is near. I can feel it.*

"I don't understand women," Mac said to Cameron, interrupting Michael's meditation. "That little WAAF in the parachute hut. You saw her? Course you did. I took her out last week. Caught a picture and a pint. She let me put my bloody hand up her skirt, but today she acts like she don't know who I am."

"Mebbe yer hands were cold," Lawton said. "I doubt a girl would want ya gropin' her nether regions with cold hands."

"How the hell would you know?" Cameron asked. "The closest you've been to a girl's skirt is the time you got lost in the department store and wandered into the women's fitting room."

"Go bugger a sheep," Lawton said. "That's the real reason you Scots wear kilts, ain't it? Easier access?"

Mac laughed and reached over and punched Cameron on the shoulder.

"At least my great-grandfather didn't get banished halfway around the world for shagging a goat," Cameron said. "I know how you Australians are. Bunch o' convicts, the lot of you."

Michael smiled as he listened to his crew's banter. It was the same before every mission. The men traded insults as a way to pass the time and ease the tension. To the uninitiated, it sounded harsh and unfriendly, but each would give their life in defense of the same man they insulted seconds before. Aircrew had a strong bond and the men held nothing back in defense of one another or their plane. Michael looked up at the nose of his aircraft. Just aft of the bomb aimer's position, a green shamrock and the words Paddy's Wagon marked it as his aircraft. Twenty-nine yellow bombs painted below the pilot's window indicated how many missions the crew had flown. *Only one more*, Michael thought. *We made it all this way. I don't think she'll get the thirtieth.*

"Jesus, can we just take off already?" Williams exclaimed. "I can't take much more of this waiting around."

"You'll wait so long as they tell us to wait, wee man," Mac said.

"Hope they don't scrub it," Graham said.

"Enough of that," Cameron ordered. "You three, just sit there in silence until the skipper gives you permission to speak."

The concrete began to dig into his back, and so Michael stood and stretched. As he did, a red flare went up in the distance.

"Alright, lads," Michael said. "Time to load up."

He stood aside and waited until each member of the

crew boarded the plane, then he gave a brief nod towards his ground crew and tossed his parachute pack inside the hatch. As his hands closed on the metal and he prepared to board, his mind repeated the words *Hail Mary, full of grace, the Lord is with thee.* The words left as quickly as they came as he lifted himself into the plane.

CHAPTER NINETEEN

"I can tell you one thing," Helen said as she sat across from Grace, crossed her legs, and lit a cigarette, "Mr. Holland is not happy with you! Says you stormed out of there like your arse was on fire."

"And that's what he let you off early for?" Grace asked.

"Oh no, not that," Helen said. "A few hours after you left, he called me into his office, all polite like. Told me to sit down and offered me a fag and a cup of tea. He said he felt bad about what happened and that after looking over the schedules and orders for the month, he thinks he can give you a few weeks off. If you're willing to come back, that is."

"I see. And what else?"

"Sorry?" Helen looked at her with a blank expression.

"I said, what else? He's got conditions, I'm sure. He made as much plain to me earlier."

"No, no," Helen said, waving her cigarette, "there are no conditions, Grace. He says you are a good worker and you deserve a wee little reward for it. Says he doesn't blame you for wanting to get married. With a war on and all, you never know what will happen. He said it was the same the last time."

"And when does he want an answer?"

"If you show up at work tomorrow, consider it done, and

you can have the next two weeks off. And there's one other thing."

"Shocking."

"You remember Miss Dobbs? His personal secretary?"

Grace nodded. Camila Dobbs was a leggy blonde with big, dreamy eyes. Her position required close contact with Mr. Holland, naturally, but she made sure to make it closer. She had a ready laugh, if a little too loud, for any witty remark he made. The two took tea together every day, and he had a habit of standing close to her with his hand on the small of her back whenever the opportunity presented itself.

"She had to leave to go and take care of her sick aunt in Manchester last week," Helen continued. "Won't be back either."

"Her sick aunt," Grace rolled her eyes. *I wonder if she found herself in the same condition that I did. It seems like that's the excuse families tend to use. I feel sorry for her if that's the case.*

"The point is she's gone." Helen shifted her gaze to the floor before she continued. "And he says if I can convince you to come back that he'll give me her position. Comes with a nice raise too. I could surely use the money."

"And if I don't?"

"Like he told you, since you won't be in a reserve occupation no more, he'll have to report it to the authorities. They might draft you to be a land girl or something awful like that. You have to say yes, Grace. You just have to. It'll be good for us both. Imagine, I'll be making more money than my father ever did. Oh, and he says he'd be willing to increase your pay too."

"I rather doubt I'm that good of a worker," Grace said. "None of this makes sense to me."

"Don't worry why. Just say yes!"

"I… I don't know. Michael will get back early tomorrow morning, and he said he'll come down just as soon as he can. We don't know where he's to be posted next. If we are married, I might try and live near his station."

"And where will that leave me?" Helen asked. "I can't afford the rent on my own."

"I'll give you December's rent," Grace promised. "That gives you, what? Six weeks to find a roommate? Surely one of the girls in the office wouldn't mind? Besides, it may be better for me to stay here anyway. I won't know until I talk to Michael."

"If you don't accept his offer, I'm afraid he'll sack me too."

"Did he say that?"

"No, not in so many words. Just that he would be very disappointed if I couldn't convince you to stay."

"I just don't think I can. Not before I talk to Michael."

Helen stood up and walked to the door. She snatched up her coat and put it on.

"Where are you going?" Grace asked.

"I'm going out for a drink. You're being terribly selfish about the whole thing. It's all well and good for you, with your man and all, but some of us are having to make it on our own."

"That's not fair. I didn't ask to meet Michael. It just happened. Come one, let me make some tea and we can listen to the radio."

"You should have told him your secret, Grace," Helen said as she opened the door. "He might not want you if he knew. Better to tell him before the wedding and give him the choice. But no, you don't think of his feelings any more than you think of mine. Don't wait up for me."

Helen stormed out and slammed the door behind her.

Grace's mind drifted back to the summer she turned sixteen. It had been an unusually warm summer. A small country lane ran past her parents' home to a small village a mile away. The village contained a small bookshop. Grace's father encouraged her to read and gave her a small allowance each month to purchase additions to her collection. The previous month, the clerk at the bookshop promised to have a copy of *Gone With the Wind* for her on Grace's next visit. She'd first heard of the novel after her father visited the United States the previous year. He told her it was all the rage among literary circles and rumored to be made into a movie soon. Grace asked him why he did not think to get her a copy while he was there. He just shrugged and walked to his office. The shop had called around ten that morning and said the book was waiting for her. Grace told her mother she planned to ride her bicycle into the village and left as quickly as she could. She peddled as fast as her legs allowed and arrived at the shop out of breath and in record time. Grace made her purchase and jumped on her bicycle to race home and dive into the book.

Distracted by her thoughts of plantation life and the Old South, Grace failed to see a young man in the road until he shouted and jumped out of her way. She swerved her bike and lost control. The bike went into a ditch along the road, and she was flung into the grass. Grace lay there stunned with the suddenness of the crash. She opened her eyes and saw the young man peering down at her.

"Are you alright, miss?" he asked.

"I think so," Grace replied. She accepted his proffered

hand and he pulled her to her feet. Grace smoothed her skirt and tucked a stray hair behind her ear. The man she'd nearly run over was stocky, with dark brown hair and the bluest eyes Grace had ever seen. They studied her with interest, she thought, and so she smiled at him.

"You were going pretty fast," the young man said. "In a hurry?"

"Not really," Grace replied. "Just terribly distracted, I guess. I'm ever so sorry. I've got a new book, you see. I was rushing home so I can start it. Are you hurt? I hope not!"

"'Tis fine," the young man said. "You're the one who took the spill. Not me."

He grinned and picked up her bicycle.

"It looks no worse for wear," he said after he checked the wheels and the chain.

"I've not seen you before," Grace said as she looked around the grass for her book.

"My parents live nearby," the young man said. "I've been away in the army for the past three years. Joined up when I was seventeen. Anyway, I'm home now on a bit of leave. They moved to the village whilst I was in India."

Grace spotted the book and grabbed it. The cover had a few smudges but was otherwise undamaged.

"India?" Grace asked. "Must have been terribly exciting."

"Terribly dull, to be honest," he said. "Terribly hot too. Oh, my name is Thomas. Thomas Clark. It is a pleasure to meet you though the circumstances are a little unusual."

"Grace Robinson," she said.

And that's how it started, she thought. The two began to meet regularly. She found weekly excuses to run into the village. He had a month's leave before he was ordered to report back to his regiment. Thomas showered her with attention and behaved as Grace thought a gentleman should, though admittedly she had little experience in that area. The night before he left, she slipped out of the house and met him beside a small creek in a field near his parents' house. As they sat there and looked at the stars, he promised to marry her just as soon as he saved up enough money. Grace had no experience with boys. Her father kept her more or less isolated at their country home. She received her education from a private tutor who lived with the family. Dr. Robinson tried to imitate the life of the titled classes with everything he did. Thomas told her it was okay if they did *that* because they planned to be married. It was only after she'd snuck back up to her room that she realized Thomas never told her which regiment he was with and so she had no way to write to him. *It was just a mistake on his part,* she thought as she fell asleep. *He'll write and tell me soon enough.* No letter from him ever arrived.

Dr. Robinson grew suspicious a month later when Grace began to suffer from waves of nausea in the mornings. Two months after that, Grace noticed her skirts fit a little tighter than normal. Always a slim girl, she soon got to the point where some of her clothes did not fit at all. Grace assumed it was all a part of growing up. When her father noticed this, however, he examined her and determined she was pregnant. His temper exploded.

"You… you… slut!" he screamed. "You have shamed this family! Do you hear me?"

Grace sat there stunned. *Pregnant? That's impossible!* She confessed to her father the name of the young man responsible. Dr. Robinson swore to use his connections with the military to ensure Thomas received the proper punishment.

"But he wants to marry me," Grace said. "He promised he would."

"He will do no such thing," Dr. Robinson said. "If he so much as steps foot on this property, I'll take the horsewhip to him. You foolish, stupid, girl."

Grace looked to her mother for help, but Mrs. Robinson stared out the window and made no effort to come to her daughter's defense. After much discussion, Dr. Robinson decided to send Grace away to his maiden sister's home in a remote part of the Scottish Highlands.

"You'll have the baby there, and it will be given over to the church for placement in an orphanage."

"What will we tell the neighbors about why she's gone?" Mrs. Robinson asked.

"Oh, we'll tell them she's touring the Continent," he replied. "Or studying in Germany."

And so that's how it happened. Grace left two days later. Six months after that, she gave birth to a healthy baby boy. During her stay, Grace's aunt spoke to her only when necessary, though she did make sure a doctor checked in each week until the baby arrived. Grace hoped to at least be able to see the child, but no sooner had the baby come, it was whisked away, never to be seen again. When she asked, begged, the nurses to let her hold the child for a few minutes, they ignored her.

Once her strength returned, Grace made her way back to her parents' house. Three months passed before Dr. Robinson would even look at her and another five before he spoke to her. Her mother was a bit more considerate to her, but only if Dr. Robinson was not around. Grace's brother followed the example of his parents, and so Grace sought refuge in books, though her father forbade her from going to the village alone. From time to time, Grace wondered what became of the child. Did he find a home? Was he happy? It was hard not to wonder as her father made a point to mention it any time they spoke. Her 'shame,' he called it.

And Michael? Will he speak to me after I tell him that I had a child at sixteen? She never gave much thought to Thomas. She understood that he picked her out as a young, naïve girl and took advantage of her. Michael was the first man to break through her defenses since that summer. *It's different with him,* she thought. *He's a lost soul like me. I'm a better judge of character than I was at sixteen. Michael and I have something special. And I believe him when he says he'll marry me. Just come home safe, Michael. Please come home safe.*

It was his eyes that drew her in. They had the look of a dog that had been beaten and didn't know why, though they also projected a quiet defiance, as if he'd take on the whole world if he had to. Though outwardly he attempt to affect a composed, brave demeanor, she knew otherwise from the nights they spent together. In a way, the terrors he dreamed of at night reminded her a bit of her own father and the lingering effects the trenches still had on him. *Wars end for some,* she thought, *but not for others.*

She's right, Grace thought as tears sprang to her eyes. *I should have told him. It won't be fair to spring it on him right before the wedding. And certainly not after. I've gone and made a mess of it. What would Michael call it? A right cock-up?* Grace felt sorry for Helen and understood where she was coming from. Who wouldn't jump at a chance to have a promotion and a raise? It was terribly unfair of Mr. Holland to make it dependent on whether or not Grace returned to work. *And why does he care so much about me anyway? He's never once showed much interest before today, and today he showed a bit too much.*

"I'm leaving," Grace said aloud to the empty apartment. "I can't stay here another minute."

She gathered her battered, gray suitcase from under her bed and opened it. When Grace left her parents' house a few years ago, this suitcase carried a couple of changes of clothes and a dozen paperback books. That's all she took to London with her. She snatched articles of clothing and tossed them in without taking the time to fold them. She placed her well-worn copy of *Gone With the Wind* on top of the clothes. Grace kept a jar with her money in it inside the bottom drawer of her dresser. She counted out enough bills for December's rent and placed them on the table so that Helen could find them when she returned home. On a white piece of paper, Grace penned a short note to her roommate.

Helen,

I've left to be at the base when Michael gets back. I'll find a room at the village inn. I've left the rent money on the table. I will try to get word to Michael so he can find me, but if he calls here tomorrow will you please tell him? I am terribly sorry for all of this. Surely you understand. And, well, I still want you in the wedding. I shall telephone tomorrow afternoon.
Grace

She left the note near the telephone and gathered her coat and scarf. After one long look around the apartment, Grace opened the door and headed for the train station. *Here I come, Michael,* she thought. She caught the underground to the stop nearest the train station. Throngs of men in uniform lounged around on the benches inside, either going on or returning from leave. A few smiled or called out to her, but Grace marched straight to the ticket window with purpose. The next train north out of London did not leave for another hour and a half, so Grace purchased her ticket and found a spot away from all of the men, where she could sit undisturbed. The nearest train station was ten miles away from the village near the airfield, but the clerk at the window assured her a bus ran from the station to all of the outlying villages. Grace asked the man if he knew of any inns in the area, but he shook his head and said, "Sorry, miss. Here's your ticket."

Grace watched young women bid goodbye to their husbands or boyfriends as the minutes crawled by. Most tried to put on a brave face, but tears often came anyway. One group of young RAF enlisted men, not aircrew as she saw no wings on their blue uniforms, played cards using a suitcase as a table. *What was it Michael said? All war is a game until you've been in one.* She tried not to think of the nightly terrors he faced in the skies over Germany. It frightened her to think of him, businesslike behind his controls, as he coldly piloted his way through flak and fighters to drop his deadly payloads in the center of German cities. *How well do I really know him? I know how he is on leave but is that a good indication of how good of a husband he will be? No, I can't be having second thoughts now. It is too late.* To stop her mind, Grace purchased a magazine from a small newsstand inside the station and occupied herself by flipping through the pages until her train was announced.

CHAPTER TWENTY

"Your girlfriend, Herr Oberwachtmeister?" Schneider asked as Karl turned away from the door, his fingertips on the spot where Ursula's lips touched his cheek.

"A friend," Karl said as Schneider appraised him with a slight smile.

"I don't mean to be impertinent, Herr Oberwachtmeister," she said, "but I don't make a habit of kissing my male friends on the cheek. If you ask me, she likes you."

The other three girls laughed, and Karl snapped, "I didn't ask you."

"Well, if you don't want her, I'll take her," one of the Hitler Youth boys called out from across the room. Karl did not see who said it as when he looked in their direction, they wisely focused on the truck.

"Silence or I'll put the lot of you on the roof during the next raid," Karl said.

He stalked towards the staircase and made it halfway up before a sudden pounding sounded from the door. *Damn. What now?* he thought as he descended the stairs and walked across the room. A tall man with narrow eyes greeted him when Karl pushed the door open. The man wore a gray over-coat and a matching fedora pulled low over his face. The man's hand extended towards him and Karl thought he meant to offer a handshake until he caught sight of the Gestapo warrant disc in his palm. A sudden chill ran down Karl's spine.

"Yes?" he asked, his mouth dry.

"You in charge here?" the man asked.

Karl nodded.

"I need a word with you."

Karl stood aside and motioned the man to enter the station. The four young women and the Hitler Youth boys froze and stared at the visitor. Though Gestapo men did not wear uniforms, they affected a certain appearance reminiscent of American gangster films. Karl's work rarely brought him into contact with them. The Kripo, the regular criminal detectives who pursued non-political crimes, investigated arson, and Karl knew several of them quite well, though with the war on, arson took a back seat to other prosecutions. What went on in the basement of Gestapo Headquarters at 8 Prinz Albrecht Strasse was no secret among the city's residents. One of Karl's Kripo contacts referred to the Gestapo as rank amateurs, but Karl disagreed. Amateurs would not instill the fear the Gestapo agents relied on as they made their inquiries. Friends denounced one another just as strangers did, on occasion to remove any suspicion which fell on them.

"A *private* word," the Gestapo man said, glancing around at the eight sets of young eyes focused on him.

Karl led him across the apparatus bay and down a back hallway which ran the length of the building. When he reached the last door, Karl opened it and walked down a short flight of stairs to the room where the crews waited out air raid warnings. He decided not to bring the man upstairs, lest he involve the others in whatever the man was here to ask. *Is this because of the wounded prisoner?* Karl wondered. *No. It can't be that. He asked if I was in charge. I don't think he's looking for me in particular. Maybe it is one of the new recruits?*

He turned on the light and offered a chair to the man.

"I'll stand," he said. "You may sit."

Karl shrugged and sat down across the room, as far away as possible. The man patted his coat pocket and then removed a gold cigarette case. He withdrew one and offered the case to Karl, who shook his head to decline. With slow, deliberate movements, the man struck a match, lit his cigarette, and inhaled deeply. He held the smoke in his lungs for several seconds before he exhaled and began to speak.

"A young redheaded woman came in here a few minutes ago," the man said. "A Fraulein Müller, I believe?"

Karl nodded.

"Why?" the man asked.

"Excuse me?" Karl asked.

"Don't play dumb, Herr Oberwachtmeister," the Gestapo man said. "I want to know why she was in here."

Karl's mind raced. *If he's asking me,* he thought, *she must be under suspicion for something. But what? She works for the government. I've heard worse things said about the Party from Baumann.* He decided to tell a partial truth.

"It's a funny thing, actually," Karl said with a forced laugh. "She was on her way home and noticed our door, the one you knocked on, was cracked a bit and light was showing. We'd had to leave it that way so the new recruits could get in. She didn't want us to get a visit from the air raid warden, and so she graciously brought it to our attention. Like a good National Socialist."

The Gestapo man stared at him and did not say a word,

so Karl continued. "Oh, the funny part is she was planning on stopping by anyway. Yesterday she had a small incident in her apartment. Not much of a fire, just a lot of smoke. In fact, she managed to put it out before we arrived. Anyway, her landlord is being a bit difficult about the matter and demanded she get a copy of my report."

"And did you give it to her?" the Gestapo man asked.

"Couldn't," Karl said. "I haven't written it yet. In case you haven't noticed, there's a bit of a war on and we are under a raid warning at the moment."

"Your sarcasm is not necessary, Herr Oberwachtmeister."

"I promised her I'd have it written tomorrow and told her she could drop by on her way home from work and I'll furnish her with a copy for herself and an extra to give to her landlord."

"And that's all?"

"What else would there be?" Karl asked. "I suppose you need to tell me what this is about."

"The Gestapo does not answer to the Fire Brigade," the man said with a sneer. "All you need to know is we are making an inquiry. I would tread carefully if I were you."

Karl pushed his chair back and stood up. He crossed his arms and met the Gestapo agent's eyes. The man took a slight step back, so Karl took one forward.

"Listen to me," Karl said as an image of the brain leaking out of the head of the prisoner shot on the street earlier flashed though his mind. "Your threats may work on others, but I served in Poland, France, and Russia. I'd be there now had my wounds not required me to return to my pre-war occupation. I have a drawer full of medals upstairs, the likes of which men like you cannot earn on the home front with the women and children. You do not come into my station and threaten me. Gestapo agent or not. Now, if you'll excuse me, I have an air raid to prepare for."

"I'll be in touch with you again," the Gestapo man promised. "And I'll be by to pick up a copy of the report you spoke of tomorrow night. Say around 8 p.m.? Be careful, fireman. Be very careful. And when you see Fraulein Müller again, you are not to divulge our conversation. I can trust your discretion, no?"

"You certainly can," Karl lied. He led the Gestapo agent back into the apparatus bay.

The man paused at the door and said, "I'll see you again" before he vanished into the darkness.

What have I gotten myself into? Karl wondered. *Does he know we met for coffee? If he does, then he knows I lied to him. Surely he'd have said something about it if he knew. And Ursula? Dear God, what has she gotten involved in? It must be serious to have the Gestapo tailing her around Berlin. I'll have to tell her to be careful next time I see her, but if she's being followed and we go out socially, they'll know I lied. That could put the entire station in danger. What am I to do?* He considered a quick dash to her apartment, but the probability of a raid along with the possibility that her apartment was under surveillance pushed the thought out of his mind. *No, I have a greater duty to the city. But I have to let her know as soon as possible. The poor girl. Does she not realize the danger she is in? Or what those pigs are capable of doing? I lost my wife. I'd hate to lose another girl I care about, no matter how short a time we've know each other.*

"What was that about, sir?" Schneider asked.

"Oh, nothing much," Karl replied. "It's about a fire we had a week or so back. They think it may have been started by a communist agitator. He wanted to know if we'd seen anything unusual in the area at the time."

"I didn't know there were any communists left in the city," she replied.

"There are communists everywhere," Karl said. "Plenty of them in Russia."

"That's why we have to kill them all," said the boy Karl had marked as an arrogant troublemaker. "I can't wait until it is my turn to kill a few."

"Everyone is brave until the shooting begins," Karl said. "You'll get your taste of bravery once the bombs start to fall. We'll see how you – all of you – hold up under that. It isn't fun, I assure you. I've seen grown men crack under the strain."

"Cowards," the boy said. "Traitors to the Fatherland."

"Why don't you shut up and focus on what you are doing," Karl suggested. He leaned against the wall and fished a cigarette out of his pocket. As he smoked, he watched the new recruits work their way over all of the equipment on the trucks. *It'll be like going into battle in charge of a company of thirteen-year-olds*, he thought. *What has this world come to?*

Before Hamburg, Karl saw the devastation wrought by aerial bombing in Warsaw and Rotterdam. He never gave it much thought before his discharge from the army because, well, it happened to other people, not Germans. At the front, men received occasional letters from home or newspapers which mentioned bombing, but never in such a way as to indicate the serious nature of what civilians faced. Upon his return to Berlin, the piles of rubble which dotted the urban landscape filled him with dread. *It's only the beginning*, he'd thought at the time. Hamburg proved him right. A week of around-the-clock raids reduced a once grand city to a smoldering ruin. No accurate information existed as to the total dead, and though he'd seen it firsthand, Karl preferred not to contemplate the human toll.

"*Flieger alarm!*" Baumann yelled down through one of the fire pole closets. "Bombers passed east of Hannover and Braunschweig. Looks like we are it for tonight."

"Damn," Karl swore. He turned to the young recruits, who looked at him with expectant faces. "You've all been through raids before at home, haven't you?"

They nodded in unison, eyes wide. Karl noticed Koch's hand shook as she ran it over her braided hair.

"Well, it's not so different here," Karl said. "You've seen our shelter already. It's quite safe. As far as going outside, well, just focus on the work we give you, and you'll find it passes quickly enough. The worst of it isn't the bombs, it's the aftermath. I was terrified before I went into combat the first time. But once the shooting started, I just focused on what needed to be done. My first fire was the same way. You'll be too busy to be frightened. I assure you."

Baumann, Fischer, and Frei slid down the poles and joined Karl and the recruits on the ground floor. After a few minutes, the doctor, the nurse, and the ambulance driver walked down the stairs and headed towards the shelter. They kept to themselves and rarely had anything to say to the firemen unless they were on a call together. *Arrogant bastards*, Karl thought. *Though I suppose they probably just want to be home, in their own countries, among their families, and not tending to the needs of the invaders.*

"I told you," Baumann exclaimed. He shifted his feet back and forth as he moved from side to side in a triumphant dance. "But no, nobody wants to listen to old Baumann. I tell you this, we are getting pasted tonight."

"You'll not find work in a cabaret with dance steps like that," Fischer said. "You look like a pregnant cow trying not to give birth."

"Any chance it is just a feint?" Karl asked Frei.

"No. It's a heavy bomber concentration, and they are apparently all headed straight for us."

"Our anti-aircraft defenses will punish them," the arrogant Hitler Youth boy said. "Just wait and see. I was hoping to be assigned to a flak battery, but they sent me here instead."

"If you survive the night," Frei said, "I'll try and get you a transfer. For the good of the service."

"And for us," Baumann grunted.

Karl assigned two of the boys to fill five buckets full of water and place them near the station doors. The other two lugged buckets of sand from a closet and placed them alongside the pails of water. If flaming debris blocked the doors, the men could use water and sand to douse it, enabling them to move the debris and respond to wherever the city needed them. The telegraph alarm system worked during raids since the cables lay buried several feet below ground. However, headquarters instructed crews to ignore such alarms and respond only to assignments made by telephone or messenger.

As the boys gathered their materials, Karl had the young women go upstairs to grab as many flashlights as they could carry. They placed half on each fire truck. Karl then sent the youths to the restroom to void whatever they could before the bombs started. If they had to stay in the shelter for several hours, the only toilet was a bucket in full view of everyone. During the raid, Karl wanted them with empty bowels as it reduced the chance of infection if they took a shell splinter in the intestines. Such wounds rarely turned out well for the recipient. In Russia, Karl saw men die with intestines spilling from their bellies while waiting for medical aid. Even the surgeons found it best with some cases to give them enough morphine to keep them comfortable and then allow them to expire. Even with large amounts of morphine, they still felt pain. A field hospital was the closest thing to hell that Karl had ever seen. He imagined civilian hospitals, with wartime shortages, could only be worse.

Karl did a quick sweep of each piece of equipment to ensure it was in good working order, then he instructed everyone to gather their helmets and gas masks and go into the shelter. The firemen also took their belts with their axes in case they needed to chop their way out of the room. During the early days of the war, as the crews converted the room to a shelter, they removed enough of the bricks to make an escape route. It led into the basement of the building next to the station, and since it contained offices which closed at sundown, the basement would not have any occupants should the firemen need to get out.

The firemen and their young recruits trooped into the shelter and sat down on the wooden chairs which lined the wall. Frei switched on the Flak Sender radio channel so the men could monitor the air battle as it unfolded. A large flak map covered the wall, and the information gleaned from the radio transmissions indicated which part of the city was likely to get hit the hardest. Of course, stray bombs could fall anywhere. A few neighborhoods in Berlin had escaped heavy damage thus far in the war, but all of them had at least one home demolished by a bomb. *You know it is your time when the only house struck by a bomb is yours*, Karl thought. *Just like in Russia. When death is ready for you, no amount of luck or fighting back can help you.*

Some men who served with him seemed to know when it was their time. They pressed last letters to their families onto their comrades before going into battle and more often than not, a bullet or a shell struck them down, just as they predicted. Karl never had such premonitions. He just assumed the Russians would get him eventually, and thus he never worried himself about it. When he'd been wounded, the only thing he felt was surprise that his wounds allowed him to leave the military and go back to his job. But that was before Hamburg. Before he'd seen what his job now entailed in a country wracked with war and under the threat of incineration. *And now I command children who do not know what tonight will mean. They will never be the same, if they survive. I don't know what I'll say to their families if they don't make it, but it is best not to think of that. Not now. Not ever.* Karl was the last to enter the shelter, and as he did, the sirens began to wail in the distance.

CHAPTER TWENTY-ONE

MICHAEL RAN THROUGH the pre-flight checklist with Cameron as each of the other crewmen checked their own positions. He knew they'd be taking off a bit on the heavy side with the bombs and full fuel load for the long trip to Berlin and back. Smitty said he had squeezed a few extra gallons into the tanks, which could come in handy, especially with a new navigator. Michael gave Smitty a thumbs-up from the cockpit window. Cameron clapped Michael on the shoulder, which caused him to jump.

"I just want to say it's been a pleasure to fly with you," Cameron said. "Even if you do prang the takeoff."

Michael pulled off his right glove and shook Cameron's hand. The gloves kept his palms warm, though the fingers were cut out to allow better dexterity on the controls. Together they started the engines as Mac crawled out of the nose and headed towards the crew bunk just aft of the wireless operator's station, where he and Lawton sat during takeoffs and landings so they would not add weight to the nose or tail respectively. Michael slowly taxied the plane with an eye out for any obstructions. He made the left-hand turn on the runway and set the brakes. A large group of WAAFs and assorted ground personnel gathered near the edge of the runway and waved. It was sort of a tradition on the station to give the lads a bit of a send-off. Some of the young women waved goodbye to boyfriends aboard the bombers – often their last glimpse of them was as their plane lifted off and disappeared into the twilight.

"Mac, I think I see that WAAF you like," Michael said over the intercom. "Want to come up to the cockpit and blow her a kiss?"

"I've moved on, skipper," Mac said. "She was a bit too tame for my liking."

A green light flashed ahead, the signal for P For Paul to start its takeoff. Michael turned and gave an insolent salute to the crowd of well-wishers and then called his crew over the intercom. "Pilot to crew. Here goes nothing."

Cameron ran the engines up to full power, and Michael released the brakes. Paddy's Wagon moved forward with all the grace of a pregnant whale. Cameron called out the speed in increments of ten as the plane moved down the runway. Michael's eyes floated from his instrument panel to the runway and back again. The plane seemed wedded to the earth, as though she preferred to be a flightless bird.

"Jesus, she feels sluggish," Michael said. "Can you get me more power?"

"Trying, skipper," Cameron said.

A wooden fence ran along a field thirty yards from the end of the runway. They moved towards it much faster than Michael liked, but with not enough speed for him to safely get the plane into the air.

"Come on, old girl," Michael urged, "don't give up on me now."

"We aren't gonna make it, skipper," Cameron warned.

"Just a little bit more," Michael said. "Come on. Come on."

As if coaxed by his words, Paddy's Wagon responded with a bit more urgency, and he slowly pulled back on the control stick. She lifted into the air with a groan and cleared the top of the fence by ten feet. Michael let out all the air trapped in his lungs during the takeoff. A crash on takeoff often delayed a mission as it necessitated the closure of the runway temporarily. Loaded with fuel and bombs, when a plane slammed into the ground, it resulted in a massive explosion which incinerated the crew. *Worse ways to go*, Michael said the first time he saw a takeoff crash. *The crew barely had time to realize what was happening. Better that than to be trapped in a plane spinning out of control at 14,000 feet. That leaves you way too long to ponder your fate.*

"It ain't your worst takeoff," Cameron said.

"Up your kilt," Michael said. On their third mission, Paddy's Wagon took off only to sink back down on the landing gear. It took almost the whole runway to get her back into the air again. The crew had given Michael a hard time over the incident ever since. The navigator called and said they took off on time. Michael began to climb in a slow circle, through the clouds, to find his approximate place in the bomber stream. Lawton and Mac returned to their usual positions and radioed to let the crew know once they were in place. Of all of the men, Michael thought Lawton's job the most difficult. Alone and isolated in the rear of the plane in a freezing turret, if the plane took fatal damage, his odds of escape were slim. Lawton's position required the best eyes as well. A hesitation of a second in determining if a speck in the sky were a night fighter or another Lancaster meant the difference between life and death. On the long flight back across the North Sea after a mission, the cold and monotony often tempted a tail gunner into sleep. The Germans knew this and often tried to bounce bombers from dead astern just at the point the crew thought they were out of harm's way. Michael made it his practice to call each of his crew on the intercom every few minutes on the flight in and out, lest any of them slip off to the land of nod.

Paddy's Wagon bumped a little as it entered the slipstream of another bomber.

"Lanc ahead, skipper," Mac said. "About a mile out. Probably McBride's bunch. They took off right before us."

If he's as off his rocker as Sterling says, Michael thought, *I don't want to share the sky with any part of him*. Below, a sheet of clouds stretched into the distance and obscured the surface of the sea sixteen thousand feet below. A few stars danced in the night sky as a sliver of moon shone down on the bombers and reflected off their wings. *It's too clear up here*, Michael thought. *If the fighters find us above this cloud cover, they'll maul us badly*. Between flak and fighters, Michael feared the latter more than the former. Flak killed in an impersonal way. A shell burst. It either killed you or it didn't. Fighters, however, were a different matter. It was a personal battle between your crew and the skill of the German pilot. Some member of your crew might catch a glimpse of the plane that got you, unlike flak where you never saw the men behind the guns.

"Lanc behind us, skipper," Lawton called. "Jesus, if she gets any closer I'm gonna give her a burst."

"Thank you, rear gunner," Michael said. "I'm gonna climb about two hundred feet. Get us out of this slipstream too."

With hundreds of planes in the night sky, it was remarkable indeed that there were not dozens of aircraft lost to mid-air collisions. In his entire tour, Michael only knew of two crews lost to what the Wing Commander listed as a mid-air accident. Over the North Sea on a trip from Bremen, one bomber drifted up into the path of a second plane. Both dropped in the sea, several thousand feet below. No one saw a single chute from either plane. It happened about a half mile ahead of Paddy's Wagon. Michael wondered if one of the pilots might have nodded off and lost control of the plane for a few seconds. Regardless of the reason, fourteen men died thirty minutes from the British coast after surviving heavy flak and fighters over the target. *The war is so fucking random*, Michael thought. *One second you are alive. The next you are dead.*

"Navigator to skipper, we're about ninety seconds behind schedule."

"I'll see if we can make it up, navigator. Thank you."

The route to the target took them straight in and straight out, no feints, no doglegs, just a mad dash to the heart of Nazi Germany and back. Michael's eyes scanned the air. Despite the steady throb of the engine, the sky seemed as quiet as a graveyard. Were he not engaged in a delivery of death and fire, he'd almost think it a beautiful night, one where you'd take your girl out for a stroll back home.

"Pilot to rear, how's that Lanc back there?"

"Drifted to starboard, skipper. Further back too. Maybe a mile."

"Enemy coast in about five minutes, skipper," Turner said.

"Lawton and Williams, keep your eyes open," Michael said.

"Navigation flares up ahead skipper," Mac called out from his spot in the nose turret.

Michael looked over and saw the green flares dropped by the pathfinders, which marked where to turn into the German coast. He saw three Lancasters illuminated by the light, which reflected off the cloud tops as the flares floated down. In the distance, sparks flashed in the sky just above the clouds.

"Flak ahead," he called out. "We're soon over Hun Land."

Michael easily avoided the flak, which seemed more of a matter of course for the German gunners than an actual attempt to down aircraft. Graham, the wireless operator, informed the crew that he suspected night fighters were out there somewhere as he heard German chatter over some of the frequencies.

"Jam the bastards," Michael ordered.

"Doing it now, skipper," Graham replied, his voice calm.

Glad he seems a cool customer, Michael thought. *Seeing as how he's not a day over eighteen.*

"CORKSCREW PORT! NOW!" Lawton screamed.

Michael half rose in his armored seat as he shoved the control stick down and to the right. Paddy's Wagon plummeted into the darkness. Then Michael whipped the controls up and to the right and brought the plane up into a climbing turn.

"Alright, skipper," Lawton said. "You shook him. I'm not sure he saw us anyway."

"Good eyes, rear gunner," Michael said. "All good?"

One by one the crew checked in to say they were fine. All except Mac.

"Talk to me, bomb aimer," Michael said.

"Oh, I'm fine," Mac said. "But I think I left my balls back there somewhere."

"Assuming you had any to begin with," Cameron replied.

Michael let the crew laugh for a minute, then said, "Okay. Knock it off. Keep the intercom clear."

More flak erupted through the clouds. Cameron pointed out a battle between a Lancaster and a fighter off the starboard beam. In the darkness, Michael could not make out the planes, but he saw the angry tracers flash back and forth. The shooting stopped, but he saw no smoke or flame. *Fighter must have broken off*, Michael thought, *or the Lanc is drifting down out of control but not on fire.*

"How far to the target, navigator?"

"'Bout an hour, skipper," Turner replied.

The longest hour of my life, Michael thought. On raids, it felt like the route in took three times as long as the flight home. Despite a million things on your mind, minutes stretched into hours. Some of the pilots claimed the time over the target was the most dangerous time on a mission, but others maintained the trip home claimed more crews. Michael never cared much for the statistics some pilots delighted in sharing with their mates. The likelihood of surviving a tour. The chances of crashing on takeoff. Your odds of spending the war in a POW camp. Some men knew all of them by heart. *You'd have to be a fool to not know the odds of survival are slim*, Michael thought. *So isn't that enough? Why go and find out the specifics unless you have a death wish?* He glanced down at the photograph of Grace, taped to the control panel. *It'll be rough on her tomorrow*, he thought. *But she'll pull through. She's a tough girl.*

"Outer port engine is running a tad bit hot, skipper," Cameron said.

"What's a tad?"

"Just a couple of degrees." Cameron's voice was so casual

he might have been giving Michael a football score. "Not serious, I'd think."

"I'd go to Berlin on two engines if I had to," Mac observed. "I don't want to go through this nonsense again."

"How's it look back there, rear gunner?"

"Fine, skipper. But my arse is fucking freezing."

The crew laughed. The only member of the crew with a somewhat moderate temperature was the wireless operator since one of the heater vents was right by his crew station. Though crews had the option of heated coveralls, none of Michael's crew wore them. They preferred the unheated suits as it removed any chance of a short circuit or a contact burn.

"If this cloud cover doesn't break up, we'll be bombing blind," Mac observed.

"Let the pathfinders worry about that," Michael said.

As the ability of Bomber Command to hit targets increased, so too did the effectiveness of German defenses. As planes approached a target, the defenders fired off flares to simulate those used by the pathfinders. Sometimes they lit large fires in open areas just outside of a city to make it appear as though bombers in the earlier stream had dropped there in hopes the following planes would do the same. It rarely worked, but their anti-aircraft defenses made great strides as the war dragged on. Berlin had a massive belt of searchlights and batteries of heavy and light flak which stretched for ninety miles in diameter. They had the ability to throw up a wall of flak which gave the bombers little chance but to fly straight through it to hit the target.

"Hello, skipper," Mac said.

"Hello, bomb aimer," Michael replied.

"Lanc on fire. About a mile out and a few hundred yards down."

"Must have been a fighter that got him," Michael said. "Can't see any flak at the moment."

A sudden barrage of explosions shook the aircraft. Since crossing the coastline, Michael had been weaving the aircraft slightly from side to side while he maintained their heading. Above the cloud tops, the shells burst with black puffs of smoke, spraying deadly shrapnel across the sky. A tremendous jolt from the middle of the plane nearly tore the controls from Michael's hands.

"I think that one got us, skipper," Cameron said in the usual bored tone he used on the intercom.

"Hello, rear gunner," Michael said. "You alright back there?"

"Fine, skipper. May need a change of drawers though."

"Gauges look okay, skipper," Cameron said.

"Hello, wireless operator," Michael said.

"Hello, skipper," Graham answered.

"Would you mind having a look back there and see if anything was hit?"

"Right ho, skipper," Graham said. Three minutes passed before Graham came back on the intercom with his report. "We've got a hole on the starboard side, just forward of the rear spare. Big enough to stick my arse in. It punched through and hit the Elsan. Everything else looks as it should."

The Elsan was a chemical toilet just forward of the entrance to the tail turret. In fact, Lawton used it as a stool to crawl over the spar to reach his station. Crews used the toilet if necessary on long flights, but without the ability to flush, it had to be emptied by the ground crew upon return to base.

None of Michael's crew ever used it, though Mac once pissed in a bottle and placed it in the bomb bay to drop with the bombs.

"Hello, skipper."

"Hello, mid-upper."

"Lanc off the starboard beam. I think she took some of the shell that got us," Williams said. "She's holding steady, but it looks like her controls might be a little shaky."

"Keep an eye on her," Michael said.

"Okay, skipper."

Turner gave Michael a slight course correct, and Michael adjusted his heading.

"Engine still a little hot, engineer?" Michael asked.

"It is, skipper. It isn't serious though."

"Put the revs down just a bit," Michael said.

"Done."

More flak burst through the clouds, but it was off to the left and slightly below their current course. Slipstream from another bomber buffeted Paddy's Wagon again.

"We're packed in tight, it would appear," Michael said to no one in particular. *Almost there*, he thought. *We'll be in the flak belt soon.* He felt the same on every mission. The butterflies tended to disappear once he reached the target, only to resume when the plane turned for home. On long flights back from Germany, his hands often shook so badly he feared they might jostle the controls enough to make it noticeable for the crew. Each fought their own lonely battle in the sky, no matter their assignment.

"Hello, skipper."

"Hello, navigator."

"We should be thirty minutes from the aiming point."

"Thank you, navigator," Michael replied. "Look alive now, lads. We'll be in their search belt soon."

On cue, the clouds lit up as the beams of dozens of searchlights reached upward. A murderous barrage of anti-aircraft fire flashed ahead of them. *This is it*, Michael thought as Paddy's Wagon pressed on into the night.

CHAPTER TWENTY-TWO

URSULA'S HEART POUNDED as if it were about to burst out of her chest and explode like a British bomb. She walked to the door in slow, measured steps as the sound of the fist pounding on the wooden door grew in intensity and urgency. *So this is it*, she thought as her hand closed around the doorknob. It felt as cold as an arctic winter. *At least Gisela and Monica aren't here to see me hauled away by the Gestapo.* Ursula turned the knob and pulled the door open.

"Have you gone deaf, child?" Frau Pederson, the landlady, stood there with her hands on her wide hips and a frown on her plain face.

"I... I'm sorry," Ursula replied after her heartbeat slowed to normal and her voice returned. "Is there something you need?"

"There is," Frau Pederson replied. "And I'm certain you know what it is. Please do not play dumb with me."

Ursula's mind worked over what might be urgent enough for Frau Pederson to pound so insistently upon the door with a raid warning on for the night. She did not know her landlady well. Gisela handled the rent. Each month, Monica and Ursula gave her their portions and she forwarded it to Frau Pederson. Apart from a curt "Good Morning" each day when she left the building, Ursula never spoke to her. Even during the long nights spent in the cellar, Frau Pederson spoke little. She occupied a spot in the corner and contented herself with a book or with knitting gloves and scarves. Gisela told Ursula once that the landlady's husband was killed in the first war. They had a son, but he too died somewhere in Poland during the first days of this war.

"I'm afraid I don't," Ursula said. "Truly."

"The rent," Frau Pederson said with an exaggerated sigh. "It was due yesterday."

"I'm very sorry. Monica and I gave our portion to Gisela yesterday. She is the one who takes care of paying it."

"And she didn't."

"I'm sure she just forgot. She and Monica are out at the moment. But I'll remind her as soon as she gets home."

"See that you do. If it isn't at my apartment by 7 a.m. tomorrow morning, there will be a late penalty. A substantial late penalty. Am I clear?"

"Very," Ursula replied. "I will make sure you get it, Frau Pederson."

With a final scowl, Fraud Pederson turned and stalked down the hallway, her footsteps heavy. Ursula let out a long sigh of relief and closed her door. After she turned the bolt to lock it, she leaned against it, letting the wood frame dig into her back. After several long breaths, she walked across the room and took a sheet of paper from the drawer in the kitchen. *This won't do much good if a bomb hits our building tonight*, she thought with a small chuckle as she scrawled a note to Gisela informing her of the visit along with a reminder to pay the rent. With space in Berlin at a premium, others who paid rent in a timely manner would no doubt be ready to swoop in and scoop up the apartment, especially if they'd been bombed out.

Ursula checked the clock. *I have to go*, she thought. Her instructions had been explicit as to the time she was to present herself to retrieve the pistol. At first, her late night courier trips brought her a certain measure of excitement. The thrill gave her life a color that it otherwise lacked in the drab streets of Berlin. As time passed and the trips grew more risky, and frequent, she began to worry more about arrest than she had in the early months. *The Gestapo aren't stupid*, she thought. *They might very well be onto me, or rather us, already. But what choice do I have? My father fought for the old Germany. That was the Fatherland I was raised to love. Not the monstrosity we have now. I have to go. For the sake of the country and myself.*

"*Achtung! Achtung!*" the voice said on the radio said. "This is the Air Defense Commander of the Berlin sector. Enemy bomber formations have passed east of Hannover and Braunschweig. Possible targets include Berlin. Stay tuned for further information."

Somewhere off in the distance, Ursula heard the first howl of an air raid siren. Typically, the city sounded the first warning when aircraft were estimated to be thirty minutes away. After a few minutes, the sirens stopped. There would be a separate warning at the fifteen minute and then the five minute marks. After the thirty minute warning, it was not unusual for bombers to veer away, or double back to hit a target they'd already passed. Most residents ignored the thirty minute warning other than to double check their items to bring with them into the shelter.

The sound of footsteps in the corridor drew her attention back to the door. She rose and walked over to it, pausing for a minute to listen before she cracked it open. A few of the residents made their way down the stairs with their suitcases and coats in hand. They wore the grim expressions of those grown accustomed to long, terrifying nights. One elderly couple paused outside her door. The woman gave a strained smile and the man a solemn nod.

"Fraulein Müller," the man said, "perhaps you and your friends should go ahead and come with us to the shelter."

Ursula smiled. Herr Rudel took a great interest in her and her roommates. He never missed a chance to squeeze their hands as he gazed into their eyes and related some story about his life. *Some of them may even be true*, Ursula usually thought as she tried to disengage herself.

"Thank you for your concern, Herr Rudel," she said with a stiff smile of her own. "But you see, Gisela and Monica are not here right now. I'm waiting for them to return, and then we'll all come down together if we need to. Besides, it's just the thirty minute alert. The bombers may still go somewhere else."

"No, no," Herr Rudel said, his face suddenly serious. "The *terrorfliegers* are coming here tonight."

"Now you don't know that," his wife said with a tug on his sleeve. She turned to Ursula. "He's just worried about your safety, that's all."

"I appreciate it. It is most kind of you to worry."

"You have such pretty hair," Herr Rudel said as his voice took on a faraway tone. "Red hair. And those curls. Why, did I ever tell you about the girl with red hair I met in Hamburg in 1900? I was a young man then."

"No, I don't think you have," Ursula lied. In fact, he told

her about it every time he saw her. "But shouldn't you go on to the shelter? I'll be happy to listen to it another time."

He considered it for a moment as his wife continued to tug on his sleeve, each pull harder than the last.

"You are right, of course," he said. With a tip of his hat, he moved on down the hall. When they reached the stairs, his wife turned and gave Ursula a nod of thanks. She closed the door and walked into her bedroom, where her own suitcase and coat sat next to the bed. She debated taking her suitcase with her on her errand, as it might lend her a bit of cover. *I'm just another person headed to a shelter. But I'll have to pass at least one public shelter and if I don't go in, that might look suspicious. Will anyone notice?* She determined it was too risky and instead picked up her coat. *I'll either be back here in the morning or never again*, she thought as she slipped into her coat. After a glance in the mirror, Ursula decided to wear her hair up and put on a hat. *Better to blend in*, she thought. In the past, she enjoyed the fact her red hair made her stand out, but this was not a time for display. *No, I need to look as much like everyone else as I can.*

The hallway was deserted when Ursula stepped out of her apartment and locked the door. The muffled sounds of talking from behind a few of the other apartment doors told her that not everyone on the floor went down to the basement with the Rudels. Outside, Ursula wrapped her coat and scarf tightly around her slender body to ward off the chill in the air. Darkness blanketed the streets. The police and air raid wardens vigorously enforced the blackout regulations, though the occasional pile of rubble indicated their efforts, while successful at eliminating light, were less so when it came to diverting enemy planes. Ursula had suffered a severe ankle sprain one night when she stepped off a curb she could not see. Three days in bed with her ankle propped on pillows and wrapped in ice served to remind her to be more careful in the future.

She moved more by feel than anything else and kept her left shoulder near the buildings as she moved up the street. A few searchlights leapt to life in the distance and pointed at the sky like glowing fingers. From their erratic movements as they swept back and forth, Ursula could tell the bombers were not yet close enough to detect. It occurred to her, as she made her way up the street, that in all this time, she had never seen an enemy bomber. *But I've sure felt their work. What do they think about while they are up there? The same as our own pilots do, I suppose.*

The address of the shop where Ursula was to present herself was a dozen blocks north of her apartment. Working late and her decision to stop and visit Karl meant she had to move as quickly as the darkness allowed. *Straight there*, she thought. *I can't take a circuitous route like I typically do. I hope the raid and the night keep me from being followed.*

With the exception of a car which looked as though it belonged to a Party functionary, no traffic moved on the streets. Her heels made the only sound save the occasional laugh which drifted out from behind closed doors and drawn curtains. Still, she couldn't quite shake the sensation that someone was following her. Her footsteps sounded a little too loud, like others were treading at the same pace as she. However, whenever Ursula paused, so too did the sound of steps. *Surely I can't be followed through a blackout. If they wanted me, they'd have come for me at the apartment. Even if they are following me, I'm in too deep to back out now, even if I wanted to.* And so she kept walking, though she did pause every block or so just to be sure. When she checked over her shoulder, only darkness greeted her eyes. Once, Ursula thought she made out the shape of a man leaning against a doorway, but the shape never moved. *It's just my eyes acting up*, she told herself before she continued down the street.

She missed the door her first time by and had to double back. After a quick glance up and down the street, Ursula's fist knocked out the code on the solid wooden door. A full minute passed, and she raised her fist to knock again but stopped when she heard a lock turn. The door opened a tiny crack, just enough to speak through but not enough to let any light out from the blackout curtain which hung inside.

"Yes?" a male voice asked.

"I'm looking for Herr Furst," Ursula said.

"I'm sorry, but Herr Furst is not here at the moment."

"What a pity," Ursula replied.

The door opened a bit farther and a hand shot out from behind it. The fingers wrapped around her arm and pulled her inside. She blinked several times as her eyes adjusted to the lights. Slowly they focused on a middle-aged man with a pair of spectacles perched atop a crooked nose. He had the appearance of an absent-minded professor, not a man involved in a dangerous game of cloak and dagger.

"So," he said, "you are the courier?"

"I am," Ursula said.

"I must say" – he turned and walked towards a counter which ran along the wall opposite the street – "I was expecting someone male."

"Sorry to disappoint you," Ursula said as she walked behind him.

"Oh, I'm not disappointed. Just surprised. You are quite

a bit prettier than what I was expecting. I don't mind saying that at all. What brings you into our little world anyway?"

"I think the less I say the better."

"Very wise. Very wise. Less to say if the Gestapo get their claws on you."

The mention of the Gestapo sent a brief shiver down her spine. The man turned in time to see it.

"I've been a, shall we say, guest of theirs before," the man said. "I'm a Social Democrat. Or rather, I was, back when we still had a choice in such things. They don't take kindly to people who insist that the old ways were better. It was 1936 when they grabbed me. Right after the Olympics. I spent a night getting worked over in the basement at Prinz Albrecht before they let me go with a broken nose and a warning not to try anything else again."

"Yet here you are," Ursula said.

"Yes. Here I am. Mind you, I waited about three years before I got mixed up in this. Plenty of time to convince everyone around me that I was a good National Socialist and had seen the error of my ways."

He gestured across the room, and Ursula turned to see a large picture of the Fuhrer staring down at her from the wall. *Just like me*, she thought, *with all my talk about the Final Victory in front of Monica and Gisela.*

"Yes, my girl," the man continued, "there are plenty of people in Berlin who use what the Englishman Shakespeare called a false face to hide what is in a false heart."

"*Macbeth*," Ursula said.

"Ah, yes. You know it? Always good to meet another lover of the written word. I wanted to be a writer myself."

"Why didn't you?" she asked, though she grew impatient with the conversation.

"Why, the National Socialists happened," he said with a laugh. "There isn't much use for writers in Germany these days, unless you write for one of the Party publications. Those are good only for paper to wipe your ass with, if you'll pardon the expression."

"I'd like to be on my way," Ursula said. "Could I please have the... package."

"You may," the man said. He reached under the counter and pulled out an object wrapped in cloth. It made a loud noise when he placed it on the wooden countertop.

Ursula moved towards it, but he waved a hand to stop her.

"What is it?" she asked.

"I don't need to tell you what will happen if they catch you," he said. "So you must be very, very careful. Leave out the back door. Understand?"

"I'm well aware of the danger."

"I wanted to make sure. This is a Luger. It came from a German officer who met with a very unfortunate accident in a dark alley while he was home on leave. Very unfortunate. Our contacts in the police tell us the Kripo think some Kozi did it."

"I didn't think there were many communists left in the city," Ursula said.

"Oh, there's still a few around," he said. He picked up the pistol and passed it to Ursula. She took it and felt the weight of it in her hand, then she slipped it into her coat pocket. It made her feel a bit off balance, and the man chuckled.

"I suppose wearing it in a holster would have been easier for you," he said.

"I'll manage," Ursula said.

A sudden pounding on the door made them both jump. He reached out and grabbed her arm as an angry voice yelled, "Gestapo! Open up!"

"Quick," the man said. "Through here!"

He led her into the back of the store and passed rows of shelves, empty except for a few canned items. When they reached the back door, he looked at her and said, "Go! Hurry!"

"Aren't you coming?" she asked.

He gave a sad shake of the head before he opened the door and pushed her out onto the street. As the door closed, she heard the sound of splintering wood as the Gestapo burst through the front door. As she walked away, fast enough to put distance between her and the shop but not so fast as to be suspicious, she heard angry shouts and an exclamation of pain. More searchlights flashed to life, and in the direction of the city center, she heard the first anti-aircraft batteries open fire, their shells adding a punctuation mark to the air raid sirens which once again began to wail.

CHAPTER TWENTY-THREE

GRACE TOOK A window seat on the train. She watched as London gave way to green fields. What had once been farmland now housed British or American bombers and fighter aircraft as though the island nation was one giant aircraft carrier. Around her, the railcar filled with laughter and conversation from the servicemen, some British and some American, filling the time as they made their way back to their bases. Grace noticed that while some of the men laughed and talked a bit loudly, especially the Americans, others looked more somber as though they were headed to a funeral. *They've seen action*, Grace thought. *And they are in no real hurry to see it again. They have the same hollow eyes that Michael does. Soon, even the happy ones will look the same.*

Though her own father fought in the trenches during the last war, he seldom spoke of it. On occasion, after too much whiskey at dinner, he might sing an off-key version of "Mademoiselle from Armentières" or "It's a Long Way to Tipperary," complete with lewd verses which shocked her mother and delighted her brother. Whenever he broke into song, it caused a tremendous row between her parents, with her father, an ass even when sober, fueled by alcohol and her mother determined not to expose her children to such shocking words. But as to the war? He never had much to say, at least not in the company of the family. When she was six years old, her mother told her never to ask her father about it. She honored the request, and never gave it much thought until this war started. She saw her father's hesitancy to speak of his action at the front in a new light given Michael's own reluctance to talk about his war. *And what of me? I'd not like to relive my own memories of the Blitz either. Not ever. I'll never speak to my own child about them, if I'm fortunate enough to have one. Another one.*

The train pulled into a small station platform and several uniformed men got off while another group got on. They milled around for a little while and then found seats as the train pulled away. A few lit cigarettes, and soon haze clung to the ceiling of the railcar. They talked of girls they'd met, or left behind, and of fun they'd had while on leave. In lower tones, they discussed going into action soon. From their uniforms, Grace deduced most were aircrew. Their young faces betrayed a sense of excitement but also of fear, a fear they took great pains not to show to their mates. She glanced down at her watch. *Michael's probably taking off about now*, she thought. *Just a few hours and he'll be safe at home. With me. Please… let him get home safely.*

"I hope the boys are smashing the Hun tonight," said the woman sitting next to Grace through the newspaper she kept raised in front of her. "They deserve everything they are getting."

Grace glanced at her, and the woman lowered the paper. Grace gave her a polite smile, which the woman must have taken as a sign of encouragement because she lowered the paper more.

"I'm from Coventry, you see. The Jerries gave us a right pasting back in 1940. Got burned out of my own house."

"I'm terribly sorry to hear that," Grace said. "I live in London, but we were fortunate not to get bombed out."

"Indeed you were. Lost everything, you see. Thank goodness we'd gone to a shelter when the sirens went off, otherwise we'd have had it too."

Grace gave a polite nod and fumbled in her handbag for something, anything, to take an interest in to get the woman to return to her newspaper. The woman leaned close enough for Grace to smell the stale odor of alcohol on her breath.

"My name's Katherine," she said as Grace pulled her battered copy of *Gone With the Wind* from her handbag, opening the book to a random page and pretending to read. She caught a few words about fire and Atlanta. *Just like the fires that burned in London.*

"Are you going to visit someone?" Katherine asked. "Lots of girls have sweethearts in the forces now."

"I am," Grace said as she turned the page with as much noise as she could muster.

"I am too. My husband. He's stationed up north a ways, you see. He's a mechanic and works on fighter planes. He wanted to be a pilot. But just between us girls, he's not the smartest man in the world. A solid, dependable type. A bit lacking in brains though."

Grace nodded and continued to pretend to read. *God, will she not shut up?*

"Well, I see you want to keep yourself to yourself," Katherine said. "I'll let you get back to your book."

"Thank you," Grace replied. Katherine lifted her paper again and buried her face behind the pages. Grace let the novel drop into her lap and looked out the window into the gathering darkness. Shapes drifted past the window, hidden in the shadows. She thought of what the woman said about her having been fortunate to escape her home being destroyed, but then Grace thought back to the line of bodies on the sidewalk. Feet poked from beneath blankets too short to cover their whole bodies. Some were bare, and others were shod in the worn shoes of working class men and women. She thought of the long, terrifying nights spent huddled in the basement as she waited for a bomb to blast them to pieces or an incendiary to char them like a well-done steak. *Yes, perhaps I was lucky to escape the bombs, but I saw what they can do.* If she closed her eyes, the smell of burning wood and flesh still haunted her nose, as did the odor of spilled blood and intestines. *We are all soldiers in this war. Whether we want to be or not. What was it the minister said? Rain falls on the righteous and the unrighteous, or something like that. So do bombs. We are all equal in the eyes of the Luftwaffe.*

At the next stop, the woman with the newspaper and most of the servicemen got off the train. Grace looked around the car and saw three young men engrossed in a card game; otherwise rows of empty seats stared back at her. The men paid her scant notice, and her gaze returned to the window. *The next stop is mine*, she thought. *I'll have to try and get word to Michael when he returns so he will know where I am staying. I'm not certain Helen will relay my message.* Grace glanced down at her watch and wondered what Michael was doing at that moment. *Maybe out over the North Sea somewhere, and getting closer to Germany.* She closed her eyes and let the slow rocking of the train lull her to sleep.

Grace jerked awake when the conductor came into the car. The man was tall but walked with his shoulders hunched forward. Even then, his conductor's cap nearly brushed along the roof. His uniform hung from his slender fame, and his face had the lines and wrinkles of several decades of work. He called out the next stop as he made his way through the car, though he paused at Grace's seat and said, "This is your stop, miss."

The train jerked to a stop. Grace rose and collected her suitcase from the overhead rack. She made her way towards the exit. The conductor offered her his hand as she walked down the steps, and she took it with a nod of thanks.

"Good night then, miss," he said with a grandfatherly smile.

"Good night," Grace replied. She walked into the station to try and find a bus. The lobby was no larger than the inside of a modest pub. It had a few wooden benches, empty now due to the late hour. An old man sat behind a counter in one corner beneath a sign which said "Tickets." The man's elbows rested on the counter, and his head slumped forward over his chest. As Grace neared him, she heard his faint snores.

"Excuse me," she said as she placed her suitcase on the floor. The man did not stir, so she tried again, louder, "Excuse me."

The only response she got was a snort. A ringer on the far end of the counter caught her eye. She walked over and pressed down on the top. At the shrill sound of the ring, the man jumped and nearly toppled off his stool. His eyes darted around the room in confusion.

"Is it an air raid?" he gasped.

"No," Grace said. "I just needed to ask you a question."

"Then why the bloody racket?"

"You were asleep, sir."

"You're bloody well right I was asleep. There's no one here. It's late. And I'm tired. Can't blame a man for grabbing whatever sleep he can. It's hard enough to come by these days."

"I was wondering if you could tell me where to catch the

bus to Thomas Green? They told me in London a bus runs between here and there."

"It does," the man replied.

"And where might I catch it?" Grace asked.

"Why out front, you silly girl! I'm sure it's parked out there now. Hurry up. It'll leave soon."

Grace snatched her suitcase off the floor and called out a thank you over her shoulder as she rushed out of the lobby. As promised, a small green bus was parked near the curb. The three men in RAF blue from the train were walking up the steps into the bus as Grace approached. The driver told her the fare, and she fished around in her handbag and handed over the money.

"Take a seat," the bus driver said with a jerk of the head towards the back of the bus.

The RAF men nodded politely as Grace walked down the aisle and selected a seat midway down. One of them, a boyish youth with a two-day-old moustache and a flash on his shoulder which said "New Zealand" asked, "Are you headed to Thomas Green, miss?"

"I am," she replied.

"Got a fella there, then?" he asked.

"My fiancé," Grace said. "He's a pilot."

"We're aircrew too," the man said. "My name's Davies. We three got a spot of leave after our last trip. We went down to London."

"My fiancé's name is O'Hanlon. Michael O'Hanlon. Maybe you know him?"

"No," the man said. "I mean, I know the name. I've seen it on the flight rosters. But I've not met him."

"Ain't he the one who is about to come off ops?" the man closest to the window asked.

"Yes," Grace said. "That's him."

"Well," he continued. "The whole group is cheering for him. That's for sure. They say they haven't had a crew complete their thirty in a long time. You've better odds of catching a taxi in Piccadilly Square on a Saturday night. I've not met him, but I do know his bomb aimer. Big Aussie named Mac."

"Right," Grace said. "I met his crew, well, most of them, a few days ago."

"Are you going to surprise him when he gets back, then?" Davies asked.

"I hope to," Grace said. "I mean, he's not expecting me."

"He's got a good crew," the man near the window said, "from what I hear around the base. I'm sure they will be alright. Besides, maybe they just nipped over to France tonight."

"I hope so," Grace said.

"We've flown ten ops," Davies said. He lowered his voice. "It's not quite like I thought it would be. *Dawn Patrol* and all that. I'm a rear gunner. I sit back there by myself and freeze my arse off. Pardon the language."

Grace smiled. "It's alright," she said. "I've heard much worse. My younger brother was with the Commandos."

"Where is he now? If it's not a secret?"

"He was killed at Dieppe," Grace said.

"I'm sorry," Davies said. "We were in Canada training when that happened. A lot of Canadians bought it on that raid. People were very upset."

They fell silent as each grew occupied with their own thoughts. *They're such nice lads*, Grace thought as she looked at the three men who whispered among themselves. *It's a pity that they have to spend their youth dropping bombs and dodging Jerry fighters. And the odds are against them, just like they are against Michael tonight.*

"You are getting off at the village, right, miss?" the bus driver called out.

"I am," Grace said.

"Your stop is just ahead about a mile."

Grace gathered her suitcase and handbag and made ready to exit the bus.

"The airfield gate is about a mile up the road from the village," Davies offered. "I don't think they'll let you on, but you never know. You could always try in the morning."

"Thank you," Grace said. "I may try and get a message to him to tell him where I am staying. As soon as I figure it out myself."

"At this hour, finding a room... well, that might be difficult," Davies said. "But there's a pub about a block from the bus stop. If they are still open, the man who runs it might be able to point you in the right direction."

The bus pulled to a stop and the door opened. Grace stood and said "Good luck" to the men before she stepped out into the night. The chill in the air bit at her skin as she tried to navigate the unfamiliar and blacked-out surroundings of the village. She looked in vain for a villager to ask directions from, but none appeared. Silence as thick as the darkness blanketed the streets. With a shrug of the shoulders, Grace made her way up the street and kept as close to the buildings as she could. The thin sliver of the moon faded in and out as clouds drifted across the sky. It barely provided enough light to read the signs on the buildings. After several minutes, she located a sign which simply read "Pub." Grace pushed on the door of the building, but it did not open.

It was a narrow stone building twice as deep as it was wide. Two windows on the second floor looked out over the street. With a sigh, Grace sat her suitcase down and knocked on the door. After a pause with no response, she knocked again, louder this time. A crash from inside caused her to jump and step back from the door. A moment later, the door cracked open just a bit. The blackout curtain inside prevented any light from escaping onto the street.

"What the bloody hell do you want bangin' on my door like that?" a man's voice asked.

"I'm terribly sorry," Grace said. "But you see, I've just arrived and I'm looking for a room to rent."

"This is pub, not a bloody hotel. And we're closed."

The door slammed shut, and she heard muttered curses fade into the pub as the man walked away from the door. *So much for that,* Grace thought. Spying a bench nearby, she walked over and took a seat to collect her thoughts. The thought of spending the night inside the train station crossed her mind, but then she remembered the grouchy man behind the counter. *He'd probably tell me to bugger off.* Given the blackout, she had no way to know which other businesses might be open. *I can't bloody well knock on every door until someone tells me where I can find a room,* she thought.

"Yes," she said aloud. "Yes, I can."

"You can what?" asked a female voice.

Grace turned and peered into the darkness but saw only a vague shape.

"I apologize for my husband's behavior," the woman said. "He's got a bit of a cold and is grouchy on a good day. Grouchier when he is sick."

"The pub owner?" Grace said as she stood up.

"Now what was it you needed, child?"

"I know you're just a pub, but I was hoping you might be able to tell me where I could find a room. I've just arrived in town and my fiancé is at the base up the road. I'm to meet with him tomorrow."

"And he didn't find a room for you?" the woman asked. "That's a bit unsporting of him, don't you think?"

"He doesn't know I'm here," Grace replied, hoping she wouldn't have to give the whole story to yet another stranger.

"Well come along, then," the woman said. "My name's Margaret. I can make a couple of phone calls. I know a few places that might rent you a room, though it is possible they are booked up."

"Lots of people on holiday up here?" Grace asked.

"No," Margaret said. "With the base nearby, we have young women visiting their sweethearts. Now mind you, since you aren't married, don't be getting ideas of the two of you sharing a room. That won't do, you know."

"I'm not that kind of girl," Grace said with as straight a face as she could manage.

"Well, let's not stand here blithering on like idiots in the cold," Margaret said. "Come along. I'll warm up some soup for you while I phone around. Don't you worry none. We'll get you sorted out."

"Thank you," Grace said as she reached down and grabbed her suitcase. For the first time since she boarded the train in London, she felt as though things might work out after all.

CHAPTER TWENTY-FOUR

"DAMN TOMMIES," FISCHER said as he settled into his chair. "What I wouldn't give for a good night's sleep."

"During the last war," Frei said, "we would say that we'd sleep when the war ended."

Karl studied the faces of his youthful charges. The boys appeared more nervous than scared, though one of them bounced his foot up and down on the floor. Determination was etched into the faces of the young women, their lips drawn tight and eyes narrowed. *I trust them more than the boys*, he thought. *Bravado usually fades away when the shit starts.* Karl remembered the day the war began. The army called up his reserve infantry unit in early August of 1939. They had a few weeks of rigorous training and then boarded a train to the Polish border. Many of the troops were older than average, like Karl, who had turned twenty-nine a few months before the call up. They still had their share of younger soldiers, little more than children, with baggy uniforms and helmets which were a bit too large. While the older men had remained silent on their journey, each occupied with their own thoughts of home and family, the younger men boasted of the thrashing they'd give the Poles. As a sergeant, Karl considered it his duty to tell them to shut up, which he had to do often. Their move to the border was supposed to be secret, although not a closely guarded one. In Berlin, people spoke openly of the grievances the Fuhrer had against Poland, though it was also with a slightly disapproving air. Years later after he returned home, Karl learned many of those in the city reacted with shock or dismay once the government announced the invasion.

On the day the war began, Karl's unit marched into Poland and encountered little resistance other than an occasional small Polish unit determined to make a stand. They quickly dealt with such nuisances, until day three. An enemy rifle battalion had dug in behind a small stream. Despite punishing attacks from Stuka dive bombers, and the fact that the panzers were already miles behind them, cutting them off, the soldiers refused to give up. Karl's company received orders to attack the enemy's front while two other companies circled around to attack each flank. His men attacked on time while the other two companies did not. The Poles turned their full attention on Karl's men.

The chatter of machine-gun fire mixed with the single pops of rifles and the screams of men as their bodies shattered from the impact of bullets. A couple of the younger boasters from the train ride went to pieces. One dropped his rifle and sat on the ground with his head in his hands. He rocked back and forth until a bullet caught him in the side of the head. He fell back in a fount of blood. Karl's company commander screamed into the radio that the other companies needed to move. Now. Another young soldier stood up and looked around in confusion as Karl and the others yelled at him to get down. He stared back, uncomprehending, until a round shattered his knee. After what seemed like an eternity, the attack on the enemy's flank materialized, and Karl's unit was able to move forward. Only a handful of Polish soldiers survived and most of them were wounded. A man from Karl's company moved among them, casually shooting them with his Mauser just as a man might shoot at tin cans. Karl took a step towards him but his company commander put a hand on his arm. He turned away in disgust and gathered the younger men who survived the attack.

"Not so brave now, are you?" Karl said. They looked away with shame on their faces. Karl felt bad. *I was scared as well. I just hid it better*, he thought. Karl continued, "Don't worry about it, men. It happens to everyone at some point or another. You've had your first battle, and you are still alive. There's a certain victory in that."

One of the soldiers looked up at Karl. "But... but some of the others..."

"Yes, some of the others are dead. Some are wounded. That's what war is. You were lucky today. You might not be so lucky tomorrow. Or the next day. Or even an hour from now. But for the moment, you are alive and that's all that matters. Now gather your wits and get ready to move out. We are at war here, not on holiday."

"Isn't that right, Karl?" Baumann's voice brought Karl back to the present.

"I'm sorry," Karl said. "Is what right?"

"That we have little to fear. Berlin is the most heavily defended city in the Reich."

"It is heavily defended," Karl agreed, "but the bombers always get through. It only takes one bomb to ruin your day."

"That's the truth," Frei said as he busied himself picking at a piece of lint on his trouser leg.

"Where do you think they are going to try and bomb tonight?" Schneider asked.

Karl smiled at her and said, "I don't know. Most likely the center of town where the government offices are, or perhaps the east part of the city with the factories."

"Or they may just dump loads of incendiaries and try to burn us all to death," Fischer said. "Just like in Hamburg."

"*Terrorfleigers*," the arrogant Hitler Youth boy said. "They are so brave, making war on women and children. Once the Final Victory comes, they will have much to answer for. I personally look forward to seeing that fat pig Churchill stood up against a wall and shot. I'd pull the trigger myself if they'd let me."

Baumann let out an exaggerated sigh and rolled his eyes. Karl shot him a look of warning. Though the station provided a safe place for the firemen to talk openly since they trusted one another, the addition of the Hitler Youth boys in particular made it dangerous to express certain thoughts or jokes in their presence. Given the amount of cheek in Baumann's typical conversation, Karl worried about him the most. *The Gestapo already has their eye on this station, though it is Ursula they are really after. Still, it wouldn't do to have one of those little shits turn in one of the men. I'd hate to lose a good fireman just because he offended the sensibilities of a true believer.*

The flak sender radio sprang to life. Voices filled the room as the controllers gave directions to the anti-aircraft batteries. The flak operators sounded excited, in contrast to the clipped voices of the radio direction finders. Karl knew the batteries would throw up a wall of steel shell splinters to inflict whatever damage they could on the enemy planes as they approached. Despite the interior location of the station shelter, the *crack-crack-crack* of the batteries atop the nearby Zoo Flak Tower reached into the depths of the room once the guns opened fire. The walls shook a bit from the vibration of the guns. Dust floated down from the ceiling.

Frei removed a package of cigarettes and stuck one in his mouth. He passed it around to the men, who each took one. He did not offer it to the young volunteers.

"May as well get a last smoke in," Frei said as he struck a match. "I have a feeling we'll be busy tonight."

"Sounds that way from what they are saying on the radio," Baumann agreed.

"Maybe they'll drop some on Wedding and bump off a few Kozis," Fischer said.

Though he was only eight years old when the first war ended, Karl remembered street fighting between communists and rival right wing groups in Berlin in 1919 and 1920. Karl never developed any real political feelings, one way or the other, apart from his dislike of communists made stronger by his experiences in Russia. The fear of a communist take-over helped propel the National Socialists into power. Karl disapproved of them in a general way at the time, though he appreciated their anti-communist stance. *But now? Now I've seen what they were really about all along,* he thought. *Death would be a relief compared to the nightmare I live in. We've much to atone for. I have much to atone for too.*

"When do you think we'll get an assignment?" Schneider asked.

"We probably won't get anything specific," Karl said. "If this raid is as heavy as it sounds, once the bombs start falling we'll know where to go."

Schneider nodded and asked, "And afterwards? How long will we work?"

"The last heavy raid it was two days," Fischer said. "Thankfully we don't have to scoop up very many dead bodies. They bring prisoners from one of the camps to do that for us. Forced labor – excuse me, voluntary labor. I never seem to remember what new words and phrases we have to describe things. In fact…"

Karl cleared his throat and Fischer fell silent. The French doctor in the room began to softly whistle "La Marseillaise." His Dutch assistant ran his hands through his hair and then leaned back and closed his eyes. *He's got steady nerves*, Karl thought. He considered telling the doctor to stop whistling but decided against it. If it kept him from going crazy during the raid, so be it. Panic in close quarters could be contagious. And fatal. A week ago, a stampede started in a crowded shelter after a near miss and killed ten people. Their bodies stacked up in front of the door like a wall of human flesh.

"Listen!" Baumann cried out. "Quiet and listen!"

From overhead, the first rumble of aircraft engines sounded. The flak radio again exploded to life as did the batteries nearby. The sound of firing intensified and soon drowned out the noise of the airplanes. The walls of the station began to shake a bit more as the guns pounded shell after shell into the night sky. Karl wondered what exploding shells sounded like to the men in the planes. He knew what the whizzing sound of shrapnel and the heat you felt from a near miss was like from his time at the front. He remembered burrowing into the earth like a child does with a blanket on a cold night. But up there? Was it any different for them?

"Christ," Frei said, "they haven't dropped anything yet. That must mean Charlottenburg's going to get it tonight."

Ursula! Karl thought. *I hope she's safe in her shelter. I should have insisted she stay here during the raid. But no, the Gestapo would've known she was here. What is she up to?* He resolved to stop by her apartment building the first chance he got. *Please let her be safe*, he mentally asked a God he no longer believed in. *She's in danger from the Gestapo. And now this. Please let her be safe.* The shriek of the first bombs as they hurtled earthwards caused a couple of the Hitler Youth boys to jump.

"Steady," Karl said. "It's true what they say. You don't hear the one that gets you. As long as you can hear the bombs falling, you are safe. The one that will blast you into little pieces, well, you'll never hear it coming."

"Little pieces we'll scoop up and send home to your mommies," Frei added.

"That's enough," Karl said when he noticed two of the boys turn a shade of pale green.

CRUMP! CRUMP! CRUMP! The nearby blasts nearly toppled them out of their chairs. Hartmann stifled a low sob. Baumann let out an oath of surprise. Even the Dutch ambulance assistant let out a startled cry of surprise. Karl took a drag from his cigarette to try and calm a heart which threatened to burst out of his chest. *Steady. Steady.* His mind repeated the word over and over. *You can't show any fear in front of the kids. It won't do to make them panic.* Instead, he crossed his legs and tried to appear as relaxed as possible. *CRUMP! CRUMP! CRUMP!* Three more bombs hit, a little further away than the first three.

"That plane has gone by," Baumann observed as though he were describing a sunset.

"One down, maybe seven hundred to go," Fischer said. "This is no nuisance raid."

"It won't last long," Karl said, forcing himself to smile at his young volunteers. "We'll leave here in a bit, and then you'll be so busy that you won't notice it at all."

"The British drop high explosives to open up the buildings and then incendiaries to set the furnishings, and people, on fire," Fischer explained. "If we don't get hold of the fires when they first start, well, then Berlin will be like Hamburg."

"One Hamburg was enough," Karl said. "I don't fancy seeing that done to my own city. So yes, we'll go out and work and we will all do our duty."

Karl stood and glanced around the room before announcing, "I'm going to take a look outside."

Exiting the room, he took a deep breath to cleanse his lungs of the stale air inside the shelter. The stink of sweating, unwashed bodies and uncared-for teeth made every shelter an olfactory nightmare, especially the smaller ones like that in the fire station. Some nights it drove Karl to almost pray for a direct hit to free his nose from its torment. He made his way across the apparatus bay by memory rather than sight, as all the station lights were turned off. The city routinely shut off the gas before a raid too, lest a gas leak merge with the fire from an incendiary to create an explosion to rival those of the bombs.

Outside the station, Karl smelled the cordite from a nearby bomb, but in the darkness, he saw no damage or fires, yet. Overhead, searchlights swept back and forth across the sky. Flashes of tracer fire stitched its way upwards and the occasional burst of a larger shell cast shadows on the ground. He looked up when he heard the sound of an aircraft almost directly overhead. Three searchlights locked onto it, and the bomber looked as though it was being held up by the lights. The doors to the bomb bay were open. Karl surmised it took no evasive action because it had not yet dropped its load. Shells burst around it, and the plane suddenly lurched as though it hit a speed bump in the sky. Smoke drifted from the two engines on its port wing followed shortly by yellow and orange tongues of flame. The plane began a slow roll onto its side and nosed downwards. The searchlights moved onto other targets, and it took Karl's eyes a minute to readjust to the darkness. *I feel bad for the people that plane is going to land on, with its load of bombs still inside.* Karl wondered why the pilot didn't jettison the bombs after the plane was hit, though he knew it was possible the pilot or bomb aimer was killed by the shell which downed the plane.

He stood listening, waiting. A tremendous blast shook the ground as a sheet of fire erupted in the distance. *That'll be the plane*, Karl said to himself. It must have had a two-thousand kilo bomb on board. He heard shouts and screams from the direction of the explosion, and he gave a slow shake of his head. *I guess that will be our first stop of the night*, he thought as he slipped back inside the station and yanked the cord to open the doors to the apparatus bay.

"What in the hell was that noise?" Frei called out from the darkness behind the fire engines. "Is it the end of the world?"

"A bomber went down with a full load on board. Looks like a few dozen blocks from here. Grab the others and let's head that way."

In a moment, Karl heard the sound of footsteps as they entered the apparatus bay. The Hitler Youth boys babbled excitedly among themselves. Karl held up a hand for silence and then realized they couldn't see him.

"Quiet!" he yelled.

Silence descended upon the station.

"Here are your orders. We'll take the engine out first, followed by the ladder and then the ambulance. Stick close together but not too close. We'll be driving blacked out and we may have to make sudden stops. I don't want to fill out the paperwork if we have an accident. Or if one of you gets hurt. Follow our instructions immediately! Am I clear?"

"*Jawohl,* Herr Oberwachtmeister," they yelled in unison.

"Get to it then," Karl said. He climbed into the cab of the engine as Fischer started the motor. He mentally calculated the risk of the fire they'd see, just as he did on every call. *Bomber. Half loaded with fuel. Heavy fire conditions. Damage from explosion of bombs. Unexploded bombs. Incendiary fires. It won't be easy. Hopefully we will get some help from the other stations.*

"What was it that Englishman said?" Fischer asked, inching the fire engine through the station doors as Karl methodically pulled the rope to ring the bell mounted on the front bumper. "Once more into the breach, dear friends?"

PART FOUR

22 – 23 NOVEMBER NIGHT

The first angel sounded, and there followed
hail and fire mingled with blood,
and they were cast upon the earth: and
the third part of trees was burnt
up, and all the green grass was burnt up.

Revelations 8:7

CHAPTER TWENTY-FIVE

"Hello, skipper."

"Hello, bomb aimer," Michael replied.

"Should be on the bomb run in about ten minutes."

"Hello, navigator," Michael said.

"Yes, skipper?"

"Are we on time?"

"Only about a minute behind schedule."

A minute, Michael thought. *That's not too bad. With an engine running hot, I won't risk increasing the revs to try and make it up.* A searchlight beam swept right in front of the nose of the aircraft, but it didn't catch them. By the time it crossed back, Paddy's Wagon was safely beyond its arc. A tremendous battle erupted off the starboard beam. Angry tracers flew back and forth between a Lancaster and a night fighter. Williams rotated his turret and squeezed off a few shots of his own, but they fell short. A burning plane plummeted earthward.

"Who was it, mid-gunner?" Michael asked.

"Looks like they got the fighter, skipper," Williams said. "Hard to tell for sure. But it looks like a fighter going down."

Flak buffeted the aircraft, and it bounced slightly in the air.

"Pilot to bomb aimer. Okay to weave a bit on the approach?"

"That's fine, skipper."

Michael moved the plane from side to side a bit to throw off the aim of the German flak controllers. A flash like a cigarette in a dark room blossomed about a hundred yards dead ahead. Michael ducked as a few pieces of shrapnel pinged off the aircraft.

"You okay, Mac?" he asked once his stomach returned to its place.

"We took a hit up here, skipper," Mac said.

"Serious?"

A minute passed while Mac assessed the damage to the nose of the plane.

"Hit the nose turret, skipper," Mac finally said. "Looks like it's going to be out of action. It's spraying oil all over the place."

"No loss," Cameron said. "You can't shoot for shite."

The crew laughed the strained laugh of men afraid but unwilling to admit it. Michael allowed it for a minute, then ordered them to clear the intercom. *No great loss*, he thought. *The fighters don't usually come at us head on anyway.*

"Could you check the temps again?" Michael asked Cameron.

"Outer port and inner starboard running hot, skipper," Cameron replied. "Just a few degrees. Nothing to worry about."

Yet, thought Michael. Up ahead, he saw dummy flares set off by the Germans in an attempt to divert the bomber stream from its target. A few fires burned in the center of the flare pattern, also started by the ground defenses. Bombing at night was a cat and mouse game. The Germans tried to guess the target and shift their night fighters to cover it while Bomber Command used a variety of tactics to mask their intentions.

Sometimes the Germans guessed right and other times they guessed wrong. It was a war of nerves as well as machines.

Some of the other pilots insisted it was skill rather than luck which brought them home safe after each flight, but Michael had seen enough to know that survival often depended on little more than pure chance. A shell or a night fighter could get you anywhere, and the randomness with which planes got hit proved that no matter how skilled the pilot, anyone could be listed as "Failed to Return." Veteran crews went west just as often as new crews, though the constant stream of replacements made it seem that there were always new faces around. Few lasted long enough for anyone to learn their names, much less mourn them once they were gone.

Michael had a hard time even remembering what his crew was like on their first operation. Scared, he was sure, but all of the missions since then blended together in his mind like a slide show of horrors. He had a hard time picking out any single raid unless something unusually frightening or funny happened. Cameron could rattle off the dates and targets they'd flown up to this point with ease, as could Mac. Michael knew only that this trip over Berlin was one too many as far as he was concerned.

"Five minutes, skipper," Mac called out.

Flak shook the aircraft again, and for a second, the controls slipped out of Michael's hands and the plane nosed down. He corrected the pitch and started to weave again. The sudden chatter of Lawton's turret caused him to jump. Beside him, Cameron froze, concern etched into his face. After what seemed like an eternity, the guns fell silent. An eerie calm descended upon the aircraft and the men inside her.

"Okay back there, rear gunner?" Michael asked.

"Sorry, skipper," Lawton replied. "Bastard snuck up on me."

"I don't think he hit us," Cameron said.

"Did you get him, rear gunner?" Michael asked.

"I punched him in the snout, and he broke off. He's not shot down, but I don't think he'll be back. I know I hit him, just not good enough."

"More flak coming up ahead," Mac said. "I think they must be expecting us. The wankers."

Michael saw the angry bursts in the sky directly in their flight path. Beneath him, fire began to merge and grow together as the incendiaries from the planes ahead of them in the stream dumped their bombs and turned for home. *We are really giving it to them tonight*, Michael thought. *I'd not want to be on the ground in the middle of this*. Though Michael had still been in the operational training unit the previous July during the Hamburg raids, one of the pilots had told him that on the night the great firestorm destroyed the city and God knows how many lives, he had smelled the odor of burning flesh from the cockpit of his Lancaster, fifteen thousand feet above the city. The thought of it made Michael shudder now as it had then. Few of the men in the planes gave much thought to what damage their bombs wrought upon the targets. Many of them had seen the destruction of German bombs firsthand during the Blitz. Michael had not experienced a raid himself, though he'd seen damage in London on leave. *Grace knows what it is like*, he thought. *And I'm glad that I don't. I wonder what it was like for Maureen the night she died in Belfast.*

In school, the teacher had shown the class pictures of Germany out of a book. It seemed like a happy place, with small houses packed next to one another on narrow streets.

The roofs were covered with wooden shingles. Perfect to set alight with a can of incendiaries. The people looked happy and even friendly. Michael remembered thinking how nice it would be to visit there one day. *Though not like this. Dear God, not like this. When we're done burning their cities to the ground, I doubt they'll see many tourists once the war ends.* He'd never met a German. His father said little about the ones he'd fought against during the Great War, other than an occasional reference to their fighting ability. *I now know why he respected them at least*, Michael thought. *They can put up one hell of a fight.*

"I've got a spot picked out," Mac called out. "Okay to open bomb bay doors and arm bombs?"

"Okay, bomb aimer. Let's start our run."

The plane grew a bit sluggish as the bomb doors opened. From the point the bomb run started, Michael had to hold the plane steady. The flak and searchlight batteries knew this and made it hell on the crews. Michael held the controls with his left hand for a moment while he crossed himself with his right. *Hail Mary, full of grace*, he repeated in his head.

On the run into the target, Michael allowed Mac to be his eyes and kept the plane as steady as he could, making the corrections in steering that Mac called out. If they failed to get a good run on the target, Michael knew he'd have to turn the plane around and try again. *I'm not flying through this hell a second time. Not for all the tea in China.*

"Steady, steady," Mac said.

Cameron slapped Michael on the shoulder and pointed off to the left, where a Lancaster plunged towards the ground, bathed in flames. Michael shook his head to ward off the sight. *Poor bastards*, he thought. Seven men trapped in a burning coffin. In the flames, he caught the aircraft number. *Christ! That's McBride's crew! So long, Sterling. I'll mail the letter for you.*

"Left, left," Mac called out, and Michael put a bit of pressure on the left rudder pedal.

"That's it. Hold her steady," Mac said.

The cockpit was bathed in a bright ocean of light as a searchlight beam caught them but failed to hold the plane. Michael let out a whistle of relief. *WHAM! WHAM!* Two quick explosions bracketed the plane. It jerked around like a puppet on a string before Michael brought it back under control. Beads of sweat appeared on Michael's forehead and trickled down his face. He blinked to keep them out of his eyes, squeezing the control column tighter to stop himself from instinctively wiping his face. His hand shook slightly. *Shit! That one got us for sure.*

"Hold her steady, skipper," Mac yelled. "We are thirty seconds out. Bring her right a bit. There you go. Just a bit more. Steady again."

The controls responded slower than normal. Michael ran his eyes over the instrument panel and saw nothing that looked out of sorts. Up ahead, more flak bursts sent shrapnel bouncing off the wings and the nose of the plane. *Jesus, they're getting close*, he thought. On occasion the flak batteries managed to get the exact altitude and course of a bomber right, and when they did, shells pounded the aircraft to pieces more often than not. The only thing worse than getting coned by a searchlight was letting the guns on the ground zero in on you.

"Okay back there, rear gunner?" Michael called.

"Fine, skipper," Lawton replied. "I think."

"Mid-upper? You okay?"

"Right ho, skipper. Felt a few pieces pass by a little too close for my liking."

"Left a bit," Mac said. "Steady. Bombs going in ten seconds!"

Michael bit down on his lip to distract himself from the butterflies in his stomach. Beneath him, he saw the flashes from bombs as they hit the ground. More red and green flares dropped off to the right as pathfinder planes dropped to keep the target area clear for the next flight of planes. *They could just drop on the fires now.*

"Cookie gone!" Mac called out as the plane rose slightly after freeing itself of the heavy weight. "Incendiaries going now! Taking photograph."

"Wireless and navigator, check in please!" Michael said. Fighting to keep his voice calm, he called again. "Hello, wireless, are you okay? Hello, navigator?"

"I'll take a look," Cameron said. He ducked through the thick black curtain which separated the navigator and wireless operator compartment from the rest of the plane.

"Photograph taken!" Mac said. "Closing bomb doors. Start weaving, skipper. Fast. They are firing at us."

More flak burst around the plane. Cameron stumbled back into the cockpit. He pulled his oxygen mask down and vomited on the floor. Then he sank to his knees in the puddle he'd made and retched until there was nothing left in his stomach.

"What is it?" Michael asked as he looked over his shoulder. "Are you alright?"

"Dead," Cameron said as he put his mask back on. "Both dead. Shell splinters punched through and hit them both."

Michael nodded as his brain tried to digest the information.

"Skipper, it's a mess. Their guts are all over the floor."

"Jesus." Michael forced himself to focus on keeping the plane in the air. "The controls are a bit stiff, flight engineer. But still working."

Another shell burst rocked the plane. *Much closer and we'll get a direct hit*. Michael continued weaving the plane as much as he dared. Two more shells burst about thirty yards from the port wing. Paddy's Wagon let out a groan of protest.

"Jesus, skipper," Mac said. "Get us out of this. Fast."

"I'm trying," Michael said. "And Mac, come up here, please."

Mac stuck his head through the hatchway that led to the flight deck.

"Can you go back and check the charts?" Michael asked. "See if any are serviceable. It may be a bit of a mess back there."

Mac nodded and ducked through the curtain. He returned a few minutes later.

"A few of them are, so long as you don't mind blood, but Jesus, Mary, and Joseph, it smells like a slaughterhouse back there."

"Engines running hotter, skipper," Cameron said.

"I could use a pint," Mac said as he disappeared back into the nose.

"Get back up here," Michael said, his voice a little more stern than usual. "You're going to have to navigate for us."

"Jesus Christ," Lawton swore from his tail turret. "We'll never get home with him doing the figuring."

"Shut up," Michael said. "And keep your eyes open."

"And what do I do with the departed back there?" Mac

asked. "Open the bomb bay doors and chuck them out on the Jerries?"

"Just lay them both on the floor and get on with it."

"I'll help," Cameron said.

They disappeared behind the curtain, and Michael tried to focus on flying.

We've got to get out of their searchlight belt, he thought. *If we don't, we are all dead men.* As if on cue, another searchlight caught them and this time, it didn't drift away.

"Hold on!" Michael called out as he shoved the plane into a twisting dive followed by a twisting climb. The plane groaned and then screamed in protest. Michael brought her up and turned into another twisting climb, and the beam slipped away to starboard. Cameron ducked back in front of the curtain and knelt before his instrument panel.

"No change, skipper," he said. "Engines still hot but holding steady. We've lost a bit of hydraulic fluid though."

"That explains the controls," Michael said. "Mac, can you give me a course to steer?"

"Working on it," Mac said. "Give me a minute."

"Hello, skipper, mid-gunner here," Williams said.

"Go ahead."

"Looks like a bit of smoke from the number two engine. No fire though."

"Did the wireless set get hit too?" Michael asked Cameron.

"No, it looked fine."

"Good," Michael said. "We may need it if we have to put her down in the Channel."

"God, I hope not," Cameron said. "I can't swim. And number two is running a bit hotter now. Should I feather it?"

"Not yet," Michael said. "Keep an eye on it, Williams. Let

me know if the smoke gets heavier or if you see any flames. And watch the gauges, flight engineer."

Mac called out a new course and Michael turned the plane, which responded, albeit slowly. For the first time, he allowed himself to think they might have a chance. As if they could read his thoughts, the Germans sent up another barrage of flak, though it was too far below them to do much more than bounce the plane a bit. The flames spreading through the streets of Berlin began to drift away to stern as the plane turned north and then northwest. An empty black sky stretched in front of the nose of the plane, lit only by a few stars. A thin sliver of moon, hardly enough to illuminate the cloud tops, shone just off to the west of Paddy's Wagon.

"There's a black shape off to our port," Cameron said as he stood over Michael's shoulder. "See it? There! Too small to be a Lancaster."

"Keep your eyes peeled, gunners," Michael said. "There may be a night fighter lurking about up here. But don't shoot unless you are sure. No need to draw attention to ourselves."

"Okay, skipper," Williams said.

"Right ho, skip," Lawton said.

"We're gonna make it, skip," Cameron said, squeezing Michael's shoulder. "The old girl will see us home. I can feel it."

"There's a Lanc dead astern, skipper," Lawton called out. "She's close too. Maybe four hundred yards."

Michael pulled back on the controls and eased Paddy's Wagon upward a few hundred feet before he leveled off. He glanced down at Grace's photo taped to the instrument panel and kissed the tip of his finger before pressing it to the photo. *What is she doing now? Sleeping, you bloody fool. Steady on. No time to think of that now. Focus.*

"We gave them a right thrashing tonight, skip," Cameron said. "They won't soon forget it."

Nor will I, Michael thought. *Coming home two missions in a row with dead crewmen on board. And they say we Irish are lucky.* His eyes swept back and forth across the horizon and then scanned the instruments in front of him. Paddy's Wagon was getting a bit stiffer and a bit more difficult to keep level. His arms and back ached from the strain of flying and the stress of the mission. *What I wouldn't give for a hot bath and a bottle of whiskey*, he thought. *Just a few more hours. Just a few more...*

Michael heard Lawton's turret open fire as a sudden explosive force shook the plane, like a terrier might shake a rat in its teeth. A scream unlike anything he'd ever heard before filled the intercom and penetrated to the deepest part of his brain.

CHAPTER TWENTY-SIX

PILES OF RUBBLE blocked the streets and forced Fischer to take a few detours to reach the large fire burning in the distance. Every few moments, Karl glanced over his shoulder at the young women who hung on to the back of the engine. He saw looks of grim determination on their faces. The smell of aviation gasoline filled his nose as the engine turned into the block where the plane crashed. A massive crater had swallowed the middle of the street. The crash and explosion had reduced the apartment buildings on each side of the crater to piles of smoldering brick and stone. Thin streams of phosphorus from the incendiaries ran down the street and dripped into the crater. He heard a few screams from the cellar of one building, buried under the bricks. The cries rose above the noise of the aircraft engines and flak batteries.

A cascade of explosions a few blocks north made Karl flinch. He signaled Fischer to stop the engine and climbed out of the cab. The young women gathered around him and awaited orders. After a moment, Baumann and Frei joined him, their Hitler Youth boys in tow.

"Listen up," Karl said. "We don't have time to worry about the fires right now. We need to try and get people out of these cellars. Schneider, you and Hartmann go ahead and stretch a hose to the hydrant at the end of the street. We'll keep it charged in case we need it. The rest of you grab every tool you can off the truck. Shovels. Picks. Everything. And the buckets of sand too. Meet me back here with it. Go! Now!"

The volunteers scattered to gather the items while Karl motioned the experienced men to stay behind.

"We need to work fast," Karl said. "Fast but safe. I don't want one of the kids getting hurt either. So be smart. Frei, take your crew to the building on the north side of the street and we'll tackle the south."

"Got it," Frei said, "And Karl…"

"Yes."

"Do you recognize this building?"

"No," Karl said. "Should I?"

"We were here the other day," Frei said. "The redhead with the cooking problem. Your friend."

Ursula! Karl flinched as though he'd been punched in the gut. *No. Don't show concern in front of the crew*, he warned himself. Karl nodded his head.

"Well, let's get to it," he said.

Frei deployed the aerial ladder, slowly raising and then extending it over the pile of rubble. The crash and explosion reduced a four-story apartment building to a one-and-a-half-story pile of crushed stone and, no doubt, crushed bodies. One of the Hitler Youth boys scrambled up the ladder, tugging a hose from which he sprayed a limp stream of water back and forth over the bricks to cool them down while the rest of the crew attacked the debris with pickaxes and hands. Karl watched them work for a moment, and then turned his attention to his own task. Overhead, the constant drone of aircraft engines mingled with the shriek of bombs as they hurtled earthwards and the crack of exploding shells created a symphony of horror which threatened to rupture his eardrums, not to mention his mind.

Another engine and ladder arrived on the scene. Luftwaffe men crewed the ladder truck while Ukrainian volunteers staffed the engine. The Ukrainians crossed the street to assist Frei's crew while the airmen approached Karl.

"Bad business, this," the NCO in charge of the ladder said as he walked up to Karl, his voice flat and emotionless. "What do you need from us?"

"Go ahead and deploy your ladder. We're going to see if we can dig our way down to the cellar. It's full of people."

"I can hear that," the NCO said. The screams of the people inside sounded like the wail of banshees shrieking in the wind.

As the ladder crew went to work, Karl motioned his own people to gather around. He had to yell for his voice to be heard over the sounds from the sky.

"We are going to start here," Karl said as he indicated a spot close to the street. "Be very, very careful. The bricks can shift suddenly and collapse on you without warning. We have some wooden braces on the truck and we'll shore up our tunnel as much as we can, but we must work fast. There's a fire burning in there somewhere. If it gets into the cellar, well, you don't want to know what that sounds like. Questions?"

"I do love a challenge," Fischer said with a grin.

The sound of an aircraft motor caused Karl to glance upwards into the sky just in time to see a plane caught in the cone of a searchlight drop its bombs. Little black sticks fell away and started towards the ground, almost overhead.

"Down!" Karl screamed. "Everybody down!"

He flopped onto his stomach. The concussion of the blast lifted him from the ground and slammed him back again. His ears rang as he stood up and took stock of his crew. They appeared okay. Karl bent over with his hands on his knees and took deep breaths for a few minutes to force his lungs to work again.

"Go ahead and put your gas masks on," Karl told them, "and then let's get to it."

Neither he nor Fischer donned their own masks, as they preferred not to use them unless absolutely necessary, but Karl wanted to spare his inexperienced crew the feeling of smoke-scorched lungs that he and Fischer were accustomed to. At a regular fire, Fischer's job was to man the pumps on the engine but as this was rescue work, he pitched in to help as well. Karl walked over and knelt down next to the spot he intended to start working from. He peered into the blackness of the rubble and caught the faint glow of a flame from deep inside the pile.

"What are you thinking?" Fischer asked as he dropped to his knees beside Karl.

"This must be where the entrance to the building was," Karl said. "See the remnants of a heavy door? If I'm right, we should find the entrance to the cellar if we can get about twenty or thirty feet inside."

"That'll take us until tomorrow afternoon," Fischer replied.

Under regular conditions after a raid, rescue workers moved into collapsed buildings at a rate of around two feet an hour, making frequent stops to both change personnel and to shore up their work with either wooden or metal framing. On occasion, the authorities even dispatched structural engineers to advise on the best route to take and to inspect the rescue work. *We'll get no help from them tonight*, Karl thought.

"We'll have to work faster than that," Karl said. *Please, dear God, let Ursula not have been home tonight*, he thought as he pulled his gloves from his pocket and slipped them onto his hands. With a heave, he shifted one large stone to the side to enlarge the opening. He stopped and listened for any sound of creaking that warned of a collapse and heard none.

"We could work a hose in there and hit that fire," Fischer suggested. "It might buy them more time."

"No," Karl said. "I can't tell, but if it's from an incendiary, it'll just make the liquid run through the cracks in the floor and down into the cellar. I don't want to take that chance."

The women walked up behind him and placed an array of tools, wooden blocks, and buckets onto the ground around him. Karl unbuckled his leather belt and removed his gas mask canister and his axe, lest they get snagged on fallen wires, before he tightened the chinstrap on his helmet.

"I'm going in," he announced. "I'll try and pass rubble back to you to remove, and you can pass me the framing when I call for it."

As Karl spoke, Fischer busied himself tying a thick rope around Karl's waist. Not only did this give Karl directional help if he had to get out in a hurry, but if something incapacitated him, Fischer and the others could use it to drag him out. Karl stretched out on his stomach and began to inch his way forward like an earthworm. Around six inches of clearance above his head gave him limited room to work. Piles of brick and concrete pressed against his sides. The air stank of phosphorus, burned wood, and cordite. He coughed and spit a giant glob of phlegm onto the ground. *I probably need my mask*, he thought. *No. There isn't any room to put it on, and I'm not going to back out now.*

After moving three feet into the building, Karl encountered his first obstruction. A small pile of bricks reduced the crawlspace to about half its height. One at a time, Karl removed the bricks and passed them back. With half of them gone, he called back for some wooden blocks and Schneider passed them forward. Given the coffin-like closeness of the walls, Karl could not turn and get them. Instead, while still on his stomach, he stretched his hand back and then pulled them up alongside him. Twenty painstaking minutes later, the obstacle was cleared.

"Fischer!" Karl yelled. "Can you hear me?"

"I can," Fischer replied.

"It looks like the lobby is open to about a meter and a half. I can see part of the staircase. The cellar entrance is probably just behind it."

"That's too dangerous, Karl," Fischer warned. "The load-bearing walls are shot. There's nothing holding that pile of bricks above you up but blind luck. If you go in there and start moving stuff, the whole thing will come down on you."

"Stop being an old woman," Karl yelled back. "Have the girls grab the first aid kits off the truck. And get a couple of the Luftwaffe men to wait right outside the entrance so they can help get people out."

"Are you sure?" Fischer asked.

"Now!" Karl screamed.

Hold on, Ursula, Karl said to himself, *I'm coming as fast as I can.* He pulled himself into the lobby and slowly raised to his knees. Radiant heat from the bricks made him feel as though he had just crawled into an oven. The sound of flames as they crackled above him in the debris coupled with the darkness reminded him of the descriptions of hell he'd read about in school. Inch by painful inch, Karl moved forward. Nails, jagged rocks, and broken glass tore at his knees and legs. Fresh screams erupted from the cellar.

"Help us!"

'We're burning up!"

"For the love of God, someone get us out of here!"

Karl tried to yell down to them that help was coming, but the trapped occupants gave no indication that they heard him. Just feet from where he thought the cellar door was, he encountered a heavy floor beam which had fallen diagonally. More wood and stone were stacked atop it. The narrow space it left was far too small for him to squeeze through.

We can't cut through it, he thought. *If we try, it'll bring the whole thing down. I can't fit under it. Neither can Fischer. Maybe one of the girls can? No. It's too dangerous. We'll have to wait for more help. I can't wait! Ursula could be in there! I must get her out!*

"Ursula!" he yelled as loud as his aching lungs permitted. "Is Ursula Müller in there?"

The only response was more screams.

"Damn!" he swore. "Damn. Damn. Damn."

As he made his way out of the rubble, he cursed the British bomber crews and the Nazis with equal fervor.

"Problem?" Fischer asked as Karl's head emerged from the hole.

"Yes," Karl said as he stood up. Fischer handed him a canteen and Karl swished some warm water around in his mouth to cut the dust, then spit it out in a brown stream. "There's a beam blocking the entrance to the cellar. We can't cut it and I can't fit under it."

"Well," Fischer said with a sigh, "There's not much we can do for them then. Other than to try and keep the fires off them."

Fischer noticed Karl's eyes roaming over the young women in his crew.

"Karl!" he exclaimed. "Surely you are not going to send one of them in?"

"I thought Schneider might make it through," Karl said.

Fischer grabbed his arm and dragged him several feet away as, above them, a flak barrage burst around a bomber illuminated by a searchlight.

"Karl, you cannot do that," Fischer said. "These girls aren't trained for this."

"Perhaps not, but we weren't trained for this either until the war began."

"I know why you're doing this," Fischer said. "You think she's in there."

"I don't know what you are talking about," Karl said as he turned and walked back to the group of women. He walked over to Schneider and leaned down, his mouth close to her ear.

"I need your help," he said.

She listened to Karl's explanation and nodded her head with a curt, "*Jawohl,* Herr Oberwachtmeister," her voice muffled by her gas mask.

Karl removed the rope from around his waist. She raised her arms as he fastened it around her.

"If something happens while you are in there, give two sharp tugs and we'll get you out," he said. "And Schneider…"

"Yes, Herr Oberwachtmeister?"

"You remember the woman with the red hair that stopped at the station?"

"Yes."

"She, well... she may be in there."

"I understand."

Schneider lay down on her stomach and began to crawl into the rubble. Karl stood there, clutching the rope in his hand as she moved inside. Fischer walked over and glared at him.

"I don't like this, Karl," he said.

"She'll be fine."

"Who? Schneider or your girl?"

Before Karl could answer, he heard Baumann yelling for him across the street. He thrust the rope into Fischer's hands and hurried over, dodging the shell crater. Baumann didn't speak, he merely pointed. Karl followed the direction of the finger and saw the arrogant young Hitler Youth boy sitting on the curb with his arms around his knees. His head rested upon his kneecaps as he rocked back and forth. Loud sobs erupted from deep within his lungs. Beside him lay the body of a young girl, eight or nine years old. Blood smeared her nightgown and a piece of brick protruded from the center of her chest.

"I sent him in to see what he could find inside," Baumann explained. "He carried her out and now he won't leave her side."

"Leave him be," Karl said. "He's done enough for one night. We'll send him home after the raid."

Karl returned to his side of the street and stood next to Fischer.

"I think she's reached the beam now," Fischer reported.

Karl nodded. He watched as the rope in Fischer's hands suddenly grew slack.

"She's coming out," Fischer said.

Five minutes later, Schneider appeared at the entrance to the tunnel. She remained on the ground, her lower body still under the debris pile. With gloved hands, Schneider pulled her gas mask off and laid it on the pavement in front of her.

"I need a shovel," she said. "I can't squeeze under the beam, but I think I can scoop out a few inches beneath it and get through. I can hear the people in the cellar. They are alive, but I don't know for how long. I'm not sure how we can get them all out."

Karl grabbed a shovel and passed it to her.

"Once you get under the beam, give three sharp tugs on the rope. I'll move into the lobby and we'll put someone else near the tunnel to help. We have to try."

"Maybe I should have joined the RAD instead," she said with a slight grin.

As she began to scoot backwards into the tunnel, a sudden vibration shook the ground. Karl reached out to grab her. Schneider's bright blue eyes, wide with fear, locked onto his. Just as he took hold of her hands, the pile shifted and heavy stones collapsed onto the tunnel, smashing her lower body. Her eyes registered brief surprise, then pain as she tried to raise herself up onto her elbows. The stones pinned her lower body to the ground. Karl knelt in front of her and tried to think of something, anything, to say. There was no way to pull her out without ripping her in two. After a moment, blood exploded from her mouth as if from a volcano, splattering the front of his uniform. He retreated and stood up, unable to look Fischer in the eyes.

"Karl! Is that you!"

A woman's voice shook him from the scene in front of him. He turned and saw Ursula running towards him. Her red hair was loose and flowing around her head. The light of the fires burning all around danced through it and made it look as if it were a fiery halo.

"My God," Karl whispered. "My God. What have I done?"

"Karl," Ursula panted when she reached him. "I'm in trouble. A lot of trouble."

"You weren't at home tonight," Karl said, unable to comprehend what he was seeing.

"No, that's why I'm in trouble."

"Yes," Karl said after a long pause. "Yes. With the Gestapo."

"You know about that?" she asked.

"They came to visit the fire station after you left."

"Can you help me?"

"Now?" he asked. "Ursula, I would love to, really. And I will. But not now. I have a job to do."

She glanced down at the growing pool of blood around Schneider's body.

"I'm sorry," she said. "I shouldn't ask."

"Go to the fire station," Karl said. "The main door is unlocked. There is a safe room on the first floor. Wait for me there. Go now. Hurry."

My God, what have I done? he thought again as he watched her disappear into the darkness.

CHAPTER TWENTY-SEVEN

Ursula hurried away from Karl, headed towards the fire station. When she left him, he was standing over the crushed body of the young woman on his crew. Stunned, somber, or angry, she wasn't entirely sure. The weight of the revolver in her coat pocket reminded her of the deadly game she played. *I'm supposed to deliver it,* she thought, *but the Gestapo knew about the meeting. How? If I take it to the warehouse, I'll lead the police straight to the others. And one of them may have been the informant.*

She determined to head for the fire station, as Karl advised. Despite the ongoing raid, groups of people emerged from some of the buildings, holding suitcases and coats, some of them clutching a handkerchief over their mouths and noses. They dashed down the street in search of a safer public shelter as their own buildings, or those around them, burned. Flak bursts mingled with the searchlights and reminded her of a fireworks show she had seen as a girl. The only thing missing was the music, though the drone of engines and the shriek of bombs provided some accompaniment.

"Get off the street, you fools!" a young policemen yelled at the people who hurried past him without the slightest intention of obeying his instructions. "It's too dangerous to be out right now. Wait until the raid ends. It shouldn't be much longer now. They never stay long."

A sudden noise made the hair stand up on the back of her neck, and without time to think, Ursula ducked into an open doorway and curled herself into a fetal position on the ground. The pistol dug into her side. A tremendous explosion shook the ground. Dust dropped from the ceiling as she struggled to refill her lungs with air. It took several minutes, though she couldn't tell precisely how long, before she regained the ability to stand. She left the building and walked into a scene of horror.

The flickering light from dozens of fires illuminated the street. The people present appeared as shadows. None of those who had been walking around her were still on their feet. A few thrashed back and forth on the ground like fish removed from the water. Their screams were barely audible over the noise of the attack. A young woman crawled on her stomach, hands clawing at the ground, as she dragged her shattered legs behind her. A young boy sat on the pavement, gazing at the spot where his right leg had been with an amused expression on his face. A few other victims now resembled lumps of meat rather than human beings. The stench of blood, exposed intestines, and seared flesh filled the air. *There's no one to help them*, Ursula thought. *The authorities are too busy with rescues. Even those that might otherwise survive will die.* The young policeman lay on his back. A large, jagged shell splinter, still smoking, protruded from his stomach. His hands pulled at it to no avail. When he saw Ursula, he reached a hand towards her. Blood dripped off his fingertips and ran from the corner of his mouth.

"Help," he said, his voice barely above a whisper. "Help me. Can you get this out of me?"

Ursula knelt beside him and patted his hand. She kept her eyes from the shell splinter and focused on his face.

"Help's coming," she said. "The firemen are just up the street. They have an ambulance with them. They'll be here soon. You just lay back and try not to move."

"You must be a Valkyrie," he said with a pained smile, "Come to carry me away to Valhalla."

He took one more ragged breath, and then his eyes fixed on some distant point. Ursula squeezed his hand and stood up. She looked around the street. Two dogs appeared and began to lap up some of the blood. A man with a jagged stump where his right arm had been stood up and began to look around. He yelled for someone to give him his arm back. A small boy, two, maybe three years old, sat on the ground next to the body of a young woman. He tugged at her coat and wailed, "Mutti! Wake up, Mutti! "

Another group of refugees, perhaps flushed out of their cellars by the last bomb, hurried towards Ursula. An incendiary burst behind them, spraying several of them with liquid fire. The human torches screamed, a sound more animal than human, and they began to run. Some ran in circles, others straight ahead, but their movements did nothing but feed the flames. After an impossibly long time, they dropped, one by one, to the pavement and lay still. Ursula swallowed the bile which rose in the back of her throat. The companions of the burning people did not stop to help, they merely increased their speed to put as much distance between themselves and the pools of fire as they could. The façade of a building a block behind her tore away from the frame and collapsed into the street in a shower of dust which soon coated everyone around. Ursula pulled a handkerchief from her pocket and pressed it around her nose and mouth.

I must get out of here, she thought. *Quickly.* Her feet moved with a will all their own, and she resumed her dash to the fire station. She hoped the raid might keep the Gestapo from trailing her as closely as they might otherwise have been able to do. *But they knew there was a raid on and still followed me to the shop.* The bell of a fire engine clanged out from the darkness ahead of her, and she moved off the street just in time to see a dark green shape drive past her. She could barely make out the faces of the crew, boys for the most part, and scared. It seemed as if the raid had been going on for days, though in truth it had not quite been a half hour.

Ursula considered going into one of the apartment buildings and trying to get into the cellar to blend in with the occupants. She decided against it, as the residents of Berlin tended to be very particular, not to say possessive, about their cellars. Each had its own cliques and its own unwritten rules. The odds of them allowing an outsider in, even in the midst of a heavy raid, were slim. *Would we let someone into our building? No. Probably not.* Only then did she realize that the spot where she met Karl marked where her apartment had once stood. *Oh, my God! Everyone inside must be dead. Lucky for Monika and Giesela that they decided to go to the movies tonight.* In the chaos of the night and her attempt to get to the fire station to find Karl, she had not recognized the pile of brick and stone as her home. Losing her apartment did not cause her much grief. True, all her possessions now lay beneath a mound of broken brick and concrete, but the spartan existence demanded of wartime residents of Berlin had robbed

her of most of her possessions long before. *My copy of* Gone
With the Wind *is all I'll miss. I'll not be able to replace it. Not
until the war is over, if even then.*

Another ripple of explosions, this time farther behind her,
shook the street. Ursula stopped and chanced a glance over
her shoulder. She half expected to see the black official vehicle
favored by Gestapo agents approaching, or a man in a trench
coat and fedora emerge from a doorway or alley. When neither of those sights greeted her, she breathed a sigh of relief
and then continued with her journey.

If anyone is following me, she thought, *maybe the Tommies
will do me a favor and drop a bomb on top of them. They've
killed enough women and children tonight, it's about time they
kill someone worthwhile.*

"We must get to the Zoo Flak Tower," Ursula heard one
man urge the woman he was with, perhaps his wife, as the
two of them each dragged a child along by the hand. "Hurry!"

Ursula shook her head. *Does the fool not know they won't
open the doors while the raid is still going on?* Her feet ached,
as her shoes were not suitable to a mad dash through rub-
ble-strewn streets ahead of the police. She took a chance and
stopped long enough to lean against a building, remove each
shoe in turn, and rub her feet. She winced as a blister on her
right heel popped and oozed a bit of slime on her hand. *If
that's the only wound I suffer tonight, I'll be luckier than most,*
Ursula thought as she put the shoe back on and started walking again, a bit slower this time and with a slight limp as the
raw spot continued to rub on her shoe.

A police barricade blocked the intersection of Kleist
Strasse and Charlottenburger Chaussee. Ursula stopped sud-

denly. An older policeman in a baggy uniform and kindly eyes waved her forward.

"You can pass, fraulein," he said. "We're letting people out, but no one but official personnel can go in. Charlottenburg is really getting a pasting tonight. We don't want bystanders getting in the way of rescue operations. Come on. Quick."

Ursula nodded and walked around the barricade.

"Do you have somewhere to go?" the policeman called after her.

"Yes, thank you," Ursula said. "I have a friend who lives just up the way. I'm going to go there."

"If they aren't at home, try one of the public shelters. Best to be off the street tonight."

"Thank you, sir," Ursula said as she moved on, not wanting to engage a police officer in an extended conversation lest he notice the bulge in her pocket. Another series of explosions erupted ahead of her, in the direction of the Tiergarten.

"I heard the zoo got hit when the raid first started," a man beside her said. "The elephants all burned alive in their cage and some of the animals escaped. Fancy that. I'm sure they'll find their way into some cookpots by tomorrow night, eh?"

As if on cue, a zebra galloped down the street, eyes wide and nostrils flaring. The animal gave no sign of stopping and forced pedestrians to dive out of the way. A zookeeper with a tranquilizer gun ran after him, but the nimble-footed animal kept just ahead of him and out of range. Then a front hoof stepped into a small hole in the street, and the animal's leg snapped with a loud crack. It tumbled forward and lay on its side. The zookeeper hurried over and ran his hands over the leg to find the break. The older police officer who spoke to Ursula earlier walked over and pulled his pistol from his holster.

"You do it," he said as he thrust it towards the zookeeper. "I can't. I know this animal. My son loved to go and see him at the zoo. I just... I just can't do it."

The zookeeper accepted the pistol without a word, placed the barrel against the zebra's temple, just behind the eye, and pulled the trigger. Then he returned the gun.

"We could use some help, you know," he said to the policeman. "We've got animals burning up. Can't you spare anyone?"

"In case you haven't noticed, *kamerad*," the police officer said, "We've got people burning up too. I'm truly sorry for the animals, but human life comes first."

Those poor animals, Ursula thought. *The adults know why this is happening. The animals, and the children, don't.* Up ahead, the anti-aircraft batteries atop the Zoo Flak Tower sent up another barrage of shells. A bomber sprouted flames from a wing and began to stagger sideways. More shells burst around it, and the plane rolled onto its side and drifted towards the ground. A few people on the street cheered. Most continued on their way without so much as a glance upward. They did not even flinch when an explosion ripped the plane apart. *More lives gone*, she thought. *Enemy lives, but humans nonetheless. All with families that will forever wonder what happened to them in their final moments, but they'll never know, just as I'll never know how my own brothers died in the east.*

The fire station loomed ahead of her in the darkness. Ursula hurried over to the front door she'd used on her earlier visit. It was unlocked, just as Karl said it would be. She yanked it open and ducked inside. Two families sat on the floor in the center of the apparatus bay, four adults and six children. They did not bother to look up when she walked in. All six children were gathered around one of the women as she read them a story from a book, something about unicorns and fairies and a time in which men did not hurl fire upon one another from the sky. The station smelled of sweat, smoke, and exhaust fumes, but the air was more breathable than the choking smoke outside.

Ursula looked around for a place to sit but found no chairs. Her eyes found a hallway near the back of the station, and she walked over to it. In the darkness, she felt her way along the wall until she reached the room that the crews used as a bomb shelter. The Flak Sender radio inside the room barked out corrections and locations for the gunners. With the door to the room closed, the voices echoed off the brick walls. Ursula found it a curious mix of voices. None sounded scared, at least not that she could tell. The large map which took up one wall indicated hydrant locations, fire stations, police stations, searchlights, and anti-aircraft batteries. Ursula quickly discovered she could tell which units were talking on the radio if she found their letters on the map, which was divided into grids. The raid took on the nature of a football game she'd listened to on the radio once with her father, at least until a nearby bomb shook the building. Ursula closed her eyes as if the darkness might protect her. *This is like being trapped in the hold of a sinking ship*, she thought. The thick walls of the station kept most of the raid noise to a minimum, though she felt the vibration of bombs and the flak batteries through the floor.

CRUMP! A bomb exploded with a massive boom that caused the station to sway on its foundation slightly before it settled back. *The families in the bay need to be in here*, she decided.

Ursula stood and walked back into the apparatus bay. She told the family that the room down the hall was much safer, but they declined to join her. One man insisted that he could not handle the confined space of a small room.

"At least let me take the children in there," Ursula said. "They'll be safer. I promise."

Their parents repeated that they preferred to stay where they were. Ursula shrugged and returned to the room. After a few more minutes, she got up and turned the radio receiver off. She stuck her hand in her pocket and her fingers closed around the revolver. The wooden grip moistened from the dampness of her palms. She withdrew her hand and wiped it on her skirt, then she slipped her shoes off to allow her blistered feet to breathe a little. *It'll be over soon enough*, she told herself. *It never lasts that long. It seems like it does, but truthfully, they come and go very quickly.*

She wondered if Monika and Giesela managed to find their way into a public shelter when the alert sounded. *Hopefully they are safe.* Her two roommates tended to regard the raids as more excitement than anything else. Public shelters were safer than a cellar, but they filled up quickly with those caught on the streets when the alarm sounded or those who preferred them to their own shelter.

Ursula heard men's voices in the hallway. *They're back already*, she thought. *Thank God! Karl can give me some advice.* Though it was unlocked, someone rapped their knuckles on the door. She stood and walked over.

"Karl!" she exclaimed as she pulled the door open.

"Good evening, Fraulein Müller," said the man in the

trench coat. Another man pushed past her into the room. He stuck his hand into Ursula's pocket, removed the pistol, and stuck it into his own pocket. Then he grabbed her upper arm. Hard.

"I believe," the man in the trench coat said, his voice low and deliberate, "that you and I have much to talk about it."

Ursula opened her mouth to speak but no words came.

"Your fireman can't help you now," he continued. "Come along. I happen to know a nice, quiet place on Prinz Albrecht Strasse where we can chat and not be... interrupted. Shall we?"

Ursula yanked her arm away from the man and squared her shoulders. She looked the man in the trench coat in the eye and said, "I can walk without any help."

CHAPTER TWENTY-EIGHT

THE INSIDE OF the pub smelled of stale beer and cigarette smoke. A single lamp cast light over the public room. The chairs were stacked upon the tables, and the floor was still damp from where Margaret had passed a mop over it. Another light shone from the kitchen behind the bar. The smell of soup caused Grace's stomach to rumble. She glanced at Margaret to see if the older woman had heard the loud growl.

"Just have a seat at the bar," Margaret said. "I'll warm up some soup and make a few calls while you eat. You look half starved."

"It isn't as bad as that," Grace said as she put her suitcase down and sat on a barstool. "It's just that I decided to leave sort of spur of the moment and didn't take the time to eat supper."

"We'll soon put that to right," Margaret said, disappearing into the kitchen. Five minutes later she returned with a steaming bowl and a plate with some rolls. "That's all I can do on short notice, but it ought to fill you up some. You look like you need a little meat on your bones."

"Thank you," Grace said.

Margaret nodded and walked over to the phone. Grace devoted her attention to her meal and tried her best not to listen in on the phone calls, but from the few words that reached her ears, it became apparent that finding a room was a more difficult proposition than she thought. *It seems like half of England has come to this little village. There's an airbase every eight miles. Why is everyone here?* She did not relish the thought of sleeping on a bench outside in the cold, damp November air, but she determined that she would do it if Margaret could not help her. She dipped a roll into her soup and chewed on it for a long minute. Despite her hunger, the food caused her stomach to cramp. *Must be nerves*, she thought. *Sunrise will put everything to right. Just a few more hours to go now and he'll be back.*

"Right then," Margaret said after her fourth phone call, "we'll be along in a little while."

"Is there something available?" Grace asked as Margaret walked over to the bar, filled a small mug with beer, and placed it in front of her.

"You look like you need this," Margaret said. "It's on the house, so we're not breaking any laws here."

Strict wartime rules dictated when and what spirits could be served by pubs or restaurants. Beer was plentiful enough, but wartime shortages made hard liquor nearly impossible to come by unless a person had a pre-war stash. Grace's father spent the last few weeks of August in 1939 stocking his own personal cellar as he remembered how things had been during the last war. Given his fondness for drink, Grace had no doubt he'd gone through it all by now and would have to suffer along with the rest of the population for the duration.

Grace took a small sip. Her stomach protested, and she sat the mug back down. Alcohol never agreed with her much, and after her overindulgence in whiskey when she quit her job, she doubted it ever would again.

"There's a room for you," Margaret said. "An older woman a few blocks from here rents out rooms. She's been a widow since the last war. Bit of a busybody, but she includes breakfast with the price of the room. Not that she can cook as well as I can. I should have asked before. You have money to pay her?"

"I do," Grace said. "I was employed up until today. When Michael gets back this morning, we'll be married within the week. I may go back to work then, but I'll have to relocate to be near his next posting. We aren't sure where he will be."

"You said he's at the base. Is he aircrew, then?"

"He is," Grace replied. "A pilot. Michael's a Flying Officer."

"Snagged yourself an officer pilot, did you?" Margaret gave her a knowing grin. "Good show, that! During the last war, the girls around here all swooned over the pilots. We had a training base nearby, you see. Close to where the bomber base is. Oh, they'd fall in love with an officer at the drop of a hat, they would."

Grace blushed. "I didn't fall in love with him because he was an officer."

"Of course not, but it makes for a nice bonus, don't you think?"

A large grandfather clock in the corner struck ten. Each gong sounded like a funeral dirge ringing out over a crowd of mourners. Margaret walked over and switched on the radio. The newsreader ran through the headlines, all war related.

"Tonight, Bomber Command smashed Berlin," the newsreader said with gusto.

Berlin, Grace thought. *It had to be Berlin for his last mission. Of all places.*

"Is your man getting a pass or something?" Margaret asked as she turned away from the radio.

"He's got one more operation to fly to finish his tour. I saw him yesterday in London on a forty-eight-hour pass, and he thought they might be going up tonight."

"They did," Margaret said. "Maximum effort from the sound of it. I'd say every plane on the base took off in a steady stream. Loud as Gabriel's trumpet, it was. The Huns are going to get a fearful prang tonight."

The boys probably will too, Grace thought, *if they went to Berlin.* She finished her meal and took another small sip of beer. Margaret collected the dishes and returned them to the kitchen.

"I think I should probably go to the room now," Grace called after her. "I appreciate your help. I truly do. I didn't fancy sleeping on a bench outside, but I'd have done it."

"Oh, I know," Margaret replied. "I was young and in love once myself."

She nodded her head towards the ceiling.

"My Jimmy came home from the last war looking like a recruiting poster with his ribbons and medals. Fell head over heels in love with him. I was just a girl. Younger than you, I'd say. If I'd have known how loud he snores, I might have cast my net elsewhere."

Grace laughed. *I wonder if he has nightmares like Michael does. I can't ask that. Too personal.*

"Grab your suitcase and I'll walk you down," Margaret said. "It's not far."

The cool air bit at Grace's face as they left the pub. Her

eyes tried to adjust to the darkness of the blacked-out village, but she found it difficult to make out much of anything. Margaret, on the other hand, moved with the practiced skill of an insider. She took Grace's elbow to help guide her. Grace glanced up. Heavy cloud cover blanketed the night sky. Had there been any light, the base of the clouds would have reflected it earthward again, but in wartime, clouds made the night seem darker and more ominous.

"When I was a little girl," Grace said, "I was terrified of the dark."

"And now?"

"I'm not scared of the dark… I'm scared of what happens in the dark."

"Scared for your man up there?"

"Terrified," Grace admitted, "but I know he'll come back to me."

"I'm sure he will." Margaret squeezed Grace's elbow. "I'm sure he will. Look here, it's just up ahead."

They stopped in front of a two-story home on the end of a side street. It had two windows downstairs, one on each side of the door, and two more upstairs. The house sagged on its foundation and gave a slight list to the left. Margaret knocked on the door, and after a long pause, a middle-aged woman opened it just enough to peer outside, then beckoned them to enter. Grace and Margaret slipped around the blackout curtain and entered the foyer. Grace saw a dining room to her left, dishes still on the table, and a parlor on the right with a fire in the fireplace. A man in a navy uniform sat in front of it, reading the paper as smoke from his pipe curled upwards and made a blue halo above his head. Across from him, a woman sat nestled deep into an armchair, absorbed in kitting a scarf.

"Good evening, Mrs. Owen," Margaret said. "This is Grace. Grace Robinson. She's the girl in need of a room."

"So I gathered," Mrs. Owen replied.

For what seemed like the thousandth time, Grace explained why she needed a room and asked for one for at least two nights, with two more nights possible. Mrs. Owen listened patiently and then walked into the parlor. She returned with a thick, leather-bound book and a pair of scissors. Grace handed over her identity card, and Mrs. Owen recorded the information in her book, then she passed over her ration coupons.

"It isn't much, I'm afraid," she said as she handed Grace the key. "All I have available is the old maid's room. It's upstairs in the attic. A bit drafty, but there are plenty of warm blankets. Breakfast is served promptly at 7:30. I stop serving at 7:45, so be there on time or not at all. Now, you say you are waiting for your fiancé to get a bit of leave?"

Grace nodded.

"You'll not be bringing him in here," Mrs. Owen said. "I normally do not allow single women to stay here. Always throwing themselves at the airmen, they are. I'm making an exception for you since you are engaged and you're to be married soon, from what Margaret tells me. But you are not to have men in your room at all, fiancé or not. Am I understood?"

"Yes, Mrs. Owen," Grace replied. *I'm sure Michael can find a way in other than the front door.* "How much will I owe you?"

Mrs. Owen considered this for a moment and then gave her a price for two nights.

"Seems awfully expensive." Grace passed the money over.

"How badly do you want a room? I could charge double and you'd still pay it."

"Her grandfather was Scottish," Margaret said by way of explanation. "That's where she gets her business sense from."

Mrs. Owen laughed.

"I'll take my leave now," Margaret said.

"Thank you for all your help. I'd have been lost without you," Grace said.

"Good luck," Margaret said as she walked out the door.

"I have no porter to carry your suitcase," Mrs. Owen said. "You'll have to manage on your own. Everyone else is in bed except for Commander and Mrs. Bahr. If you'd like a night-cap, I believe there is some sherry in the parlor."

"No, thank you," Grace said, "but I might like to sit in front of the fire for a bit."

Mrs. Owen led her into the parlor and introduced her to the couple. Commander Bahr half rose from his chair and nodded. His wife looked up from her knitting just long enough to make eye contact and smile. Grace placed her suitcase in the corner and then sank into a chair next to the commander.

"We're here on holiday," Commander Bahr said, pointing towards his wife with the stem of his pipe. Though his eyes were bright, his face bore the lines of a man who'd spent many sleepless nights with thoughts of death. "Just came off convoy duty. Haven't had a leave in nearly eighteen months."

"I would think a village near an airbase might be a little noisy for a holiday," Grace said.

"It is at that," Commander Bahr said with a laugh. "But I'm an old navy man. A cottage by the seaside won't do for me. I've spent too much time staring at the ocean of late. No, a place in the country, airbase or not, was just the ticket I needed. Isn't that right, Norma?"

"Mmmm," his wife said without looking up.

"Gets involved in her projects, that one does," Bahr said.

"You must get dreadfully lonely out there on the ocean," Grace said.

"You get used to it. Truth is, the war makes for a more exciting cruise than peacetime ever did. Dangerous, of course, but exciting nonetheless."

"Is it as bad as the wireless lets on?" Grace asked.

"Worse," Bahr replied. "But the tide is turning. Slowly but surely. Early on, the Jerries gave us a right thrashing every time we went out. But now, our losses are going down and theirs are going up. I don't envy the men in the U-boats now. We knock them out as fast as they come off the factory line. Just like they were doing to us in 1940 and 1941. I'm lucky. I've only been sunk once, but some sailors have had three or four ships shot out from under them. I'm not sure if that counts as bad luck or good, truth be told."

Grace made a few more minutes of conversation as she allowed the heat from the fireplace to penetrate into her core, then she stood and bade the couple goodnight. With suitcase in hand, she made her way up the stairs to the second floor. Tucked away in the back corner of the hallway was a rickety staircase which led to the attic door. The key stuck in the lock for a moment before the door popped open. Grace felt around until her hand brushed against the light switch and she flipped it on. Mrs. Owen had told the truth. The room wasn't much. It contained a narrow iron-frame bed with a thin mattress and pillow, a wooden dresser with a porcelain wash basin, and a small wooden desk. The room only had one tiny window, up near the roofline, but it stayed hidden behind a thick black curtain, though with the clouds no moonlight would have entered the room anyway. The room smelled musty with a twinge of mildew. It brought to mind childhood visits to her grandmother's home in the country.

I certainly hope there are no rats, Grace thought as she placed her suitcase on the bed and opened it. The room lacked a place to hang the clothes she'd brought with her, so she laid them out across the top of the desk instead. After closing the door, she slipped out of her blouse and skirt and into her nightdress, a white cotton gown that reached to her ankles. She left the light on as she crawled into the bed, beneath the scratchy wool blankets. A clock struck the time from somewhere downstairs. *He's probably headed back by now*, she thought. *Bombs gone and making his way home to me. At least I hope so.*

She picked up her book and tried to start where she'd left off on the train. Visions of dashing young aristocratic cavalrymen filled her mind, but the image of a burning city kept drawing her in, closer and closer, until she could almost see the population fleeing hungry flames which devoured all in their path. *Am I seeing Atlanta during the American War? Or where Michael went tonight?* Growing up, her parents always said she'd had a vivid imagination. As a child, it was a blessing, but as an adult, it was a curse. *Just a few more hours*, she told herself, *and I'll hear the sound of the planes coming back and I'll know he'll be alright.*

Grace placed the book on the desk, turned out the light, and tried to sleep. She lay there in the dark with her eyes closed, but no sleep came. Her mind drifted over every memory she had of Michael, from their first meeting to their last. She saw the faces of his crew, young, eager, and scared despite their efforts to hide it from each other. As the clock struck four,

Grace heard the first drone of an approaching aircraft. The throb of the engine caused the house to vibrate a bit as it flew low overhead. *The boys are home*, she thought. *Thank God!* An hour passed, and with each minute, the sounds grew louder as more bombers felt their way home through the clouds. Some landed at Thomas Green while others flew on a few miles to the north where another squadron made its home.

Twenty or thirty minutes after the sound of the bombers stopped, with dawn's early rays beginning to peek through the window and around the curtain, Grace heard another sound. It was a bomber, but unlike the others whose engines gave a steady hum, this one flew with an almost choking noise, as if the engines were ready to quit, ground or no ground. They sputtered and coughed and grew louder as the plane flew overhead, so low that the whole house shook. Grace got out of bed and pulled the desk chair over to the wall. She climbed on it, pulled the curtain aside, and peered out the window.

CHAPTER TWENTY-NINE

"Corkscrew starboard! Now! Now!" Williams yelled.

Paddy's Wagon screamed in protest as Michael shoved the plane into a twisting dive. *Come on, old girl,* Michael said to himself, *stay together for me.* The plane responded as if she'd heard his plea and completed the difficult maneuver without breaking apart in midair. *Thank you.* Michael gripped the controls tighter to keep his hands from trembling.

"Did we shake him, mid-upper?" Michael asked as he leveled the plane.

"Think Lawton got him, skip," Williams said. "I saw a spurt of flame right before we corkscrewed. But I think he got hit too."

"Mark the position, Mac," Michael said. "Pilot to rear gunner."

After a few seconds of silence, Michael tried again. "Come on, Lawton. Answer me."

"Either he's out or the intercom is, skipper," Mac said.

"Go take a look, would you, Mac?" Michael asked.

Michael turned his attention to the sky in front of him. The controls felt stiffer than before and responded a bit slower every minute. The engines still ran, but with considerable less throb than before.

"Engines still hotter than a Glasgow whorehouse, skipper,"

Cam reported as he looked over the panel on the starboard side of the cockpit.

"Sheep can be quite warm, engineer," Williams answered.

"Keep your eyes open, mid-upper," Michael said. "I think that last fighter pass knocked out the rear turret."

"Okay, skipper," Williams answered.

A cool hand if there ever was one, Michael thought. *Too bad he's got twenty-eight more ops to go on after this one. His odds aren't good.*

"Permission to give the plane a quick look over, skipper," Cam asked. "I wanna give you a full damage assessment."

"Get to it then," Michael said. In the darkness, he felt rather than saw Cam grab a portable oxygen bottle and disappear into the nose compartment. A few minutes later, he emerged and just as quickly disappeared behind the navigator's curtain. He nearly bumped into Mac, who was making his way forward from the rear of the plane.

"Lawton's dead, skipper," Mac said as he stood alongside Michael. "Cannon shell exploded inside the turret. It's out of service. And he's pretty well nothing but paste. Fancy they'll have to wash him out with a hose."

"Thanks, Mac," Michael replied. He swallowed hard to force the lump back down his throat.

"He was a good man," Mac said. His voice shook slightly. "Damn Huns."

"Keep it together, Mac," Michael said. "We need you to get us home."

"Hold her steady for me," Mac said after a long pause. "I'm going to try and shoot a fix. Haven't done it since training. Let's see if I remember how."

The plane contained a small glass dome just aft of the cockpit which allowed Lancaster navigators to shoot a position fix at night using the stars. It was a difficult task for trained navigators, much less bomb aimers pressed into navigation duty. Though members of the crew had cross-training in other areas, it was no substitute for a person with specific skills for the job. Combat, however, called for improvisation, and crews that managed to adapt to each new deadly situation survived while the rest did not.

"Got it, skipper," Mac said after three minutes passed. "Stand by and I'll give you a new course to steer."

"Try and get us close to England, would you?"

"Oh ye of little faith."

Michael diverted his course a bit to the west to avoid a small cluster of searchlights as they swept the sky in the distance. Unlike the flight into the target, where he could feel the presence of other bombers in the sky around him, now the air felt empty, almost lonely as though Paddy's Wagon was the only plane in the sky. *With the damage, we probably are*, Michael thought. *The airspeed's dropped, and we are no doubt behind the main stream.* A few flak shells burst impotently off the starboard beam, well above the height of the plane. *Missed us, ya bastards.*

Mac called out the new course, and Michael made the necessary correction. The controls grew stiffer with each passing moment. Cam emerged from behind the curtain and walked up beside the pilot's seat. He shook his head.

"It's bad, skip," Cam said. "Nose and rear turrets out of action. We're hulled in well over a dozen places. Hydraulics are leaking. Two engines running hotter. Oh, and the Elsan's out, which pains me to no end."

"Why?" Michael asked.

"I've need of a massive poo," Cam said. "Ate too much at lunch."

"Anything you can fix?" Michael asked.

"Not at all," Cam said. "It's well beyond my humble abilities. She'll need a total refit and maybe the scrap yard."

"Still airworthy?" Michael asked.

"Aye, she'll hold up for a bit longer. Not sure how much though. Wings look a bit rough too from what I can tell."

"How are we on fuel?" Michael asked.

"Oh, we've plenty of that. The tanks aren't leaking. It isn't running out of petrol that I'm worried about. It's the two engines. If they go, you'll not be able to keep her up for long."

"You think we should bail out then?" Michael asked.

"No," Cam replied with force in his voice, "I think she'll make the Channel at least. From there, who knows. Maybe a swim. And maybe we can make it back home. I don't fancy a dip in the Channel in November."

"Me neither," Williams added from the top turret, where he'd been monitoring the intercom. "Truth be told, I can't swim. Never had much cause to learn back home."

"Bloody useless, the lot of you," Mac said. "I've been swimming since I was three."

"You grew up on a bloody island," Cam said.

"Isn't Great Britain an island too?" Mac said.

"Keep the intercom clear," Michael said. "And report any new problems. How far are we from the coast, Mac?"

"I'd say about an hour, skipper," Mac said.

"About an hour? Can you be more specific?"

"No," Mac replied.

The German-controlled coast held the last dangers from searchlight and flak batteries, but their anti-aircraft fire was usually perfunctory and posed no real danger. The more skilled crews worked in the Ruhr and around Berlin. Night fighters were a different matter. On occasion, German pilots slipped in behind the bomber stream on their return trip and pounced on weary crews as they circled the airfield, awaiting landing instructions. Given the cloud cover, Michael hoped they would be free of that threat once they crossed over the Channel. Night fighter pilots did not like to fly in heavy cloud cover and he hoped the cold, damp night would keep them close to their stoves in their dispersal huts. *We've seen too many of them already tonight*, he thought.

"Lanc to port, skipper," Williams called. "About a quarter mile out. She's losing height fast.

"Tracer fire?" Michael asked.

"No," Williams replied. "Engine trouble, I'd say."

Michael turned and caught a glimpse of the twin tail of the bomber slipping lower in the sky as if being pulled to earth by a kite string. *That'll probably be us soon enough*, he thought. He glanced down at Grace's photo. He began to wonder what she was doing at the moment before he willed himself to focus on his job. *No distractions*, he said. *Stay on top of it.*

Minutes felt like hours. Michael's arms, shoulders, and back ached as he fought to keep the plane on course. She was difficult enough to steer under optimal conditions, but with hydraulic problems and battle damage, it took every ounce of strength he had, and more, to stay aloft. A mile ahead, a few searchlights reached through the clouds. From that distance, they looked like fingers as they swept back and forth.

"Searchlights up ahead," Michael said. "Are we nearing the coast, Mac? Can't tell from the clouds."

"Should be, skipper," Mac answered. "If my calculations are correct."

"I'm going to alter course a bit to get around them," Michael said. "Give me a new heading when you can."

"Okay, skipper."

Michael altered his course a bit to the west to avoid the searchlight belt. The plane was soon free of them and, as best he could tell, out over the Channel. *Now for the hard part*, he thought. *We're clear of the Huns. Now we just have to make it home*. The last few hours of a mission took an eternity, with crews often lulled into complacency by the nearness of home.

"Mac," Michael said on the intercom, "just in case we have to set down in the drink, go ahead and start broadcasting our position every few minutes so the search and rescue boys will know where we are."

"No can do, skipper," Mac said. "I flunked the Morse code exam. That's how I ended up a bomb aimer. Harder to muck that up than the wireless."

"I can do it, skipper," Cam replied.

"You'll have to go back and forth," Michael replied. "I need you up here too."

"I'm a man of many parts," Cam said with a laugh. "Just you worry about keeping us in the air, and I'll make sure they know where we are. Assuming Mac does, that is."

"I heard that, you bastard," Mac said. "I can still open the bomb bay and toss you out to the fishes, you know."

"Okay, that's enough," Michael replied. "Go ahead and make the first broadcast, Cam."

Michael gently nudged the control column forward to begin the long, slow descent as Cam ducked behind the curtain to make the broadcast on the wireless set. *Thank God it's still working*, Michael thought. *At least we had one piece of luck tonight.* Every few seconds, he glanced down at the altimeter and watched the needle spin to the left, quicker than he would have liked. He knew the plane would not be able to climb much with the damage, so every meter lost was lost forever. Through a gap in the clouds, he caught sight of the water, a glistening black force which seemed to beckon to the plane to merge with it.

"Cam," Michael called.

"Yes, skip?"

"Make sure the IFF is on. I don't fancy getting blown out of the sky by the Royal Navy or our own coastal batteries."

"Done, skipper," Cam replied. "On my way back up."

When they dropped below ten thousand feet, Michael told the crew it was safe to come off of oxygen. He unsnapped his own mask and left it to dangle by his face so that he could still speak into the intercom.

"We'll have to feather number three," Cam said. "She's way too hot."

Michael nodded and told Cam to handle it, which he did with speed.

"How's number two?" Michael asked.

"Still hot, but not that bad."

With only three engines, the amount of time to reach home extended, though by how much Michael could not readily gauge. *Too much, I reckon*, he thought.

"You still awake up there, mid-upper?" he asked.

"I am skipper, but me arse is cramped."

"We'll get you down soon enough," Michael said.

Beads of perspiration ran down his face and dripped off his nose and chin. It formed a damp pool in his lap. Cam left to put out another distress call.

"Is anyone answering you?" Michael asked.

"No, skip," Cam replied. "They must be taking their tea or something. Useless fecks."

"We should be seeing the coast in about twenty minutes," Mac said.

"Which coast?" Williams asked.

"Up yours, you Welsh bastard," Mac answered.

"Pilot to crew," Michael said. "We've our first decision to make. I don't know how much longer we can stay in the air. We can either keep going or we can ditch as close to the coast as we can. Let's take a vote?"

The crew unanimously decided to stay in the air.

"I've got a date this evening with a tasty WAAF corporal who works in the control tower," Mac explained. "If we ditch, I won't make it back in time. I've been after her for weeks, and she only just agreed to go out with me earlier today before our check flight. Think of all the time I'll have wasted if we end up in the drink."

"A true hero," Cam said.

"Sod off," Mac replied.

"I was talking about her," Cam said. "Fancy that, agreeing to go out with an ill-bred Australian buffoon such as you. When we get back, I'll have the Wing Commander put her in for a gong."

Michael knew he should again remind them to stay off the intercom, but with the condition of the plane, not to mention three of the crew, the banter helped break the tension. *If that's what keeps them going, then so be it. It would be foolish to put a stop to it now.*

The English coast slipped beneath them and Michael breathed a sigh of relief. *Forty minutes and we're home free, assum-*

ing I can get the old girl on the ground. Engine two sputtered and then the prop slowly came to a stop.

"Guess we won't have to feather that one now," Cam said. "One less thing to do."

"Should we find the nearest airfield and put her down?" Michael asked.

The crew answered in the negative, with Mac again giving his reason for wanting to return straight to the base. Michael began to try to raise the base on the R/T. After twenty minutes and numerous attempts, a woman's voice filled his ears.

"Good morning, P for Paul."

"I've got two engines out," Michael reported. "And three dead. My hydraulics are shot to shit. We need priority clearance to land."

"You're the last to come in," she said. "You are cleared to land. Watch for the flare path. We'll have a crash truck and ambulance standing by. Good luck, P for Paul. God be with you."

"Roger," Michael replied.

"Any wounded, P for Paul?" she asked.

"Negative," Michael answered. "Just dead."

A flurry of activity filled the plane. Williams climbed out of his turret as he and Mac tried to secure any loose objects in sight lest they break free and travel forward in the event of a crash landing. From the darkness below them, Michael could make out the flares which lined the runway and pointed the way home.

"Wheels down, Cam," he said.

Cam fiddled with the lever for a few seconds.

"They're stuck, skipper. You'll have to bring her in on her belly."

"Try and lower them manually," Michael said.

"No time, skipper," Cam said. "You'd have to circle around, and I don't know that we can stay up that long."

"Pilot to crew," Michael said, "the landing gear won't lower. I can either bring her in on her belly or I can point her out to sea, get whatever altitude I can, and let you bail out first. I'm staying with the plane. I don't want to leave the bodies alone. Once you jump, I'll set her down wherever I can."

"Not on your life, skipper," Mac said. "We're a crew. We go together."

"Roger to that," Williams said. "I'm not going if you're not."

"Me neither," Cam said.

Michael felt his eyes grow damp. He glanced down at Grace's photo before he replied, "That's settled then. Assume crash positions."

He expected the crew to retreat to the crew bunk just aft of the wireless operator, but instead Mac and Williams crowded into the cockpit with he and Cam. They sat down with their backs against the port bulkhead, and Mac slipped his arm around Williams's shoulder.

"Flaps to middle," Michael said as he struggled to line the nose up with the runway. His path took him straight over a sleeping village.

"They aren't responding, skipper," Cam said.

"We're going in hard then," Michael said as he watched his airspeed. He knew he had to reduce the throttle to land, but he needed every bit of power to make it to the field and not set his plane down atop some unsuspecting civilian's house. *Damn bad show, that*, he thought. Michael eased off the throttle just enough to reduce a few miles per hour.

"No matter what, skipper," Cam said, "I'm proud to have flown with you."

Over the noise of the engines, Michael heard Williams's voice, soon joined by Cam, who took a spot on the floor next to Mac and put his hand on Mac's shoulder.

Nearer my God to thee. Nearer my God to thee.
E'en though it be a cross that raiseth me.

They continued to sing as Michael watched the ground approach. *Fast*, he thought. *Too fast.* He reduced the throttle and the number one engine coughed and then stopped. *Jesus!* Michael swore to himself. Paddy's Wagon nosed down at a sharp angle and began to accelerate. With every ounce of strength he had left, Michael heaved up on the controls. The nose lifted just a bit, but only for a moment. He glanced down and behind and saw the three men in his crew, their eyes closed, as they continued to sing.

Still all my song shall be. Nearer my God to thee.
Nearer my God to thee. Nearer to thee.

I'm sorry, boys, Michael thought as he continued to fight with the controls. With the heavy vibrations of the damaged plane, the tape holding Grace's picture to the instrument panel broke free and the photo drifted towards Michael's feet. He took one hand off the control column and tried to grab it, but he was too late. He looked back up and saw the ground as it rushed towards him. *Hail Mary, full of Grace, the Lord is with thee. Blessed art thou among women.* He did not have time to finish.

CHAPTER THIRTY

Ursula sat in a chair which wobbled slightly from side to side. She was behind a wood table, her right wrist attached to a metal loop on the chair by a pair of cold metal handcuffs. Despite the air raid, the Gestapo agents had managed to summon a car to the fire station. They bundled her into the backseat. The agent with the scarred face got in the back alongside her while his companion joined the driver in the front. Before he drove away, the driver glanced back at her and smiled. He was a squat man and resembled a fire hydrant. He had the flattened nose and hard facial features of a boxer. He gripped the steering wheel with ham-sized fists, and the car lurched away from the station into the night. When they arrived at Gestapo headquarters, the agents took her down to the basement, cuffed her to the chair, and left. She'd lost track of how long she'd been in the room. *That's probably the point of it*, Ursula thought. *I guess I'm about to find out if all of that is true.*

The room smelled of urine and fear. A single bulb hung from the ceiling in the center of the room and provided just enough light to cast shadows on the wall. Dampness chilled the room, and Ursula shivered as goosebumps erupted from her arms. When they brought her into the room, the agents confiscated her coat, and her thin dress provided little warmth. Occasional screams and angry shouts penetrated the tomb-like silence. *Not even an air raid can stop their interrogations*, she thought. On the drive to Prinz Albrecht Strasse, the bombers left, though whether or not they'd return was anyone's guess. Sometimes the British sent multiple waves as much as an hour apart in an attempt to lull the population into a false sense of security; thus when the next wave hit, their bombs caught rescue personnel out in the open and massacred them. *Karl... I've put him in danger. They'll get him too. Fireman or no fireman. That won't matter to them, and it won't save him. What have I done? I chose to risk my life, but I had no right to risk his. But he was a soldier once, so maybe he will understand.*

She watched as a cockroach crawled up the leg of the table and paused, a foot in front of her. Its antennas swept back and forth as it seemed to consider what her presence meant to its own existence. As if satisfied she meant no harm, the roach turned and crawled down the opposite table leg, crossed the floor, and took up a position on the wall. Ursula jumped when she heard the sound of heavy footsteps from the hallway, but they continued on past her door. She heard the jingle of keys as they entered the room next to hers, followed by shouts and the sound of a person being slapped around. *Is that someone from the warehouse? I imagine they lifted the lot of us. Unless... unless someone in the group was an informant.* Ursula tried to picture each member individually and thought of her interactions with them to find something, anything, that should have indicated they worked for the Gestapo, but her mind failed to turn up suspicions of any of them. *They seemed more concerned that I was the informant*, she thought, *as if I'd spend any time at all around those thugs in their trench coats and fedoras.*

Twenty minutes passed as slowly as twenty hours, and then the door opened. The scarred agent walked in, followed by the man who'd driven the car. The driver crossed the room and stood behind her chair, so close that she smelled his perspiration. The scarred agent closed the door and sat down across the table from her. With slow, deliberate movements, he produced a pack of cigarettes, put one in his mouth, and lit it. He exhaled and blew the smoke across the table towards her face. A full minute went by before he spoke.

"My apologies," he said. "How rude of me. Would you care for a cigarette? I think you'll find this brand to your taste. They are American. My brother is in the Luftwaffe and took them from a downed American pilot. Take the pack if you'd like."

Ursula declined with a shake of the head.

"My name is Schiller," he said. "I've been following you for quite some time. It's nice to finally get a chance to meet, yes?"

Ursula did not reply. Schiller opened the folder he carried with him and took a pen from the inside pocket of his coat.

"I must ask you some questions," he said. "Mostly routine background information. Let's start with your name, address, and occupation."

Ursula gave him the answers, and he scribbled them on a sheet of paper.

"And your parents? Their names and address?"

"They are both dead," Ursula said. "Before the war."

"My sympathies," Schiller said. "And how about the names of the people you live with?"

Ursula considered insisting that she lived alone, but gave Monika and Gisela's names anyway.

"Excellent," Schiller said. He drew the word out and made it sound as if it had five syllables. "Now, onto the reason for our meeting tonight. Who were you planning on shooting with the pistol, Fraulein Müller?"

"No one," Ursula said.

Schiller sighed and shook his head.

"If you are honest with me, I can assure you it will go much easier for you. Sure, a prison sentence or perhaps a stint in a labor camp, but you'll be given the opportunity to show your dedication to National Socialism and earn your release. If you lie or withhold information, well, let's just say it will go much harder on you. I would regret that very much. I'm sure you understand. I'm just here to do my job. I bear you no ill will and would hate to resort to more extreme measures. I truly would."

As if on cue, the driver reached out and placed his hands on both her shoulders. He squeezed them, hard, for a moment and then let go. *He's the muscle*, Ursula thought. *Schiller must not want to get his hands dirty.*

"I know who you were working with," Schiller said. "The individual who gave you the gun was well known to us already."

"Was?" Ursula could not stop herself from asking.

"He was shot while attempting to escape," Schiller said, stubbing out his cigarette and lighting another. "Most unfortunate. It happens more often than you might think. Some people have no respect for authority these days."

"I'd never seen him before tonight," Ursula said.

"We doubt that very much," Schiller said. "Your associates are here too. The people you met with in the warehouse. Some of them have proven to be most cooperative. They say you were the leader of their group and set the whole thing up. No doubt you were influenced by your father's politics."

"I led nothing," Ursula protested. "They are lying."

Ursula's head snapped sideways, ears ringing and eyes blurring as the driver slapped the side of her head. She bit her lip and felt blood well up inside her mouth.

"Don't make us question you more urgently," Schiller said. "Let's talk as friends."

"We'll never be friends," Ursula said, "and I have nothing to say. You know what I was doing and what I did. So why the questions? If you truly have the entire group under arrest, then there isn't much for me to add that you don't already know."

"Oh, but there is plenty," Schiller said. "Who were you going to shoot? Who were you getting your directions from. Yes, we have much to talk about."

"I wasn't going to shoot anyone," Ursula said, "and I was not in charge. I have no idea who was giving directions. I just served as a courier. That's all."

"Would you care to hear my theory?" Schiller asked. Ursula shrugged and he continued, "I believe that fireman friend of yours is the mastermind of your little group. He has the perfect cover. A decorated veteran, who works for the government. Few would suspect him of anything. Perhaps we should bring him in too."

"He has nothing to do with this," Ursula said. "I just met him the other day."

Schiller focused his attention on the folder in front of him and shuffled a few papers. Every so often, he pulled one out and read over it before he stuffed it back inside. Ten minutes passed before he spoke again.

"You know, Fraulein Müller," he said, "that we have other ways of making people talk. I decided to give you the opportunity to be honest with me, but you are proving to be a bit too headstrong for my liking. I've always been told that was the case with redheads like you. Perhaps we should move down the hall? There is another room that contains some instruments which we find most useful. Maybe a little electricity to, shall we say, stimulate the conversation? Or perhaps a pair of pliers might convince you to talk."

"I cannot tell you what I don't know," Ursula said.

"It's sad, really," Schiller said as he gathered up the papers and put them back into the folder, closing it slowly. "Such a waste. A pretty girl like you should be working to help secure Final Victory, not involved with anti-government agitators bent on helping our enemies win. Is that what you want? To live under the Bolsheviks?"

"I'm a loyal German," Ursula said. "The old Germany. The real Germany. Not what your people have made it. My brothers died for the Fatherland."

"And what would they say about you being in the basement of Gestapo headquarters? As to being loyal, well, loyal people don't find themselves here. We deal with traitorous elements from within our own society. Berlin is full of such people these days. Defeatists, communists, Jews in hiding. It's my job to ferret them all out into the open so we can crush them."

"I'd think a patriotic person such as yourself would want to serve at the front," Ursula said with a slight smile.

"Duty demands different things from different people. I

am worth far more here, doing my job, than I would be freezing my ass off in Russia. Or picking grapes in Italy."

Schiller rose suddenly and walked to the door. He stuck his head out the doorway and called for someone named Friedrich. When the man appeared, Schiller whispered a few words to him, too low for Ursula to hear. The man nodded and walked away. Schiller shut the door and returned to the table. He sat down in his chair and gave her an almost friendly smile.

"I've just given word for your boyfriend to be picked up and brought here," he said.

"Boyfriend?" Ursula asked. "I have no boyfriend."

"Your playing dumb is wearing on my nerves," Schiller said with a sigh, "You know exactly who I mean. Your fireman."

"I've told you he's not involved," Ursula protested. "I just met him. And besides, there's a raid on. Not that you seem to care how many people have died tonight."

"Defeatist talk," Schiller said. "Your attitude has been duly noted."

Ursula placed her free hand flat on the table and leaned forward in her chair.

"All I know is what I have told you. I was asked to pick up and deliver a revolver, which I did. Or rather, I picked it up. You know from whom and you know who I was bringing it to. I don't know why or what it was to be used for. You'll have to get that from the others. Now, either charge me with something or let me go."

Schiller laughed, a sharp, jilting sound.

"That's not how it works," he said. "This is the last chance I'm going to give you. If you fail to cooperate, it'll be Plötzensee Prison and the guillotine or a bullet in the courtyard. Either one would be a shame for such a pretty girl as you. I'd hate to have to see your head severed from your body. Now please, Fraulein Müller, please cooperate."

The thought of the guillotine turned her stomach, but Ursula had nothing else to tell him. *I've said everything I know,* she thought. *I don't even know the names of the others, nor what they planned to do. How can I convince him? No, it's no use. He's made up his mind.*

"You've nothing more to say?" Schiller asked.

"I've told you all I know," Ursula insisted.

Schiller gave a nod to the driver, who had kept his post behind her chair. He leaned down and unfastened the handcuff from the arm of the chair. For a moment, she thought Schiller intended to free her. When the driver hauled her to her feet and pulled her other wrist behind her, she realized how wrong she was.

"Follow me," Schiller said as he walked out of the room. Ursula did not have much of a chance to follow under her own power, as the driver seized her arm and dragged her along the corridor. They stopped outside a steel door at the end of the hallway. Schiller fumbled in his pocket for a key and opened it. As the driver dragged her into the room, Ursula gasped. A metal frame on the opposite wall greeted her, a set of steel restraints in each corner of the frame. Two cables were clamped onto the frame as well, and she followed the lines back to a battery on the floor. A few feet in front of the frame sat a wooden chair with restraints on the arms and legs. A table next to it contained hideous-looking instruments with dried blood on them. An open drain on the floor in front of the chair served as a means to catch the blood.

"What should we start with, boss?" the driver asked, his voice eager.

"Just stick her in the chair for now," Schiller said.

Rather than strapping her to the chair, the driver just pushed her down into it and left the room with Schiller. *What now?* Ursula thought. *Should I make up a story? No. He'd figure that out quickly. Surely they'll believe me if they've talked to the others. They have to. But what about Karl? Are they really going to pick him up tonight? Or tomorrow? If he's still alive.*

The door was flung open and Schiller, followed by the driver, stormed in. Schiller walked up to her, grabbed a fistful of her hair and tilted her head backwards. He put his face close to hers. His breath reeked of pickled herring and champagne.

"Tell me the truth! Now!" he screamed.

"I can't tell you what I don't know," Ursula gasped as she tried to twist her face away.

Schiller strengthened the grip on her hair in response. "You talk, or I'll leave you in here with Gunther."

From over his shoulder, she saw the driver smile and lick his lips. Ursula made no reply.

"Gunther, I'd start with the electricity if I were you."

"My thoughts exactly, boss," Gunther snarled.

Schiller stepped aside, and Gunther advanced on her with a wolfish grin. A rap on the door brought him up short.

"What is it?" Schiller yelled over his shoulder. The door opened and a spectacled face appeared.

"I need a word," the man said. Schiller swore and walked out into the hallway. A few minutes later, he came back into the room and looked at Gunther.

"The other girl in their group talked. We've gotten who they were working for. Apparently, Fraulein Müller really doesn't know much other than who she picked up the documents and pistol from, which we already know."

"So I can leave?" Ursula asked, though she knew the answer.

Schiller answered with a laugh and Gunther joined in, his hands clutching his sides as they shook.

"No," Schiller said. "You made your decision to betray your country. Now you will suffer the consequences. Come on. Stand up."

Ursula got to her feet and Gunther grabbed her arm.

"To the courtyard," Schiller said. Gunther nodded and pulled Ursula down the hallway and then up a short set of stairs. The early rays of the sun made an attempt to penetrate the cloud cover as they walked outside. The air smelled of smoke and a faint whiff of gas. Across the courtyard, in front of a wall made of sandbags, Ursula caught a glimpse of the woman from the warehouse. Like Ursula, her hands were cuffed behind her. A group of soldiers stood in a cluster a dozen feet away.

My God, Ursula thought. She felt her bowels turn to water. Her knees began to shake. Gunther tightened his grip on her arm to keep her from falling. He released her arm when they reached the wall. Then he shoved her forward. Ursula stumbled into the other young woman but managed to stay on her feet.

"Where are the others?" Ursula whispered.

"Dead," the woman said.

"I told them nothing," Ursula said.

"I know. You didn't know anything worth telling. Makes no difference now."

Ursula turned and saw Schiller appraising them with his

arms folded across his chest, his face tight and mouth drawn into a frown. A uniformed officer walked over and gave a short order to the soldiers, who drew themselves into a double line facing Ursula and the other woman.

"I guess this is the end," the other woman said. "All for nothing."

"No," Ursula said. "Not for nothing. For Germany."

CHAPTER THIRTY-ONE

KARL, FISCHER, AND the three remaining women auxiliaries stood over Schneider's body. Karl reached up and removed his helmet. He tucked it under his arm and then ran the back of his left hand across his eyes, which stung from smoke and emotion. Koch sobbed softly, her tears smearing the dust on her face.

"I thought it was safe enough," Karl said. "I would not have sent her in otherwise." But he knew that was a lie. *You let your concern for a woman you've just met cause the death of an innocent girl.*

"It probably would have been," Fischer said, "had more bombs not come down. Listen. I think the raid is over now. We can work without being blasted to splinters."

Karl concentrated for a moment as his ears adjusted to the sudden emptiness in the sky. The air still rang with the sound of hungry flames, collapsing walls, and screams, but the steady drone of aircraft and flak was gone.

"They may come back," he replied.

"I don't think so," Fischer said. "As hard as they hit us, I doubt they have enough aircraft in reserve for a second strike."

"We won't be able to help the ones in this basement," Karl said. "Go ahead and mark it, will you?"

Fischer produced a piece of chalk from his pocket and

scrawled a message on the brick just above Schneider's body to alert other rescue workers that people were trapped, and most likely dead, inside. Later, in the daylight, crews made up of political prisoners or prisoners of war would come along to collect the remains. In cellars filled with charred corpses, soldiers sometimes employed flame throwers to finish cremating the remains before they were scooped up for disposal.

"Should we try and get her out?" Fischer asked as he turned back to face the group.

"I don't think we can," Karl said. He walked over to the fire truck and removed a tarp, then he gently spread it over Schneider's torso and weighted the ends of it down with bricks. He glanced across the street and saw Baumann making his way towards him, his entire crew minus the shell-shocked Hitler Youth boy in tow. Dirt streaked the boys' faces, and they all had a certain hollow look in the eyes, a look Karl had seen countless times. *They are veterans now*, Karl thought. *They know the score. Poor kids. They didn't realize it would be like this.*

"We pulled three live ones out," Baumann reported. "They say the rest are dead."

"Good work," Karl said. "Let's move on down the block a bit. Fischer, tell the Luftwaffe crew and the Ukrainians what we are doing and ask them to come along."

Karl put his helmet back onto his head and led his mixed bag of firefighters and recruits down the street. For the first time, he had a moment to consider what had happened just after Schneider died. *Ursula's in trouble*, he thought. *Trouble enough that she asked me for help in the middle of a raid, and I couldn't give it to her. She'll be safe enough at the station until later, though it might be a day or two before I can get back. Surely she can take care of herself until then. Even the Gestapo has to get off the streets when a raid is on, don't they?* He stumbled and nearly fell as his right foot caught a piece of concrete in the middle of the street. Some buildings still stood in defiance of the bombs. Others had their facades ripped away, exposing the lives of the occupants to all who passed by, while some had collapsed completely. Fires burned inside several of the buildings. Karl thought about having the trucks moved, but with little water pressure, the hoses would be no more effective than a garden hose. *We might as well piss on the fires to try and put them out for all the good we'd do.*

A group of dazed civilians sat huddled around the entrance to an apartment building. Karl walked over to them and knelt down.

"You need to get moving," he said. "Can you walk out of here? Head towards the Tiergarten. I'm sure there is something set up near there already to get you sorted out."

An elderly man slowly turned to look at Karl. Over the man's shoulder, Karl caught sight of a young girl. She lay on her back with her head in a woman's lap.

"My granddaughter," the man said. "Look, her leg is badly broken. She can't walk."

Karl studied the group. An elderly man and woman and two younger women he judged to be in their mid-twenties, and the girl, eight or nine years old.

"Is she in any pain?" Karl asked.

The girl moaned as if she'd heard the question and squeezed the hand of the woman who held her.

"What do you think, fireman?" the man asked. "Surely you have a bit of morphine you can give her."

"I do not," Karl confessed. "But I may be able to get her some. Just a moment."

Karl walked over to the group of Luftwaffe fire personnel. One of them carried a first aid kit, and Karl returned to the civilians with a syringe of morphine. He handed it to the old man.

"Here," Karl said. "Just stick this in her arm and push the plunger down. It's a healthy dose and will probably put her to sleep for several hours. During that time, I'd advise you to find a way out of here. And move her while she is unconscious."

"Thank you," the man said.

"Over here, Karl!" Fischer shouted as Karl stood up.

Karl looked and saw Fischer, Baumann, and Frei gathered around the front of an undamaged building.

"What is it?" Karl asked as he approached them.

"Their cellar door is locked," Fischer said. "I stepped in and had a look. I can't hear anyone inside, but I'm sure people are in there. Let's get them out."

"Right," Karl said. With his flashlight beam to guide him, Karl made his way into the darkened lobby. He found the cellar door just behind the staircase. He pushed on it, but it did not give. Karl handed Fischer his flashlight and then took several whacks on the door with his fire axe. It splintered and gave way after the third swing. He took his flashlight back and stepped through the door frame.

"Fire Brigade!" he yelled. "Can anyone hear me?"

Silence greeted him as he made his way down the steps, with Fischer close on his heels. Karl's flashlight beam caught the first face – a young woman who looked as though she were asleep with a small baby in her lap. Neither of them moved. Karl shone the beam around the room and saw a dozen other faces. The people sat on benches with their backs pressed against the walls. A few of them had their heads titled back, a few others forward. All looked sound asleep. If not for the rosy cheeks they all had, Karl would not have known they were dead.

"Carbon monoxide," Karl said over his shoulder. "All dead."

"Let's get out of here," Fischer said. "It's giving me a headache."

They walked back out to the street and Fischer chalked "13 Tot" on the wall. *Damn*, Karl swore under his breath, *they never even had a chance. All they had to do was open the door and get some fresh air in, but that might have drawn the fire in too. Those poor bastards.*

"Is there anyone to save?" asked Hartmann, "Or is the whole city dead except us?"

"There's people alive," Karl said. "We just have to find them and tell them to get out of the area. It's too dangerous to stay here, but a lot of people don't want to leave their possessions or their apartments behind, or what's left of either of them. You can't blame them. When they walk away, they know they'll not be back. Sometimes I wonder if the government understands what it is asking people to endure."

"Of course it does," one of the Hitler Youth boys replied. "And the Fuhrer appreciates the sacrifices made by the German people on behalf of the Fatherland."

"Shut up," Frei snapped, and the boy fell silent.

"What did your friend want?" Fischer asked as they moved down the street. "I thought I heard her say something about needing help."

"She did, but she didn't elaborate. I sent her to wait at the station."

"Let's hope it isn't police trouble," Fischer said. "They won't be in a happy mood after tonight."

"Are they ever?" Karl asked.

A small fire burned on the ground floor of the next building. Karl took a bucket of sand from Hartmann and walked inside. He grabbed a few handfuls and tossed it onto the fire to no effect. Frustrated, he dumped the entire bucket onto the flames and watched as they sputtered out. He walked over to the cellar door and pushed it open. Voices drifted from the darkness below.

"Fire Brigade!" Karl shouted. "Everybody out. The building isn't safe. Best to head out of the neighborhood quickly. Watch your step on the way up."

Twenty people filed up the stairs, past Karl, and out the door. None looked him in the eye. They clutched suitcases, coats, and handbags. Their faces bore the same stunned expression he'd seen on the faces of soldiers on the front lines in Russia. *Their bodies are responding,* he thought, *but their brains can't process what they've just been through.* Outside, Frei gave them directions on the clearest route to take and the line shuffled away into the darkness.

"If the Tommies keep this up, we'll be out of rooms in the city before the year is out," Fischer said.

"I think that might be the point," Karl said. "Workers can't do their jobs if they don't have a place to stay. Rather than destroy the factories, they destroy the homes. There's a certain cruel logic to that."

"There is," Fischer said. "Bastards."

The crews moved off down the street and stopped outside of a building where fire burned on the top three floors. Only the ground floor remained free of the flames.

"Come on," Karl said as he led his crew inside. Heavy smoke conditions forced him to don his gas mask. It helped him breathe, but obscured his vision at the same time. Fischer found the cellar door and yelled down for the occupants to get out. Four people emerged, likewise wearing their gas masks. Like creatures from a horror movie, they left the building and moved off down the street. Karl followed them outside and pulled his mask off.

"Should we try and stop the fire?" Fischer asked. "At least we could keep it from spreading."

"With the people out of the building," Karl said, "there is no need. If we try to fight every fire burning tonight, we'll be busy for ten years. They'll have to burn themselves out eventually. Life, Fischer, is what's important now."

"Ours or theirs?" Fischer asked with a laugh.

"We're expendable. The city isn't," Karl said. "We're firemen. We die so others may live."

Across the street, lit by the flickering orange glow of the flames, Karl watched as Frei, Baumann, and their Hitler Youth volunteers led a group of elderly people out of another apartment building. Frei clutched a small dog, which he handed to a gray-haired woman once they reached the street. She gave him a nod of thanks as Frei wiped his hands on his pants. Some of the Hitler Youth boys held suitcases, which they returned to the owners before the line of people moved away.

"What a night," Fischer said. "Is this the heaviest we've been hit?"

"To be honest, the raids all run together in my mind," Karl replied. "But I think this one will stand out."

"Still nothing like Hamburg," Fischer said.

"We can count our lucky stars for that," Karl said. "And the government can thank us for being the best Fire Brigade in the Reich."

The two men watched as a car pulled up alongside the curb

across from where they stood. Two men in leather trench coats and fedoras pulled low over their faces got out. One stayed with the car while the other approached Karl and Fischer.

"What's the meaning of this?" Fischer asked as the man got close.

Gestapo, Karl thought with alarm. *Maybe this is what Ursula was talking about when she said she was in trouble. But what are they doing out in the middle of an air raid?*

The man dodged a line of refugees and walked up to Karl and Fischer.

"Oberwachtmeister Weber?" the man asked as he extended his right hand. Karl caught sight of the warrant disc the man held with the words *Geheime Staatspolizei* stamped on it.

"The Gestapo has decided to pitch in and help with cleanup?" Karl asked. "What's this world coming to?"

"Are you Weber?" the man asked again, his voice flat and emotionless.

"I am Oberwachtmeister Karl Weber, yes," Karl replied. "And who do I have the pleasure of speaking to?"

"My name is not important," the Gestapo man said. "You are to come with us right away."

"Not possible," Karl said. "As you can see, we are a little busy here."

"That wasn't a request," the Gestapo man said.

Fischer stepped close to the man as Frei and Baumann hurried over from across the street.

"The Oberwachtmeister told you he cannot go with you now," Fischer said as he pointed a finger at the man's chest. "I'm sure he will be happy to report to Prinz Albrecht Strasse when his work here is done. Isn't that right?"

"It is," Karl lied. *I have nothing to tell them other than I know Ursula. What in the devil was she involved in? Whatever it was, it was important enough to get the Gestapo out during a raid. But you cannot convince them that you don't know anything. They just manage to persuade you to say something, anything, before they whisk you off to a labor camp or worse. I'd sooner go underground than go visit those gorillas.*

"I have my orders," the Gestapo man said, his eyes darting back and forth between the faces of Karl and his fellow firefighters.

"And I have mine," Karl replied. "Do you forget that we too are under the control of the police? We report to the Security Office, just the same as you. Your commander does not supersede the authority of mine. Now, if you'll excuse us."

Karl turned away, and the man reached out to grab his arm. Fischer's hand shot forward and closed around the Gestapo man's wrist.

"Assaulting a firefighter in the performance of his duties," Fischer said, gripping the man's wrist as hard as he could. "After an air raid, no less. I'd say we could have your little tin badge for that, you sawed-off pig."

"Let go of my wrist," the man said, "or it will go hard on you."

"Hard on all of us," Baumann said as he stepped forward, along with Frei. "We are a crew. What concerns one of us concerns all of us. Is that clear enough for you? If you persist in this, I'd suggest you go get some more men. You'll need them. We've all seen service at the front in this war or the last, unlike you lot."

"Be reasonable," the man said. "All we want to do is ask a few questions. It is routine, I assure you."

"If it is routine," Karl said, "you would stop by the station tomorrow rather than track me down in the midst of a raid. How stupid do you think I am?"

Karl glanced up and watched the upper floors of the apartment as they continued to burn. *Ursula... I hope she's okay. Maybe she's evaded them and that's why they want me. They want to know where she's gone. No, they aren't stupid. They would know to check the fire station.* The thought of her in the clutches of the Gestapo turned his stomach in a way not even the worst sights he'd seen during the war ever had. *If they have her, she is as good as dead. Just as dead as Schneider. Jesus! I killed Schneider tonight, and I can't save Ursula. How much more am I expected to have on my conscience? I bring nothing but death and misery to those around me.*

"Is there a problem?" The second Gestapo agent had crossed the street to stand next to his colleague.

"Oh," Frei said, "here's your girlfriend. I rather doubt he'll be much use to you in a fight. He looks like the runt in a litter of puppies – not that you are much bigger, eh?"

A sudden cracking sound echoed from overhead. Everyone froze, their eyes searching the sky. As if in slow motion, the façade of the burning apartment building began to crumble. The bricks started their descent towards the ground.

"Move!" Karl shouted.

The other three firefighters turned and ran up the street, but the Gestapo agents remained rooted to the spot as if paralyzed.

"Move!" Karl yelled again as he reached out and shoved them, his hands breaking them out of their trance. They turned and ran as well. Karl looked up at the waterfall of bricks tumbling towards him and smiled. *Now I'm finally free.*

CHAPTER THIRTY-TWO

GRACE DRESSED IN the pale gray light of the dawn, the image of the crippled Lancaster flying low overhead still fresh in her mind. She glanced at her watch as she stood in front of the wash basin. 6:30. *Too early for breakfast,* she thought. *But I rather doubt I can eat anything.* Before she left the room, Grace slipped the watch she'd bought for Michael into her handbag. The stairs creaked under her feet as she made her way down the stairs. The sound of pans clanging drew her into the kitchen, where she found Mrs. Owen standing over the oven. Sweat glistened on her brow as she looked over at Grace.

"It's a bit early for breakfast," she said, "but the kettle's on and the tea should be ready if you'd like some."

"I would," Grace said. She watched as Mrs. Owen poured the dark brown liquid into a white mug with stains on the handle.

"Go on to the parlor," Mrs. Owen said. "I'll call you when it is time to eat."

"I was wondering if I might ask for a favor," Grace said hesitantly.

"Yes?"

"Could I perhaps use your telephone? You see, my fiancé doesn't know I'm here, and he said he would call my apartment when he got back to let me know that he is okay. My roommate should be there, and I want to check in with her to make sure he's called."

"The phone is in the hallway," Mrs. Owen said. As Grace started out of the kitchen, Mrs. Sterling call after her. "Keep your conversation short!"

"I will," Grace promised. She found the phone on a table adjacent to the entrance to the parlor. She picked it up and asked the operator to connect her to her apartment. After a few seconds, the line began to ring. No one answered. Grace placed the phone back into its cradle. *Helen must not be home*, she thought. *What if Michael's tried to call and got no answer? How will he know where to find me? Damn you, Helen! I thought you'd be there!*

The rational part of Grace's mind told her that, given how she'd parted with her roommate, it was unreasonable to expect her to serve as a secretary and relay messages. Still, despite Helen's desire to dance and go on as many dates as possible, she usually managed to make it home before dawn, though not always. *Where is she?* Grace thought. *I doubt she got up and left for work this early. She must have gone home with someone last night. Another one of our friends, no doubt.* Grace carried her mug of tea into the parlor and sat in front of the fireplace. A few minutes later, Commander Bahr joined her.

"I was planning to sleep in a bit this morning," he confessed as he sank into a chair, "but I heard the most frightful prang over at the airbase. Woke me up. Did you hear it?"

"Yes," Grace said. "I was looking out the window and saw a plane that appeared to be in trouble fly over very low. Then I heard a crash."

"Dreadful business, that," Commander Bahr said. "My

wife didn't hear a thing. She's still asleep. Gabriel could blow his trumpet right now and she'd sleep through it. I doubt she'll even be up in time for breakfast."

"Have you been married long?" Grace asked as she sipped her tea.

"Ten years," Bahr said. "We got married right after I got my commission. We've spent much of the time apart with me being at sea, but we did get to spend a lovely year together in Gibraltar when I had a shore posting. That was in '38. Peacetime. Odd, but I hardly remember what it was like to not be at war."

"I know what you mean," Grace said. "Do you think the war will be over soon?"

"I don't," Bahr said. "At least not for a few more years. When the Yanks along with our boys are finally able to land in France, well, that'll wrap things up for sure. But until then, all we can do is tread water. The Russians are doing their bit too and chewing up the Germans. Every Jerry they kill is one less for our boys to worry about. Last night you said you had a fiancé in Bomber Command?"

"Yes," Grace said as she stared at the fire.

"Did he fly last night?"

"I believe so," she said. "He said he'd call to let me know he got home safely, but there's no one at my apartment and he doesn't know I'm here."

"What are you going to do?" Bahr asked.

"I was considering going to the base after breakfast," Grace said.

"They won't let you on the base," Bahr said, "but maybe they could get a message to him. How were you planning on getting there?"

"I was going to walk. They say it's only a mile or so up the road."

"I've a better idea – I'll run you up there myself."

"Oh, you don't need to trouble yourself. I don't mind walking. Really."

"Nonsense," Bahr replied. "It's the least I can do, and it'll give me something to do with my time while I wait for my wife to wake up. Besides, I'm certain that your fiancé would do the same for my wife if our roles were reversed. I've met a few of the bomber boys, and they are dreadfully nice chaps."

"He hoped to fly Spitfires," Grace said, "but they needed bomber pilots more."

"Every pilot wants to fly Spitfires, even some of the Yanks have told me as much. Lovely plane, the Spit."

"I've not seen one up close," Grace said. "During the Battle of Britain, we'd see contrails overhead, and I saw a few German bombers caught in the searchlights, but I've never been up close to one of our own planes."

"Ask your fiancé. I'm sure he could figure out a way to sneak you onto the base and maybe even take you up in his bomber. I hear a few crews have given the occasional WAAF an unauthorized ride."

"I'm not sure I'd like that much. Too dangerous for my liking. I'll leave the flying to Michael."

"Breakfast is ready," Mrs. Owen called from the dining room. Commander Bahr stood and allowed Grace to walk ahead of him. They found a plate of eggs, rolls, and a single piece of bacon at each seat at the table.

"Sorry there isn't more bacon," Mrs. Owen said. "I had the devil's own time getting any."

"Where'd you manage to find it?" Commander Bahr asked.

"Best I keep that to myself," Mrs. Owen said. "It wasn't exactly legal."

"Everyone uses the black market these days," Grace said. "No shame in that."

She nibbled at a forkful of runny eggs and then took a small bite of her breakfast roll. It did not sit well in her stomach, and Grace spent the rest of breakfast pushing food around her plate with her fork and not eating any.

"Not hungry?" Commander Bahr asked with a raised eyebrow.

"Not terribly," Grace said. "Nerves, I think."

"Understandable. I suppose you are anxious to get out to the base to find out about your man."

"That's right," Grace said.

"Pass your plate to me and I'll finish it for you, then we can be on our way," Bahr said.

Grace slid her plate across the table. She watched as Commander Bahr shoveled food into his mouth as quickly as he could. Once the plate was empty, he drained his cup of tea in one long swallow. Mrs. Owen came back into the room and placed a cold cup of milk in front of each of them. Bahr drank his as quickly as he'd drank his tea. Grace managed to swallow about half of her cup before her stomach issued a stern warning in the form of a severe cramp. She rubbed her abdomen with her right hand for a moment and the cramp subsided.

"Are you sure you aren't ill?" Bahr asked, studying her face.

"Quite," Grace said. "I've just got a nervous stomach this morning. It'll pass soon enough. Once I see Michael."

"Grab your coat and we'll be off," Commander Bahr said as he pushed his chair back from the table and stood up.

Grace walked over to the coat rack near the door and slipped into her red overcoat. The Commander put a heavy dark blue coat over his uniform and grabbed his hat.

"Mrs. Owen," he called over his shoulder.

"Yes?" came the reply from the kitchen.

"If my wife comes down before I return, would you be so kind as to tell her I've stepped out for a few minutes. I shan't be gone too long. I'm going to drop Grace off at the base and then see if the bookstore in town is open. I've a need for some new volumes to take with me when I return to my ship."

"I'll tell her," Mrs. Owen promised. "I hope she comes down before breakfast gets cold."

Commander Bahr led Grace outside and around the corner to a black sedan. He opened the door for her, and she got into the front seat. He walked around and got behind the wheel. Bahr produced a pack of cigarettes and offered her one. Grace declined with a shake of the head.

"Do you mind if I..." he asked.

"Go ahead," she said.

Bahr stuck a cigarette in his mouth and lit it with a match before he started the car.

"I always find a smoke after breakfast aids with the digestion," he said, pulling the car away from the curb. "What do you plan to do when you get to the base?"

"Ask if they can get a message to him," Grace said. "I know they won't let me on the base, but I'm sure they could pass a message along."

"Perhaps," Bahr said. "I'm not sure how secretive they are

about their personnel, but seeing as how they have the run of the village, I think it won't be a problem."

Grace nodded and looked out the window. The village passed by, most of the houses appearing still in the early morning. The houses disappeared as the road crossed over a narrow bridge. A thin layer of fog clung to the empty meadows. The air felt damp, and the faint odor of motor oil floated on the breeze. A few cows grazed lazily along the side of the road behind a low stone wall. The scene reminded Grace of her home. *Father always liked living in the country*, she thought. *It's got the best air and is good for the constitution, he said. I wonder what he would have done if they'd commandeered his property and dropped an airfield on it. No doubt he'd protest all the way to Parliament or the King if he could get away with it.*

"Nice morning, this," Bahr said. "I fancy retiring to the countryside when the war is over. Maybe doing a bit of teaching."

"I grew up in the country," Grace said. "I found it dreadfully boring as a child."

"And now?"

"The silence appeals to me," she said. "Especially after living in London for three years. All the hustle and bustle of the crowds and everyone rushing around like mad has a way of grating on the nerves."

"That it does," Bahr said with a chuckle. "I grew up in Portsmouth. A navy town. Ships coming and going all the time. My father was a merchant captain, so it was pre-ordained that I'd go to sea, though I chose the navy instead of the merchant fleet. My father never quite understood why. I'm not sure I do myself."

"Is he retired?" Grace asked. "Your father, I mean."

"No, he's dead. His ship was torpedoed by the Germans in 1940, and he went down with his ship like a good English captain."

"I'm sorry I asked," Grace said.

"No bother," Bahr replied. "Here we are. The entrance to the base is right over there. See the guard shack?"

She followed the direction of the finger he pointed and saw a small wood-frame hut near a road blocked with a wooden gate painted black and white. Bahr stopped the car across from the shack.

"Shall I wait for you?" he asked.

"No, thank you," Grace replied. "I can manage my way back. And thank you terribly for the lift."

"My pleasure," Bahr said. "I'll be seeing you back at the inn."

Grace smiled at him as she shut the car door. As she walked up to the guard shack, a man in a blue RAF uniform stepped out of it. He had two stripes on his sleeve, and he clutched a rifle across his chest.

"Can I help you, miss?" he asked.

"I hope so," she replied. "I'm looking for my fiancé, you see."

"And he's on this base?"

"He is," Grace said. "A pilot. O'Hanlon. Flying Officer Michael O'Hanlon. Do you know him?"

"I don't run around with officers, miss," the man said.

"Is there any way I might get a message to him?" Grace asked. "It's frightfully important. He thinks I'm in London right now, but I came up here to surprise him. I want to let him know where I'm staying."

"I don't know… we ain't supposed to do that. Take messages and the like."

"I'd be ever so grateful," she said, "as would Michael, I'm sure."

"I guess I can call the duty officer," the man grumbled.

She followed him over to the shack and waited outside as he picked up the phone. He asked for the duty officer, and after a series of yeses and I sees, the man hung up the phone.

"Someone will be along to talk to you in a minute, miss," he said. "You can step in here and have a seat. I'll wait outside."

"Thank you," Grace said as she entered the shack and sat atop a wooden stool. "Is it really necessary for someone to come and talk to me? Couldn't you just pass on my message over the phone?"

"Orders, miss," the man said as he kept his eyes focused away from her. "That's what the duty officer said."

"He's alright, isn't he?" Grace asked.

"Don't know, miss," the man said. "I just guard the gate. That's all. I have no idea who flies and who comes back."

Ten eternal minutes passed before a dark blue car pulled up to the gate. The guard walked over and lifted the wooden arm. The driver, a WAAF sergeant, moved the car forward just enough so the gate could close behind it, then she got out and opened a rear door. A tall, thin man in the uniform of a Wing Commander got out and walked over to the shack.

"You must be Grace," he said. "I've heard Michael talk about you. I'm Wing Commander Simpson, his CO."

"Is he alright?" she asked. "I just wanted to get a message to him. That's all."

"Why don't you come have a seat in the car, and we can talk," Simpson said.

Grace tried to stand but found her legs would not cooperate. Simpson gently reached down and took her arm, steering her towards the car. The WAAF sergeant opened the back door and Simpson helped Grace sit down, then he walked around to the other side and got in beside her. The sergeant shut the doors and stood outside the car.

"Please tell me what is going on," Grace said. "Please!"

"I'm terribly sorry to have to tell you this," Simpson said after a pause, "but Michael's plane crashed on landing a few hours ago."

"Is he alright?" Grace asked.

"I'm afraid he's dead." His voice cracked as he continued, "All of them. His whole crew. Dead."

It took a moment for the words to sink in. Grace felt her eyes begin to water, but she willed them to stop. Simpson's own eyes glistened as he spoke.

"He was a fine pilot," he said. "One of the best. We're all a bit shaken up, to be honest. Him on his last operation and all. Dreadfully bad business."

"Yes," she whispered.

"I wanted to tell you in person because since you aren't married, his father would be his next of kin and you might not hear anything. I felt we owed you that much."

"Thank you," Grace said.

"Shall I run you back into town? I'm sure some of the lads would like to come by and pay their respects tomorrow. We usually have a bit of a dust up when one of the crews goes west. You'd be welcome."

"No. Thank you," Grace said. "I can walk back."

"Are you sure?" Simpson asked. "It's no trouble."

"I am," Grace replied. "And thank you, Wing Commander. I appreciate you taking the time to talk to me."

"If there's anything I can do, you need only ask," Simpson said.

Grace opened the door and got out of the car. In the distance, she heard the drone of engines as aircrews began testing their planes for the night's mission. She pulled her coat tighter around her shoulders and began to walk down the road towards the village. Tears stung her eyes as she turned and faced the morning sun. With its warmth beating down upon her face, she smiled at the memory of Michael and his crew joking with each other at breakfast, of the night they met at the film in London, and of the few nights they'd spent together. She reached into her handbag and removed the watch. The sun reflected off the face as she slipped it onto her left wrist. *Goodbye, Michael. I'll never forget.*

AUTHOR'S NOTE

For much of my adult life, I've had a foot in two entirely different worlds. As I spent a career in public safety, both as a firefighter and later as an arson investigator, I had a front row seat to human nature and its accompanying misery. A thousand small tragedies played out in front of me. A thousand scenes too funny to be believable to a person who wasn't there still cause me to chuckle at inappropriate times. But my left foot was firmly planted in a very different world. I received an MA in History in 2003 and the following year, I began to teach part time at a community college, something I continued to do throughout my firefighter days. In later 2012, I suffered a serious injury which required me to hang up my helmet for good. In the spring of 2018, I joined the full time ranks at a local college. It was the merger of these two worlds which gave rise to *So Others May Live*.

Given my work background, I spent a lot of time researching the history of the fire service, particularly how departments handled working conditions during wartime. I've had the honor to speak with individuals who fought fires under the bombs in London and various German cities. From professional firefighters to civil defense volunteers, they all exhibited the very definition of courage and devotion to duty.

In January 2017, I awoke from a particularly vivid dream in which I saw a crippled Lancaster struggling to land as the crew softly sang a hymn in their crash positions. Later that day, the image merged with a particularly horrifying story told to me by a man who had been a teenager auxiliary firefighter in Germany during World War Two. It created a strange visual juxtaposition of the bombers and the bombed. That, Dear Readers, is how this novel was born.

So Others May Live is a work of fiction, though it is a novel partly grounded in hard facts. That said, I do feel it is necessary to mention here where I may deviate slightly from the historical record. Bomber Command did smash at Berlin on the night of November 22nd, but the details of the raid are a little different than what is described in my book. Charlottenburg did receive a frightful prang that night, but the raid happened earlier in the evening than I describe. Also, heavy cloud cover obscured much of the target which kept the night fighters at bay. 26 bombers were lost, around 3.4% of the attacking force, and around 175,000 Berlin residents were left homeless. The Zoo did suffer damage and several animals died, as I describe. However, I intended to depict this raid as being more of a representation of raids across Germany in general rather than a blow by blow account of a single raid. That is why I deviated from the historical record, though I hope my readers will both understand my reasons and forgive me for doing violence to history.

The sources I utilized in researching this novel include books, videos, audio recordings, photographs, interviews, and my own experiences on the job. Unfortunately, the day to day operations of German firefighters during World War Two can be difficult to nail down as they have not received near the same level of research attention as, say, the London Fire Brigade during the Blitz. I pieced together factual nuggets from several sources, but at times I had to use what amounts to a SWAG (Scientific Wild Ass Guess). In those instances, I used my own knowledge, training, and experience to fill in the gaps with how a firefighter or department would likely respond to something. I can only hope that I got it right, or somewhat close to right. I'll let you be the judge.

Now comes the hard part. In almost every book I've ever read, the author lists all the people he or she would like to thank. I desperately want to the do the same, but I'm terrified of leaving someone out. Just know that if I forget to include you, it wasn't intentional and I still love you. The first person I must thank is my grandfather, a decorated World War Two veteran. Not only do I look like him, but I also act like him, which can be both good and bad. I'm the man I am today because of the example that he set. He passed away on Easter Sunday, 2009. I would give up everything I have just to talk to him one more time. Like most men of his generation, he was tight lipped about his service, but towards the end of his life, he opened up to me so that I could write his story down. I owe a thanks to the rest of my family as well.

I spent a long time as an adjunct professor, overworked and underpaid. Since 2013, I applied for full time positions at various colleges no less than twenty times only to strike out. Oh, sure, I'd be a finalist, but never the selection. I'm living proof of why you should not give up. I got there eventually. To that end, I have to thank my long-time friend and current boss Ken for not only being a constant source of encouragement, but also for making sure I could focus on editing my book without worrying about where my next meal was coming from by hiring me full time at his college. I've known his wife Abbie for many years as well, and she's been a great help to me, both personally and professionally. I'm fortunate to work with some great colleagues at my current institution. They welcomed this shell-shocked old firefighter into the fold. When I had to miss the first few weeks of class during my first full time semester due to an emergency surgery, they all jumped in to help. I've found a closeness and a unity of purpose that I thought only existed in the fire service. To my former colleagues at San Jacinto College South and Alvin Community College, I would like to say that I enjoyed my time toiling away in classrooms alongside you, and the hours we spent solving all the problems of the world in the faculty lounge. Some of you have likewise gone on to other institutions, but I'll always remember those years we spent together. I wish I could thank all of you individually, but time and space prevent it. Just know that you are a big part of my eventual success.

In 2013, the history chair at ACC, Chris, hired me almost sight unseen to teach dual credit courses at Turner High School in Pearland. What followed was the most remarkable four and a half years of my life. I thank him for the opportunity. I grew both as a professor, but also as a person. The students I taught there were truly special. I probably learned more from them than they did from me. I wish I could thank them all individually. They mean more to me than they'll ever know. Two of my ACC colleagues, Keith and Andrew, have been a big help to me. Keith took the time to comment on a small excerpt and assured me that it did not suck. Andrew and I exchange cat photos on a daily basis and he's helped me rethink some of what I do in the classroom. When I reach the end of life's journey, I will look back at those years I roamed the hallways at THS as among the best in my life.

I cannot state with certainty how many students I've taught over the years. Given that I deal with constant pain from my injuries, the time I spend in front of a class is the only pain free moments I have, because the distraction pushes it out of my mind. For that, my students will always have my thanks. Some of them have taken the time to read and comment on sections of the novel, and their feedback has always been insightful. Teaching has helped me grow as a person which has also helped me grow as a writer. Though I have a graduate degree in history, I do not consider myself a historian. Instead, I think of myself as a storyteller. Perhaps not a great one, but I hope I am at least decent at it.

My editor Kristen Tate can wield the red pen of death with the best of them! She's the caliph of the comma splice, the potentate of plot, and the mogul of the manuscript. Her suggestions about the overall story arc, character development, and my grammatical miscues served to make this book better. Her assistance extended beyond editing. Kristen also filled the role of consultant, confidant, coach, and cheerleader. If you find yourself in need of a professional editor who will push you to put your very best product out there, look no further than Kristen.

Some people are family by blood, others are family by choice. I was a late comer to social media and the mysteries of the iPhone, but I got there eventually. My extended network of social media family includes some individuals that I know in person and others known only to me through the internet. I would like to specifically mention Tim and Samantha who took the time to comment on an early draft for me. Anyone who follows me on social media has had to endure frequent posts related to my progress with the book over the past eighteen months. They deserve a medal, or at least a mention in the dispatches.

Lastly, I must thank two special people. My wife Elizabeth took the time to read the first draft, and each subsequent one. With Teutonic bluntness, she was not afraid to point out parts of the manuscript in which things did not flow as well as they could have or should have. When we got married on March 2, 2008, little did we know how much our lives would eventually change. At that time, I was at the top of my profession with my dream job as an arson investigator. I was comfortable, happy, and generally excited about life. It all went away in the blink of an eye. With my injuries, Elizabeth must not only go to her job during the day, but also serve as my caretaker when she gets home. Though outwardly it doesn't look like much is wrong with me, all of my injuries are there, just below the surface, and I'm hampered in my day to day activities because of them. Our vows said "in sickness and in health" and its mostly been sickness. Likewise, the "for richer or poorer" part has mostly been poorer. She's stuck by me through it all, even when we spent our tenth anniversary back in the emergency room. This book would not have happened without her help and support, but most importantly, her love. She's my wife. My best friend. My confidant. My soulmate. My savior. And my hero. On those days that I really need a swift kick in the ass, she gladly provides. Every day I fall in love with her all over again.

The final person to thank isn't actually a person. She's my little princess Anastasia Colleen Hutchison. Throughout the long days of typing away at the computer, she "helped" me in the way only a cat can. Usually this took the form of her laying down on the pages as I printed them out, or knocking them out of my hands when I tried to read over them. I wake up every morning to her licking my face. Every night we watch television together or listen to a Red Sox game on the radio. When I'm home, she's by my side. I know they say that dogs are man's best friend, but in my case, it is a cat. I know Anastasia is happy that I've finished the book, as it means more time spent with her, but eventually I'm going to have to tell her that I'm writing another. I hope she'll forgive me.

As always, any errors, omissions, or mistakes in the book are entirely my fault, and not those of anyone mentioned above. That sounds a bit high-brow, so here's how I would really say it. If the book sucks, it is all my fault. Check out my website where you can follow my blog as I write about books, cats, history, or anything else that strikes my fancy. From the website, you can find my social media links as well. Keep chasing your dreams. As my friend Burt, a true warrior if I've ever met one, says, "Never ever quit."

L.H.
http://leehutchauthor.com

CPSIA information can be obtained
at www.ICGtesting.com
Printed in the USA
BVHW040956180419
545902BV00009B/57/P